thule

FINBAR'S
ISLE

hiBERNIA

BRITANNIA

ROMA

PARADISE

PARADISE

A Novel

For Paul and Jean,
with warm regards from
one voyager to another ...
whether our destinations be

by

Dikkon Eberhart

Paradise or the Barreds!

Dikkon

Undercliff August 1983

Stemmer House

PUBLISHERS, INC.
OWINGS MILLS, MARYLAND

Inquiries should be directed to
Stemmer House Publishers, Inc.
2627 Caves Road
Owings Mills, Maryland 21117

A Barbara Holdridge book
Printed and bound in the United States of America
First Edition

Library of Congress Cataloging in Publication Data
Eberhart, Dikkon.
    Paradise.

    "A Barbara Holdridge book"—Verso of t.p.
    I. Title.
PS3555.B463P3   1983   813'.54   83-4392
ISBN 0-916144-52-6

For Channa,
with love

1

BEFORE MORNING, THE GALE blew itself away. The man on the raft scarcely saw the change, however, for the three days since the foundering of the Roman ship had been savage to pass. His limbs were numb from exposure to cold. The rope by which he had tied himself had chafed through his jerkin and into his skin. His eyes were glued by mucus and salt. The change occurred, and he guessed it in the dim revolutions of his mind only by the passivity of the wind. He did not care. That about which he cared now lay deep in the green cold of the Western Sea; on the bottom, where cod motivated this way and that, and where the slow, shelled ooze snailed its way across sword and axe, hoe and pail.

Dawn came. Only slightly did the sea drop. The sun broke higher into the eastern sky, filling the wet air. It was the warm season of the year, and its rays gentled the winds still more. The raft rose, as always, and fell, as the man lashed to it passed from dark to light, from cold to brights, and then back down again. He slept.

He heard the surf, but he did not know what it was. He knew that it was different in sound and in the new rhythm it imparted to the pulse of the sea's wild heart. It entered his dream. Where his spirit had been poised toward the leap at death, now it was pulled back once more to the sea. Of a sudden, he was cascaded forward and dashed such a blow against the rock as should have killed him. He choked. The raft was above him. He began to drown. Barnacles ripped his flesh. He felt seaweed in his face and clutched it. The sea dropped, and his face emerged. He gasped a breath, choked, went under. The raft battered him. He tore at the rope that tied him. The seas crashed, driving him down. He drew air when he could; more often it was water. His fingers clutched the rope and frenzied themselves at the knot. A handful of seaweed kept him near the rock. Thought came again, and he thought he would stop. This was too hard a struggle. His chest, and his arms, and his face were raw from the rock. The sea wanted him: it could have him. Everything he was in life already belonged to the sea. It would clean his clay quickly, now that it owned his steel as well.

The knot was loose. Even as he succumbed, the raft was pulled from him, and he discovered himself half out of water, arms entwined as tight as any lover's in the clammy, rubber hair that swirled around him. He hauled himself higher, that the seas might not trouble his bleeding legs: not with thought of rescue, only that the pain should cease. He had been washed upon a point of rock. His eyes, rolling, perceived the rocks running along in the sea. The waves grumbled against them, now and then with a spurt of spittle white in the sunlight. Off somewhere to his right was a hint of land, the green of trees seen through eyes still washed with grey. He could not focus; he could scarcely breathe. He vomited. The scend of the sea washed him clean. He could breathe more easily. Suddenly, it occurred to him that he might live.

An hour later—or more, or less—he moved again. The tide had dropped, and he was dry enough. His cuts hurt fiercely when he moved. He hauled himself on hands and knees to the top of the point of rock, eight feet above the sea. He had come ashore near its farther end. Twenty feet to the left of the spot where he had hit the rocks, he would have missed the land forever. There was no sign of his raft. Looking eastward, he saw that the waves marched onward somberly toward the horizon, and that there was no land that way. Looking westward along the rocks, he saw that his land was a very small land in the middle of the sea—he would guess no more than two miles in length. He was looking at its thickness from where he knelt. Its thickness was half a mile. Its height, he judged, would not exceed one hundred feet. Beyond it to the west, the horizon was as blank as it was to the east. Looking round the compass, he saw that the same lonely prospect existed to south and north. He saw no sign of human beings. There were thousands of birds.

Wearily, he groped onto his haunches and began to pull himself toward shore. The rock was fissured, which made the going hard for a man in his condition. He rose shakily to his feet. He stumbled. Where his hands hit the rock, they left blood. He struggled upward once more; though he was not a tall man, he was broad, and still powerful. Crossing the rocks, he used his hands as well as his feet, and he carried his head low from pain and exhaustion. He felt his curling hair matted with salt and seaweed against his face. Something had gone wrong with his left leg: the limb did not support him so well as the right.

He neared the shoreline and looked up. He tried to grasp the shape of the island. His vision was hampered by the screeching wheels of gulls that revolved angrily around him. For the first time, his ears caught their strident clamor, and his nostrils the sun-warmed scent of their guano. There were other scents of the earth as well, even of this miniscule earth in the sea, and they penetrated his dazzled brain. He stepped onto the stones. His blood drained away downward. He was standing at one end of a beach one hundred yards wide to his left. At its other extremity, another point of rock jutted out into the sea. The beach was steep below the high-tide line and flatter above. The demarcation line was marked with whitened drift logs and brown tangles of dried seaweed. The beach was composed mainly of large, washed pebbles with a strain or two of medium boulders mixed through. In color, it was grey, but with the sun shining on it, sparks of brightness here and there were illuminated: a pearly mussel shell, a bit of rounded coral, a shark's egg case, a reddened crab shell, the translucent bones of a dead gull. The man looked upward. The top of the beach was backed by a stand of bramble trees: furze and bog myrtle. These gave way as the land rose sharply to the bare, eroded cliff of a sandbank one hundred feet high. The bank backed the entire beach, looking as though some great maul had cloven the island in two at the formative day, and that the other half had sunk. The top of the bank was heavily wooded: old spruce mixed with hazel and yew. In spots where a momentary root could be dug in, there were sea campion and sea pink in big, soft clumps, and even wild roses clinging to the cliff. Mainly, though, there were birds, nesting, hatching, strutting, screaming, preening. The cliff was a perfect spot for them, giving them height, protection and a lee from the western wind.

He turned around. The water between the two arms of rock was a pool in the sea, beautiful, dancing. Out there, ever and ever, the formless grey rolled on. The man heard the seas rumble in patient umbrage against the island's rocky flanks. Occasionally, the sun lit a tossed mare's tail where a particular crest met a rock in passing. He looked between the arms at the horizon. His viewpoint was so low that he saw it jagged with retreating seas, not as a line against the sky. He wondered whether that was the way back to Ireland, to Drumhallagh with its monastic cells like beehives on the bare rocks, and its fat sheep grazing beside the streams.

Ireland must be somewhere east or south, but the gale had driven the Roman ship far from her planned position, and, when she foundered, she might have been anywhere. Not that he minded where he was. The Battle of Cul Driemne had soured him to Ireland's charms, and he had been in passage for the Mediterranean's olive shores—he and all his tools. He coughed an ironic laugh. He who had for eleven years resisted the Christian importunities of Drumhallagh and its brethren was now as bare and lonesome upon a seagirt rock as any holy *peregrinus* in anchoritic ecstasy at the prospect of uninterrupted communion with his Lord. He sat down on the stones and laughed some more. He hurt.

When his laughter subsided, he stared out at the pool. Across it, eiders led out their ducklings. Into it, shags dove. Fleets of herring sought to escape the beaks above only to be driven to the seals below. Sheerwaters and fulmars fought for tidbits. Terns lanced and yelled in the sun. Guillemots tossed up their red feet like children waving flags. Puffins strutted on the cliff and gaped their remarkable beaks. And the great, white herring gulls took their arrogant places on dead limbs and rocks, screaming at all who passed by. Always, the big, male gulls rose and tasted the air. A dozen would rise up the edge of a wind, a dozen hang just above treetops with eyes spying out clues to the gale, a dozen slip away sideways in long, descending arcs to brush the tips of swells with their wings, to beat their way back into harbor. No bird heard the sound of the wind, for the sound of the wind was its blood, but all birds knew the ebb of the wind, its rich, aboriginal flow.

A gull bumped against him and waddled away. He saw that the bird's leg was broken. It hobbled. The man was hungry. He rose and pursued it. He trapped it against a bend of the rocky point. It retreated, shielding its hurt side and hissing in terror. It cowered, too feeble to scrabble up the side of the rock and away. The man lurched, caught the gull, wrapped it in his arm, and made to twist its neck. It was the work of seconds. But the man stopped —in mid-twist, as it were—and sat down on the stones, the gull still hugged beneath his arm. A wave rolled near his feet. Blood disappeared into the earth, leaving hardly a trace, save a faint tinge in the froth of the retreating surge. The man sat for an interminable time. Eventually, the gull ceased to struggle. It sat in his arm with its neck in an awkward manner, turned to the man.

By the turning of the tide at mid-morning, the island was as quiet as it ever became. The air was still. It had been washed by the gale and was soft to the nostril. The sea continued to recall the rage of the past days, but, with its waters low on the rocks, it made less noise. The sky complemented the round of the sea with a sphere of its own, soft, blue and warm.

Finally, the man loosed his arm. "Go," he rasped to the bird.

The bird swayed on its legs.

"Here," said the man, and, with care, he ripped the tatter of his sleeve away and bound a stick round the bird's leg, by way of a splint.

The gull hopped aside, awkward. Soon, it made its way to the rocks and, with wings and beak, it pulled itself to the top and began to preen its feathers.

"I'll bring you a crab," the man called.

Later, he examined himself. His clothing was almost

gone. He could see his skin and, it seemed to him, even his muscle and his bone through rags. He felt bent and scoured. He bathed his cut feet in seawater and used his other sleeve to bandage them. He stood and walked. He limped still but not so badly. Carefully, he climbed again onto the rocky point that had saved him. Working along its opposite side, he was able to get a view of another shore of his island. The far western end of the island was composed of a rising meadow along which he could watch the wind blow, by the ripple in the surface of grasses and ferns. Here and there grew a small stand of stunted trees, or the brown of sedge cotton, but in the main the land was barren along that weather edge. Void of the larger flora as it was, that end of the island also supported its colony of birds. He saw flocks of skylarks snap like hair across the sky. Interesting as a circumnavigation of the island might have been, neither his feet nor his will would have borne it. Too, he was mindful of the eventual return of night, and he desired a shelter of some kind. He returned to the familiar beach and its leeward attractions. Choosing a spot at the top of the beach, he hollowed a shallow pit in the stones, ringed it with heavy baulks of driftwood, and topped this primitive hut with lighter pieces of driftwood and what thatch he could acquire. He fashioned himself a pallet of hazel feathers. Work with sticks brought him fire.

The tide dropped. Afternoon became dusk. The man wearied of his exertions. He dragged himself to the edge of the sea. He sat on a rock and stared across the flattening water at the pinks and golds that drained so quickly away from the eastern sky. Three bands of orange clouds reflected the sun dropping behind his cliff into the sea. Swells disappeared into the eastern night. The man saw them go. Close-to they mirrored momentarily the hot lights of the sky, but farther out—and his horizon was not far away—the world became grey and lonesome. The sun was gone. A fulmar flew across, like a curtain to the night, and the sky blew away into stars.

There was a triangular boulder near him. Starlight reflected on a slight stream issuing from beneath it. The man rose to investigate this phenomenon, bent to taste, and then, eagerly, dropped to his knees and drank hunched over like an animal. The fresh water was gritty, however; he hollowed out a small bowl in the sand, and, when the grit had cleared, he returned to drinking. It was a long time before he had had his fill. When he rose again, he walked to the very edge of the sea, and he stood for a long time with bent head. Then he laughed. It was not a full-lunged sound, but it was startling to the birds, and they shrilled at him, rustling their wings and desiring to sleep. The man stood still after his laugh with his arms stretched out to either side, his body tense, his poise expectant: the ragged man before the sea. Then he walked to his nest at the top of the beach, buried himself in hazel and warm pebbles, stared into his fire, and slept.

The sun, the next morning, found him there. A gentle day was given to Finbar, and he recovered his strength. Thirty years in the mines and at the forge had bestowed upon him, despite his bad leg, a physique that needed little rest to recover from any exertion. He drank when the tide was low. He explored his lonely island and found eggs enough to sustain him. No sign of man befouled the island, and for this at first he was glad. He had seen enough of the traffic of man. Slowly, while he wandered the island, snatches of the immediate past returned to him with a vividness that caused him to stagger. He recalled the sinking of the Roman ship and knew himself to be unmoved by the fate of its crew. When he remembered once more the carnage of the battle at Cul Dreimne, he sat down and stared at the sunbaked surface of a rock on top of the hill until the vision went away. He saw that the rock was granite, that it was white and grey, that there was a crack in its side out of which grass was growing. He drew his hand across the rock's surface—his black skin in strong contrast—and felt the roughness of rock smoothed by time's grit. He raised his head and stared out across the sun-glint sea. He would die in this spot, he realized. The idea caused him little regret, for he had seen his tools— his anvils, his hammers, his tongs, his bellows, his buckets —cast into the sea to lighten the gale-tormented swanship. It had been blasphemy to him. To leave his bones on this lonely island was a fate like any other. He might have left them at Cul Dreimne; he almost had. He might have been drowned, along with fat Basil, that arrogant merchant, when the swanship broke apart. Indeed, he thought, in all of his wanderings since his birth in the Carthaginian hills, he had rarely been far from death. Still, that his industry should be sunk in primal ooze through time—that defeated his will and wit. He sat on the boulders at the top of the island watching the clear days fly, and his single anger was for the lack of a tool.

The sea and the sky offered him infinity, but, after a passage of days, he shrank from infinity and deserted the hilltop in favor of the earth at the foot of the cliff. He set his back against it. Gradually, with sticks and a flat stone, he dug his way back into the cliff. The days came and went. He scooped out a shallow cave. Now, he rarely emerged from his cave; he heard the calling of the birds from shadow. He thought of nothing.

Summer became autumn.

The sea grew rougher. Wind stung the silver pool into grey arrows speeding. The nights were sharp; the breakers banged and surged against the rock points, occasionally making the island shudder with their weight. Cold spray flew across the rocks and sometimes entered Finbar's cave. Finbar crouched before his hearth, and he cared for nothing. The nights were longer now, and the sound of the sea closer to him. He felt the fear he had felt in the Thessalian forests. That panic laughter around him then, that wild piping, was here in the boom of the breakers. He dug.

The cave sank deeper into the cliff. It sloped downward for many feet from the light, and from the wild, cascading breakers, before it widened to become Finbar's nest. There his fire smouldered day and night. Soot and grease coated the soft rock through which he had dug. In the nights, he squatted before the fire, and he looked for day as a respite from the hammering of the sea. In the day, though, he did nothing more: soon night would come with its welcome black. He was naked now, having laid aside his attempt at a cloak of grass. He smelled of fish and smoke, his black body shone with oil. When driven from his cave to hunt or drink, he went about crouched under the weight of the sun, the splash of the wind, the clangor of the gulls. He had built a fish wier in the cove, and he pursued the trapped creatures with a slender spear, throwing his withering body after them in frenzied spasms. He hated the touch of the sea, crawled from it with his flapping fish as quickly as he could. He ate orach, and goose-tongue, and rose hips. He found beds of clams, and he tore mussels from the rocks. But these excursions into the world occupied him less as the autumn drew toward its close. More time was spent huddling in silence at the bottom of his cave, staring into the red glow of his fire. All his life had been fire-enriched, and now, at the end of it, he desired only that eye that had named him.

He missed the first snow. It had melted before he emerged from the cave. But the second and third he knew, though dimly. Then came a blizzard, and the wind whistled into his cave, and the fire died. This aroused him. He climbed into a white, a driving world. He dragged stones and bushes to cover the mouth of the cave. The snow piled on his naked back and ran off with his sweat. He was afraid of so white a world. The wall done, he plunged once more into the gloom of the cave and fought with sticks the death of the embers. He shivered, and chattered to himself, and stamped around the hearth. It took a long time, sweating over the sticks, trembling, but at last a small shoot of yellow flared up from the ash. Finbar tended it carefully, poking small strips of half-dry wood into it, drying them, then igniting them. Time passed outside the cave, day to night and back to day again, before the fire burned well. Now, finally, he squatted, his knees hugged to his emaciated ribs, and listlessness came over him once more. As the fog settled down over his mind, he felt a resolve never to leave the cave again. He was close to the earth and to fire. He was content. His mind slipped away. Automatically, as it became necessary, he tended the fire, but he was unaware of his actions. His mind was nearly gone; his soul would be next. Outside the cave, the days came and went. More snow fell. Ice built up in jumbled tide-powered heaps along the shore. The breakers were grey with rotten ice as they broke. The island congealed in onto itself, stilled its life, and waited.

Light! Finbar looked up. There was a tearing sound. More light. The light hurt him. He tried to look away, back to the fire, but the fire was nearly gone. Its red embers could not compete with the . . . light!

The tearing sound again. Finbar shrank back. The whole hillside before him seemed to give way and fall. White light speared him. He screamed: a thin, sick sound.

Finbar wound his arms around his knees and drew into a ball, staring. His brain could not function in the light. Snow fell into the entrance of the cave with a whoosh, and, when it hit, white crystals fanned out and splashed his fire, his shanks, his cheeks. He screamed again. And now the air came in, cold, vigorous air, full of sea sounds and rioting scents. The wind whipped the fire into life once more, and smoke swirled around the hollow that had once been a cave. More snow spilled in. Finbar tried to hide in the smoke, but the air spun too fast. The fire had been scattered by the blast, the ashes begriming the snow, and the heat had gone forever. There was no place to escape the light and the cold.

A sound like a trumpet blared. Finbar looked up. An angel obscured the light. A halo surrounded the figure. The angel was tall, tall. He spread out across the opening. He blared again. Finbar understood that he had died, and that this was the Angel of God come to collect him. He did not scream any longer but sat huddled, his eyes never leaving the shape above him. The angel waved his arms, and the cry came once more. Mildly, Finbar was amused. A touch of his ironic nature was kindled. It was the Nazarene apocalypse after all. They had been right all along. He wished he might have one more moment in Greece to report this knowledge. Now, though, the angel began to descend into the hollow. Finbar saw that he did not walk, as mortals do, but that he glided down. Death was not so bad, Finbar thought, as the angel reached down for him. What did the Nazarenes say? "Unto Thee I come, O God."

But he was not lifted up as he expected to be. Instead, the angel's hand touched his face, pushing aside the tangle of hair, touched it tentatively. The blaring came again, but out of the harsh sound, Finbar distinguished words. The angel was speaking to him. The light, and the air, and the clarion shrill of the voice combined to render the words indistinguishable. He wished the angel would speak more slowly. The angel ought to be accustomed to the incapacities of the newly dead. Finbar wanted to answer the angel's pleas—there was eagerness in the angel's eyes—but he could not. He fluttered his hands, as though to communicate his readiness and at the same time his inability. The angel squatted down on his heels, seemingly pleased. The angel and the dead man watched one another with no more sound. An especially loud crash of sea on rock shook the air. Finbar flailed at the angel, clamped onto the angel's arms and neck. He screamed his thin and horrid terror. The angel thrust him back, very strong for an angel, gripped his shoulders, shook him. Again, the noise, the voice, came in Latin, calm, calm.

Finbar relaxed slowly. His eyes opened. His nose was running. His bladder had let go. The angel was kneeling away from him. Finbar's eyes grew more accustomed to the light of the hollow. He realized that it was daytime, near noon, and that much of the brightness of the air could be explained by the thick crust of snow and ice that overlay everything. Now that the entrance of his cave had been ripped away, he could see one point of rock sticking out to sea. The ocean was wrinkled, the tide was high, the rocks were congested with ice. He looked back at the angel's face. It *was* a face, not a glow as originally he had supposed. It was a calm face, and attractive, as one would expect of an angel, though it was deeply browned and lined. Greying red hair escaped from a hood around his head. The hood was attached to a thick woolen cloak, patterned with stripes of red and blue. The angel was very human-like, Finbar thought. He looked again at the face. The eyes were blue. There might well have been freckles under the hard brown of the cheeks. The nose was long and boney, and the lips were thin, though beautifully drawn. There was a square chin. The angel opened his cloak at the throat, and Finbar saw that his chin was softened almost to a feminine degree by the grace of his neck. Underneath he wore a white, woolen garment, much discolored by use. The angel's hands were long and fine. They, too, were burnt the reddish brown of the face. The angel had a bandage around one thumb.

"Can you speak?" the angel asked.

Finbar nodded. The angel had addressed him in Latin, as was proper for an angel.

"Who are you?"

"Finbar."

"How did you get here?"

"I died."

The angel shook his head at Finbar. "You are not dead."

And then Finbar realized that it was so. The anomalies of which his senses had become aware in the last minutes coalesced into a certainty that the angel was right: the sight of the rocks and the sea, the angel's stained clothing, the lively edge of the wind, the light off the snow, the bandage. These things were too real, too filled with life, to be death. Finbar began to weep. It was a painful, wracking sob that shook him.

"Here." The angel—or, as Finbar supposed he must now call him, the man—unfastened the rest of his cloak and tried to pull it around Finbar's body.

"I don't want it." Finbar attempted to push it away.

"You must. You'll freeze."

Finbar relented, slowly. The pain was beginning to overpower him. For months, he had not felt the cold. Now he felt it. Now he felt the wasting of his muscles, the starving of his system, the thirst that was in him. His bad leg came back to him with its old pain. Welcome back to life, he thought bitterly. He drew the stranger's cloak about his shoulders and wept.

The stranger knelt down beside him, taking Finbar's hands and holding them gently in his own. "Pray," he said.

"No."

"Pray for thanksgiving for your deliverance."

"From what am I delivered, and into what?"

The stranger did not answer. Instead, he bowed his own head, and Finbar watched his lips move. The position was awkward. Finbar remained curled into a ball, the stranger on his knees. The prayer continued for some time.

"Amen," the stranger finally said, looking up toward the sky. "All is well."

Finbar said nothing, but he was swept by tears once more. "I don't want it," he groaned. "I hurt."

The stranger sat down beside Finbar and drew his shuddering body into an embrace. "Rest," he said. "Lay your head against me, and rest."

Overcome with sadness, and washed with the intoxication of the smell and feel of another human being, Finbar did as he was told. He pressed his hands and his face into the stranger's chest and felt the man's arms around him. Finbar had a vision of his mother, who had died as soon as he was born. The memory of his lonesome life brought tears once again. He pressed himself against the man's chest, and then he realized, suddenly, that it was a woman who embraced him. He felt soft breasts under the tunic. For a second, he tried to pull away, but, as her arms tightened around him, he relaxed. Still only half-conscious, not quite alive, Finbar lay in the woman's arms feeling nothing of her except her warmth.

Many minutes went by, perhaps an hour, before he stirred. The pain was coming back. As he stirred again, he felt her breasts move beneath his face, sliding softly under her tunic. His sex came back to him, along with the pain. So, now, knowing himself a man, he did pull away.

"Who are you?" he asked.

She smiled at him. Her face was softened, and he swam for a moment in the milk of his mother. "Ide," she said.

"Ide."

Finbar reached with his fingers and touched her lips.

Ide smiled again, and then she asked him, "How did you come here?"

"Our ship sank, I was washed ashore."

"How long have you been here?"

He took his hand back and concentrated. "It's winter now?"

Her eyes expressed tenderness. "Yes. Early winter, anyway. November."

"Half a year or more. It was April, I think. From Ireland."

"Ireland!" she started. "You're a black man. You're not Irish."

"No. I'm a smith. But I lived in Ireland. At Drumhallagh."

"Finbar? Are you Finbar, the smith? I've heard of you. Everyone's heard of you."

"Yes, I'm Finbar." He realized that she had switched from Latin to Gaelic. "You, too? You're Irish?"

"Of course. I'm Ide, Abbess of Ailech on Lough Corrig. We are on our way to Thule."

"We?"

"Brendan, Abbot of Clonfert, is our leader. We are six."

"Here, on this island?"

"Why, yes."

"Have you been here all along? No, that's stupid. I'm dazed. I'm not thinking right. You didn't come to find me?"

Her smile was gentle. "We are on a voyage. We stopped here to repair the curragh. There was a great blizzard, and we lost a mast. I saw your smoke. We'd never have known you were here. You ought to have looked out each day at least."

"I never thought of rescue."

"We must never abandon ourselves. God does not admire us if we do."

Finbar shivered inside his robe. "It's cold," he murmured.

Ide was solicitous. "Can you stand?"

"I don't know."

"I'll take you to Brendan. We have food and warm drink."

Finbar smiled for the first time. "I'll stand for that."

"I'll help you."

With the woman's assistance, Finbar found that he could rise. The bad leg tottered under him, threatening to give way, but he could walk when he leaned heavily upon Ide's shoulder. A few steps took them out of the hollow and to the lip of what had been the cave, before Ide pulled away the rocks and the earth that Finbar had built up before it. Finbar was able to brave the light and the air now, though his feet were cold, bare in the snow. He looked around. The cove, the furze, the cliff all were covered with snow. The sun shone high from a clear sky. No wind moved on the surface of the sea. Finbar straightened his back and breathed a lungful of the vigorous air. His ribs and back ached with the exercise, but he felt blood warm his face and head.

After his six months on the island, everything about the physical scene before him was well known to Finbar. What riveted his still wavering attention, though, was the shape of a large curragh drawn up like a black sausage on the snowy shore of the cove. Two tents made black squares against the white foreground. A pair of men was walking between the tents and the curragh. Another man was bending over a long pole supported on two stones next to the boat. Finbar realized that it must be the new mast. Calm voices floated in the air, matter-of-fact conversations. Smoke and steam came from a pot suspended on a tripod over a fire between the tents. It was on this that Finbar's astonished gaze finally rested. He felt saliva jet in his mouth, and the ache of his hunger consumed him so quickly that he staggered.

Ide struggled to hold him upright. "Atla!" she called. "Joseph! Help me, please!"

The two men who had been nearing the curragh turned and stared in her direction, and then they cried out. They pointed toward Finbar and began to run. The third man stood up, and then he, too, began to run. Another man emerged from the tents. Before Finbar could grasp the situation, he was surrounded by men from whose eager and anxious faces came rapid questions and expressions of well-wishing. Ide answered questions and gestured toward the pot of food. Finbar was swept up and carried to the tents. They seated him inside one of them, surrounded by a litter of expeditionary stores. Someone thrust a bowl of steaming liquid into his hands, and for a time he knew no more than the delight of broth sliding into his body. Before he had even tasted its contents, it seemed, the bowl was empty. It was taken away and brought back full. This time, he began to taste the food, a fish stew. Then the bowl was empty again, and he was gesturing for more.

"Not yet, Finbar," Ide said. "Wait. You'll sicken yourself."

He looked up at the faces surrounding him, listened to the jumble of conversation and inquiry. He smiled, and then he must have fainted, for everything went dark.

When next he knew himself, he was lying under blankets with hot stones surrounding his body, someone was singing a hymn next to him, and it was deep night. He could see nothing in the tent. The voice of the singer was muffled. The wave wash on the shore, also, was muffled. There were no other sounds; no wind seemed to be blowing. Finbar lay in the darkness. His body pained him, but, still upon the edge of sleep as he was, the pain troubled him hardly at all. It was incredible that he should, so suddenly, find himself among men once more. Men! On this island! Perhaps, though, it was still a dream, or still death. Ide had told him he was alive, but perhaps the dead do not know they are dead. Perhaps they live on, in the other world, and they do not notice the change. That could be. Ide, after all, had seemed quite as comfortable as ever death could want her to be. First an angel, then a man, then a woman. If he called for her now, she might come to him in the form of an owl, or of some other night creature. He had heard of women in Greece, priestesses, who changed their forms at will, and who lived in and out of the shade. He began to feel that he must be dead, after all. The thought did not distress him. Outside, the smooth, baritone voice of the singer continued in the dark, as though time had no meaning. The sound filled the tent. Finbar's spirit rose with the melodious offering, became a part of its being, and pulsed like waves against the shores of a far haven.

It was Ide who woke him, in her natural form. She bore in her hands a bowl of the stew he had eaten the night before. With it, she had brought cakes of potato flour and a section of honeycomb. A warm light penetrated the hide of the tent and lit the planes of her face. She squatted beside Finbar's cot.

"Here," she said. "Soon you will be well."

He watched her as he ate. Her face, he saw, was a serious one. The cheeks were lined with the strokes of a lonely life, or at all events of one given to melancholy. But there was nothing hidden in the face at all. He had encountered few women in his life with open faces: She would have integrity, her features told him, a thing rarely to be found.

"Last night I thought again I was dead," he said when he had finished.

She smiled, as he had hoped she would. She stood up and took from him the bowl and trencher. "It is time for matins. I must go. For now, you may remain here."

When she drew the flap of the tent aside, Finbar saw that the day was fine. "Would you like it open?" she asked.

"Please."

Outside, in a moment, Finbar heard the sound of the morning observation being made. The psalm, "Praise the Lord from the Heavens," wafted into the air, sung by melodious male voices, with one female alto in accompaniment. Finbar raised himself on his elbow and looked around. Here inside the tent were comforts of the human kind. All were neatly arranged. There were stacks of woolen clothing: cloaks, tunics, leggings, leather boots and skullcaps. In addition, a good quantity of foodstuffs and of cooking equipment was in evidence. It appeared that the curragh had been emptied, so that the stores might be organized anew. Roots, onions and dried meats were in one spot; honey, preserves, fruits and nuts in another. Cookware was sorted into size and packed carefully. Soap, candles, oil, pitch, salt and every sort of valuable for a voyage was in evidence. Also there were the nautical items: spare hides, cordage, twine and tar. The jumble of equipment, to the eyes of a naked castaway of six months' tribulation, was wealth unbelievable. Finbar merely allowed his eyes to rest upon these homey, man-made shapes, and happiness filled him. The sight of a hammer brought Finbar up to a sitting position. There were tools! He rose from the bed, weakly, and tottered to its place. He raised it and felt the weight of it in his hand. It was light. It would be of little use at a forge; but the fact of it, the presence of it in his hand, was more stimulating to Finbar almost than the broth had been. With a tool in his hand, he was himself again. He even laughed.

Immediately, Ide was at the door of the tent. "Are you well?" she asked.

Finbar was well enough to be aware of his nakedness. Though a rough cloth had been draped round his loins, he covered himself further by collapsing back into his bed.

"Better," he assured her. He still held the hammer in his hand. "I was looking at these tools. Mine were lost when the ship sank," he explained.

She came to him, took the hammer, and returned it to its place.

"We have prayed for you," she said.

"Thank you."

She looked at him with a tenderness that somewhat embarrassed him. "Have you prayed?"

"I suppose not."

"You must."

"I'm not of your faith, Ide."

She lifted one eyebrow and made a caustic return: "There is only one faith, Finbar."

"As you wish."

"Forty-two years I have known what I know now."

"I'm tired, Ide," he replied.

"Then I will leave you, but think on this: why have you been spared, and why have you been rescued by us? These things are not without reason. History is not a series of random events. God is your savior."

Finbar felt querulous. "I don't know the reason. How should I know?"

"You're tired, too tired for talking. Nonetheless, there is a reason." She turned away.

Throughout what remained of that day, Finbar rested. Now and then, one or another of the men visited him. As often as not, Finbar lay in a stupor during these visitations, unconscious of anything except the mere presence of another human being. At such times, the visitors merely watched. Now and then, one twitched a cover of his blanket more snugly around his legs, or by some other hospitable motion sought to ease his return to the world. At other times, when he happened to be conscious yet alone, Finbar allowed himself the luxury simply to hear the commonplace sounds around him. He felt somewhat as a baby must feel as it explores with its first senses the world to which it has been given. No single sound, or object, or circumstance meant more to Finbar than any other. Each factor of life carried the same weight in his mind.

The day was waning when Finbar woke from another sleep. The air was colder now than it had been at noon, and the sunset sky shone into the tent through the doorway, making the hide red. Out of that red eastern world there came the dun voices of monks in song: "Hear us, God, our Savior, our hope throughout all the boundaries of the earth and in the distant sea." The Spotless Lamb was offered, and all took communion, the sun fading. "Take this holy body of the Lord and blood of the Savior for everlasting life." At the end, a small canticle welcomed the first star, and then the voices fell silent, leaving only the gurgle of retreating wavelets across the sand.

Shortly, a figure filled the door of the tent. It was an old man, whom Finbar had seen before, during his half-conscious hours. The figure was bent and supported itself upon a shellagleigh. It came in through the doorway with a sideways motion and then paused, looking around, swallowing, in the dim manner of the half-blind.

"Are you there?" a dry, ancient voice asked.

"Yes."

"My name is Barinthus."

"I am honored."

"Joseph will come soon with food."

The elder moved aside, carefully, assisting his steps with the stick. He found an upturned bucket, and he sat. He hunched himself like a toad: thin shanks high, knees beside his head, his chin resting on his hands, which, in

turn, rested on the knurl of his staff. Evidently he watched
Finbar in the dimness of the tent, but Finbar was not
certain that the eyes rested where the mind desired them
to rest. Uncomfortable, Finbar adjusted his blankets.

The old man said, "You are a black man, child of
Cain."

"I was born in Africa; my father was a desert trader."

"How came you here, to this rock?"

"Shipwreck."

"And to the ship?"

"I was bound from Ireland to Greece."

"They say you are a smith."

"Yes."

"They say you are Finbar the Smith. He who armed
our dear Brother Columcille for the Battle of Cul
Dreimne."

"That is so."

"Yet you are not a Christian, they say."

"I confess that this, too, is so."

"You are he who armed the force of God against the
satanic power of Dairmait mac Cerbaill, and you are not
a Christian?"

"A smith only."

"I say you are a liar."

Finbar, suddenly, was frightened. He flushed hot.

The old man continued, his pale eyes unhinged. "I
say you are Judas Iscariot, traitor to our blessed Savior. No
Christian. No smith. A black fiend on a rock in the sea: It
is not the first time I have seen the like. I was fooled
before, yes, I was, but I warn you now, you scourge of God,
that I cannot be fooled again."

Finbar did not know what to do. The elder's voice
remained dry, as though he were reciting to an enemy as
much dreamed as seen. Though darkness was approaching quickly, the old man's eyes continued their odd caress
of Finbar's wasted form. Finbar saw that there were yellow rings in the irises; almost they were the fey eyes of a
goat.

"My name is Adeodatus," Finbar said, sullenly.

"Gift of God!" Barinthus snorted. "Curse of God,
more like."

"My mother was a Christian."

"Your mother was a crone, spawn of Pluto on Perse-
phone."

"You? You speak of the true gods?"

"Ah! You are caught, fiend. I am quicker than you.
Old wit is mightier than your pagan cunning." With triumph softening the etched bleakness of his face, Barinthus stood. "You are known, Judas Iscariot. My brothers
and I know you now. Pagan, curse of God, we see you for
what you are. No tricks will suffice. You will not get off this
island. Go back to your cave and wait another year. Go
back, for you have failed."

So saying, the old man made his way toward the
mouth of the tent. Finbar could think of no reply. As
Barinthus reached the door, a thin, stooped figure came
in, carrying trenchers.

"Go back, Joseph," Barinthus cried. "Look not upon
the evil one."

"Brendan asked me to feed him," the man replied.

"Go back to Brendan and tell him that I have discovered the identity of this . . . this man. Tell him all is
known."

"I was instructed to feed the castaway, Barinthus."

"Blessed food ought not to strengthen one whom the
devil feeds."

"Perhaps you should tell Brendan yourself."

"My nephew is slow to learn," Barinthus agreed, nodding. "I will find him now." He passed out of the tent.

The monk with the trenchers and the smith looked
at one another. The darkness was almost complete, and it
occurred to Finbar that he could see more of the man,
silhouetted against the late sky, than the man could see of
him. Courteously, to equalize the situation, Finbar sat up
and swung his legs to the earth. The monk retreated out
the tent door.

"I'm sorry, I didn't mean—" Finbar began.

"I came to feed, not to converse."

Aggrieved, Finbar said, "My name is Adeodatus. I am
no devil."

"Will you eat?"

"Please."

"Lie back again."

Finbar did so. The man brought him the food, potato and onion soup, spruce beer, barley bread and honey.

Seeing the quantity of the repast, Finbar asked, "Will you sup with me?"

"I do not eat."

"I beg your pardon?"

"My Lord feeds me with His breath from heaven."

"But surely you must eat something."

"Once in forty days, as our Father Brendan prescribes."

"And you sail that way?" Finbar bit into the thick, rough bread, feeling the sweetness of the honey break across his tongue. "Sailing is hard work, hungry work."

After a pause, the man said quietly, "I do get hungry sometimes."

"Here. Have a piece." Finbar held out the bread.

The man almost touched it, and then he drew back. "No."

"You're too thin."

"I am as it pleases God."

Finbar broke off another piece of the bread. "A strict god, that."

"You mustn't speak that way."

"Especially not with, what's-his-name, Barinthus, around, eh?"

"Barinthus is a good man."

"I'm certain he is."

"He has been here before."

"Here? Where?"

"Out here in the sea, not on this island. He has made this pilgrimage before."

"To Thule?"

"What makes you think that?"

"Ide told me that was your destination."

"That's her destination."

"What's yours?"

"We are sailing to Paradise."

Finbar swallowed incorrectly and had to cough. When the paroxysm was over, he looked at the thin monk standing defensively in the dark. "To Paradise?"

"Yes. And you will not stop us."

"Why should I?"

"I've heard the tale—we've all heard it—of Barin-thus's last voyage."

"There's a misunderstanding here. I'm not whoever you think I am."

"You are a black man living on a rock in the sea. You are no Christian, by you own admission, God protect you. Barinthus recognized you at once."

"My name is Finbar. I am a smith."

"Before, you said Adeodatus."

"Adeodatus is my real name. I was born so. After I forged the weapons for the Christians at Cul Dreimne, your own Brother Columcille gave me the name Finbar. For Finn, you know, Finn the hero, but with a curly top." He rubbed his thick, kinky hair to emphasize the fact.

"How came you in Ireland for the battle?"

"I've lived there eleven years. I move around, all smiths do. One vein is exhausted, and then you move. You learn a technique here, a technique there. But I was at Drumhallagh for eleven years. I was born in the city of Hippo Regius—"

"Saint Augustine's city!"

"That's right. I was born there, but I went to Egypt. From there I traveled to Greece. I lived in Greece a long time, mining silver and tin. Greece is a rich land. Then I followed the Danube through Gaul. I got to Ireland eleven years ago."

"You were born in Saint Augustine's city?"

Finbar nodded. "The City of God."

"I don't think it proper for you to pun upon the memory of the blessed saint."

"I guess not."

There was a pause, and then the monk asked, "And now?"

"I was going back to Greece. I'd grown weary of the damp, green, dreary hills, all divided by little stone walls."

"That's my home."

"I meant no disrespect."

"Actually," the man said wistfully, "I suppose my home is with Brendan, and that is with God."

"In any case, you understand my point."

The man laughed. "It's very green."

"Very."

The two chuckled together. By this time, Finbar had finished almost all the food. He relaxed back against his pillow, replete, and swigged the beer. He was pleased to have a laugh from the stiff, self-conscious man. "Are you certain you won't eat?"

"I told you."

"All right. It's your body."

"It's God's body."

"I won't argue."

"There's no argument."

Finbar drank. "Where were we?"

"I must go."

"Don't you want the rest of the story?"

"If it's your desire."

"Never mind."

"As you wish."

"I've offended you. I'm sorry."

"I shall pray for you."

"My thanks on it."

"You're very casual."

"You're very bitter."

The monk looked hard at the smith for a moment, and then, turning, he said, "Good night."

"Wait!"

"Well?"

"Nothing."

"Are you comfortable?"

"Yes."

"Then, goodnight."

The night was dark. The air was still. No sound of man came from outside the tent. The thin man had closed the flap when he left, and Finbar was completely alone, except that he was aware by smell and by remembered vision of the pile of stores around him, the pile of equipment for the cruise to Paradise.

He was half asleep when music came to his ears. This was not the chanted hymn of last night, not that baritone exultation of the Nazarene God. At first, Finbar thought

that he had dreamt it, so low and so airy was it. He thought
perhaps it was a snatch of tune from the Thessalian hills,
those open, piney woods of sun, and warm rocks, and
sandled feet light with spring. He thought of the miner's
widow he had known there, of how she had been Finbar's
after the miner choked out his life on dust and hard work
and bad air. He thought of the way she had lain on the
earth with him—to feel the voice of the Goddess at her
back, she said—and of how his skin had prickled when the
Goddess had come into her, and of how her hair had been
loose.

As he thought of her, the music came again, but it was
not of the past. It was a wild, mad, building shrill such as
might come from a Pan pipe or flute, a night-music of
dance, and of the twinkling of hair like whips in the moon.
It excited him. It took his breath. He could not lie still. He
jumped up. His skin was hot. The tent reeled around him.
He tripped and whirled, catching his balance, losing it
again, falling. He hit his head. His mind spun faster. He
was frightened. He was not a well man. Life burned in
him too fast, too hot for him to control it. He struggled to
orient himself, to sit. The music built still higher. It came
from nowhere, was everywhere. His skin shivered, now
hot, now cold. He blundered into the tent pole. He clung
there as the sound washed through his feverish mind. This
was how the gods felt. This was too much for man. This
was too much for Finbar. He must get out. He must get
out into the night, to find the music, to stop it, to make it
stop before he lost his mind with fever and awe. The
inside of the tent was hot. He was burning up. He knew
the way to the doorway, he thought. He launched himself
away from the pole, tottering forward into a rush. He hit
the door at full speed and burst through it into the night.

The outside air was like ice water to his flushed body.
Suddenly, the sound of the music dwindled until it was no
longer a universal madness but became a whistle played
in a certain direction and from a certain distance. Finbar
flailed himself to a halt, off balance, awkward. He looked
around. He was standing on the shoreline, just above a
lazy tide. A quarter moon in the east showed peaceful
shapes of land and sea, the loom of tents and curragh. Off

to his left beside the first tent the cook-fire was a red glow.

A voice called from behind him. "Atla, please! I need to sleep."

It was Ide's voice, and Finbar spun around. The woman was just emerging from the tent next to Finbar's. She was close to Finbar and had not seen him. She straightened up.

"Oh!"

Finbar cleared his throat.

"You startled me."

"I'm sorry."

They stood too close to one another for a second. Then Ide stepped back. "What are you doing?"

"The music, I—"

"You couldn't sleep?"

"That's it."

"It's Atla. Always in the middle of the night. He knows Brendan hates it." She raised her voice and called toward the point of rocks at the end of the beach. "Atla!"

Finbar was growing calmer now. "I heard music last night, too. Singing."

"The night is a good time for closeness with God. That was Barinthus, Brendan's uncle."

"Really! I wouldn't have thought that Barinthus had such a voice—"

"You know Barinthus?"

"He came to my tent this evening. I would have thought that he . . . I mean, he has an old voice."

Ide chuckled. "There are two Barinthuses, as you'll see. At least two. He's a very old man, it's true, but sometimes it's as though he were possessed by God. Do you understand what I mean?"

Finbar nodded. "Absolutely."

Ide looked at him sharply. "You said you were not a Christian."

"There are different ways of possession."

"Demonic ways."

"Now you sound like Barinthus."

"How?"

"He thinks I'm the devil."

"And you aren't?"

"Ide!"

"You had better get to bed. Your teeth are chattering."

"I'm not! I've told everyone. I told him; I told that thin man—"

"Joseph?"

"Yes, Joseph. I told him. Do I have to tell you?"

"It's yourself. That's whom you have to convince."

Ide took Finbar's shivering arm and led him back to the door of his tent. The music had stopped, and all was quiet once again on the island in the middle of the sea.

"Can you find your own way?" the woman asked.

"Yes."

"Perhaps tomorrow you can join us for matins."

Finbar nodded stupidly. "Yes, perhaps."

"Sleep now."

Shivering under his blankets, his body thin and strange to him after its release from the music, Finbar wished that it would all go away: the monks, the gods, the music. He had no gods. He denied all gods. Yet, he knew, negation is no victor over affirmation, and these holy travelers would see in him negation only. They would wear him down. He could repeat his unbelief—today, tomorrow, the next day—but they would have him in the end. They would not make him Nazarene, perhaps, but they would strip him of his own decision, for he was without his tools to sustain him. He would be a nay-sayer in the company of yea-sayers, a lonesome and futile life. Better he should have died in the cave: then, at least, he had had peace among the given things of his own world—the fire, the rock and the ore.

Far away, perhaps from the other end of the island, he heard the Pan music once more. This time, he slept.

2

DURING THE NIGHT, THE AIR grew colder, so that when Finbar awoke, he was shivering under his blanket. It seemed to him that the hour was early. As the tent flap was closed, there was little light, merely a greyness at the center of the tent. The paraphernalia of the expedition loomed around him in somber heaps. Boots, leggings, tunic and cloak—the costume of the wandering, sea-drift monk—had been left for him the day before. With his thin limbs quaking, he pulled the garments on. Then, standing, he paused. He felt that the clothes separated him from his island. The wool was warm enough, but for months he had sensed the play of air against skin. His nakedness had grown so familiar to him that now, accoutered as the human world thought right against the rigor of cold, he was frightened of an encroaching comfort. An Irish monk in all but his black face and his scattered hair, Finbar rubbed his sleeve. He should have been dead by now. How often does a man return from the dead? He should have died many a time; instead, he was a monk. It was the middle of the sixth Christian century, and for years he had been confronted with the charnel worship of these Nazarenes. It was the middle of the sixth Christian century, and death was harder to come by than anyone would have expected.

Finbar pressed the tent flap aside and stepped out into the day.

"Don't move!" came a yell from behind him.

He froze. The second stretched long. He was facing the sea. He saw pink in the sky. It was dawn. A javelin clattered to the earth just before him. Its point tossed up a divot of half-frozen, snow-covered sand. He turned to

look in the direction from which the warning cry had
come.

His anger was cut off by the sight of the longest man
he had ever seen bounding across the snowy beach. The
man slowed his career as he came before Finbar. He
blurted, "Sorry! I'm Atla. It slipped. Follow me." He
picked the javelin from the sand and leapt away.

Before Finbar realized it, he, too, was running, very
clumsily, in the wake of the capering man. "How could it
slip?" he called, but his boots were heavy, and his legs
were weak. The snow was crust above and mush below.
It was difficult to run through it. His voice was lost in his
sudden breathlessness. He slipped and fell. He cut his
hand on rough ice. Atla whirled and, running back, urged
Finbar up. The smith rose, staggered when his cloak tangled his legs, and ran again. "What are we running for?"
he panted. Atla led across the top of the beach and then
turned and made a jerky, long-limbed way up the edge of
the cliff to the wooded top of the island. Finbar was only
half-way up when Atla gained the summit. The tall man
turned back and called for him. Breath hurt Finbar's
throat. He had a stitch in his side.

"Too long in bed, my sluggo," Atla cried, slapping
Finbar on the back when the smith wheezed to a halt on
the lip of the cliff. "Open those lungs!"

"I'm sick," Finbar gasped, still clutching his throb-
bing side.

"The devil! Look there!"

"What? Where?"

"Out there, pagan. The sun. Isn't that your sun?"

The ball of fire was two fingers above the eastern
horizon. A measure of breath came back into Finbar's
body.

"It's not my sun."

"What?" Atla looked genuinely puzzled. "I thought
all you people drew your strength from the sun."

Finbar straightened his back halfway, but the stitch
caught him again, and he stood ridiculously contorted.
"What am I doing here? I'm not interested in the sun."

"We're going for geese, that's what."

"What do you mean?"

"They've roosted on the other side of the wood for two nights. We'll see. Take this." He thrust the javelin into Finbar's hand and turned to dive into the wood.

"But wait—"

Already Atla had disappeared into the trees, leaving no mark of his passage, though how he had managed with his windmill limbs to avoid knocking even the delicately balanced tufts of snow from the low yews was something Finbar could not understand. Finbar swept one glance at the sun, and then, finally in some control of his wind, he shoved himself through the outer fringe of trees.

Inside the wood the ground was nearly clear. Finbar walked on needles and wintering moss except in those spots where a thinness in the canopy overhead had allowed a trickle of snowflakes to make its way down to the ground. The air was stiller than it had been on the edge of the cliff, and it was colder. Finbar's breath hung mistily around his head. Sweat on his forehead dried, and he felt the cold acutely, as one does when emerging from a fever. He saw the man before him swimming between the trunks with the liquid flicker of a fish through eel grass, and, even as the fish is camouflaged, so the man's rough, brown robe merged with the background of the needles and the winter trees.

"Wait!" he called out, but the hurry and the tension in the other's manner hushed the sound even as he uttered it. It came as a whisper through the heavy, chill trees, and Atla swung around at once, motioning for silence.

Finbar trudged forward until he stood next to Atla. He resented the man, and his side still ached. "What do you mean, it slipped?" he asked again. "I could have been killed."

"Never mind that now," Atla muttered. "No time." Atla bent his head next to Finbar's. "Look through there." Despite himself, Finbar was fascinated by the man's visage. Atla's face was as disproportionately long as the body. His skin was burnt a deep reddish color, and he was missing his two top front teeth, so that when he opened his mouth to speak, he looked from the front like the fish he had resembled from behind. His hair was red and tightly

curled, and his tonsure was growing out. He had a thin
beard through which the skin of his cheeks could be seen.
His lashes were long and curved, like a woman's, and the
eyes they guarded were Ireland green. Each eye sported
purple flecks like petals around the pupils. They were the
oddest eyes that Finbar had ever seen. They were so ab-
sorbing, in fact, that Finbar missed what it was that Atla
whispered to him.

"What did you say?"

"We'll have the wind, I said, so don't worry about
that. It's motion that will spook them. Be careful." Atla
straightened and turned away.

"But what are we going to do?"

With an air of only barely restrained anxiety, the
monk whispered, "You'll take the right, see? There.
Creep out into the open, but go handsomely, handsomely!
They're usually on the crest, with the lead gander on the
rocks watching. Be very careful. I'll be coming in from the
left. We want to get as close as we can before they spot
us."

Finbar hefted his javelin. "I'm not much of a shot."

"Never mind. Get close enough, and that won't matter."

"Maybe you'd better take this, and I'll drive them to
you."

"No. I have these." Atla pulled four birding spears
from under his robe. Finbar arrested the man in order to
examine for a moment their three-pronged, bone tips
lashed onto the shafts with rawhide, and the fired clay
rungs that were slipped over the shafts to give the spears
proper heft and balance.

"Did you make these?"

"I have to have something to do. It gets dull aboard."

"Beautiful work."

"My father taught me."

"You mean Brendan?"

"No." Atla smiled. "Not he. He knows a lot, but he
doesn't know how to make a spearhead from a fish bone.
He just waits, and pretty soon God gives him the fish, or
the fulmar, or whatever it is, without his having to catch
it himself."

"Does he really?"

"What? Wait?"

"No. God. Does your god give him things?"

Atla grinned again. "If you want the answer to that, just watch Brendan's face when we give him the geese."

· Atla motioned Finbar to move off to the right side while he took his own course left. Finbar did as he was bid, dropping to his hands and knees as he approached the open.

In a few moments, Finbar had crawled to the very edge of the wood. One yew only remained between him and the crest of the hill where the geese must be. He stretched out on his stomach in the snow and wormed his way around the base of the tree. The crest was ahead of him and to his left about twenty-five yards. Somewhere on the other side of the crest, he knew, Atla was crawling forward. He assumed Atla could see what he saw: twelve or fifteen geese resting in the snow, the sun only now beginning to play on their bodies and the snowy ground around them. The lead gander was in the lookout position that Atla had promised. The nearest goose to Finbar was at about a twenty-yard distance, much too far for an accurate cast of the javelin, at least for Finbar.

Finbar studied the situation. The geese appeared to have no knowledge of the hunters as yet; the lead gander stood his watch without any sign of nervousness. At present, however, Finbar was well screened by the boughs of the yew around which he peeped. Finbar would have to come into the open to get closer to the geese. There was one avenue open for that maneuver. Ahead of Finbar and downhill to the right was a fold in the ground running away from him across the slope of the hill. If he could worm his way into that fold without being seen, he ought to be able to creep in relative security until he was at a spot downhill from the flock but only about ten yards to its side. At that point, he would no longer have the wind, but from there he could attack, so the wind would not matter. It occurred to Finbar that he and Atla had arranged no signal by which to inform each other that they were in position.

Finbar suffered a rush of anger. It was just like a cursed Nazarene to assume that everyone existed to carry

out the work that he selected as the will of his god. Finbar
had no desire to slaughter geese. He wiped snow from his
face. Now he was the puppet of a Nazarene goose-hunter.
Half of Finbar wanted just to stand up and scare the
damned geese away.

However, his humor rekindled, Finbar thought of fat
goose sizzling on the spit and realized that his body was
tingling with excitement at the exercise. There was, after
all, something rousing about this whole stalk.

He had to slither five yards before he reached the
fold. Had the geese glanced in his direction, Finbar surely
would have been seen. He was open to view the entire
way. He was camouflaged only in the fact that he was
partially covered by snow. He moved forward with ex-
quisite slowness, scarcely breathing. Since his face was
hugged to the snow, he was unable to see what reaction
the geese might be having. He felt their eyes with his
mind, however, gleaming beadily over the white surface,
seeing his slight shift of weight from toe to knee, wondering, gabbling, raising their necks . . . and then would come
the startled squawk, the bell-beat of air, the rush of their
bodies away. He ached forward toward the fold that
would protect him from their gaze. The five yards passed
slowly. Then the ground began to fall away under his
hand, his arm, his face, his chest; and, like a snake, he
slipped down into the minute crease he had been making
for. The snow was deeper here: it covered him entirely.
Still squirming, still low, still blinded by the whiteness,
and still soaked by the melt where it flowed in at his collar,
he made a somewhat more rapid way along the fold until
he judged he had come far enough.

Finbar gathered himself carefully before raising his
head. He expected the alarm to be given at any second.
Carefully, he positioned his arms and legs in the best
situation for a sudden stand, a sudden dash, a sudden cast.
He poked the spear forward through the snow until it lay
in just the way he wanted. He paused and concentrated
on his breathing, stilling it, waiting for the clamor of his
heart to cease. He fought away from his mind all distrac-
tions of cold, wet, ache and restlessness. He lifted his head
until his eyes broke from the clinging snow.

He was looking up the slope at the flock. He was

farther than he had planned to be from them, about twelve yards. Still there had been no alarm, but, focusing his eyes on the gander, he knew that there would be at any second. The big male's eyes were staring straight into his own. For a long second, the two looked right inside each other's heads, and then the gander opened his yellow beak.

Finbar burst up through the snow and yelled as loudly as he could. His shout drowned the gander's cry, but the bird got in a second high, frightened call as his wings spread, and he leapt into the air. From the corner of his eye, Finbar saw Atla's form plowing chaotically forward through the snow, his arm drawn back to throw. As the gander beat a second time with his wings, the hunter's arm lanced forward, and the spear sang across the hill crest. It caught the gander in the breast, just under his left wing, and the sudden weight and pain caused him to roll over in the air. He struggled to catch the wind again, beat frantically, calling in horror to his flock. The tines deep in his flesh confused him. The haft was too heavy. He fell out of the air, still fighting, and landed in the snow with a whirling, frightened thud. The snow was kicked into blizzard by the terrified beating of dozens of pairs of wings.

Finbar saw Atla throw a second time, and a third, but he did not see the results of those casts, for he was dashing forward himself, all weakness gone, closing the gap between himself and a goose on his side of the flock, who was having trouble getting into the air. The goose was running away from him, down the open slope of the hill, her neck stretched out across the snow, her beak open, her wings beating hard. But the snow was too deep for her, and every time she almost lifted off, her feet tripped, and she came down running once more. Finbar panted behind her. He was gaining. He was nearly close enough; closer. He was running so fast downhill that he was on the verge himself of tripping or flying. He pushed harder. His breath was beginning to get ragged. Only minutes before, he had been a sick man in bed. Now, he was sprinting through crusty, deep snow after a terrified goose, the hill going steeper and steeper, the shore below and the sky brilliant with the new day. He pushed harder, gained, drew near, remembered his spear and brought it up. His wind was nearly gone; his eyes stung with cold-air tears; he saw her black eye staring at him in mad terror as he ranged alongside; he tensed his arm; he threw . . . and, just at that moment, she launched upward an inch. Finbar saw the spear flash just under her breast, missing her, but her feet hit the shaft, and it tipped her right over. She was down, struggling in the snow to right herself, unharmed but tangled by her own wings, and feet, and panic. Finbar pounded almost past her before he could reverse himself and fling himself at her. He closed. The goose retreated, hissing, her neck arched, the snow whirling in the back-beat of her wings, balancing her upright. Finbar reached out with his hand. He dove at her. He felt a hard blow on the arm, and then he had her, and he was rolling, and kicking, and shouting in the snow. He had got her by the wing. Her strength astonished him. He felt the bones in her wing bend as he squeezed and she thrashed. He was trying to roll his weight on top of her. She was calling with all her might. Finbar was nearly choked with snow and excitement. He managed to trap the wing between his side and the ground. He reached out blindly, flailing with his hand to grab her neck and throttle her. He felt her become tense, struggle fractionally free, and set herself for a moment. He looked up and saw her neck arch above him. He reached for the neck. She lashed at him with her beak once more. The blow took him on the side of the head. It was like being slapped with a log. Finbar's mind went dark. His vision reeled from the blow. His hand relaxed, and the goose was gone.

Finbar lay exhausted in the snow. Way up in the sky, far, far above him in the whirling blue air, the shapes of the geese spun round as they disappeared. He watched them go. Their calling grew thin, and then it, too, disappeared. After a bit, Atla's face came into the circle of sky above him. His grin was grotesque with the teeth gone from the middle of it, but his remarkable eyes were on fire, the purple petals shimmering with excitement.

"I got the gander! And a goose. I saw yours. Too bad."

Finbar smiled and moved his hand.

Concern suddenly broke across Atla's countenance the way rain breaks across a glittering sea in a squall. "Are you all right?"

Finbar nodded. He made no motion to get up.

The sun came out after the squall. "What a chase! I was sure you would have her."

Finbar looked away from the hunter's face and into the sky again. It felt so warm, so satiatingly warm to lie there in the snow. He had never known that snow was so warm.

"Come along," Atla urged him. "Get up."

Finbar raised his hand to his head. The spot where the goose had hit him was numb, but when he brought his hand before his eyes, he saw that there was blood running freely along his thumb. He must be bleeding intensely for such a light touch to gather such a gout of blood. He stared at it for a second, and then he said, "Look. I'm bleeding."

Atla appeared embarrassed. "Get up," he repeated.

Finbar still stared at his hand. "Blood."

Atla straightened himself up and made as though to turn away. "I have to get the kills," he said. "Come."

He disappeared from Finbar's view. Finbar rolled over onto his side. The snow was deliciously warm. He lay his wounded head down on it. But then the snow suddenly turned cold, and the ache of it went right through his brain. He rolled himself the rest of the way onto his stomach and pushed himself to his hands and knees. He stared at the bloody snow under his head and realized, gradually, that the red drops were falling from his own chin. It was an odd sensation to watch them spatter one after the other into the hole they made. They steamed when they hit the snow. Finbar moved his chin a bit and watched another hole drilled by the drops. "I'm bleeding," he murmured.

"Finbar! Let's go. Help me with this."

Finbar looked up. Atla was standing on the crest of the hill, a goose dangling by the neck from each hand. Finbar pushed himself off his hands and rocked back onto his heels. He stood up. He felt very tall, very thin. The whirling was happening in the sky again. "I'm coming," he mumbled, and he started up the hill.

He reached the top of the hill a long time later, or so
it seemed. As he climbed, the whirling of the sky became
faster, and at the top, he saw that the horizon and the sea
were being planed off by the spinning air. The sun was
brilliant, a steady point in the middle of the wheel. He
stared at it. It was bright. Vaguely, he felt a goose thrust
into his arms. He stood with the goose neck-down in his
embrace while Atla bled the creature. A deft twist of the
knife up inside the throat, and the blood began to gush.
It is incredible how much blood a goose holds. Finbar
watched as the cooling liquid poured ceaselessly down
into the snow. It seemed to his shaking mind that the
blood he felt running from his own head mingled with the
goose's blood, and that together the two streams soaked
down through the snow and into the ground, turning it
mucky, and, in his imagination, fertilizing it with his life
and with that of the goose.

When the second goose had been bled, Atla reversed
the bird in Finbar's arms so that the limp neck and head
were lolling at the top. He knelt, and, with a thrust of the
knife between the legs, ripped upward to open the cavity.
Intestines, fat, and tentacles of blood sagged out into the
hunter's hands. Atla knelt as though in prayer, his head
bowed, his arms thrust to the forearm inside the steaming
holes, working by touch. Plying rapidly with the knife
blade along the insides of the ribs, he disengaged stomach
and crop. The extracted guts slithered to the snow as
grotesquely as a placenta will ooze out after the convul-
sions have ceased. One goose was done, and Atla dropped
it aside, where it lay crumpled on the blood-soaked snow,
feathers dull and broken. Finbar took up the second, and
the supplicatory process was repeated. That done also,
Atla stood. "Here," he said, and he dropped a liver into
each of Finbar's waiting hands.

Holding the steaming, dripping organs, greasy between his fingers, Finbar stared at them, still dazed. They
were of such a deep red as almost to be purple, slightly
veined or convoluted, labial in their flapping valves, the
surface of one embedded with globules of yellowish fat.
Finbar knew that the configurations of those surface
markings meant a great deal. Hundreds of times in

Greece he had seen this very scene: the priest in his bloodied robe, his arms wet to the elbow, holding out the grisly
organ of some wretched calf or goat to the slant of a
just-risen sun. All around in the dell would be the hushed
expectation of the faithful, the rocks and the pines themselves almost bending forward in their eagerness to hear
the verdict. There would be dogs and boys lapping at the
trough. The smoke would rise from the fire as the smell
of singed meat carried in the faint, dusty air. And the
omen. The omen would be . . . the priest bends forward
studying . . . the omen would be . . . .

From his high, dazed, whirling situation on top of the
hill in the middle of the sea, Finbar looked at the two
goose livers, and he knew that they could tell him something, and he realized he would never learn what it was.
He was not an interpreter of omens. Atla had been cleaning his knife in the snow, washing his hands free of the
muck of the slaughter. Now the monk rose and turned
back to Finbar, sheathing his knife. "Ready?" he asked. "I
can carry the geese, if you'll take the livers. Barinthus
especially loves the livers." With that he started down the
slope of the hill toward the beach.

The sea was calm and the tide was half out when the
two men came off the bluff and onto the shore. They
walked in the wet strip between the snow above tideline
and the soft curling wavelets coming in from the southwest across the Western Sea. Atla carried the geese slung
across his shoulder, his other shoulder supporting a vari-
ety of quiver, in which the spears were lodged. Finbar
walked beside him. Because he could see no other way to
do it, he was carrying the livers in his upturned palms.
Atla, so spindly and tall, was as vigorous in his movements
after the fact of the hunt as before it. Finbar needed to
hurry, almost to scamper, in order to keep up. His whole
body ached with the unaccustomed exercise of the morning, and now, especially carrying these awkward hands-
ful, he found himself winded and clumsy. The shoreline
curved outward for several hundred yeards before it
reached a point created by a portion of the hillside being
eroded by wind and weather. Around that point, Finbar
knew well, there was a small, jagged, steep-sided cove

before another point, which was the one that turned and elongated itself and became the southern of the two rocky points that hemmed the lagoon and the beach at the island's eastern side. The portion of the shore upon which they walked at the moment was sandy and strewn with large boulders and logs.

They drew near to the point. Everything about this place should have been as familiar to Finbar the castaway as is the hut of a blind man to the questing hands that serve the man for eyes. On the point, however, there was a configuration of stones that was new to Finbar. There was something human in its regularity: large boulders laid down one beside another to form a sort of wall. Finbar drew Atla's attention to the spot.

The hunter grunted. "Sebastian," he said, and he spat.

"Who's Sebastian?"

"No stomach."

They were closer now. Finbar saw that the wall of rocks extended in a semi-circle outward from the hillside, enclosing a small space, and returning once again to the hill.

"Sebastian's hut," Atla said.

The hunters came up to the wall. Sebastian had begun his hut carefully. Each rock fitted nicely the rock next to it. A second course of rocks had been started at one end of the wall where it closed with the cliff. A gap facing the sea, presumably a doorway, had been left in the wall. The snow and sand in the area were well churned with the footsteps of the builder, but of that man—whoever he was—there was no present sign. Finbar, winded, took the opportunity to collapse upon the wall. Atla, his energy goading him, quested this way and that, the geese flapping grotesquely against his back. "Sebastian!" he called. "Hoy! Sebastian."

After a few minutes had passed, Finbar's wind returned. He sat with his livers on his thighs, hands sticky now with blood and mucus, staring out to sea at the flat horizon. The day was well commenced, the sun two hands above the sea, the streaks of warm-weather cloud lazy from the east. There was very little sound, just Atla's

scuffling and his grunted shouts. Finbar fancied he could
hear the sound of snow melting.

At one point, when Atla crossed back before him,
Finbar renewed his question. "Who's this Sebastian?"

"One of our party. He *was* one of our party, anyhow.
Now, he's off on his own, the poor fool."

"And he's building this hut?"

"I'm not helping him. Only Brendan understands it."

"But why build it? I mean, I thought you were going
on, to Thule, or—"

"Or what?"

"Well, I've heard that you are going to . . . to somewhere that—"

"To Paradise."

"Yes."

"We are, but he's not."

"You mean he's staying here, on this island?"

"That's right."

Finbar looked around himself, astonished. "But
why?"

Atla grunted and swung the geese impatiently from
one shoulder to the other. "You cannot reach a spiritual
goal by physical means."

"Isn't it Paradise you're sailing to?"

"Yes."

"But, don't you see—"

"He said that. I didn't. He's the one who believes we
can't get there. We've been sailing now for almost two
years—"

"Two years!"

"—and Sebastian thinks we haven't gotten any closer
to Paradise after all this time than we were when we set
out. He always wanted us to go into the Mediterranean
when we were south. He's a traveler. He's been to all
those places—Greece, Egypt, Africa. He's been there, and
he thinks this is a physical voyage, a cruise of some sort to
a physical spot."

"And Paradise isn't?"

"I follow Brendan. And Barinthus. He's seen it!"

"What was it like?"

"It was a shoreline, a landfall, but not like any other

one. You should get him to tell you. There are birds; and
the smells! I can imagine the smells."

"You mean it's a physical spot."

"Of course, it's a physical spot. What else would it be?
It's Paradise. What do you think? It's where we came
from, and where we are going back to, with the help of
sweet Jesus, our mainstay."

"You're going there now?"

"Why not? Brendan is called there, you can tell. He's
a mighty man, is Brendan; he's a friend of God."

"I don't see what Sebastian has to do with it."

A noise of falling rock came from the other side of the
point. Atla dropped the geese on the sand. "Sebastian was
one of us." The hunter turned to Finbar and motioned.
"Here. Come here. I'll show you." He set off with long
strides around the end of the point. Finbar followed, still
carrying the livers in his hands. They rounded the rocks,
and the inner, jagged little cove opened up. Initially,
there was no sign of anyone. As the two men clambered
back into the narrowing notch of the cove, the air grew
damper and cooler. The sun was still too low to touch this
spot. The waves pulsed in along the rocks, the narrowing
shore forcing them into steeper size without lending
them at the same time more force. Thus, they broke
against the rock at the end of the cove heavily but, as it
were, listlessly. The steep sides of the cove formed a dank
bowl in which the sound of the waves echoed.

"Sebastian!" Atla shouted, and the echo repeated,
"Se-bas-bas-bas."

"I don't see anyone," Finbar replied.

Atla raised his voice higher, "Hoy!"

Whether there was any echo that time, Finbar did
not know, for the sound of Atla's voice frightened a hundred terns, who suddenly, from nowhere, leaped into
flight around them, wings and beaks darting, calling,
swirling through the air. As quickly as they had filled the
space of the cove, they were gone, drawn like a scarf
across the sky. In their place stood a naked, bearded man.

The man was so close to them, and his appearance
was so unexpected, that both Finbar and Atla jumped.

"Yes, Atla?" the man said. His voice was flute-like in

its clarity coming through air still crinkled with tern-brushed facets.

"Sebastian."

"Yes, Atla, what is it?"

"I've brought Finbar."

"Who?"

"The castaway."

Sebastian bowed solemnly to Finbar, who, discomfitted not so much by the man's nakedness as by the ridiculousness of the entire situation, bowed back.

"Your servant," said Sebastian.

"And yours."

Sebastian was older than Finbar, his hair greying and thin where it was not shaved away in his tonsure. His figure was bent by the double burdens of asceticism and age. He squatted on bandy legs over a rock. "I have been getting stones," he said.

Finbar stepped forward. "Let me help."

"No need," the man said, and he straightened with the rock, which was a heavy one, casually balanced in his hands. "You have your own burden."

Finbar looked at the livers in his hands. "What am I supposed to do with these?" he asked Atla impatiently.

"They're for Barinthus."

"They're horrid. You take them."

"I have the geese. Wrap them in your cloak."

Sebastian stopped next to Finbar on his way back toward the point and the hut, the rock apparently of no concern to him. He was considerably stronger than he appeared to be. "You should wash the blood off your face," he said to Finbar.

Finbar gestured helplessly. "I can't. I don't know what to do."

Sebastian smiled in a benevolent manner. He glanced at Atla and said, "You see? That is why I stay. That is the fate of man: 'I can't. I don't know what to do.'"

"Staying here until you die will solve that?" Atla bristled. Finbar was surprised to hear the anger in the tall man's voice.

"Will sailing?"

"When we reach Paradise—"

"If you reach Paradise."

"When we are there, it will be solved."

"For you. But for this poor man?" Sebastian nodded at Finbar and resumed his walk toward the point.

"He'll come, too," the tall hunter replied impatiently.

"What?" Finbar gasped.

Atla was paying no attention to him. The man leapt after Sebastian, harrying him with angry questions. The two made their way to the point, the one walking firmly and quietly, the other as jerky and explosive as an exclamation mark.

"I will not!" Finbar called after them.

Finbar looked around himself and then, disgustedly, dropped the goose livers on a rock. He made his way down to the wash of the sea and bent to clean the dried blood from his skin. The sea was cold, and the wound on the side of his head ached when he kneaded it with his fingers, but the blood came away, and it felt as though the flesh was not too badly ripped. He began to feel clearer of mind than he had all day, actually than he had since the moment of his rescue by Ide. Dallying, he squatted by the sea, cleaning hands already clean, watching the spend and surge of the slow waves, realizing that he was alive. After a time, the sun brought its yellow line down the wall of rocks on his left and found him in the damp hollow.

Finbar stood up, and, disdaining the silly livers, he walked back to the point. Arriving there, he heard Atla's and Sebastian's voices in argument, although it was a conversation as curiously ill-assorted as their physiques: the one voice anxious and high, the other almost inaudible, phlegmatic. Finbar saw that two or three stones had been added to the course of the wall, and that Sebastian was filling chinks with careful applications of mud. The naked man was as unperturbed by Atla's insistent hammering as he was by the sea breeze or by the snow through which he tramped. Looking at him, Finbar felt that there was something extraordinary about him. He seemed to fit the environment in a way that Finbar usually ascribed only to a bird. It occurred to Finbar to wonder why the terns that had been disturbed by his own and Atla's presence in the cove had apparently been content with Sebastian's. But there was that about the man which made Finbar feel, had he himself been a bird, that he should have been content to sit in Sebastian's hand, to build a nest there, to raise his children there, and to teach them to fly. One could be certain that Sebastian would hold himself silent through the entire process, that he would only, at the critical moment of the first flight, flick his wrist in such a way as to speed the fledgling on its way.

As Finbar stood there watching, taking no particular thought of the argument itself, observing instead the characters of the protagonists, a voice called from behind him, "Sebastian!"

Finbar turned. He saw Joseph top the ridge on the opposite shore of the cove, wave his arm and call again, and then scurry down across the rocks.

Sebastian turned to Finbar and smiled ironically. "All men come to Sebastian."

Atla snorted. "No men will come after we leave."

The other turned back to him and said, softly, "You mustn't mistake the value of your company, my brother. Christ's society is diversion enough for me."

In a moment, Joseph hurried up, out of breath. He nodded to Finbar and Atla and addressed himself to Sebastian, full of the anxiety of his commission. "He wants you."

"Then he will come to me," Sebastian replied, and he bent down on his old shins to work mud into a stubborn crack.

"But he said right away."

Sebastian looked up, his face smiling. "Brendan and I have known one another for many years. He will come to me. There is no more hurry in the world."

Joseph was nonplussed by this flat response. He dithered.

It was Finbar's first opportunity actually to see Joseph in daylight. The monk appeared at first to be tall, but, seen in contrast to Atla, he was of normal height. What produced the erroneous appearance was his unhealthy thinness. His movements were graceless. His wrists, looking brittle, extruded from the sleeves of his robe, and his fingers were long and inarticulate. His skin had not the

deep brown of his fellow seamen's. Rather, it was pinkish,
as though never accustomed to the light, and it contrasted
strongly with the blackness of the hair on his forearms and
fingers. Joseph's thinness made it easy to observe death in
the man: his head was little removed from a skull. He was
already balding. His beard was dispirited. There were
sickly patches of peeling skin on his temples. He wore
several thicknesses of wool, and, even so, a blue chill hovered near his lips.

Finbar began working with Sebastian to muscle the
rocks into place, as much for the pleasure of tutoring them
as for any interest in the finished hut. The sun was higher
now, hotter, and the snow was mush. The work was heavy
for Finbar. He removed his cloak, and then his tunic, and
the heat played along his arms and back. Atla sat on the
slope of the hill above the foundation and continued his
disquisition, although the argument was growing desul-
tory for lack of a sharp response from his antagonist.
Sebastian moved rock and mud as though born to the task,
never hurried, ever cunning in his engineering. Now and
then, he shot a barb at Atla, and the tall man lurched and
attacked again.

Some time later, silence fell over the group. Finbar
was the last to notice it and to look up from his work. A
man stood beside the foundation. He was a short man and
a broad one. When Finbar straightened his aching back,
he found that the top of the man's head was less high than
his own chin. The man's face was round, red, wide, and
surrounded by a thick, red beard. His cheeks and jaw
were muscular, his neck a bull's heavy one. He gave the
impression both of enormous physical power and of un-
swerving drive. He stood solidly, his weight evenly distributed on his thick, athletic legs. His arms were akimbo,
great fists on hips. In order to look side to side, he shifted
his deep hogshead of a chest back and forth, rather than
turning his head on his neck in the more normal way. In
his vitality, he could not have been more opposite a
human being from Joseph.

"This is where you will stay?" His voice was bass.

"This is where I will stay," Sebastian answered.

Sebastian and Brendan were almost of a height, although Sebastian gave the impression of having shrunk to that height, while the man who would sail to Paradise gave the impression that in fact he might have been far shorter than he appeared, except that the power of his purpose so inflated him that he swelled upward. One was naked and the other was clothed; they stood a fathom apart across the wall. They eyed one another for a long time.

"So be it," Brendan said, eventually.

"You know me, Brother Brendan," Sebastian replied.

"And you know me."

"I wish you well. I hope you find this place you're looking for."

"We shall."

"It won't be easy."

"It never has been. Our Savior requires strength."

"You have that strength?"

"So I believe."

Brendan turned his attention away from Sebastian and focused on Finbar. "You are the smith?"

"Yes, sir." Finbar surprised himself. There were few men he had addressed so in the past twenty years.

"You will come with us to Thule, shipping as Sebastian's replacement. It is the will of God that we should find you here, where our brother had been called to make his own peace. Your coming was predicted and expected." Brendan looked more closely at Finbar. "You will build up your strength. As you have heard from Atla, no doubt, you are going to need it."

"Thank you."

"I merely follow the dictates of the Lord. He has provided you at the time when we need a man. Thank Him. Were it not for His provision you would never have this opportunity to serve His Divine Will."

"Was it He, then, who saved me from drowning?"

Brendan studied the smith's face for a moment. "I have heard your case," he replied. "My uncle, Barinthus, also, has made his judgment. I understand that you are not a Christian. That is of no concern to me. You may espouse whatever gods your pagan ignorance suggests to your own fancy; your fate is your own to choose when you sail with me. Witness this man"—he pointed to Sebastian—"and his place of rest. It was the good Lord

God who saved you when all others drowned. It was He who deposited you on this island. It was He who sustained you even when you ceased to work for your own salvation. The Lord may use even the pagan for His own purpose, and it is not for me, or for anyone else, to gainsay Him. As you are now, so you shall stay, but aboard my vessel, you shall be an arm of the Lord, whether you consider yourself so or otherwise."

Brendan turned back to the naked monk. "Brother Sebastian," he said, "we have known one another for thirty-one years. Our paths will never cross again. Whether you will find your desert in the sea, I cannot tell. I have been shown nothing. But you make this choice of your own free will. Abide happily in this fertile spot. It is a freer one than many our tired eyes have seen. Keep yourself well. We shall pray for you. Your theology is strong and honest, and we respect you for that, though ours differs. You bring man's spirit to Paradise without regard for place, the road being only in your soul. Perhaps yours is the purer truth, but I cannot forget the power of place, and I see a road before me when the sun sinks down into the sea. You remain; we go; but we both sojourn for Christ. Let us sing the Mass this one final time together, and then we shall depart. The new mast has been stepped. We sail on tomorrow's tide."

The moment thrilled Finbar. There beside the noontime sea, the voices of the monks rose in holy song, bass and tenor, strong and weak. The sun shone down. The smith felt the shiver of holy dread upon him, which he had felt before only in the clutch of earth, or else in the mad music of the darkling hills. Though absolved by Brendan of responsibility, he longed for union. He watched their faces, ogled the scrap of bread, the splash of wine. He saw the hands flicker through ritual signs. He saw for one quivering instant that the naked and the clothed were one.

When it was over, the monks embraced Sebastian, one by one, with Brendan last. The captain stood holding his friend by the shoulders and staring at him. "Are you sure?"

"I have no fears. God will provide for me. He will not refuse one who comes to Him with so light a step."

"We envy you a bit, but we have our own course to steer."

"Thank you, Brendan, my father and my friend, for our years together."

"It is you who have fathered me, Sebastian. Be at peace."

Brendan embraced the naked man once more, and then he turned away. Without gesture or backward glance, he led the march back to camp. Around the point and out of sight from Sebastian's hut, Finbar saw Atla put down his geese for a moment in order to remove his four birding spears and stick them in the sand above the tide-line.

Atla seemed embarrassed when he caught Finbar's eyes on him. "He would never have accepted them if I had offered," the tall man muttered. Finbar saw a deepening of the red of the man's ears and cheeks. "Well, what am I supposed to do? He'll starve otherwise. He wouldn't make himself a spear; it would take his time away from prayers."

Finbar nodded and bent to retrieve the livers he had left on the rock. One had been stolen already by scavenging gulls, but the other remained, though knocked into the sand. Finbar held it up and tried to brush the sand from it. "I'm sorry about this," he said.

"Never mind. Liver is rich food. One will be enough for Barinthus."

Finbar and Atla walked in silence the rest of the way. Before them, the four-square figure of Brendan stumped solidly along. Joseph lurched from side to side of the captain like a moon tethered to its parent planet, spinning helplessly in a reflected glow.

When they neared the beach and the cliff where the camp had been set up, Finbar sighed. "So I am one of you now."

"You are one of us."

"Where is Thule?"

"Northwest of here. No one knows for certain. It's the last land on earth."

"Isn't it late in the year to sail? Especially northward?"

"You are with Brendan now. It is incredible what that

man is able to do. Have no fears about sailing with us. We shall reach this Thulean spot because Brendan desires it."

"You are very certain."

"I am. We have been at sea for two years, and the things we have seen have been remarkable. Brendan has never been wrong."

"Who is he, anyway?"

"Abbot of Clonfert, founder of the monastery at Iona, founder of other sanctuaries from Brittany to the Scottish islands. Mainly, though, he's what you see there. He's a seaman. I've seen him thirty hours at the helm in a gale, and he meets each sea—each sea for thirty hours!—as nicely as the first. Once, way south of here, we were bowling along in the night, driving hard with the sheets started, and the sea was livid with fires around us. It was hypnotic. There was nothing in any direction except infinite stretches of sea, all of it lit by pale green flames wherever a fish jumped or our wake churned. Suddenly —he was asleep—Brendan leapt up and ordered us to tack, instantly, instantly. We were all so hypnotized by the beauty of the fires that we hardly knew how to respond. So Brendan grabbed the helm from Sebastian and threw it across. When things began luffing and slapping, we caught on, and we settled her on the new course. Then, what do you suppose? The first light of dawn came across the sky, and there, right where we would have been had he not awakened, there was a low, jagged reef, like shark's teeth piercing the surface. Right where we would have been in another minute. Even now we were just barely coasting along its edge, only just able to point high enough to skim past. How did he know? That's what I wonder. How did he know?"

"There are ways," Finbar said slowly, "that a man can hear the sounds of the earth, that he can listen to its language. In the mines—"

"It was God," Atla interrupted him. "Brendan is in God's hand. He has been chosen. That's all I know. Where he goes, I shall follow."

Finbar looked up at the man's great, odd head nodding beside him. He sighed. "Now I go there, too."

"You're a castaway. You have no choice."

"No."

"God wills it."

"Oh!" Finbar grunted. "Very well."

Atla stared at him as they lurched down on rocks slippery with rotten ice and seaweed. After a moment, he said, "In Thule, you shall decide."

"Are there ships from Thule to the Empire?"

"There is a monastery there."

"So there is some communication?"

"As little as possible. Our people do not delight in the Empire's ways. They are in Thule because it's as far away as can be."

"Then what am I to do?"

"You shall have to decide."

"Decide what?"

"Decide what to render to whom."

"That's your language, not mine."

"The language is unimportant. To be submerged in bliss: that is important."

With that, the party came around the last headland and the camp spread out before them. Walking across the beach toward the curragh, Finbar glanced up at the base of the cliff. There was the hollow, now partially collapsed, where he had hidden himself from the outside world. He was astonished to see how tiny a spot it looked. There before him was the boat that would range the world, and even beyond the world, to Paradise. There were the men, whose imagination encompassed much. Finbar looked once more at his grave. At the last, a man needs so very small a piece of the world that there is an element, one tiny element, that yearns for that six-foot slice even while the arms are spread wide and the eyes water in the sun. Finbar wanted to tell someone of this simple thing he had learned, but Atla and the rest were gathered around the curragh, their senses technical as they admired their shining mainmast, newly pitched and neatly stayed. So, he clustered with them, nodding awkwardly to Ide and to Barinthus.

Though no sailor he, Finbar was starved with a castaway's longing for the seduction of manufactured things. A block to him was as a woman's breast might be to another man, and he fondled it, and smoothed it, and tried what it might do. Through the afternoon, he observed a process similar to that which he made happen in the forge. In the same way that the potential of ore became the realization of steel, the curragh's hull, stripped of rigging and spars, came from that state into full life. It seemed that the professionalism of her crew coaxed her, tickled her, seduced her into an expectant state, and later that day, when she was rolled down the beach and out into the water of the pool, she came to rest there like a living thing, another gull among the wheeling flock.

In the meantime, while the others performed esoteric tasks upon the rigging, Barinthus guided Finbar in the restowage of the stores. The old man's partial blindness did not stop him from feeling out the proper location of each item, nor did he exact less than high performance on the part of his pupil. Each boot, each coil of line, each hide or jar had its own spot; each action, Finbar felt, was as ritualistically observed.

The job gave Finbar the opportunity to examine the curragh. His years at Drumhallagh had familiarized him with the ship-building technique of the Irish, but he had not seen so large a curragh before. Commonly, the curraghs were about twenty feet in length and were used for inshore fishing and crabbing. They boasted only one small sail, and that was raised on a mast that was easy to unstep in the event of rough weather. They were open boats, propelled by oars. Rarely were they even partly decked over against heavy seas, for offshore work was rare: the Irish were a contented people, not longing for adventure upon the highways of the world. It was true that mission activity drove monks and nuns to hop island-to-island in search of fertile soil in which to plant the Christian seed, but their wandering rarely took them out of sight of shore. Anchorites were known to have ventured beyond the horizon, but they cared nothing for seamanship. Their goal was mystical union with their god, and anything that might float was suitable for their enraptured waftings. Contrarily, upon Finbar's examination, Brendan's voyage to Paradise seemed to have been organized with care. He learned from Barinthus that the curragh had been built expressly for this journey. She was nearer forty feet than thirty, and she was correspondingly wide, which, the old man said fondly, made her a steady sailing platform. She was constructed, as were all curraghs, of a basketwork hull of ash withes over which was stretched and sewn a skin of ox hide. The seams between the individual ox hides were treated with pitch, and the entire hull was smeared with wool grease. The grease protected the hull from the corrosive action of the salt in the water, though Finbar knew the Nazarenes believed their god to be responsible for the preservation of their ships when even half a mile offshore. As was appropriate in a ship that was built for blue-water work, the curragh was permanently decked over in the bow and stern areas. She had a rowing well amidships that itself might easily be tented over at need. And, because she went out upon the open sea, the curragh was built to be sailed: she had two permanent masts, each with a large squaresail to which lighter panels could be added in gentle airs. She was steered by an oar that was lashed to a frame athwart her cockpit.

"A Roman ship, it was, you say?" Barinthus asked Finbar after a time, handing him another water bag.

"Yes. We had left from Ardmore and were past Sceilg Mhichil when the gale came up. After that we never knew where we were."

"Pigs!"

"What's that?"

"Those swanships. I've seen them. Built like barrels, they are. You want to sail—I mean *sail*, even if it's not to Paradise—you want a ship that bends. Take this ship now. This ship bends. This ship uses the wisdom of the sea itself: go the easiest way and rely on God. Those Roman tubs just butt their way through the ocean, and if they hit something hard, they burst apart like a barrel dropped off a cart."

Finbar shook his head and hefted another bag. "You really believe that business about trusting god with your sailing, I can see it. I wonder. . . ."

The monk's old face grew youthful in the dim, reddish light under the decking. "When we get there, you will see."

"I'm just going as far as Thule."

Barinthus paid no attention to Finbar's remark. Instead, he said proudly, "This is a very unweatherly boat, by the Good Lord, and we mean to keep it that way!"

"But I thought—"

"Ho! You are like all the rest. You think weatherliness is all there is."

"But how can you get to windward?"

"We never go to windward."

"What do you mean? Everybody goes to windward sometimes."

"We are sailing to Paradise, boy. Remember that. We sail downwind. God is a mighty wind. He is the wind, and we go where he propels us. We trust in the God wind."

Finbar could think of nothing more to say.

However, in the evening when all was ready and the curragh was prepared for launch, Finbar had a curious and disturbing experience. The curragh slipped down her rollers and breasted out into the calm pool. Just as she did so, there came a brilliant bar of light from behind a golden cloud, and the bar played upon the curragh and lit her rigging until it glowed. It seemed then to Finbar that some one of the gods, to whom the sky must still be sacred even in this faraway spot, smiled upon the departure. He was not certain which god it might be, having none any longer himself, but he half turned to catch Atla's eye and make him understand that the old powers were yet active here. Whereupon, as the monks burst forth in prayer and lauded the Father, Son, and Holy Ghost, three fulmars fled across the sky, one after the other, and seemed in their passage to draw a curtain across the golden bar, for that light was suddenly extinguished.

Finbar lay down to sleep for what he knew was to be his last night ashore for many days, in a state of tension so unexpectedly great that it gave him stomach cramps, and annoyed him for its presence as well as for its effect. He hated a life that he did not control.

3

SOMEONE SHOOK FINBAR. It was Ide. The camp was bustling. Finbar pushed the blanket off his body and swung to his feet. "Here," the woman said, thrusting a crust of hard bread into his hand. As he ate, he made his way through the dimness of the tent to the door flap. He pushed it aside. The air was cold, with flurries coming suddenly out of darkness. Even as he stood there, Atla and Brendan came to strike the tent.

"Morning," Finbar grunted, lending a hand with the pegs.

"Not yet," Atla sighed.

The captain rumbled, "It's a fair breeze."

"I hate to leave in the snow," Atla replied.

Finbar swallowed the last of his bread and wished for a cup of something hot to wash it down. He and Brendan struggled with the damp and stiff leather as it flogged in the irregular blows of the wind. The captain worked feverishly, as though so strong was his yearning to be away that he could not spare a moment. Atla pressed the wind out of the collapsing tent with his long arms.

"Get it aboard," Brendan panted. "Get it folded and aboard."

"We will," soothed Atla. "We will."

"I'll check on Barinthus."

Brendan disappeared into the darkness.

"Why's he in such a rush?" Finbar asked.

"This is God's moment, not his. God is in a rush."

"God?"

"God's work, anyway. A man should not wait to be about the work of the Lord."

The curragh had been hauled in until her bow nosed

the shore. Brendan completed the final stowage and jumped down off the foredeck onto the sand. The entire crew was gathered there. A little greyness had come into the black world, enough to see the loom of the curragh's hull and less clearly the intricacy of her masts and lines. She snubbed impatiently against her painter. Small swirls of snow stirred the cloaks of the waiting crew. Brendan gathered his crew's hands together in one grip between them, and matins was sung. Finbar's discomfort was acute. He drew his fingers from Barinthus's horny palm as soon as he was able.

"Finbar," the captain ordered, "get into the cockpit and stay out of the way."

Crouched in the corner of the cockpit, the smith watched his newfound companions go about their familiar routine. Brendan manned the steering oar; Barinthus was on the bow. A combination of arms—Atla's, Joseph's, Ide's—raised the yards. Brendan directed the action with soft commands. With all prepared, Atla dropped into the water alongside and waded ashore. He freed the lines. A gust took the bow and swung it away from the beach. The tall monk took a step or two and leapt for the forestay, clung, and then, with Barinthus's assistance, hauled himself inboard. The gap between the curragh and the shore widened further. Brendan swung his craft until he was quartering away from the land, having gained steerageway with windage on his hull and top-hamper alone.

"Loose the brails," he called, as Atla made his way aft and another gust struck.

The sails filled with a bang. The craft heeled and became a lively, charging thing. The rocky point rushed toward them. Brendan hauled them around until they took the wind over the stern. For a moment, everything was obscured by snow. Then the flurry passed them, and Finbar saw that they were already streaming between the tips of the rocky points, their bow dipping toward the horizon, and their stern tossing carelessly at the island shore that had been his home for the time of a long death and a birth.

He crawled awkwardly into the stern, conscious of his unseamanlike posture and envious of the obvious delight with which Atla and Ide danced from line to line on their unsteady platform. He cowered there, staring back into the wind and the storm at the last glimpses he would have of his island. Still more light had come into the sky now: one might almost call it day, but a grey and filthy day given to cold, and sleet, and hardship. Across the tops of rearing seas was his home—so small an island in the desert of the sea! Half a mile downwind, caught already by the pulses of the deep, nothing of the island remained, not its scent, no flotsam, hardly even the sight of it. From a crest, the rocky points were yet visible; from a trough, no more than the pointed pines.

A gannet followed them, keeping station off the port quarter. Now and again, the bird accelerated past them, low down across the waves, until his white back was obscured in a flurry of snow. Time passed. Finbar grew more steady on his feet, and he rose from his crouch to stand braced against the pitch and roll, his face still sternward, his memory yet master to his dream. In the sky, the gannet appeared close beside him. The bird hovered in perfect stillness six feet away, a tremble of white on grey. Finbar stared straight into its eye. Neither the man nor the bird wore an expression. A moment passed. Then the stern began to rise before the wall of a sea. Finbar leaned outboard. Up and up he swooped. The sea boiled and thrilled below him. The power of the wave began to catch the curragh and surf her forward and down. At that instant, the gannet tucked its wings and darted right at Finbar. The man felt a sharp pang in the cheek, let go the shroud to sweep the fluttering bird from his face, and lost his balance when the curragh reached the crest of the sea. He tumbled into the cockpit, oversetting Barinthus and Joseph, who were coiling lines, narrowly missing Atla at the helm.

"The bird attacked me!" he cried, as he extricated himself from the heap.

"Stay inboard where you belong," Atla growled.

"Damn the bird."

"Do not blaspheme!" Joseph cried.

Startled and apologetic, Finbar assisted Joseph to prop Barinthus on his seat again.

"See that you know what you're doing another time," Atla said. "We'd scarcely have a chance to find you, if you went over the side."

Barinthus nodded. "The bird meant no harm."

"No harm!" There was blood on Finbar's cheek.

"It was a warning. Use care in God's wilderness."

Finbar turned away disgusted.

For five days, Finbar was bruised by the curragh. The motion, the wet, the cramped conditions, all contributed to his wretchedness. The one overarching fact of life aboard the boat was that nothing was ever still. All day and at night, in the rain, in the snow, whenever the sun shone: the curragh tossed and crashed so that there was always a thwart barking Finbar's shin, always a line snubbing his buttocks, always a spar to prod him. Anything unsecured disappeared overboard. Finbar lost a knife and two cups—losses the expedition could ill afford—before he learned. The motion made him hungry but robbed him of his food. The muscles of his neck and shoulders ached with the force of his empty retching. He was perpetually wet. He possessed one suit of clothing. The air was cold most of the time, and there was wet wind or snow every day. What portion of himself Finbar managed to keep dry grew damp in any case because of the salt that suffused everything. His horrid off-watch hovel, a narrow portion of flooring twisted with scraps of woolen cloth, was musty and damp. On the fifth day, Finbar found mold growing on the tail of his cloak. Worst of all was the enforced togetherness. Until three days before his departure from the island, Finbar had seen no human during the length of a spring, a summer, and a fall. He had been blown clear of human habit by an eight-month nakedness. Now, wrapped in human fumes, he was always in the company of two or three. No half hour of sleep passed over him but that he did not suffer a kick or a snore; no motion of his arm or leg that was not arrested against another human's flesh. His most intimate gestures and actions were shared perforce, and with a horrid, wanton indifference as though this swinish living were unremarkable. What eye did not trace his embarrassed handling of a line, his sluggish instinct at the helm? Finbar had made himself accustomed to many differing hardships during his wandering existence, and he attempted now to perform his varied duties with competence. But the damp, and the motion, and the prickly nearness of his own kind defeated him.

Arising on the fifth morning to go on watch, Finbar found himself exhausted not only by the physical conditions of the cruise but by his own reaction to them. It was time for a change. He took a breath and rubbed his grimy eyes. This morning he would give himself a good bucketful of cold water in the face.

Coming into the cockpit, he found himself confronted by Brendan. The man's short, muscular presence fit the cockpit precisely, as though he and the curragh and the sea were all made of the same stuff, all measured by the same rule. His very muscularity and competence gave him an inscrutable quality. Finbar had rarely exchanged a word with him, which was unusual—though they were on different watches—considering the easygoing atmosphere aboard. Most of Finbar's instructions and support had come from Atla, with whom he shared his watch.

He and Brendan were alone in the cockpit for the moment. The sun was two fingers above the horizon astern of them, hanging red just under a line of purple cloud. The sea was still dark with its nighttime hues, except where the top of a wave caught a faint glimmer of the new light. The curragh was wet from an unseasonable dew. The wind was steady in the northeast.

Brendan smiled. It was not a felicitous expression for that wide, red face to adopt: there was too much solid flesh for the smile to transform the face, so it remained oddly concentrated around his lips and eyes.

"The wind will be steadier today, Finbar. God has heard your anguish."

The black man drew himself erect. He was nervous in confrontation with Brendan. "The days have been horrible," he muttered.

"Not so." Brendan's face retained its smile, but he took a more solid stance, as though to preach. "The days have been whatever it pleased God to make them. They are not designed for us. You may or may not be desirous of a certain sort of day, but if the day is not to your liking, that hardly puts the day in the wrong."

Finbar tried to smile. "Where's Atla?" he asked.

"Here," came the hunter's reedy voice from behind. Atla straightened his great height from the damp of the cabin and reached for the bucket. Slinging it over the side, he drew up a bubbling bowl of their wake. He thrust his hands into the water and dashed it against his face.

"Me, too," Finbar said.

"You? You're fooling."

"Go ahead."

Grinning, Atla slung the water at him. The shock left Finbar sputtering.

"Feel better?"

"Much." He smiled. "Yes, I do."

Atla chuckled and turned to take the steering oar from Brendan. The captain came forward, and Finbar found himself confronted once again.

"It's time you understood the sea," Brendan said, serious as always. "It's time you began to make your way without hurting yourself."

"I've done what I've been asked."

"So you have. But it's time you were easy. I understand that you're not a seaman, but you're not a smith either. No, don't interrupt. You are here aboard my vessel, a castaway, and you are as naked before the deep as any man ever is. This is the land of God that you see around us. This wilderness is the place that God has given us to try us in. Look!"

Across the dawn sea, a school of bluefish, driven upward by tuna below, streaked the dark surface into silver spume. Now and then, a dark back slashed into the school, and the frenzy doubled as the prey fled their tormentor. One such pursuit brought a bluefish close to the curragh. In desperation, ten feet from the side, the fish shot out of the sea, up and up into the morning, twisting and flashing, seeking escape. The tuna followed right behind, his larger body bent almost double with the force of his jump. The two met in the air five feet out of the sea, just as the bluefish began to descend. Finbar saw the fearsome jaws with their rows of white teeth snap shut across the bluefish's body.

Brendan's deep voice rumbled beside Finbar. "No matter how hard you try," he said, "escape is impossible.

Come to your senses. Allow the Lord the power of his wilderness. Seek to become a new man. Do not dwell on the terrors below."

Indeed, almost as though Brendan's words had made the difference, a new pleasure began to swell in Finbar from that morning. Perhaps the explanation was the weather, which offered three days of clear northeast winds, of sun, of regular seas. Perhaps it was the simple effect of time working on what was, in the end, a resilient spirit. The small trials were gone—just like that. Damp though he was, he felt perfectly warm. Cramped though he was, he was content with the presence of others aboard. Vigorous as was the motion, he could make his way above and below the deck without discomfort. The only pressure on him now was from the hunger that came doubly raging when his seasickness vanished. The holy voyagers ate very sparingly—Joseph, in fact, nearly always fasted—and Finbar had yet to feel full at the close of a meal.

On the eighth day, the curragh was bashing along before a quartering wind and a following sea. She rode dramatically, almost surfing on the faces of the great combers as they rolled up in musical order behind her. Finbar was at the helm, and he could see them come. All the way from the blue, tossed horizon they made their way, regular as the tolling of some liquid bell. One after another, hour after hour, the wet blows continued. One heard the chime with all the senses of the body, but more so with the deeper senses of the blood: that wild, eager wish to be plucked from human fate and allowed the sound of the Goddess' own heart unceasingly, a wish expressed in every sinew, every vein. It was a wish so transforming to the soul as almost to alter the very structure of man. It was the lust for Paradise, and it was without evil.

Finbar clung to his oar. The sun lay against his skin. His tongue tasted salt. He was thin, and strong, and beautiful. He felt a very god.

Only Atla and Ide were on deck at the time, the former rippling his way through ethereal tunes on his bone whistle, the latter keeping time to the music with nervous fingers, while trying to keep her face turned to the winter sun. The wind blew her grey hair around, where it had escaped from its clasp, and she tried repeatedly, exasperatedly, to gather it again. It was a companionable moment in all, with the surge of the sea and the press of the wind bearing them westward into a new world.

As a personality, Ide interested Finbar. He watched her as she took the sun, and wondered how she came to be in such an odd company. Perhaps she wondered, too, for he had observed that in some way she kept herself apart. Her self-effacement in this masculine company was no more than necessary under certain circumstances, but even during the dog-watch relaxation after the evening meal, when all sat casually in the cockpit and remarked on the course of the day, Ide was aloof. Finbar was aware that she did not sleep very much. She worked hard at her seamanship, and she showed more than usual concern for the comfort of Barinthus, her watch-mate. To Joseph, she scarcely said a word. Earth makes use of man for her own purposes, Finbar thought, moves man about, brands him, stretches him, without allowing him to know why, or, worse, without seeming to care. There was this woman caught up somehow away from her life. This was no place for her. It was not her sex that disoriented her, he thought, though certainly this was an odd pursuit for a woman. In fact, it was her melancholy, and her quietness, and her privacy—none of these comported easily with the bare, unwinking certitude of the cruise.

"Look!" Ide shouted, pointing. "Dolphins!"

Fifty yards away, the face of a sea leapt with a sudden coruscation of rippling bodies. The dolphins flew over one another in their eagerness to drop down the wave. They came on like arrows, singing. A sea reared between them and the sailors, but they burst from that as they had from the first, and then they were upon the curragh, pirouetting at the bow.

"Barinthus!" Atla shouted. "Fish, old man. Come out!"

Finbar heard coughs and murmurs as the elder dragged himself from sleep. Soon, parting the leather curtain that shielded the below-decks, his thin, white head emerged. There was heat in his wintry eye. "Fish, you say?" He rose to his knees on the cockpit deck, swayed with the rush of the ship against the coaming, and leaned outboard. The wind caught his lank, white hair and slapped it against his cheeks. Grandly, Atla gestured with his whistle to the dolphins. Barinthus rose uncertainly to his feet and, startlingly, he began to sing. Soon, as the play of the dolphins grew more intense, his voice attained the baritone that Finbar recalled from the night hymns. The song completed the dolphins' arabesques, the sound and the motion intertwining like smoke and wind.

Finbar bent toward Ide. "What is it with Barinthus about fish?" he asked her.

She turned a startled face to him. "You haven't heard the story of the last voyage?"

"I've heard mention of it, but nothing about fish."

Ide's face crinkled when she glanced at the old man. "Ask him about it."

Finbar straightened and looked at Barinthus's back. "Barinthus?"

The man did not answer. Indeed, he was so intent upon the view of the dolphins, so powerful in his song, that it seemed useless to address him.

Ide answered for him. "It was a great fish, an enormous, divine fish that guided him to Paradise last time. Since we left Ireland, Barinthus has been waiting for the fish to reappear. We always tell him about fish."

For two hours, the dolphins danced at the curragh's bow. Their game was an ecstasy to them, it seemed, and their mercurial flicker in water and air was as glorious to the sailors.

By and by, the sun began to get low in the sky, and the air—which, though it had never been warm that day, at least had not been cold—acquired a sharp edge. The dolphins made one final sweep around the curragh, and then they hied themselves eastward. Finbar had quit the helm by that time, surrendering it to Ide, and he now sat on the foredeck with his back against the foremast and watched the sea before them. The wind was somewhat more hearty than it had been at midday, when Finbar's watch had come on deck, and it had veered several points eastward. Nevertheless, the curragh sailed along with all the verve that she had shown since this favorable weather had come upon her three days before. Finbar luxuriated in the sensation of the downward sweep on the face of the seas. He was cold, and he felt that soon he should shelter himself in the cockpit, but for the moment, the sensations were too acute, the solitude too satiating, for him to move.

Finbar touched the straining sail above him and luxuriated in the experience he had had that day: the first release of his person from its chains of habit that he remembered in many years, saving the days of his death and birth on the island. For hours on end, he had not thought once of himself as a smith, nor remembered Greece, nor longed for the known conditions of a land-locked tramp. Instead, he merely existed on the sea. He was a spindrift mote. One sea after another had raised his stern, rushed him forward, dropped him behind. He was nothing but blue and air.

The sun was close enough to the horizon now for it to be partially obscured by the seas when the curragh was in a trough, and for it to leap again into the sky when she soared up onto a crest. The sky was brilliantly colored in reds and oranges, with small, fair-weather clouds like angel hair loose and airy above.

In the cockpit aft, Finbar heard Brendan's deep voice say, "Before we repair our bodies, we shall fill our souls with divine food."

"Lord, open our lips," the others replied.

"Praise the Lord, all His angels; praise Him, all His powers."

And the others answered him: "Sing praises to our God, sing praises! Sing praises to our King. Sing praises in wisdom."

"May the radiance of the Lord our God be upon us."

And, with that, the baritone splendor of Barinthus's voice carried the others in hymns of joy.

Shortly, Finbar felt someone approaching across the leather deck. Ide's face nudged his world at the bow, her skin lit red by the setting sun.

"Hello," she said. "I prayed for you."

"For that, I always thank you."

"Joseph is preparing the meal."

Finbar smiled. "And he won't eat it."

"He lives by penance. Discipline is beautiful to him."

Finbar shook his head. Ide smiled, and he watched with pleasure the play of wrinkles across her wind-burnt face. Grey hair blew forward across her cheeks.

For a time, the man and the woman sat side by side. The sun was gone, except for its upper rim when the curragh was high on a sea, and the first of the stars hung low before them, pearly in the thinning, pink air. The minutes passed slowly. Gradually, the color of the sky succumbed to the encroaching night. Finbar was mesmerized by the process: when he moved his eyes, he saw that the whole sky was lit with stars.

"We should go aft," he remarked. "Supper will be ready."

Ide continued to stare into the western night. Finbar could barely see her now against the sea, just the glint of her hair as it caught the stars. Then he saw her eyes turn toward him, the pupils lit with liquid reflection. "How can you doubt that there is something out there?" she asked.

"I don't doubt it. I simply don't know what it is."

"Open your heart to the Lord. Paradise is there."

Awkwardly, Finbar placed his hand on hers. "Perhaps Paradise is here instead. Perhaps this is all there is to perfection."

"No. It's a place." She did not move her hand, but then neither did she seem to be aware of his.

"Perhaps it's in the process of going there, not a place."

"You're wrong, Finbar, but I'm glad you're content."

"Your entire theology is based upon the specificity of things. The actuality of the resurrection. The absolute hierarchy of priests. The perfect transmission of election from Jesus to the Apostles and on through them to the Church. Now this insistence upon a place, a particular spot that can be reached by boat, which is called Paradise. I take a looser view of things."

Ide glanced at him with some surprise. Now, she removed her hand. "You know a lot of words," she said.

"For a smith?"

"Don't be offended."

Finbar stretched his shoulders. "Oh, I'm not," he sighed. "I was showing off."

She said, "There's no reason you shouldn't know the words," and her voice was apologetic.

"I've seen Christianity, Ide. In Egypt and Greece, I've seen it. I lived eleven years in Drumhallagh. I've never been among the *religiosi,* but even we of the *familia* learn the forms and the usage."

"You're more articulate than many smiths."

"I'm more interested. It was philosophy I followed through those lands, not iron. I thought it was iron, but in truth it was the mettle of the gods. I realized after Cul Dreimne that this was the case. That's why I was going back to Greece."

"What's in Greece?" Her voice was that of a wistful stay-at-home.

"Air. Light. I'm not sure . . . the gods."

"The pagan gods."

"They are older gods than yours," Finbar replied with a grin, "older by far."

"Older is not better."

"Ha! You see? Even for you to say that—even to imagine a comparison—is anathema. I may, but you mayn't. *Deus semper meior.*"

"You should not use the formulae of the Church against me."

He grinned, "I have no intention to do so. I merely observe. What, for example, are you doing here?"

"Going to Thule."

"And the others?"

"On their way to Paradise."

"Paradise . . . a Persian word, a garden of birds and tame animals where women in veils bring sherbet in stemmed glasses. Is this what waits for Brendan?"

"Of course not. Our Paradise."

"The concept is relative, then?"

"You lay traps."

"No. I tell you who I am."

The two were silent for a time. A planet was rising

through Pegasus. After a time, Ide said, "Perhaps Barinthus is correct about you."

"I hope not," Finbar chuckled.

But Ide was not amused. Her voice had another tone than before. "Perhaps your coming is the fall from grace of our pilgrimage: the snake in our grass."

Finbar, not for the first time, was afraid.

"Ide?" he queried.

"I think I shall speak with you no more."

Just at that moment, Atla's voice came from the stern, like a flute trilling across the water. "Our meal is prepared," he called. "Come to table in the name of the Lord."

The two rose to a crouch and made their way aft. Before they dropped down into the cockpit, Ide urged Finbar, "Ask Barinthus about the last voyage, if you doubt Paradise."

Accordingly, when the group had given thanks and was eating, Finbar turned to the old man and tried to draw him out.

Barinthus gummed his salted cod for a time, his thin, old head swaying under the stars. The water jug was passed. All continued to eat. Brendan helped himself to a johnny cake. Atla drank and passed the jug, and he broke off a piece of honey comb for his own cake. Joseph, abstaining as usual, was at the helm.

"You want the story of Paradise?" Barinthus asked finally.

"Tell it; do," Ide said, laying a hand upon Barinthus's knee.

"It was many years ago. A long, long time ago. I was quite a young man then." His voice trailed off into silence. The wind caught a line and snapped it against the canvas cover of the cabin until Brendan reached forward and silenced it. Atla ate more honey. Barinthus moistened his cod in whale oil and chewed.

"Please tell us," Ide ventured once more.

"I could see Paradise," Barinthus said quietly, so quietly that Finbar needed to stop eating to hear. "It was as close as . . . as that!" He snapped his fingers. "There were birds flying round its top, and they sang in many voices, but I could understand them, every one. And the smells! I shall never forget the smells of Paradise."

Into the silence that followed this lyric, Finbar asked, "How could you be certain that it was Paradise?"

"The fish told me. The fish led me there. You see, I set out from Lough Corrig to find the Lord. I just pushed myself out in a boat. I never knew where I was going. I desired only to go where the Lord, my blessed guide, was glad to send me. I had neither meat nor fish, nor wine, nor water. When I hungered, the fish came to me and gave me food. When I was dry, my chalice was filled with water so sweet I drank but one drop each day." He broke off and said, "Pass the jug."

Finbar took the jug from him when he was finished, and he, too, drank.

"Sweeter than that," Barinthus continued, and Finbar could hear that he was smiling.

"The fish told me which way to steer," Barinthus continued. "That's how I knew that it was Paradise. I had been gone a long time, a very long time, and I was weary, but the sight of Paradise so near kept me eager." The old man sighed. "I was unable to come there, though." Barinthus concluded, "There are many evils in the world."

When it seemed that Barinthus would not go on, Finbar reached out in the darkness and touched the old man. "Then you didn't go there?"

"I saw Paradise."

"But you weren't there yourself?"

"I was close by. I was as close as fire is to water."

"That is poetry. Those two are different stuff."

"It's as I have said. There are many evils in the world. I am one of them."

"You?"

"Yes."

"What do you mean?"

"I think I will sleep now."

"But what do you mean?"

"God be with you." Barinthus stood, creakingly, and he turned to make his way down into the cabin.

"Good night, uncle." Brendan's deep rumble came from a corner.

Finbar turned to the captain after Barinthus had
gone and asked, "What did he mean that he was evil?"

"I think, if Barinthus will not say, it is not for me to
do so."

It was Brendan's and Joseph's watch, so Ide and Atla
made their way below. Joseph relinquished the helm to
Brendan and set about clearing the meal away. Finbar sat
at the forward edge of the cockpit, his arm laid along the
roof of the cabin and his chin resting on his arm. He
looked forward into the night, feeling the heavy rush and
sigh of the vessel. He looked up. The sails swung back and
forth across the stars, obscuring them and then allowing
them to emerge. He had been struck by the intensity of
the elder's quiet voice, by the vivid unreality of the memory. The scend of the seas beside him beat against his
mind, pulsed through it with images of a Paradise nearly
attained, a transformation nearly accomplished. What
was the evil in the man that kept him from perfection?
The sea around him, the night, the scurrying curragh on
its fantastic journey, the horizon that dropped down
ahead and pulled up behind without altering its perfect
circle one whit: for the first time, Finbar understood
Brendan's reference to this place as a wilderness. It was
the earth stripped of causality, laid bare as a bone. It was
raw power, the earth's unhumaned energy, and, as such,
it must be the abode of perfection, if perfection existed at
all.

"You should sleep," Brendan coughed.

"I guess I will."

He bent to thrust his head through the flap and nearly
banged into someone coming out. "Oh!" he cried, startled.

It was Barinthus. "Help me," the old man begged.

Finbar took the frail arm in his hand and assisted the
man to stand and to make his way to a thwart. Barinthus
was panting. In the stillness of the rushing night, Finbar
knelt at the elder's feet, watching the thin skull against
the stars. The man's mouth opened. "You asked for the
tale," he gasped. "You ought to have it."

"Uncle," Brendan's muffled rumble came out of the
darkness by the steering oar, "don't tire yourself."

"*I* am not tired, good my Brendan. My body is."

"As you wish."

Finbar glanced at the captain's silhouette. Brendan
had not moved in some time. His figure, as ungainly as a
lump of rock against the sky, swung up and down as the
seas passed below, the stars making the backdrop for the
motion. Brendan's face was staring forward into the night
with the perpetual alertness that characterized him.

Taking a cue from the captain, Finbar said, "Another
time, perhaps. We will have another time when neither
of us needs so much rest."

"No. I shall tell it now." He put his hand out blindly
and caressed Finbar's wooly cheek. The intimacy startled
the smith. "For perhaps tomorrow we shall be in Paradise."

Finbar rose quietly and sat beside the ancient monk.
"What did you mean by evil?" he asked.

"I mean, I was tempted and found wanting. That is
the reason why I was never allowed to land on the blessed
shore."

"But how were you tempted?"

"I discovered someone out there on the sea, quite
close to Paradise. It was the moment of my temptation,
but I was unaware of it. You see, I was very young. I had
been sailing within sight of Paradise for many days. I
sailed as craftily as I knew how, but I could never come
any closer than I had been when I first spotted the shore.
I could see the birds, smell the holy smell. . . ."

He broke off, and his body seemed to sway in remem-
brance of the sensation of that closeness to perfection.

"I could draw no closer," he continued. "The fish had
deserted me. However, after a time, I saw a rock in the
sea some distance off. I turned my bow that way and,
when I had come close, I found that there was a man on
the rock, a black man, a man clothed in nothing except his
own hair. His hair was so long that he had wrapped it
around himself for a skirt. I knew by that that the man had
been on the rock for a long time. I desired to speak with
him, but even though I sailed right around the edge of the
rock, he showed no sign of seeing me. He was staring
across the sea toward the tip of Paradise, which could just

be seen, barely lifting its peak above the billows. I landed. I stepped ashore on the rock. Though there was barely room for the two of us to stand without wetting our feet, he still did not notice me. It was a very curious adventure. I scarcely knew what to make of it."

"What happened?"

"Well, the sun went down into the sea, and the night came. I stood on that rock all night, getting no response from my companion. Finally, the sun came up from the other side of the sea, and it was then that the other man appeared to come to life. He moved, and shook himself, and subsided against the rock as though he had been suddenly bereft of his bones.

" 'Who are you? How do you come to be here?' I asked him.

" 'My cursed name is Judas Iscariot,' he replied.

"Of course, I recoiled. It was a horrible thing to meet such a man. 'But what do you here?' I cried.

" 'This is my fate,' he told me, holding my foot so that I could not leave the rock. 'I am doomed to spend the rest of time here in the vicinity of the Land Promised to the Saints. I may see the place, but I may never go there. One day each year, I am allowed to move my limbs, to eat, to drink, to curse my fate. For the other days, I am frozen still. I stare at heaven, unable to curse, unable to weep, unable to mourn. Today is that one day during which I am free, insofar as ever I am free. I have seen your boat these last days, and I saw when you turned toward my rock. You have no idea what passion boiled in me then, struggling to get free, struggling to move, struggling to speak, so that you should not leave. You are the first of my own kind I have seen in 500 years!'

" 'We may be of similar types,' I answered him, trying to move my foot, 'but we are not of similar make.'

"You see, I was very young.

" 'Brother,' was how he answered me.

"There was nothing I could do to dislodge his grip. That man held me there all through the morning while he recounted the horrors of his imprisonment. They were horrors, Finbar. I won't detail them. The poor soul had suffered terribly, in ways that I did not even understand at the time. I did understand one thing: I knew the pain of seeing Paradise and of not being able to go there. Poor Judas had endured that pain for 500 years.

"At noon, the fish came across the sea, the same one who had led me thither. He had in his mouth a bit of bread and a skin of wine. This, that otherwise should have been Eucharistic fare, he tossed onto the rock in a contemptuous fashion, and he made off despite my entreaties. You see, I had fallen somewhat under the spell of friend Judas, and I desired to confront the fish with the injustice of the man's curse.

"However, the fish departed, and we were left on the rock. It drew toward evening. Judas continued his recitation. I became increasingly wroth. Finally, Judas noticed that the sun was about to dip into the sea. He had not even touched the bread and wine, so eager had he been to pour out his story to me. Now he moaned and wept at the shortness of his respite. I begged him at least to eat before he should become frozen once again for another year. But he turned upon me and desired me to take him with me from the rock. If I took him with me, he assured me, the curse would come to its end, and he should be allowed to die, as he so desperately longed to do. His passion was unquenchable. He dithered and spat in his furious longing.

"What was I to do? In the course of the day just spent, I had come to see him as a man such as myself. His misfortune had come upon him through his own sin, but he had paid heavily, and it was my feeling that he ought not to be forced to pay through eternity. Enough had been extracted. The deed had been done, and I was certain it had been paid for. He excused himself in the most winning way. He thought Christ had desired the betrayal. He was logical. He was articulate. He was humorous. He was human so completely, and I was lonely—I had failed to reach Paradise—that I did as he bade me. I took him aboard my boat just as the sun sank into the sea."

Barinthus fell silent once more. Finbar stared out across the cockpit and the deck at the black sky. The curragh continued in her uninterrupted rush into the west. The sea and the wind were the elements through which this tale wound itself. Finbar felt himself stitched up inside a coat made of this cloth, a coat from which he longed to burst the shoulders but which he was powerless to rip. A sense of pity overcame him for the withered, exhausted monk beside him, not on account of his tale— for who knew what of it was true?—but on account of the need that he felt to have the tale at all. A sense of the frailty, of the fearsome powerlessness of man came to him there in the middle of the night, in the middle of the sea.

"I took Judas Iscariot into my boat," the old voice continued, "and I set my course for home. I, Barinthus, son of Rudhraighe, took it upon myself to alter the structure of the world. Yes, I was young, but I was a fool.

"We sailed and sailed. Judas grew increasingly nervous as the journey approached its end. He hardly dared believe that he was so easily to be set free. I was beginning to regret my hasty decision, but I had no choice now but to follow it through. The man's whining voice grated on my nerves. Then a great storm blew up. It was a bad storm, and we were sorely pressed. Judas was little assistance to me, so totally was he caught up in the moment when he would set his feet upon human soil once more. In the middle of the storm, at the crucial moment, the fish appeared just beside the boat. We were leaking, and I was bailing, and I did not see the fish at first. I heard him call to me, though, and I looked over the side. There he was, his great head sticking out of the sea, his eyes like moons watching me. He asked me what the trouble was, and I told him we were badly damaged by the storm. He was not surprised. I begged him for assistance. He asked me why he ought to bother. He had never been that way before. I cursed him and called him a false friend. Then he told me that the storm was no natural disturbance. It had been sent by Christ Himself, my Lord and Master, for He was angry with me. The fish told me that I must turn about and repair once more to the rock. I must return Judas Iscariot to his incarceration there. Only then would I be allowed to return to my home. If I refused to do that, both of us would die."

"What did you do?"

"I was cursed either way. That is the evil of which I spoke before. That is man's fate, to be cursed either way."

"But what did you do?"

"I took him back."

There was a long silence. Joseph, who had come into the cockpit during the tale, rose and switched places with his watchmate, Brendan. The captain sat down beside his uncle and stretched his legs.

"It's cold," he said softly. "You ought to be in bed."

"I hardly feel the cold any longer, my boy."

"Still, you ought to rest."

"A man of my age sleeps very little."

Silence fell upon the group again. The constellations wheeled overhead. A shooting star sliced down toward the western horizon. A stray cupful of seawater slopped over the rail and wet Finbar's legs. He stood up.

"That is why you look for a fish," he said.

"That is why."

"I hope we see that fish."

"We will. Never doubt. That is as much man's curse as anything else. Does the sea doubt? Do the stars doubt? Does the wind, however it blows, doubt? Never doubt, Finbar. Doubt is the beginning of the end. Have faith. Believe. Never doubt."

"You doubt me. You told me so."

"I don't seriously think you are Judas Iscariot. I do recognize that we have found a black man living naked on a rock in the sea. I note that we are taking you with us. This time, though, we are taking you *to* Paradise, not away."

"I'm only going to Thule."

Barinthus waved a hand. "As you wish."

Finbar stood in the middle of the cockpit, moving his weight easily to the surge of the sea. He was tired. "Good night," he said.

"Bless you," Barinthus replied.

Even as Finbar turned to pass below, there came a sudden lurch to the side, and, with a bang, the sails slapped free of wind.

"Wind shift," Brendan muttered. "I've felt it coming."

Everyone set about trimming the sails to the new wind, but as they did, it veered again. The curragh shied sideways on the crest of the sea it had just climbed.

"We'll have to do some work now, Joseph," Brendan chuckled. "Go to sleep, Finbar. The two of us can cope. It will be calm by morning."

"More rain?" Finbar asked.

"If it's not snow."

Finbar groaned. He looked at the old monk sunken into his bony thighs, the wind flapping a loose fold of rough wool against his flaccid hands. "We'll see that fish," he murmured, from pity.

Barinthus's queer eyes were hot when he looked up. "That is the other curse," he said, "the real one. Everything begins again. Always it is repeated. We cannot stop."

"But you want the fish!"

Barinthus said nothing.

"You have almost been in Paradise. You must want the fish."

"Did Jesus want the Cross?"

"I am not a Nazarene; I cannot tell."

"I am, and I can do no more."

"If Jesus wanted the Cross, then your rescue was valid."

Barinthus only watched him. Finbar stared back. Finally, the old man said, "It was Jesus' storm."

Finbar burst out: "Your God is too hard to hurt you this way! You Nazarenes have made too high a thing of him. Subtlety, yes. I can agree with subtlety. Orpheus had subtlety. Athena, Hermes. But this is too much! Who can worship a being like this? Who would want to? The cunning of Orpheus is a triumph! All your Jesus does is punish."

No one replied. The sea banged against the leather boat, and the wind shifted again. Down in the cabin was to be heard the quick flippancy of Atla's whistle.

"Silence!" Brendan roared. "You, Finbar, go to bed."

Finbar stood his ground. "Why silence?"

"We need no augmentation of the harmony of God."

"I am sorry for you. Eurydice learned otherwise."

"What did it avail her?"

"You know the tale?"

"I am not a stupid man."

"Yet you argue for this Nazarene god?"

"Nor am I a missionary. I argue about nothing. Nor apologize. The world is as it is. You shall see, if we get there."

"If?"

"When, if you prefer. It alters nothing. Go to bed, Finbar, or trim the foresail."

Finbar smiled. "I'm off watch."

"Then go below. And don't you be a stupid man."

"How, stupid?"

"You cannot *think* the truth into existence. The truth is. You can think what you like, but you cannot make a south wind of a wind from the north."

"You perceive me trying?"

"I perceive you wishing to try."

The sail banged free of air again.

"Just sleep, Finbar. Sleep and look at the sea."

4

FINBAR WAS AROUSED BY passionate singing from
the deck. He recognized Barinthus's voice. The old
monk must be late awake. Finbar's dreams had been
of Paradise denied, and he wished the man well in his
hymnodizing, but he wished, too, that Barinthus might do
it more quietly. Finbar rolled over and pulled the musty
comfort of his blankets more tightly around himself. Yet
the singing grew more intense and more pointed, more
exultant, until its character was undeniably different from
what it ordinarily was. Curiosity drove the remains of
sleep from Finbar's brain, and he extricated himself from
his bed. It was difficult to squirm his way aft in the complete darkness of the cabin because of the sleeping bodies
around him, a difficulty accentuated by the rolling motion
of the curragh, but he managed to do it without awaken-
ing any of the others. He shoved the door flap up. Outside,
hardly anything was to be seen. The stars were partially
obscured by a building overcast from the north. The wind
had dropped during the past hours, as Brendan predicted
it would, and the motion of the curragh was sluggish.

As Finbar peered around, the sails lost their wind.
They slatted erratically until, surging to the top of a following sea, they filled with a weary rustle. There didn't
seem to be anyone at the steering oar. Finbar stuck his
head higher and rubbed grainy eyes. The singing came
from forward along the deck. Neither Barinthus nor Ide,
his watch companion, was to be seen. Finbar craned his
head to see forward. Everything was blanketed by the
impenetrable darkness. However, to his nostrils came an
odor of fish. Finbar pulled himself completely from the
cabin. He wore only his jerkin and leggings, and the air

outside was damper and colder than it had been earlier. He crawled forward along the deck. Off the starboard side of the boat Finbar saw a round shape humped up from the sea. It appeared to be a rock, but it shimmered in the lurid glow of the phosphorescence around it in a way that seemed to give it motion. The size of the object was hard for Finbar to judge, for its color was the same black as that of the surrounding night. It was either a small object close by, or a bigger one farther away. In any case, it dwarfed the curragh. While Finbar watched, it seemed to grow larger still. It was so large to windward that the curragh lost her wind completely and fell to rolling uncomfortably in the irregular chop the object cast up below itself.

Finbar could not move his eyes from the apparition, but he felt someone crawl from the cabin and stand beside him. Brendan's voice came, gutteral and sleepy, asking, "What's going on? Why are we falling off?"

Finbar tore his eyes from the object and looked at Barinthus. The man was leaning far over the side, clinging with one skinny arm to a stay, and calling out anxiously. In the eerie light from below, his face and thin hair were lit green. His eyes were as bright as those of a lover, his coaxing calls as plaintive.

It appeared that the remainder of the crew had come on deck. A movement behind Barinthus caught Finbar's attention, and he saw that Ide was crouched there in an attitude of wonderment. Finbar could feel Atla's and Joseph's presence beside him now, though his eyes had returned irresistibly to the shape above them, a shape that continued to grow. The odor was stronger. It thickened in his throat, and he feared he might choke. He brushed against Atla, and he realized that the hunter crouched beside him as tense as a bowstring, his arm in casting position, a spearhead gleaming in the green loom. It was then that it occurred to Finbar that the object might be alive. Just as he was wondering about this, an eye, an unmistakable eye, emerged from the sea and glared at them. The eye was as big across as Finbar's shoulders, and it was intelligent. A mind was behind it. Finbar heard himself shout.

In that instant, several things happened. Atla uncoiled. The spear leapt toward the eye. Brendan yelled, "No!" and brought his hand down on Atla's arm, interfering at the last moment with his aim. The spear, instead of piercing the eye, thudded deeply into the wrinkled skin just below it. "You fool," Brendan shouted, as Atla grabbed up another spear.

In an instant, the curragh was tossed into the air as though she had been a fly whacked by a bull's tail. She came down again, on her side, partially swamped. The sailors looked up. A mouth twice as long as they were, a mouth armed with teeth each as tall as a man, opened out of the sky and the sea. The mouth began to close on the curragh. Finbar had a momentary vision of Barinthus balanced on the rolling, wet deck, his arms open wide and his mouth calling imprecations, before the maw closed. There came a rending and a tearing of the boat. Atla cast again, at the last moment, and the monster took the second spear in its throat. It hesitated before crunching down, the curragh held crosswise, almost casually in its jaw. The water frothed, and the boat filled. Finbar saw Joseph swept over the side. A flailing arm reached from a breaker, white against the dark water, and then it was gone. The foremast broke off short, the broken spar and yard like pins annoying the monster's enormous jaws. Another spear sank into the flesh of the animal's lip. Another. Finbar grabbed up an axe while more spears sprouted from the lips and gums of the great animal. It was nearly impossible to stand in the tangled boat. The only light was the green of the agitated sea. The monster began to shake the curragh as a dog does a rat. Finbar's entire universe became crashing water and breaking wood. He found purchase and swung and swung with his axe. He saw Brendan beside him hewing. The ship was below the sea as often as she was above.

Suddenly the great jaw opened once more. The monster backed away. Dripping thick blood from its head and jaw, it held a position a few feet away from the wrecked curragh. The men stood in exhaustion, their arms hanging, their fingers slipping in the blood on the axe helves, watching the monster for its final lunge. Instead, it turned, and, without hurry, it disappeared into the night.

Unbelieving, the three of them looked at one another. A very little light was beginning to appear in the
eastern sky, although all was overcast by now, and by this
light they saw the horror in one another's faces. The monster was gone, perhaps, but the curragh was sinking. Already, smashed and ripped below the water, she was half
full, wallowing in the troughs. There was no sign of Barinthus or Joseph. Ide could be seen clinging, conscious or no,
among the wreckage of the foremast.

"Bail," Brendan croaked, and the two others set to it,
still too dazed entirely to grasp their predicament.

Brendan surveyed the damage. He pulled Ide from
the deck into the well of the cockpit. She was alive, and
slowly she came back to awareness of where she was.
Brendan thrust a bucket into her hands. "We're sinking!"
he shouted into her blank face. "Bail!"

Stripped of top-hamper and full of water, the curragh
was moving hardly at all across the sea. Instead, she settled ponderously into the troughs and as heavily muddled
across the crests. Wreckage was strewn around her; her
foremast, still attached by its stays, was trailing away up-
wind and acting as a further brake to her motion. Other
wreckage littered the swells.

As fast as they were bailing, their attention was on
Brendan. The captain clung in the shrouds of the mainmast and bellowed for Barinthus and Joseph. The lonely
cries seemed to be absorbed in the humid cold of early
dawn. At last, the mariners heard an answering voice.
Sweeping their gazes around, they saw the form of Barinthus, with Joseph in tow, rising and waving on a low sea
twenty yards to leeward. Less heavy in the water than the
curragh, and dependent only upon Barinthus's failing
strength, the two were being swept inexorably away. Motioning his intention to Atla, Brendan knotted the end of
a line around his waist and plunged over the side.

Brendan's stroke was lusty, and his direction was
good, but even as he drew close to the struggling men—
while his lifeline steadily paid out over the curragh's side
—the two began to disappear below the surface. Finbar
saw Joseph surface once more, his mouth wide to gasp a
breath, and saw him slapped in the face by the broken top

of a passing sea. Brendan was only four yards away then, still swimming. The end of the line came up from the cockpit and snaked over the gunwale. Without a thought, Finbar leapt overboard after it, catching it as it fell into the sea, and allowing himself to be drawn away from the curragh with it in his hand. Finbar was not a good swimmer, and the sea was icy. He put the line through his teeth and windmilled toward the boat. Atla was leaning over the side unsteadily, waving a spar in Finbar's direction. The motion of the waterlogged boat made the flailing pole a danger more than a help. Finbar felt it crash against his shoulder before he was able to grab it on its next pass. He got it and held it, and Atla drew him steadily in toward the curragh. Finbar knew Brendan was still on the line behind him, because he could feel the captain's weight, but he was too low in the water to see across the crests to where Barinthus and Joseph ought to be. Not until Finbar had been drawn to the side of the boat and dragged across her swamped gunwale did he have a chance to stand and look behind him. He passed the line he had rescued to Atla, and the other hauled in the catch. Indeed, Brendan did have the other two in tow. When the line had been drawn back in, he was discovered at its end with an arm around each. Barinthus and Joseph were nearly drowned. Hardly a word had been exchanged by any of the members of the crew since the monster's departure.

Finbar felt himself grow warmer with the bailing. Joseph revived, and he too was put to bailing. Much more slowly than Joseph had, Barinthus became conscious, but he was stunned. He sat awash to the chest on a thwart in the rowing well, his head down, and he failed to respond when Brendan spoke to him. His ancient frame shivered violently, and everyone knew he would die soon unless he could be made dry and warm. There was no way to get dry. The water was holding steady in the curragh, now that four were bailing, just eight inches below the gunwales. Bail as they might, they could not get ahead of the inward rush of the sea. There was nothing for Barinthus to do but sit, up to his chest in the winter ocean, wavelets lapping at his neck.

Brendan explored the damage. Most of the cracked

stringers and ribs, and most of the torn hide, was right amidships where the monster's mouth had closed on the curragh. He felt that if they could fother a sail across the bottom of the boat, they might be able to stem the leak a bit. With Ide's assistance, he found a sail stowed forward, and the two of them quickly bent lines onto the four corners. Then everyone stopped bailing for a moment as two of the lines were strung under the bottom. The sail was positioned carefully, and then the lines under the bottom were hauled in. This pulled the sail down the other side and across the bottom.

Once securely in place, the patch did some good. Three bailers, now, could keep ahead of the sea, and four actually lowered the level in the boat. Very gradually, as dawn came, the curragh rose out of the water and began to feel once more as though she were afloat. As the hull came free from the water, fewer holes lay below the surface. At the same time, with less water in the curragh, Ide and Joseph were able to make their way along the inside and stuff blankets and other items into leaks. By midmorning, with only one person bailing, and he not so vigorously as before, the curragh was alive.

Meanwhile, Barinthus huddled in the bow underneath what little shelter the forward decking provided. He found very little protection from the wind and from the occasional gouts of spray that broke over the side. His condition had been dire enough when he was hauled back aboard; but now it steadily deteriorated. By the time the sail had been fothered under the keel and the curragh was beginning to rise out of the sea, Barinthus had become delirious. In shaking voice and amid mad rumblings, he called to the great fish, begging for the guidance he so greatly craved and which he believed the fish had the power to offer. Frequently during its efforts to save the boat, the crew bent over the old, sick man and chaffed his limbs or called to him. But he was far away, and there was no response from him. Of the crew, Brendan was the most acutely hurt by Barinthus's weakness: he was torn between seamanship and pity for his dying uncle. Finbar and Joseph took it in turns to force wine upon the old man, but the warming liquid simply gurgled back from his blue lips and ran down his chin. His face was grey and sunken. His almost toothless mouth no longer chattered. The violent shivering passed away, to be replaced by a stillness that was the more unnerving to his well-wishers. The power to control himself, even to respond humanly to the intense cold, had passed from him, leaving him hanging on the edge of his demise the way a withered leaf hangs from a twig after the winds have passed, and then lets go.

Barinthus's wet garments were stripped from his body. Blankets and cloaks that had not been commandeered to caulk the vessel were wrung as dry as possible, and he was wrapped in them. Morning became noon, and the sea subsided while the overcast thickened. There was almost no wind. A thin rain began to fall; the deep heaved around them, grey and cold. Everything was wet. Atla worked at the erection of a jury rig. Ide did what she could to construct a shelter for Barinthus, but most of the materials had either been swept away in the fight with the sea monster or had been used to repair the curragh afterwards. Little could be done to keep the old man dry.

By late afternoon, the rain had chilled to sleet and it fell more heavily. The condition of the crew in general was miserable, but the condition of Barinthus was worse. No longer was there any response from him at all, of any sort. He neither moaned with the cold, nor cried out for the fish. He knew none of the crew. He ate nothing. He drank nothing. He was alive, as Brendan would periodically discover by feeling for the faint, ragged beating of his heart, but it was as though he were only momentarily so.

The light began to be extinguished from the day. The curragh lay dead in the water, her makeshift sail limp, the sleet sizzling into the sea around her and dripping with irritating persistence everywhere. Wet snow and ice built up, rotten with melt water, on the rigging and the spars, only to fall off at the slightest shift of weight aboard, usually to drench anew someone who had just managed to dry one part of his body.

"Brendan, we're taking water again," Atla called softly from the stern.

The sea had managed to dislodge the fothered sail sufficiently to open up some of the rents in the hull. Two men constantly bailing could keep ahead of the new influx, but it was apparent that the condition would grow worse instead of better. Brendan had been resting with Barinthus, trying to coax him to drink some wine, but now he rose and moved aft.

Passing stiffly by the silent, bent bodies of Joseph and Finbar, who were bailing, he pressed Ide's arm. "Warm him, Ide. Please. He mustn't die. Do what you can."

"Of course." The woman rose and made her way forward.

They spoke in whispers, the crew. No one raised his voice. In the eerie, still air, their voices carried well. Hardly any light was left at all in the sky. Bent forward on his knees in the bilge, awash to the groin with chilling water, Finbar could see almost nothing. He bailed mechanically. He dipped the bucket down, filled it with water, and cast it over the side. Only his arms and his back moved. He was weary to the bone, chilled beyond any memory he had of cold. His eyes were closed. Forward of him, Joseph bailed, bent over into the same aching position, chilled by the same wash of new sea with every bucket thrown out.

Finbar found that he was in mind of Greece. Images of the dry, rocky land, of the warmth of the sun, moved slowly through his brain. He thought of the woman there. Probably she was dead. He realized they would all die. First, Barinthus. Barinthus was nearly dead already. The others would all be dead in a day or so. How long could they continue this bailing? How long could the curragh hold against the sea? Suppose a wind came, any sea at all? That would be the end. There was nothing they could do. Over his shoulder, he heard Brendan and Atla whispering. Now and then, he heard a word or two of what they said, but he cared little about it. It was bitter to die in the sea. Once already he had given himself to its embrace, and he had been saved. The word brought a flood of anger at the Nazarenes. They would consider his extra time a Grace—they did, in fact: Ide had told him so—but they were wrong. There was no resurrection, only transformation, its mundane cousin; better to die in the realism of the ancient way, to know the earth as fundamental and the gods only its ephemera. Better to recognize in chaos what chaos is, than to fall to the fantastic claim of the Nazarenes that there was their god first, and their god active, and their god to be thanked. He paused in his bailing. Sleet dripped from his hair. His back ached. He eased the muscles by stretching his arms over his head. No, he thought, the strong, the honest belief was in the face of some Titan behind this scene, the bland face of a careless cosmos. This Christianity was pap, for snivelers who dared not stand free in the winds of the world.

"Finbar." A whisper came from the bow. "Finbar, I need you."

Finbar looked up. His eyes could hardly focus. The world had rolled over into night. He saw a form in the bow, a woman's form, he thought. It was the Greek girl, naked.

"Finbar, please. It's cold." But the girl spoke with Ide's voice, and, stiffly, he stood. His leg was on fire with pain.

"It's the only way to warm him, Finbar. Please. Take off your clothes."

He stepped forward. Joseph, too, was on his knees, staring at the apparition of the naked woman before him. Her form seemed to the weary smith to merge in and out of the clouds behind her.

Standing beside Joseph, Finbar croaked, "I must bail."

"Go, Finbar," came Brendan's voice soft behind him. "We are holding our own."

Finbar knew this was not true.

"Joseph," the voice came again from the stern, "take a rest. Atla and I shall bail."

Joseph was too exhausted even to stand. He merely sank back on his heels, the water to his waist. His eyes never left the woman's shape. He coughed.

Finbar made his way forward. When he reached the bow, Ide took his arm and pointed down to the huddled shape of the old man. "I've been lying with him, but he needs even more heat."

"What can I do?"

"Take off your clothes. We'll put him between us."

Finbar did as he was bid. Ide had made a temporary bed with planks across two thwarts, and it was on this that she had been warming Barinthus. The blankets were still warm from her body, where they were not wet. Finbar, shivering, lay down on them.

"Joseph," Ide called. "Please wrap us when I lie down."

There was no answer.

"Joseph?"

A strangled sound came from him. "I can't," he muttered.

"You must." Ide's voice was calm. "Come," she urged, and she moved aft to hold her hand out to him. Sleet washed down her back. Her voice shuddered with the chill.

Finbar called, "Joseph! Help us. It's cold."

"Joseph," Ide said again, softly. "Do not be ashamed."

"*I* am not ashamed," the man rasped.

"Please," she said.

"Cover yourself, woman."

"I will cover myself with blankets, but you must wrap them, for I cannot do it myself. It's dark, Joseph. We are in extremity. Barinthus is dying."

"Better to die than—"

"Than what? I ask nothing of you that you cannot give."

Brendan, bailing in the stern, now became aware of what transpired forward. "Joseph," he commanded, "do as she says."

Still the monk was reluctant.

"Ide," Brendan said, "go back and cover yourself. Next, you'll freeze. Joseph, go with her and wrap the covers. That is an order."

Joseph stood, shakily. Ide turned and collapsed herself into the blankets.

"Quickly," she rasped at Joseph. "He's cold again."

The man moved forward with tremendous reluctance and drew the blankets and the waterproof covers around the forms of the three others.

"I'm sorry," Ide whispered to him.

"I am a follower of Christ," he replied.

"I know."

"I shall follow Him until I die." His voice was proud.

"You are to be honored, Joseph, commended for your faith."

"I don't want honor from you," he retorted. "I am alone with my God." With that, he turned and retreated to his place amidships where he commenced again to bail.

Finbar and Ide wrapped their arms around one another, with the cold body of Barinthus between them—shivering again, a good sign—and tried to ignore the pattering of the sleet against them, the runnels of icy water across their faces and down their necks, and the knowledge that the curragh was again awash. It was good for Finbar to lie down and to stretch his leg out straight, but he felt the hopelessness of the gesture they were making. Even if Barinthus should revive, there was nothing in store for him except a cold death by drowning, probably before the next day was out.

Finbar and Ide whispered together as the shivering in the old man's body grew less violent and finally, peacefully, he passed into sleep. In the background of their conversation, the only sounds were the faint creak of the curragh's injured hull as she sank in the long, flat swells, the continuous hiss of sleet into the sea, the gurgle of bucketsful of water over the side as the others bailed, and the occasional mutterings between Brendan and Atla from the stern. Eventually, there was no more sound of the sleet, for the air grew less liquid, and, as the night deepened, the overcast thinned. Close to morning, a few faint stars appeared in the west.

Finbar spoke of Egypt and of Greece and of the drear, thick forests of the Gaulish mountains. His voice was a murmur, his memory piecemeal. After a time, he realized that he was telling Ide the story of his life. It was a tale he rarely told, being a private man, and he told it as much to anchor himself at this moment of slow, wet death as to inform the woman beside him. The two of them had pulled the blankets and the canvas covers over their heads to keep out the wet, so Finbar could not see

Ide. Pressed against his chest was the frail, naked back of
the sleeping man. Pressed against Barinthus's front was
Ide. Her head lay in the crook of Finbar's arm. Her hair,
which was damp and smelled of salt and fish, lay against
his cheek. Their faces were only inches apart in their
warm cocoon. Finbar breathed Ide's breath. When he
moved his upper arm, his hand slid across her ribs. Her
feet were large and cold and calloused.

He had gone to Egypt, he told her, because as a young
man he was in love with gold. He tried to explain to her
what the nature of his reverence for the perfect metal
was. He spoke of its purity, its malleability, it weightiness.
She whispered her questions. He told her that he had
been an eager smith with an adventuresome turn of mind.
He had desired not only an Egyptian education but an
Egyptian sophistication. Hippo, even Carthage, was a village compared with Alexandria! So he had ridden the
length of North Africa all the way to Egypt. His skill with
gold was not of the nature that he had hoped. In Egypt,
however, he met traders from the East. He shared their
food, worked their camels, loaded their ships in the Reed
Sea. It was with them that he began to see that there were
other ways of understanding the world than prevailed
around the Mediterranean. These men followed the gods
of the East. They believed that time was endless, both
backwards and forwards. Ide was fascinated. How could
this be, when it was known that God had created the
world before the time of Adam?

Finbar's whispering became more heated. He told
her that the world had been created by a sacrifice: the
Original Man had been killed by his sons and his body had
been cut up. The mountains and seas, the stars and the
sun, all the birds and the beasts, everything had been
created from his parts. This was inconceivable to Ide, but,
in the damp and holy darkness of the sinking curragh, she
allowed Finbar to continue the tale. Finbar told her about
dangerous, thin men of the East with jewels in their ears
and lips painted like those of a Persian pleasure girl, with
whom he had debated questions of religion and cos-
mology that were as new to him as were their answers.
Whereas earlier in his life he had been content with the

techniques of the smith, now he began to understand that there was still more significance to the art of creating beauty. These acts were in keeping with the creative power of a regenerative universe. As a man of twenty, he found that his calling lay in the direction of philosophy, though his profession remained that of smith. So he had gone to Greece, the home of philosophy, and he had mined tin and silver in the hot, pine-forested mountains.

"Were you ever at Rome?"

"No."

Ide shifted her weight gently. She rolled more onto her stomach. Barinthus stirred, and the two were still until he settled once more into sleep.

There was a girlish quality about her voice that Finbar had never heard before when she whispered, "I should like to have seen Rome."

"I seem to have followed around the edges of the Empire, never gone to its center."

"It's Saint Peter's city."

"I know."

"That's the only thing I should like to have done. Otherwise, God has granted me a good life. I was proud to be an abbess." She moved again. "Are you comfortable?"

"I don't feel the sleet anymore. Let me look outside."

When he pulled a corner of the blanket back, he felt the cold night air. He saw that the overcast was thinner. The night was very dark. He heard water being bailed slowly. It occurred to Finbar to exchange his warm situation with that of one of the other men, but instead he pulled the blanket back across his face. Ide was moving more now, and he was growing physically aware of her.

"It's cold out there," he whispered, "but the clouds are moving."

"I don't feel any wind."

"It will come."

"Then we shall sink."

There was no answer for that.

After a few moments, Ide whispered, "Tell me about Greece."

Finbar described the forms of the land. It had a heaviness that was relieved by the extraordinary, Olympian quality of the light, almost as though the land were both mundane and ethereal at the same moment.

"Like Paradise," she murmured.

"Perhaps."

Finbar described a vein of silver he had discovered in an abandoned mine. He told her how he had worked it secretly to discover its extent. It had proven to be rich, and for a few months he was a wealthy man. This discovery occurred soon after he had taken up with the miner's widow, and, in the end, it was she who had stolen the mine away from him. A year later, he was as poor as he had ever been, walking north, away from Greece; but he carried more affection with him for that woman than he did resentment. He told Ide that she had saved his life. There was a cave-in in the disused mine, and he was trapped under the mountain, his leg pinned by a boulder. It was she who came for him, being impatient of waiting. She had had no premonition: it was her very selfishness that saved him. His leg had never healed quite properly, but he still considered himself in her debt.

"Yet she robbed you."

"It was like her to do so."

"Forgiveness is divine."

"No. It's not forgiveness. It's understanding."

"What did she look like?"

Finbar thought a minute. "I don't remember," he said. "She was shorter than you are. She didn't bind her hair; I remember that. It was a long time ago, Ide. It was a long time ago, and I was a younger man." He realized, under the heat of the blankets, that he could smell Ide distinctly, and that he was beginning to sweat. He pulled his cramped arm from under her head. He rolled more onto his back. He pulled the blankets down sufficiently to open a hole for his face to look up at the sky.

"Her skin was very white," he murmured.

Ide, too, put back the blankets. Barinthus slept like a baby between his parents.

Astern, there were sounds of slow bailing. The curragh lay half-swamped in a turgid, silent sea. There was only occasional motion as a lazy swell idled past. Stars filled the northern and the western halves of the sky.

After some time had passed, Finbar whispered, "I

ought to go aft and bail. Barinthus will be all right now."

"We both should."

Still, they lay at ease for a little longer.

When some time had passed in silence, he asked her, "Why did you come?"

"I'm going to Thule. I told you. I am called there."

"Is that the reason?"

"I am a sister of Christ. What other reason can there be?"

"But isn't there something of you, you alone, in the decision? Are you simply commanded?"

Ide raised herself on one elbow. Finbar could barely see her silhouette against the stars. "It is forbidden to separate oneself from God. We are creatures of God."

"The trouble with you Nazarenes is that you all surrender too much of your own will."

"Look at you," she whispered. "You are a castaway. What will do you have?"

"Brendan thinks he is using me; no, I am using him."

"How?"

"This is merely a way to get back to the Empire, for me. I care nothing for this Paradise business. And neither do you, or you would be going there, too. You are going to Thule, if we ever get there. Not that we will, now. So what does it matter? Tell me the truth. We are all going to die anyway. Tell me, why are you here?"

There was a long pause. After a moment or two, Ide sat up and leaned her elbows on her raised knees. She held her chin in her hands and stared out into the night dampness. "When I was a young girl," she said, "before I was a sister, there was a boy with whom I used to go walking. Oh, he was a lovely boy. He used to climb down the cliffs along the shore and gather duck eggs for me. And I would hold them in my apron, and he would talk to me. He was so earnest! We were so young." She turned her face toward Finbar. "I could have gotten to Thule more directly, I suppose. But that boy's name was Brendan." She laughed. "And here we are now."

Finbar reached across the sleeping form of the old man and touched Ide's shoulder. "You see?" he said.

She slumped down onto one elbow again. "But the call is real."

"I don't doubt it."

They were quiet. Shortly, Ide rolled over onto her back. "I don't think he remembers," she whispered, with her forearm hiding her eyes. It was odd for Finbar to conceive of their four-square captain as a callow lover, dreaming with a pretty girl in an Irish summer.

Finbar watched Ide. Starlight lay softly on her strong chin and the slopes of her throat. It played along her raised arm. Its forgiving light pared away the slackness of her years, and it gave her flesh vigor. Finbar was aware of intimacies of her body: of the froth of hair in her armpit, of the weight of her flaccid breast. He found himself growing tender in his examination of these things, and he was excited by the tenderness. Who is this woman? he wondered. The more he knew of her, the more comfortable she became. He was surprised at the erotic intensity of his imagination. He seemed to examine the shape of her under his palm and on his tongue. He stirred restlessly against the wet blankets, suddenly aware of every sensation of his skin.

Her arm came down, and he could see her eyes in the starlight. "Maybe he can't remember who I am."

"Who?"

"Brendan, of course."

"Ide. . . ."

"Yes?"

Finbar coughed. "I . . . you . . ." He coughed again. "Of course, he remembers."

Ide was looking at him intently. He realized that the faintest daylight must have crept into the sky. He could see the truth of her skin. The tenderness flowing from him was no whit diminished.

"Thank you. That was not what you were going to say, Finbar. What were you going to say?"

He laughed uncomfortably. "I've never said this before, and it sounds odd, but lying here with you has been like lying alone."

Her eyes watched him for several seconds without expression, and then she laughed. It was a good, full laugh. "Thank you," she smiled. "I've rarely had so fine a compliment."

A few minutes passed in silence.

In time, Ide's hand slid across Barinthus and sought out Finbar's. She squeezed. "It's good to die as friends," she whispered, not looking at him. Finbar squeezed back.

"So tell me more," he said, feeling drowsy now and satiated with his new-found intimacy. "Why did Brendan make this choice, to go into the Church?"

"He could have been a fisherman; his father was. It was Barinthus who really turned the tide. It was when Barinthus returned from his first voyage. Brendan never looked back after he heard that tale."

"Then his life has been spent preparing for this voyage?"

"Yes."

Finbar digested this singleness of resolve, and then he asked softly, "But if he had been a fisherman?"

Ide laughed and shrugged, a Greek gesture which a moment before would have stirred Finbar's memories from the present. "I was an *oblate*. It wouldn't have mattered to me. I was given to the convent by my parents. There was nothing I could do."

Finbar could scarcely recall his parents. "It's a different life, Ide, yours from mine. I can't understand your life."

The woman raised herself onto her elbow, and Finbar's eyes went to her breasts as they sagged free of the blanket. She noted his glance and gathered the material around herself more securely. "It's not a hard life to understand," she said. "I've done what was asked of me, and I've done it well."

"Myself, I've always done as I pleased."

"And look at you," she said. "Poor thing, you are the worse for it."

"Maybe. And you?"

"I go to God."

"You're very certain."

"I've never doubted it."

Finbar looked away. "I doubt everything," he murmured.

"Just so."

A great gasp coming suddenly from the night made Finbar wonder whether one of the bailers had breathed his last over his bucket. He looked around to see. He noticed that a bit of light now illuminated the sky. He saw the crumpled figures of Brendan and Atla in the stern. Between himself and their forms were the stark, motionless bars of the jury mast and yard, the idle slump of the jury sail. Everything was wet. He twisted farther and saw that the curragh was deeper in the ocean than he had thought. The water was nearly up to the thwarts. Soon the bed upon which he lay with Ide and Barinthus would be afloat. Amidships there came a rustle of movement and then a splash of water. Joseph subsided into stillness once again. Some minutes passed. Joseph bailed another time. Finbar was ashamed. He had spent the night in warmth and comfort, comparatively, and he was stronger than Joseph. He pushed back the blankets. The air was cold against his skin. As quickly as he could, he pulled wet clothing on.

Finbar swung to his feet, thigh deep in the water, and sloshed aft. He shook Joseph's shoulder and told him to go forward and lie down. The man's body felt as cold as stone. There was no response to Finbar's suggestion. Instead, as though nothing had occurred, the man bent forward, filled his bucket, and slopped it against the side of the boat. Half of what he had dipped up fell back inside. Finbar looked aft at Brendan and Atla. They, too, seemed in a mindless state. He tried to call to them, but his voice was a croak. Instead, he turned his attention to Joseph again.

"Joseph, rest."

There was still no response. The bucket was lowered again and again filled. Finbar took the man's hands in his own and stopped the awkward motion. That alerted Joseph. The monk turned his eyes up toward Finbar, although his stare was blank. Gently, Finbar withdrew the bucket from the chilled fingers that grasped it and then stepped to the gunwale and emptied it. He repeated, "Go rest, Joseph. You've done enough."

Comprehension was beginning to show on Joseph's face.

"Finbar?"

"Yes?"

"I can't move."

"Let me help."

"It's my legs. They won't move."

Finbar slid his hands under the man's arms and tried to lift him. The footing was bad, and he struggled awkwardly. Joseph did not seem to be able to straighten himself, even when Finbar had his weight lifted off the bottom of the boat.

"I'll have to carry you."

"I'm sorry."

"Don't be. You've done enough. Too much."

"I tried to bail."

"You did, you did. You've been like a rock."

"I want him to depend on me, that's all. I must be dependable."

"Who?"

"Him." Joseph moved his arm fractionally toward the stern.

"He does, Joseph. I know he does."

"I tried."

"He knows you did."

Meanwhile, Finbar lifted the thin man bodily in his arms and began lurching forward with him toward the bed in the bow. Joseph was bent at the knees and the waist into a kneeling posture. He could not straighten himself.

"Do you hurt?" Finbar inquired softly.

"No." Then Joseph realized where Finbar was taking him. "Not with her," he said firmly.

"Joseph, you must get warm."

"Not with her."

"Look, I'll just put you here beside Barinthus. You needn't think of her, but you must lie down. I'll cover you then."

"I . . . can't. I mustn't."

"You will, Joseph. You'll save yourself. What would he think," Finbar nodded astern, "if he knew you hadn't the courage to save yourself? How could he count upon you then?"

"All right."

"You needn't be afraid of her, you know. She's asleep."

Joseph was indignant. "I am not afraid."

Finbar set him down on his side facing away from Ide.

The man still could not move, but his features were animated as he hissed, "For two years, she has distracted us from God."

"Surely not."

"You haven't seen it. None of them have seen it, but I have. I've watched her all the time, and I know what she is."

Finbar pulled coverings across the wet monk. "Rest now," he said. "I must bail." He turned away.

Joseph snatched at Finbar's cloak. "She keeps us from God," he repeated. "I know she does. That's why we are tried this way." He motioned around them. "We are to die because of her."

"Let go, Joseph. You're tired. I must bail."

"What good is bailing with the devil aboard?"

"I don't think she's the devil."

With scorn, Joseph returned, "You are not even a Christian."

"No," Finbar admitted, and he twisted his cloak free. "But I can bail. At the moment, that may do you more good than my conversion."

"Don't speak so."

"Don't you be a fool, Joseph. Rest. Don't fear Ide. Let me bail. If we survive this, then we can discuss women and Christianity."

"It's not women; it's her. And we won't survive unless the Savior is pleased. Don't you see? Our survival is not in our hands."

"Then, if it makes no difference anyway, let me bail."

"Don't patronize me."

"I'm sorry, but Joseph, this is not the time. We're sinking."

"This is the best time."

Finbar turned away. "I'm going to bail."

All this conversation had been carried on in a whisper. The sounds around the curragh that originally had alerted Finbar had continued, but Finbar had been unconscious of them. As Finbar turned his back on Joseph, the monk said in a louder tone, "Someone must understand!"

Finbar looked out over the side at the sea, now visible in the gathering, grey light.

"Oh, no," he said.

"What is it?" Joseph hissed.

Finbar did not reply. He continued to stare over the side. Finally, he turned back to Joseph. "You must be right after all. We are doomed."

"What do you mean?"

"Out there. Dozens of them."

"Dozens of what?"

"Whales. The monsters from the other night. Here, I'll lift you up."

The sea was flat and woolly in the partial light. On each side of the curragh, ahead and behind as well, the surface was dotted with smooth, enormous, black backs. The gasping that Finbar had heard was the breathing of the creatures, quiet breathing in the quiet dawn. As the two watched, more of them appeared from out of the sea. Their backs would slide into view, and their breaths would sigh in the cold air. Vapor would mist for a moment, and then the back would lie there motionless in the sea. Now and then, interspersed with the gasps, odd sounds seemed to fill the air as though of singing, sounds that appeared to have no point of origin but echoed still inside the ear.

"Wake Barinthus," Joseph whispered.

"You wake him. I must tell Brendan." Finbar looked aft and saw that the two men were slumped as they had been before, unaware of the leviathans around them.

"Not her."

Finbar did not have time to spare on further discussion of Ide. He slogged toward the stern as quickly, but as silently, as he was able.

"Brendan," he whispered stridently, "Brendan, Atla, wake up." He made his way through the tangle of broken equipment. "Brendan! Look!"

"What? What is it?"

Finbar was beside them now. "Look around us." He pointed out over the side. "Look. Hundreds of them."

Brendan and Atla, their faces white with fatigue, their eyes ringed with grime and salt, stared out into the horrifying dawn.

"We won't survive another attack," Brendan whispered, and he laid his hand on Atla's arm.

"Don't worry," the latter smiled. "I learned my lesson."

A noise from forward caught their attention. Barinthus was on his knees staring over the side, and he had begun his crazy singing. Ide fumbled at him to drape him with blankets, her own body shivering with cold. Joseph, still unable to straighten his legs, supported himself on his hands and tried to get as far away from the woman as he could. In lurching away, he pulled too far and fell with a splash into the bilge. There came a grasping and a fumbling, and he hauled his head above water. Ide reached across to take his hand, but he struck her aside.

"Don't touch me!"

His voice cut across the stillness of the water like a blade, separating the night from the day. Everyone except Finbar looked at the man in astonishment. Joseph stared hatefully at the nude woman bending above him. Barinthus was caught in mid-hymn with his mouth open. Then the moment changed. With dignity, Ide withdrew behind her blankets, turning her back on the boy and pulling damp clothing across her body. Barinthus recommenced his song. Brendan started forward through the water toward his uncle. Atla merely shrugged and stared out at the creatures of the sea.

Though movement aboard testified to the beginning of the day, all felt a hand of silence laid upon their backs. So horrified were they to discover themselves surrounded by beasts who, at any moment, might finish the work they had begun, that they hardly knew how to breathe. Finbar and Atla fell to bailing, but they emptied their pails into the sea as gently as though they contained explosives. Brendan caressed Barinthus, joyful at his recovery, and the other whispered his song to the fish. Avoiding any contact with Joseph, who had managed to pull himself back onto the bed, Ide made her way aft and took up a bucket. With Barinthus safe, Brendan fell to massaging Joseph's stiff legs. All the while, more of the creatures appeared around them, and the dawn came on with watery light.

The sun had just appeared in a small rim above the horizon when Brendan suddenly stopped what he was doing and stood up, his face a study of puzzlement and speculation. Barinthus had turned to him and was whispering urgently. Brendan's movement was so abrupt that he caught everyone's attention. As the curragh rose and fell in the faint swell, the shadow of the sun played up and down his wet body. His face gradually showed an eagerness that brought a flush to the round cheeks, so that, as he made his way aft, he looked once more the Brendan of the fair wind and the following sea.

He gathered Atla to the stern of the curragh and fell into low-voiced, eager debate with him. His gestures, at Barinthus and at the animals in the sea, were emphatic. Atla appeared at first to be doubtful, but a gradual excitement spread also on his face. Then he, too, was the old Atla. The two broke apart, and Atla made his way forward, with a grin on his lips, looking for oars. Brendan called the others around him. His announcement was made in a hushed voice, but a thrilling one.

"We have a chance. Barinthus says so. You all know we will sink in the next day if nothing more is done to make the curragh shipshape. Even if we can bail her dry again, which would seem to be impossible, there's nothing we can do to make her strong enough for any sort of wind or sea unless we can get some new hides sewn across her bottom. With new hides and new grease, we ought to be able to get her going once again, even if she is tender because of the loss of some ribs and stringers. I have been trying to figure some way to sew the hides on, but I haven't been able to do so because there's no way that we can get outside her, and there's certainly nowhere that we can haul her out.

"Now, perhaps, there is. Look around us. This is Barinthus's idea: If we can row her close beside one of these animals, and if someone can go over the side onto its back, perhaps we can get the job done right here in the middle of the ocean. At least, it's a chance. Otherwise, we'll sink for sure."

"You mean, walk on the animal's back?" Ide asked.

"That's right."

"But think of what happened last time we had anything to do with one of these creatures."

"There's a difference."

Barinthus interrupted from the bow. His voice was pointed. "The difference is love for the animals, not violence."

Atla bristled. "How was I to know?"

"You're a man who kills; I am a man who heals."

"You eat what I kill," Atla replied defensively.

"I eat what Christ puts before me. But we have spoken of this before."

"How did I know this would happen?"

Brendan intervened. "It was foolish, Atla. You know it was. But once done, we must save the situation, if we can. You will be the one to go over the side." Brendan turned. "Finbar, you and Joseph will row. I want to bring us up to that big one over there." He gestured to a lumbering, great back glistening off the starboard bow. "He hasn't moved since we first saw him, so I think he's asleep. Barinthus, you are the only person aboard who has actually spoken with the fish. I'll want you in the bow doing what you can to keep him calm once we're aboard him. Atla will do the work, with Ide as a back-up. Ide, you'll stay aboard here and feed Atla equipment as he needs it. I want everything he'll need immediately ready: awls, needles, palms, rawhide, grease, pitch, wax and, I think, two sections of hide. You and he sew the hides together into a patch right now before we come alongside."

Ide and Atla moved forward, and together they began searching the mess of waterlogged equipment awash in the bilge for the necessities of the proposed operation. A sense of hushed and urgent excitement had, in a minute, replaced the crew's dazed anticipation of death. Brendan's low, tight voice urged them about their various tasks. The man was everywhere, checking to see that all equipment was available, moving back and forth through the sinking vessel, himself like a boat, complete with bow wave and wake that kicked up and jostled floating bits of debris.

With no one bailing, the curragh was truly swamped. There were fewer than six inches of freeboard. When they had taken their stations at the oars, Finbar and Joseph could find no purchase while sitting chest-deep. Instead, they were forced to stand, bent at the waist, and to drag the sweeps across the surface of the sea. Heavy as she was, the curragh scarcely stirred. Atla and Brendan lent a hand at the oars, and, ever so slowly, the swamped boat dragged herself across the few yards intervening between herself and the fish's back. No more than a half-hour after the proposal had been made, Brendan was able to move away from the oars and into the stern, where he steered the curragh gently against the side of the vast sea creature. A slight, occasional ripple was sucking and breaking against the blue-black hide. The curragh's side, manipulated by the slight sea, brushed the giant, moved away in a wash, came back, brushed again. There was no tremor from the great body. The two sluggish objects, rolling slightly in the sea, were an inch apart. No one moved. The curragh brushed again, this time with more of a lurch. Still no motion came from the fish.

Brendan nodded to Atla. "Go," he whispered.

Watching the tall hunter shift his weight carefully onto the gunwale and swing his legs across, Joseph began to pray aloud.

Atla hesitated for a second when he was outside the curragh, supporting his weight on his hands on the gunwale, and then, ever so gently, he let himself down and into the sea, feeling ahead of himself with his toes. The curragh rolled toward the monster again, and Atla's feet touched his side. The man tried to get his balance on the slippery, downward-sloping flesh, but he could not. He clung still to the curragh, although his body was too low to be supported by it. Instead, he was now floating in the sea between the two, his hands on the rail, his feet seeking once more for a hold on the creature's side. Atla put his face in the water and looked down. Then, with water dripping from his beard, he whispered to Brendan, "Take me forward two feet. There's a flipper there . . . Lord, it's cold."

With tremendous caution, Finbar and Joseph, at Brendan's direction, took up the off-side oars and pulled the boat forward along the creature's side.

"Stop."

Looking again toward the side, Finbar saw Atla stand with his whole weight on something in the sea, hesitate, and then let go of the curragh's side.

"Patch," he said to Ide, not waiting for anything.

The patch was fed underneath the curragh, with Atla, up to his neck sometimes in the frigid sea, adjusting its position so that it covered the entire area of the ripped hide. Before going into the sea, while the curragh was being rowed to the creature's side, the patch had been liberally smeared with wool grease, which would act both as glue and as caulk. The patch was laid right on top of the sail which had earlier been fothered across her bottom, the hope being that the sail would increase the effectiveness of the patch, even if, under the difficult circumstances, Atla should be unable to make a perfect job of the sewing.

"Begin," Atla whispered, when the patch was snugged up against the hull.

Working as quickly as possible, he and Ide began to sew, he from the outside, she from the inside. They both used awls and palms, thrusting holes through the two layers of hide and the sailcloth between them, and then alternately pulling and pushing the rawhide thread through the holes they made. The job was exacting. Because of the awkward positions they were forced to assume, as often as not completely under water, it was exhausting as well.

After a few minutes of watching, Brendan motioned Finbar and Joseph to begin bailing once more. Any water they could get out of the curragh, in order to raise her higher, would make the job that much easier. Already, working down around the curve of the bilge from the outside, Atla was below the surface more than he was above. His face, when he came up for air, was white with cold, and his teeth chattered. This was perhaps as much from anxiety as it was from the temperature, but it was clear that the job would be eased by even a fractional raising of the curragh.

With Brendan lending a hand, emptying their buckets stealthily into the sea, the water level in the boat moved downward quickly. Soon the thwarts again were above water. Atla, having sewn as far under the hull as he could get, was now above the surface and working down the other side of the patch. He and Ide could go more quickly this way. Brendan, Finbar and Joseph continued to bail. The water level sank still more, until the bilge was no more than ankle-deep. Sodden equipment and clothing littered the boat and hampered the patchers as well as the bailers. Atla, more confident now and trying to increase his pace, was moving around on the fish's back more than he had been. The bailers had the curragh almost dry.

"Careful!" Barinthus's voice barked suddenly from the bow. A tremor ran through the fish's great body. Atla lost his footing and splashed into the sea, clinging to the curragh's side, now high above him.

"Get me out of here!" he yelped.

The monster below him heaved, and he was pressed painfully between its back and the curragh's bilge.

"Pull me in!"

"Move off, Brendan," Barinthus called. "Quickly. He's waking up."

Ide leaned over the side and grasped Atla's arms. Finbar rushed to assist her, but Brendan's voice stopped him.

"No, Finbar! The oars. Row."

Finbar looked helplessly at Ide and turned back to the oars. Joseph took up one and plied it mightily. Both oars, however, were still on the side of the curragh away from the fish, and Joseph's pull, now that the boat was lighter, drove them against the fish instead of away.

"Joseph!" Brendan called. "Stop. Don't row until I say. Finbar, ship that oar across. Quickly now."

Finbar ran up with the oar.

"He's awfully cold," Ide warned softly of Atla. The monster heaved again. Atla groaned, as once more he was butted against the boat.

"Finbar," Brendan ordered, "shove off against his side."

Finbar thrust his oar against the rolling hillside of flesh beside him and felt the curragh turn outward.

"Now ship the oar and . . . ready . . . Joseph, attention . . . . Give way!"

The curragh moved. The space between them opened. Finbar was able to get a better bite with his blade for the next stroke. They pulled farther off. Now there

were ten feet of dark water, choppy with the wash of the
creature's movements, between them.

"Stroke," came Brendan's voice from the stern.
"Stroke."

When they were thirty feet off, Brendan gave Finbar
permission to help Ide muscle Atla aboard. Atla came up
slowly, both he and Ide too tired to assist very much.
Finally, Finbar heaved him onto the gunwale, and Atla
toppled down into the bilge. He lay panting there while
Finbar returned to his oar and helped pull the curragh
into the pool of sea between their creature and the others
around him.

"Avast," said Brendan, when they were well clear,
and he stepped down into the waist to help Atla to a
sitting position on one of the thwarts. Everyone gathered
around the man, congratulating him and rubbing his
limbs to restore his circulation.

Soon, Atla raised his strained face from off his chest,
and looked at Ide out of sunken eyes. "You did a good
job," he muttered. Then there came a twinkle, and he
made as though to untie his belt. "Get some blankets," he
said. "I'm terribly cold."

To Finbar's surprise, Ide blushed. Barinthus and
Brendan laughed, and Joseph turned away. Brendan
cuffed his tall friend on the cheek and said, "He's all right.
Don't let the attention go to his head."

The group relaxed now, with the curragh afloat for
the first time in hours, the sun above the horizon and
warming the wet, still air. Around them, the creatures of
the deep continued to snore and roll. Their own creature
was quiet again. Barinthus kept an eye on the fish while
the rest of the crew joked and chuckled. The relief of the
tension of the past hours was intoxicating.

Eventually, Brendan turned the conversation to the
patch and to what Atla could report concerning the condition of the hull.

"I wasn't able to get underneath all the way," the
latter said, "but we sewed down both sides of the patch
as far as the third stringers. I think it will hold where I
sewed it, but the patch certainly won't hold long where
it's only glued on. I think we'll have to try again, this time

working down from the other side. I don't know what we can do about the area right below us. I can't get there at all without hauling the boat up on something."

"We're going to do it again?" Joseph asked, his voice frightened.

"We have to," Atla replied.

"All right now," Brendan said. "We'd better go about it before the creatures disappear or something else happens. We've been very lucky with the wind and the sea."

"Not luck," Barinthus commented.

"However it is," Brendan replied, nodding to his uncle, "we'd do better to have the job done quickly. Is everyone ready? We'll keep the same duties, I think. Finbar, you and Joseph will bring her up against the other side."

Once again, the curragh was rowed quietly up to the side of the monstrous beast. Everything went as before. Atla swung himself over the side and, gasping when he entered the water again, lowered himself until he was standing on the creature's fin. Ide thrust her awl through the side just above the waterline, and the two commenced to stitch up the patch. Barinthus sang to the fish. Finbar and Joseph, having no more bailing to do, set about putting some of the stores and the litter to rights.

Time passed quickly. Atla and Ide worked their way down one edge of the patch as far under the hull as they had been able to do from that side, and then they began on the second edge. A little order began to appear amidships. Joseph hung cloaks and tunics on the rigging to dry in the sun. Finbar stacked the food stores, separating out from the main bulk of goods the dried meat and fish that were unusable now after soaking for thirty hours in seawater.

Barinthus broke off his song to report, at the same time as Atla did, that the fish was growing restive once more.

"Can you hang on?" Brendan called. "You're almost done."

"I think so," Atla replied. "Sew like a demon, Ide."

Their fingers fairly flew as they plied the rawhide, pulling it tight, grunting and slapping the hull, working in

effective rhythm down the side. Finbar and Joseph left off
their clearing efforts and stood by.

The water around the curragh began to chop once
again as the fish twitched and rolled. Finbar watched the
shine move up and down the whale's flanks as his breathing grew more rapid. "Sew, Atla," he called.

Atla found it necessary almost to dance on the creature's hide as the footing continued to change. His work
with the needle and palm slowed considerably. The fish
began to move forward, making it necessary for Atla to
work his way back, looking for footholds. He was off the
fin now, slipping along the flank itself. Brendan put Finbar and Joseph on the off-side oars in an effort to keep
pace with the monster, but their success was minimal.

Barinthus broke off his song again and said, imperi-
ously, "Swing me in."

"No," his nephew replied.

"Swing me in, Brendan. I'm going aboard."

"You can't."

"Don't argue. Swing me in now."

Brendan hesitated.

"I will be obeyed."

The old man stood right up in the eyes of the bow
now, his cloak swept back, his feet poised for the jump.
"Do it!"

"All right," Brendan assented. "Swing him in."

Finbar and Joseph glanced at one another and then
gave a pull with their oars. The bow of the curragh pulled
in close beside the black body, and Barinthus jumped.
There was nothing delicate about it. He landed with both
feet right on the creature's back, out of water, up near the
single nostril. For a moment, he staggered as he adjusted
to the new motion. The creature itself, feeling the sudden
weight, flurried its tail and twisted in the water. It appeared that it would dive immediately.

"Barinthus!" Brendan yelled in warning.

Atla leapt for the side of the curragh across the widening sea, falling heavily against the gunwale.

Barinthus paid no attention. He stood firmly on the
monster's back, wreathed in the steam of its breath,
opened his arms high and called out in a strong, clear

voice, "Fish! Oh, Fish, hear me. It is Barinthus, Fish; Barinthus, whom you know. Fish, our ship is sinking, and we need your assistance, Fish. Hear me, Fish of Paradise! We ask your patience. We need your strong back."

The others watched him apprehensively, but the movements of the fish slowed, and then they came to a halt. The fish lay still in the ocean once again, and Barinthus gestured to them with an eager hand while continuing to harangue the fish.

"Pull back," Brendan whispered. "Quick."

Almost immediately, the curragh was against the side of the fish, and Atla was over the side. This time he made no pretense of caution. He jumped onto the monster's side and walked about there familiarly. He thrust his awl through the side and, with Ide's expert assistance, had the patch sewn down to the farthest point he could reach in a few minutes.

"That's it," he said. "Come on, Barinthus."

"No," the old man said. "Haul the boat back to the stern of the fish."

"What?" Brendan called. "Come back aboard, Barinthus. We've done all we can."

"You have, but I haven't. Do what I say."

With a shrug, Brendan gestured that they should obey. The curragh was hauled swiftly into a position astern of the creature's back, just over the enormous tail.

"Roll forward, O Fish!" Barinthus yelled. "Roll forward that we may continue our work."

Hardly believing that Barinthus was attempting such a thing, but ready, nevertheless, should he be successful, Ide and Atla waited to stitch the unsewn edges of the patch across the bilge as they came free of the water.

Barinthus worked his way forward on the fish's head until he was standing just at the forward edge, right on the break of the sea. He continued his coaxing, and the fish responded. So gently that the observers could hardly see the motion, the fish slid forward in the water. A flurry occurred in the region of the pectoral fins and, with the greatest delicacy, the fish's back arched. Silently, the tail moved upward through the water under the boat until it brushed against the curragh's bottom. An extraordinary sensation passed through all those aboard: they were being lifted from the sea by the raising of the whale's tail. Before they had time fully to grasp their situation, they were free of the water altogether, balanced on the flat, wide tail, their hull dripping and sweating in the sun. Atla was the first to respond.

"Careen her," he hissed.

The others tumbled over the side to stand on the tail itself. Taking lines from the mast, they hauled the curragh over on her side until the raw edges of the patch were exposed. Inside of five minutes, although it seemed an eternity, the edges were neatly and snugly stitched, grease was rubbed into the stitching, and pitch was spread thickly over all. Brendan and Joseph and the others allowed the curragh to roll back onto an even keel.

Barinthus, meanwhile, had continued his conversation with the fish. A great and continual agitation of the water came from the monster's sides, where he was exercising his pectoral fins to maintain his balance in the awkward position he had assumed. Toward the end of the five minutes, Barinthus had grown restive.

"Hurry," the crew heard him call in the midst of his soothing murmurs to the fish, "he's tiring."

Indeed, the tail had begun to sag back into the sea by the time the stitching was done.

"Get aboard," Brendan whispered stridently. "Quickly!"

The tail drooped still more until it was itself awash. Atla and Joseph came aboard. Finbar rolled himself across the gunwale and held his hand out to Brendan. The curragh began to slide down off the tail stern-first into the sea.

"Jump, Brendan!" Ide called.

Brendan leapt for the rigging as the boat slid off its makeshift ways and breasted back into the sea. Wet to the waist, he pulled himself across the side and tumbled into the bilge.

"The oars," he cried, before he even stood up. "Pull for Barinthus."

When he rose to his feet, he saw that his uncle was perfectly secure. Grinning, the old man watched the faces of the crew across a widening stretch of water. When they had shipped their oars and bent to them, he turned back to his fish. He still stood right forward on the fish's head, just where the water broke upon its skin, but now he seemed taller and there was a new vitality in his stance. The sunlight, coming in aslant from the low, climbing sun, set his face and his wet garments aglow. He waved to his nephew as the curragh neared.

"To Thule!" he called, and then, laughing, he turned his back on the curragh. The fish began to move.

"Barinthus!" Brendan yelled. "Come back."

The man only laughed again, and the fish took on more speed.

"After him," Brendan urged his crew, bending forward as though he would add his eagerness to their efforts on the oars, but the fish's motion was too fast for them. Twisting and darting between the great, black backs of his companions, the fish led them a circuitous chase for most of a mile across the oily swells. At times, Barinthus was way ahead, his upright form, with its cloak flapping in the wind of his passage, seen across the tops of long waves interrupted by scores of glistening bodies. Once or twice they brushed against these bodies in their eagerness to follow closely on Barinthus's heels, but they feared the monsters no longer. They had become familiar with the great fishes, seeing them now only as predictable circumstances of the deep. They even chided them when the creatures blundered into their way, and once Finbar, in exasperation, unshipped his oar and swung it against the side of a particular fish that persisted in obstructing the curragh. The fish moved to one side, grudgingly, it seemed.

It was not until they neared the edge of the pod that the rowers began to gain back some of the distance they had lost. Barinthus guided his whale to the open sea, pulled out perhaps a cable's length or so, and then slid to a standstill. He waited, rolling slightly in the somewhat larger seas outside the pod, for the curragh to approach.

When Brendan thankfully drew the curragh alongside and the rowers dropped their oars, Barinthus grinned at their gaping faces. Casually, he gestured a few points north of west. "Thule is that way," he said. "Oughtn't we to go?"

He issued a gutteral command to his whale, and the animal rolled a bit so that his dorsal fin on the side toward the curragh lay on the surface of the sea. Barinthus walked down the fish's back and onto his fin. "Lift!" he said. He was raised up until he could step, with all dignity, across the gunwale and onto a thwart. He sat down on the thwart, composed his robes about himself, dismissed the whale with a word of thanks, and turned to look back at the crew, which still watched him unbelievingly. Nothing was said. The whale departed. The sun hung in the air. No breeze stirred. The curragh rose on the back of a swell and settled gradually into the trough.

Barinthus sought Finbar's eye. Raising one of his eyebrows, he murmured to the black man, "Still doubt?"

5

THE WHALE HAD INDICATED to Barinthus that Thule lay northwest of them. There was a mild breeze from the north. Brendan lay off on the starboard tack, and the curragh forged her way across the building seas in her search for a winter home. For the moment, she was secure. The patch held back the leaks, and she rode on the waves instead of through them. However, she was jury-rigged, and her progress on the wind was worse than it had been before. The helmsman's job was made more difficult by her unbalanced rig. With all her sail aft, he had to struggle to keep her from coming up into the wind and stopping short. Many of her ribs and stringers amidships were broken or cracked. As a consequence, the curragh was much less rigid a structure than she had been. The forces transmitted to her hull by the shrouds, the mast and the steering oar tended to bend her out of shape. As often as not, there were sags or wrinkles in her hull surface. In the short run, these eccentric curves obstructed the free passage of the water along her hull and by so doing slowed her down. In the long run, the danger was greater. Little by little, despite everything the sailors could do, the curragh was being torn apart by her own flexibility. As day followed day, her seams opened farther. The rawhide stitching stretched and tore its holes. Each noon, more water needed to be bailed out of her than on the day before.

It was December. Across the northern vastness of the ocean the days came with increasing cold. A wind that would have been fresh and invigorating six months before now cut through five layers of wool and ran its sharp fingernails across the ribs. After two days with a fair northerly, the wind swung into the northwest, and it hung there day after day. There was nothing the sailors could do. Their weariness was almost unendurable. At the change of each watch, they tacked. Making a bare seven points, they knew full well that four hours of bashing into cold seas with the wind beating them down had put them perhaps half a mile to windward of where they had been eight hours before. At night, their anxious, tired eyes stared at the Pole Star, willing it to come higher off the sea, but the difference they were able to measure from one night to the next was pitiably little.

There was hardly any talk among them. They had been saved from certain drowning by Barinthus's extraordinary control over the whale, yet it seemed that they had been saved from what after all would have been an easy death only to be sacrificed to a hard one. They were angry with Brendan for taking as truth the direction Barinthus claimed should be their course: their previous habit had been off the wind. Brendan stuck as fixedly to his heading as he did to anything else, and their anger increased as their exhaustion made them stupid. Coming off watch, they fell like axed trees into the rumpled mat of blankets that tangled the cabin floor. They were asleep almost before they had time to drag painfully at the matted strips they had bound around their hands. They stayed in whatever position they landed until shaken awake for their next watch. There was little to eat, less to drink. Sleeping and waking, the time was all the same: cold more bitter than they had imagined before, weariness of muscle and of will, emptiness so deep they hardly felt their insides eating them up. They began to suffer from bodily ills: their limbs and buttocks were agonized by salt-water boils. The slightest motion dragged stiff wool across the tops of these sores. Nine-tenths of their attention at any one moment was on the impossible task of forcing themselves not to shiver, in order to relieve the boils, but they were too cold not to shiver. Their eyes grew raw. Their lids were pus-caked and red. The salt of wind and spray needled the inflamed flesh. Their gums swelled and grew sore. They itched, for they had not been out of their rank garments, wet and dry, since leaving Finbar's island.

Their feet, continuously inside their boots, were swollen, white and peeling.

Contributing to their attitude of defeat was Barinthus's ill health. Rather than invigorate him, his magnificent performance with the fish seemed instead to have robbed him of what little vitality he had possessed. Since the first night after the incident, he lay in the decked-over rowing well, hardly speaking, hardly moving, more often than not completely unconscious of what went on around him.

Joseph, too, seemed to have retreated from the present. Though the regular Christian services were carried on now with brevity and an impatient stamping of feet, Joseph's own observations were meticulous and prolonged. The anchoritic imagination was strong in him, and he could not be forced to eat. He remained as much as possible below, though he hardly slept. Duties that were thrust upon him often went undone, and Brendan existed in a state of exasperation with him. With Barinthus comatose, and Joseph as good as useless, the entire handling of the boat fell to the four others, and thus their hours of sleep were severely cut, their hours of exposure dangerously increased.

So it went on for eleven days. The wind held steady, now and then blowing up almost to gale force but never wavering in its direction. Eleven days of beating in winter seas can kill from sheer strain. One more day of it and there might well ensue a mutiny, notwithstanding the Christian discipline of the mariners. To turn and run, no longer to fight, and to search for a more southerly sea: this was a longing in them as strong as their longing for a hot drink.

One of the more tedious and dangerous duties was chipping ice off the bow. Spray, as well as the normal wash of their bow wave, froze against the hull, especially at night. It was possible during a very cold spell for the ice to build up so quickly that one could almost see it grow. In a sense it was beautiful, thickening the lines, frosting the hull; but it was dangerous because it was so heavy. The added weight made the curragh sluggish and brought her down by the bow. At regular intervals, someone had to

crawl out along the ice-covered leather deck until he lay
in the bow, and then, while being drenched with seas that
came aboard and struggling for balance against seas that
did not, he had to chip away at the ice with a chisel, being
careful all the time not to stick the instrument through
the side of the boat. It was hideous, one-handed, despairing labor.

On the eleventh day, chipping ice on the foredeck,
Ide found a piece of seaweed frozen into the block at
which she was hacking away. The find was momentous.
Back in the cockpit, the exhausted woman shivered in
excitement while Brendan, Atla and Finbar fingered the
trophy. It was a fresh piece of vegetation. The part that
had been ripped from its rock anchor was clear to be seen,
still ragged, still new. Somewhere nearby there was land.

The four sailors stared at the seaweed and then at the
horizon. Their faces were grey and their backs were bent.
The men's beards were ragged and filthy. In each of the
eight eyes was a new glimmer, a light that had been extinguished days before. It takes little in the way of hope to
bring life back to a corpse. But, of course, there was nothing to see out under the rim of the sky. The seas reared
high with the same regularity, the blue had the same
intense, cold opacity that they had learned to expect. Still,
out there somewhere, over one small stretch of the horizon, there must be land. Thule: the last spot on earth
before the final, endless sweep of the wilderness. It was
tantalizing.

Their new taste of hope added salt to the emptiness
of the horizon. For hours, they stared at nothing, seeing
only the tangling tops of sea mountains. No further sign
of land came to them. Perhaps they were already past the
lost island. Toward dark, they turned their eyes back inboard, and the cold ate at them while their hope drained
away.

That night the world changed. On watch, Finbar
knew it with his body an hour before his brain understood
it. The wind blew hollow for the first time in almost a
fortnight. The seas became confused. By morning, the sky
was thick, and the wind was puffy from the southeast. It
was a perfect slant. The curragh chugged along, butting

her way through erratic waves. It began to snow. Fat, wet flakes built up everywhere. Visibility was nil. Man is perhaps most alone on this earth when in a heavy snowfall at sea.

When Finbar came off watch in mid-morning, he was so cold and so exhausted he could scarcely see. He tumbled below and collapsed without so much as brushing the snow from his clothes. Much later, it seemed, he had an extraordinary sensation. He could feel something wrong with his feet. It was a feeling that began at his soles and traveled up across his toes and his instep to his ankles and beyond. He couldn't imagine what it was. It was not unpleasant, just odd. Summoning tremendous energy, he raised his head and squinted down the length of his body. He saw Joseph, whom he had hardly noticed for days. That solitary man sat cross-legged at Finbar's feet. Joseph had opened his own clothing, stripped off Finbar's boots, and held Finbar's soles against his own stomach. He was praying, and his eyes were shut. Finbar's head fell back. He didn't know what to think. The sensation he had not recognized was heat.

At dusk, as was their custom, the four active crew members gathered in the cockpit. Snow was thick on all surfaces, even on Atla and Finbar, who had been on watch. The snow was not falling so heavily, however, and there were signs of a break in the overcast. This far to the north, the night began early, and the spot where the sun cracked the clouds was low down and southwest of the curragh. It was time for the evening meal. Brendan made a quick prayer, and then the frugal repast was distributed. Into each grimy palm, Brendan poured a small mound of their last millet flour. In addition, there were two sips of slimy water. It did not take long to eat. What talk there was came in gutteral, hoarse ejaculations. All were convinced that Thule was there, just over the horizon in some direction; but that they would hit upon the right direction, they were not so certain. Everyone's fear was that Thule would be passed by. It made them jittery, and they searched what they could see of the ocean and the sky for any sign. Their longing was so great that, again and again, they thought they saw something, but it always proved not to be there.

The sun broke through the overcast just as it was setting, and it sent a single ray straight across the water into their startled eyes. For an instant the world showed clearly: the tossing and grey-topped seas all around, the furred clouds low and sailing, the golden-pink opalescence of the sky outside. The snow stopped. The sun sank. Everything gleamed in its white coat. Red suffused the bottoms of the low, scudding clouds. The red was reflected in the sea; all the world was red.

"Tomorrow!" each thought, shamefacedly hiding his hope from the others. "Tomorrow we shall come to the end of the world."

The red began to fade, the hole in the clouds to close. Just as it was closing, every one of them saw the same thing. They each cried out. All four of them had seen the gull, a single gull black against the red sky, winging his way home for the night.

"Did you see him?" they cried. "Was it real?"

Brendan was anxiously craning forward, seeking to get some bearing on the gull's direction.

"I think he was more westward," the captain said.

"Northward," Atla argued.

"I think westward," Brendan repeated. "We'll swing westward a bit."

The world quickly went dark when the clouds closed. There was little to give the sailors a direction in the night. There were no stars. The wind and the sea, they knew from the last few hours, were erratic. Blindly, hoping they had struck the line that the gull was taking, they butted and splashed their way through the sea. No one left the deck. Each face craned and peered into the murk ahead, each ear strained for the sound of breakers, each sense made minute calculations from the varying strength and direction of the waves and the wind. Later, about the middle of the night, the snow began to fall once more, blotting out whatever slight visibility they might have had otherwise.

The wind dropped slowly, and the snow fell more heavily. The curragh rolled and pitched in uneven seas. Before dawn, Finbar went forward on ice patrol. The night was totally closed. More acutely than ever, Finbar felt the smallness of himself and of man. He and the exhausted sailors behind him were in the very middle of total, unlimited chaos. Mechanically, he began shoving heaps of snow from the deck. He hardly felt the weight of the work. Time passed. A faint light came into the air, turning it from black to grey. The snow fell as hard as ever. A puff of wind filled the sail with a muffled thump. The curragh gained way across bubbling seas.

Finbar pushed more snow into the sea. And, when he looked up, land was right there in front of him, so close he could not see its top. It was so huge, so much higher and broader than he was prepared for that at first, he could not speak. The curragh was sailing straight into a maze of ledges and rock towers, behind which rose the cliff that had stunned his sight. It was too big, too close, too sudden in the billowing air.

Warned perhaps by the shortening and steepening of the waves, Atla sang out, "Land! Wear! Wear the ship!"

The curragh tried to wear. She was sluggish, her blocks ice-choked, her sail heavy with snow. Rigid with fear, Finbar lay on the foredeck and gripped the stay. His mind, slowed by privation, could not accustom itself to so sudden a plight. Finbar did nothing but stare ahead at the rime-grey explosions of winter seas met by hard, black rock. Caught and powerless, the curragh swung sideways upon the curl of a breaker. Her shoreward side rolled down until Finbar slipped across the crackling deck and felt his leg, then even his arm and shoulder, dragged into the sea.

"Broach!" he heard Atla yell. "Jesus save your sailors now."

"Pull!" Brendan roared. "Pray later; pull!"

With her steering oar dug in, the curragh regained a moment of control. The crest of their breaker frothed and spat around them. Finbar's arm vibrated with the ferociousness of his grip on the forestay: almost his whole body hung over the side.

The curragh broke through the grip of the breaker, shuddered down its backside, and hung still for a moment in the trough. She quivered upright. Finbar, suspended now from the bow, clawed at the slippery leather and ice for a means to pull himself inboard.

"Help," he croaked, but his lungs were full of spray.

The curragh was rising on the next sea. Atla, Brendan and Ide were struggling to get an oar shipped to give them some way. As they soared higher, Finbar glimpsed a ledge before them, sucked free of the sea, rubbery hair swirling. It was right below the curragh now, would be under them when they came down.

The curl of the breaker plucked them. They were pushed sideways again. The ledge rushed up at their exposed bilge. Desperate, flinging himself between the two, Finbar attempted to fend the ledge off with his feet. The impact was enormous, bending his exhausted body until it broke, but the ledge shied away.

Finbar relaxed his grip. His leg shrieked at him. His head swam. His lungs were filled with salt. He felt one hand trail, caressingly as it were, along the gunwhale of the rushing curragh as he was left behind. Then nothing: just the velvet cold of the sea.

An instant later, he was jerked into awareness by a grip on one ankle and the horrid tug of his body through the water. Ide, struggling to lower a leeboard, had seen him swept away, and she had flung a despairing hand after him. By luck, she had him by the foot, but the force of his weight against her nearly dragged her overboard as well. Yet, with the help of Atla pulling her from behind, she managed to get Finbar's legs along the leeward deck. His head trailed in the sea until Brendan, with a mighty and impatient heave, spun the smith's scarcely conscious body into the cockpit.

There was no more time among them for Finbar. The next breaker was throwing the curragh high. Straining on the steering oar, the leeboards, the lines, Brendan managed to get his bow around sufficiently so that the comber took the curragh on the forward quarter. Spray burst like an explosion over her and she shuddered to a standstill. But she had succeeded in breaking through the white water and now lay with her course off shore. The oars bit. She gained way, and the next breaker she was able to take right across the bow. Gradually, falling off for more speed in the troughs and hardening up to take the combers bows-on, Brendan conned his ship through the region of breakers until he was about a half mile off shore. There, no longer feeling the landward pull, he called a halt.

Finbar, trampled in the cockpit, lay half-dead; his teeth rattling so hard that they hurt his tongue when he thrust it between the rows to stop the echoing in his skull. The others were in little better case: having reacted to the emergency with automatic seamanship, they were again conscious of themselves, and fell to miserable sniveling. Everyone was wet through, and, now that they were no longer running, the small wind seemed horridly strong.

"And we were afraid we would miss it altogether," Atla panted. He broke an icicle off the tip of his nose, leaving a raw spot where another immediately began to form. "Is this Thule?"

"It had better be," Ide stammered.

"It must be," Brendan announced, looking around. "Nothing else, at any rate, would be here in the sea. It must be Thule. It is."

"Little good it will do us, if we can't land."

"Atla, all will be well. We are in God's protection."

"Oh, Brendan, I'm so tired."

"I know, my friend. I know." The captain put his arm around Atla's thin shoulders and squeezed the man. Oddly assorted in size as they were, the taller man seemed to huddle for the moment into the embrace of the shorter one. "There's a monastery here. We will rest there."

"Where is it?"

"We shall find it, Atla. Never fear."

In the meantime, Ide and Finbar clustered together under the slight protection of the break of the cockpit. The woman was chaffing Finbar's hands and face.

"I can't feel it," he kept moaning. "I can't feel your hands."

Gradually though, the blood began to come back into his fingers, and pain with it. His leg hurt terribly.

"Is it broken?" she asked.

"I don't care."

"It's almost over," she soothed. "Soon we will land."

"I don't like this place," was all he could say.

Into the midst of this pitiable scene stepped Barinthus, on his feet for the first time since the whale-walking, seemingly years ago. He stood straight, looking calmly through the dissolving overcast toward the white and black cliffs of the island. The small wind whirled the long, white hair around his face.

"Thule," he breathed, satisfied. "Make way along that shore."

"You know where to go?" Ide looked up.

"Go with the wind."

Ide groaned and looked away. "*Now* go with the wind," she grunted.

"As always," Brendan said blandly, stepping away from Atla and laying his hand once more on the steering oar. "Go with the wind, now we shall."

The curragh lay off and adjusted herself to sailing. She skirted the outside of the breaker fringe, and made her way along the shoreline. Dawn was fully come. The clouds scaled up until they revealed the detail of the coastline, and occasionally, through a rent, the excesses of the heights. It was a volcanic coast, with now and then a smoking shoulder or mountain peak to evidence the fact.

"This is your land," Barinthus laughed at Finbar, pointing to the smoke. "This is the forge of God."

"The forge of God it may be." The man was weary of Barinthus and of the whole Nazarene struggle. His leg quivered. "But if it is, then I am the alchemist."

"Alchemy is anathema."

"Oh, stop." He went below and tried to find heat at least, if not sleep, in the mat of sodden woolens that littered the cabin sole.

After noon, warmer and less tired, he came once more to the deck. A winter sun shone without heat. The sea danced around them. There seemed to be a current against them, and with the wind behind them, the sea was lumpy. Nevertheless, Brendan had put the curragh into better order. Her lines were coiled down, her decks swept of snow, and fishing lines were trailing along in her wake. Already, Atla was at work filleting an enormous cod. In all, it was a better world than Finbar had known for some days and weeks, and he felt more tolerant of Barinthus, who repeated his joke about the forge.

The coastline they followed through that day and the

next was more barren than any Finbar had seen before. Vast, wide valleys came down from the interior into the sea. Where they disappeared back into the highlands far away, their slopes were rounded and snow-streaked. In the distance there were mountains, but more often at the ends of these long valleys were the flat, white surfaces of glaciers. No tree showed itself. The interior was hung with low, grey clouds. It was a rocky, somber, awful place, silent with a silence rather deepened than otherwise by the threnody of wind and by the teeming passage of sudden gulls as quickly gone as come. The sea abounded with fish of all descriptions—jumping, schooling predators and prey—and the sailors made great use of them as food.

They noted oddities about the spot, which proved its righteous character: even in this northern spot, they found themselves in surprisingly warm seas, inviting, as their god would have desired for them. A current flowed against them, but, keeping inside its edge—for it was like a river along the shore—they sped forward in its backwash in hypnotic and majestic proximity to a timeless shore. Best of all, Barinthus was with them again. Though often heard, his tales of the former voyage kept them thrilled, for they believed in him more than halfway at least, now that they were so much on the verge.

No sign of man relieved the solemnity of the scene until, mid-morning of the fourth day, they hardened in around the end of a long point of land to find that the coastline turned north, no longer ran east, and on their right, tucked in behind the finger they had rounded, a bay opened up. Islands were scattered around the bay, but what riveted their gaze was the sail they saw backing and filling with the unmistakable, casual energy of a fisherman impatient to pull the next pot.

6

F OR A WEEK, BRENDAN AND his crew did nothing
except eat, and sleep, and rest. They were lent a
hut that served as a summer barn for the monastery's
sheep. The place was more spacious than their curragh,
but it was colder. The men did what they could to im-
prove the draft of the smudgy fire, and they sought to
insulate the walls with hay. After the manure was cleared
away and the walls chinked from the outside with moss
and muddy snow, the barn was comfortable enough.

There Brendan held court to Thule's brothers. With
Atla on one side, Barinthus on the other, and Joseph serv-
ing as clerk, the captain questioned each monk whose
work took him offshore. There was a Testament and a
map spread out on the table before Brendan, and he extracted much of interest for the future of the voyage
about currents, temperatures of the sea, conditions of fog
and wind, migration habits of birds and fish, and the dan-
gers of whirlpools, waterspouts and icebergs. Each item of
information was carefully plotted on the map and its testa-
mental implication drawn. The discussions were lengthy,
intricate, and beyond Finbar's patience. What astonished
Finbar, indeed, was the fact that the Thule community
stood in perfect awareness of the existence to their westward of the Land Promised to the Saints. No living man
had visited the Holy Shores, but that Brendan intended to
do so was treated as a mere nautical, instead of a spiritual,
ambition. And Atla did not omit to underline this fact to
his skeptical ironsmith friend.

The sisters of Thule were not so much in evidence to
Finbar as the brothers. Ide herself he rarely saw. Excited
by its new abbess, the convent flickered around its own

flame. Still, the sisters did not fail occasionally to make their way to the shoreline, to touch their fingers against the side of the curragh and with their prayers bless her on her journey to come. Finbar now and then saw them, and several times he sought to speak to them, making an effort to send greetings to Ide. But the attempt was never successful, for the sisters would look at him defensively and hasten away.

To the monks, though, the crew did not seem to pose such a threat. As much as they were proud of their isolation from the Empire, a spasm of jollity seized them when the mariners came ashore, and the mood lasted some days. It was only natural that this should be so: the time was arctic winter, and life otherwise was parceled out at one regalement to the day. That is, before retiring for sleep to their small huts, the monks were in the habit of gathering to sing a lay that reminded them of their Irish home. Other waking hours were dutifully filled with the repair of summertime hoes and rakes, the carding of wool, and the slow nurturing of cheese. It was into these careful lives that Brendan and his men burst, smelling of seafaring and cocked for Paradise. The monks sat at their feet. News of Ireland only two seasons old thrilled them, but they hated to hear of the wars. To them, war was a metaphor; it ought not to be waged with swords—certainly not, at any rate, by Christians. They disapproved of Finbar as a man of war, despite the fact that he had armed their own side at Cul Dreimne.

It was after ten days or more had passed that Finbar visited Ide for the first time. The monastery and the convent were separated by a mile and a half of tussocky sea-plain, the former right on the coastline, and the latter inland. A small brook meandered slowly along the base of a ridge of hills that angled inland from the shore. Where the brook debouched onto the beach, the monastery had been built. One followed the shore of the brook inland to reach the convent. It was late morning—and dark—when Finbar trudged to Ide's new home. A hard wind blew from behind, throwing the skirts of his cloak before him and pelting him now and then with small, spitting snow. Thule could boast no trees on its shoreline, and there was nothing more for Finbar to see in the half-light than an occasional clump of bracken too stiff to be beaten down by snow, along the shore of the brook. To his right, the anonymous ridgeline tucked itself into the clouds.

The sisters had raised two transplanted spruce trees on either side of the entrance to their convent. Finbar passed between these, and the wind troubled him less. He was able to study his surroundings more carefully. Like others he had seen in Ireland, the convent was built of stone and was unmortared. There were dwelling cells, a commissary, a chapel and several barns. Stone walls divided one area from another. As was the case at the monastery, the paths beside the walls were swept free of slush and scattered with sand. Small terraces were built into the sides of the walls, where Finbar guessed the nuns tended summer flowers, columbine and camomile that would bob merrily in the breeze. In the almost perpetual darkness of arctic winter, however, the terraces were buried in rotten ice and blown debris.

There was light coming through the chinks in the commissary wall. Loath to appear just at mealtime, Finbar hung back from entering. A late sister shooed him inside ahead of herself, however, as she might a strayed hen, and he found himself bent under a low ceiling where smoke stung the eyes and the odors of mutton, onions and —was it savory?—fought for attention. Finbar looked around. He saw Ide. He was startled by her severe habit. She was sitting at the head of the table with a lamp beside her. The only sound in the room except for the hiss of the turf fire was her voice, reading the psalm. The sister who had pushed him inside gave him a bowl and spoon, motioned to the soup pot, and sat down. As Finbar ate, he watched Ide's face. Though aware that he was present, she did not interrupt her reading of the Bible, nor did her sisters appear to pay him more heed. The stew was delicious, and he was hungry. He listened to the sound of her words without hearing their sense, and he felt the rich mutton fat coat his teeth.

Ide said nothing to him until, at the conclusion of the meal, her sisters had filed silently out of the building. She busied herself in wrapping the Bible carefully in sheepskin, depositing it in its niche, and cleaning the stew bowls with a cloth. Made uncomfortable by her silence and by the liturgical humility with which she performed her chores, Finbar sat on the bench and began to perspire. The portion of his cloak closest to the fire was steaming, and he took the garment off.

Ide sat down across from Finbar. Suddenly, she was transformed. A smile erupted across her face such as he had never seen her wear, and, grasping his hands, she blurted, "I'm so very glad you've come!"

He was startled. "Hello," he said.

Ide winked. "I'm afraid that for my sisters, the thrill of my arrival has somewhat palled. It's good to see someone from before."

"You're not unhappy here?"

"No, no. It will pass, this mood among them. There are jealousies that need to be watched, and there are those who think I am . . . insufficiently gentle."

Finbar laughed. "Good for you," he said.

"Come, let me show you this place."

The next hour passed easily. Finbar enjoyed the tour, and he suspected Ide enjoyed the covert inspection that he elicited in her sisters.

The slight daylight was fading. The wind, which had dropped, was increasing once again. Stars began to appear overhead as the clouds were torn away. Finbar and Ide stood between the spruce trees. Finbar held a torch, the flame of which spun and flared in the wind. Neither wanted to initiate the parting.

Picking up a thread of earlier conversation, Ide said, "You may never find a ship back to the Empire, you know. This may be where you stay."

Finbar kicked at a stone. "I haven't actually asked Father Asolf yet. He thinks I mean to continue with Brendan in the spring."

After a pause, Ide murmured, "Be prepared to live out your life in Thule, that's all I say."

There was a new vividness about Ide's face when she said this that struck Finbar. He was not certain whether it was the effect of the torchlight or whether there was an emotion behind the words for which he was both unprepared and, on the whole, grateful. He took her by the arm, and she did not resist. They were equally tall, and their faces were not far apart. Had he been able to put down the torch, he might have embraced her. As it was, he felt the blood suddenly run through his fingers, and he thought he saw an answering wideness of her eyes. Releasing her arm, he said huskily, "You are a beautiful woman, Ide."

Her face moved. "Don't say that," she whispered. "Not that way."

"It's the truth."

"I'm not what you say. I'm old; and I'm a nun."

"A nun, yes. But you are also a woman, and you are beautiful." He left her standing between the spruce trees.

When he had gone several yards, he turned and saw her still standing there. He could not see her face in the gloom, but her stance made him sing. His heart leapt at her across the snow. Her hand moved, as though she felt it so. Then she waved. "Come again, Finbar," she called. "You bring me . . . air."

Finbar nodded and turned away. When he looked back a minute or two later, she was gone.

The following day, the mariners were invited for the first time to inspect the monastery's scriptorium. This was the site of much winter work, when the world was too dark for farming. Here the Book of Thule was being illuminated, letter by intricate letter. Father Asolf and several monks led the visitors after Mass to the low, warm room where five men sat at easels. Finbar was intrigued by the lighting. Instead of the somewhat ineffective oil lamps that otherwise served the monastery, the scriptorium was lit by lamps made from shells ground so wonderfully thin that the light of the flame inside was both magnified greatly and made more soft. As a result, the artists worked in circumstances anyone who inhabited the long arctic night would envy. And the work they produced was beautiful.

Finbar watched Father Asolf draw Brendan's attention to the work that was being done at one easel to illuminate the letter M. Cadaverous, with bushy eyebrows that met over the sharp ridge of his nose, the abbot bent beside Brendan.

"Masterly," Brendan murmured, "masterly."

To Finbar, the two men seemed brothers at that moment, despite the width of the Western Sea that separated their normal abodes. It was something about the Nazarene presence, and it angered him. In sudden dejection, his mind slid from his own envious lonesomeness to a curiosity that had piqued him many times in the past years: it bewildered him that so spiritually narrow-minded a race as the Irish Nazarenes should at the same time have evolved so sophisticated an art of design. It was with this lesser thought that he contented his mind during the remainder of the inspection.

Walking back toward the chapel with the others, Finbar found himself close by the abbot, and he addressed the man.

"Father, I believe you are laboring under a misapprehension about me."

"You are a smith, my son. I am aware of that; and I have prayed on the subject."

"Yes, that is true, but I was referring to my part in this mission of Brendan's."

The abbot slowed his pace, and the others flowed around them. When he and Finbar were free of the group, Father Asolf asked, "What do you wish to tell me?"

"I was a castaway, and—"

"I am aware of that. God saved you for a greater errand."

"It's that I want to talk about. The errand. It is not my desire to continue on this voyage. I wish to stay here. You see, I was trying to get a boat back to Greece. That's why I was at sea in the first place. I was trying to get to Greece because I was, well, exhausted by Ireland, and I needed rest."

"I should hardly have picked Greece for that. What I hear is . . ." The abbot waved his hand vaguely.

"I did pick Greece," Finbar said. "Anyhow, I still want to go there. I would like to wait here until there is a ship going back to the Empire. Going anywhere. It doesn't have to be Greece. I can make my way there once I am back."

"And so you desire to stay here."

"I am asking it."

"To be part of our community."

"I have skills that I can use for you, skills with metal."

"I know you are a smith."

"I have worked for monasteries before."

"That was in Ireland."

"Of course, but in Gaul as well."

"You are a traveler."

"It is a smith's life."

"I will pray."

"But may I stay?"

"There is time to decide. God will guide me. Have no fear of that."

Somewhat ill at ease after this meeting, Finbar returned to the sheep barn. The atmosphere was thick with smoke. Wind from the southwest defeated the fire's draft system; Finbar and the others had been unable to conquer the problem. A southwestern gale was building up. Seas broke against the shoreline heavily enough even to be heard inside the barn. What little light the day had offered had passed away. Finbar sat in a corner and tried sporadically to repair his clothing. His leg hurt him. Joseph and Atla discussed their visit to the scriptorium, and Brendan bent beside a wick and studied his map. Barinthus snored gently in the background.

Several hours passed, and Finbar allowed himself to doze. The storm continued outside: the whole world of the Western Sea moaned. Finbar scratched lice and slept.

He became aware that his name was being mentioned. His consciousness began to return. A sudden, sharp blow in the ribs wakened him. He rolled onto his back, propped on an elbow. Above him loomed the skeletal figure of the abbot in the darkness, almost invisible for smoke, and shadow, and Finbar's own muzzy head.

"Not baptized," came the thin voice once more, and the knurl of the man's staff again prodded Finbar's ribs. "You say this man has not been baptized?"

Brendan appeared beside the abbot. "Finbar, it's all right." He gestured at the smith to stay down. "No," Brendan repeated to the abbot, "not baptized."

Finbar pulled himself to his knees, anger growing at

the fact that the abbot's staff remained against his chest. "I am not a Nazarene," he muttered.

"This is a Christian community," the reedy voice replied. "All here are baptized. We have none here unbaptized."

Finbar rose. "You have now."

Brendan interposed himself between the two, trying to steer the taller man away. "Finbar, be calm," he ordered over his shoulder.

Atla and the second monk drifted near through the choking atmosphere. Finbar could see Joseph in the background, his face eager. It was dark in that corner of the hut. Bodies jostled one another. Finbar's eyes caught the light, luminous as those of a wraith. "Tell him to stop poking me. I'm no sheep."

"Brother Asolf—," Brendan began.

"We may be small, Brother Brendan," the abbot interrupted, "but we are strong in the service of the Lord." He turned away from Finbar, and, gesturing to include the rest of his community outside, he said, "We have just now become concerned over the presence of an unbeliever among us. This person has asked about staying with us indefinitely. You will understand, Brendan. We are a small community living in harmony, but the nights are long, and the winter cold. Thule is not an easy place to live, and we have been taxed heavily in the last years. It concerns us to have a pagan with us here. Our success is hardly won."

"I am a smith!" Finbar answered in the darkness. "I don't threaten you."

"My boy." The abbot turned back to him. "You may indeed be a threat, albeit without intending any such thing. The workings of God are more complicated than any of us expected."

"I was shipwrecked. Brendan picked me up. He brought me here. You know all this. I am not an instrument of your god. I am not a test, Father Asolf."

"No one man can be certain of the manner in which God is using him. I believe you say what you think to be true. I daresay it is true. But, Brendan, we have felt concern since your arrival here with this man, and now I learn for certain that he hasn't even the basic protection of baptism." Here the abbot nodded at Joseph. "I feel myself even more greatly worried."

"What worries you?" Brendan asked, glancing at Joseph.

The abbot didn't answer for a few moments. He prodded at the dirt floor with the end of his staff, seeming to organize his thoughts. Finally, he said, "We receive visitors now and then, pilgrims such as yourselves, or brethren eager to join us. The last time was six years ago. A boat arrived from the old country, just as you have, but it was less lucky. Its crew was nearly all dead when it came ashore. We did what we could to nurse the survivors, but, one by one, they died. All of them. Then we began to die, too. It was a test. Our population was cut down by one-third before we were able to rid ourselves of the evil that was killing us. We had been lax in our observances before that terrible visitation. This is a hard land, and we had turned more attention to the provision of creature comforts than we had to the rigorous, and the more necessary, followings of Christ. So we were tested, and, barely, we have survived." The abbot turned his eyes toward Brendan. "You are an abbot, sir. You will understand our concern."

"We have been here nearly a month," Brendan replied. "I do understand your concern, but ought we not to have earned our security by this time? Finbar is no threat."

"A month is nothing. I have sat for six months on one rock and watched one spot in the sea. Six months! I learned only the most rudimentary things. Only the beginning of knowledge. A month is nothing. The winter is long."

Finbar shook himself and took a step toward the abbot. "I am not evil."

"As to your intentions, I am convinced, my good fellow. It is a question of God's action on earth that concerns us, a question upon which, as a pagan, you cannot pronounce."

"If I am a pagan, I am one after I am a man. First, I am a man like you. Next, I am a smith. Then, perhaps, I am a pagan. Those are my credentials. As a man, I can say that I am no threat to you or to your community. Thule will suffer not one whit from me. My interests are in survival as a man; and, as a smith, my interests are in the forging of useful tools. In fact, though I myself say so, I contribute to the good of the world as actively as you do yourself."

"You contribute to the good of man's world, to be sure. I am aware of that. For that, you are to be applauded. We here are making our way in God's world. We have left man's world, left it to the smiths, I may say, and we have hied us here to neighbor God's world. As a man and as a smith, you have no pronouncement to make concerning the functioning of God's world. I speak for that world, and I say that we are worried. For all that you are unaware of it, you may be a snake in our grass. I must patrol my lawn, Finbar, with an eagle's eye."

"A very earthly metaphor for your holy task," Finbar muttered.

"True, but not inappropriately so. The earth is God's. We have found ourselves a piece of unmanned earth. Its winds, its geysers, its eagles, the summer flowers blooming in the hot, clean sun: these are the messages of God writ large across our land. We have no snakes here at all."

The company in the hut was silent for a few moments. The words of the abbot, so forcefully spoken in his willowy voice, kept everyone in thrall except Finbar. The abbot stood to his whole height in the center of the hut, his face and torso wreathed in smoke, his shadow cast disproportionately and erratically upon the roof by the tiny, yellow flame of the lamp.

"Join us, Finbar." The abbot walked to Finbar's side. "Join us, won't you? Take the protection of the Lord upon you. Give your soul to Christ."

"I am not a Nazarene."

"Only there lies peace, Finbar. In forgiveness, in meekness, in love: there lies peace. I offer it to you. Think about it. We will be watching over you until you decide, but make it a decision for Christ. Simply say, 'I believe,' and you will have peace." He made the sign of the Cross in front of Finbar's face, and then he turned. "Come, Brother Cadoc, let us leave the man to his conscience."

The abbot and his brother monk strode to the doorway, thrust through it, and disappeared into the night. The four sailors stood in the attitudes they had held upon his departure, while the smoke eddied thicker, agitated by the gusts that came through the door.

Shortly, Brendan turned to Finbar. He opened his mouth to speak, but he was interrupted.

"Don't!"

"Listen to me."

"I'll not be baptized, Brendan. You must understand that. A man can't change what he is. I am not a Nazarene." He turned to Joseph. "And you, you bastard—"

"Stop!" Brendan commanded. "I'll not have that. Be still, Finbar."

Such was the force of the captain's command that Finbar closed his mouth. Brendan turned to Joseph and gestured for the man to withdraw.

"Father Brendan, I—" Joseph began.

"Leave us now, Joseph," Brendan said softly. "I will speak with Finbar alone. And, in the future, please allow me to talk with Father Asolf myself concerning these matters."

Joseph cast a furious look at Finbar, but he turned with stiff-backed dignity and disappeared into the dark end of the hut. Soon his voice could be heard in prayer.

Brendan turned back to Finbar. "You say you are not a Christian. Men have changed before. Saul became Paul."

"We are not in Damascus."

"The location doesn't matter, and, if it did, you heard Brother Asolf say that this is the country of God."

"Oh, Brendan, I despise this charnel worship! Don't you see? Forgive me for speaking this way to you. I owe you my life, but I don't see the logic of it, this worship of a dead man."

"He's not dead," Brendan interposed, "and logic is less great a faculty of man than faith."

"I just don't grasp it. Logic must be appropriate. You

say that Christ has risen eternally, but nothing rises eternally. This very earth that Father Asolf speaks of: it isn't eternal. One hundred years from now, the rocks that hang out over that point will have fallen into the ocean. What of that for eternalness? The sun moves, the planets move, the stars move. They all rise, yes, but then they set again. That's what I mean by logic. Logic is not a mental trick, not some gymnastic convulsion of the mind practiced to surprise and distract. Logic is the way the world works. Everything has a season, everything dies. To be a Nazarene, I would have to deny that. I would have to argue against every fact I know. Against everything I see! I don't bring logic forth to counter some other belief of yours: logic is, that's all. Logic just is."

"Let me bring up another matter, Finbar, something that your logic doubtless will already have shown you." Brendan walked across the hut and sat down upon the pile of woolens that covered his own pallet. He motioned for Finbar to come closer, and he lowered his voice. "We are an expedition here, five men. We represent five mouths to feed, five spaces on the floor. It's winter out there. The curragh is battered. We are living on the charity of a very small, and a very poor, community. They are out of touch with much of the world. They are nervous about us. They ache for the comfort of your baptism. We haven't anywhere else to turn until summer opens the seas again. Barinthus is ill; Joseph is . . . well, Joseph. I appeal to your conscience. Think seriously about baptism. I understand and respect your views, as you know. I never attacked you for them while you were aboard my curragh, and I don't attack you for them now. If you cannot become a Christian in good conscience, then you mustn't become one at all. Understand, though, the pressure that the Thule community is under when they look at you. Don't despise them for their uneasiness. There have been times, I suspect, when you, too, have looked on outsiders with some disdain. Understand them, Finbar, and we'll try to work together in this place, at this time. If you can come our way, with Christ, we welcome you. If you can't, so be it. You consider yourself a practical man. I'm speaking of practical things."

"I can't sell myself for your pragmatism. I never wanted to come on this expedition in the first place."

"Oh, you were eager enough to leave that island, I may remind you. You could have stayed. You could have stayed with Sebastian. The two of you could be starving there at this very moment, close beside Paradise, right there on the edge of the sea, right beside Sebastian's moveable Paradise. You could have been left there, my angry fellow, and you know it. So don't accuse me of unwanted charity."

Finbar swore and turned away, scratching frenziedly at his head. "I just wanted to go to Greece! Where there are men of intelligence."

"You're not in Greece. You're in Thule, and it is winter, and you ought to be baptized."

"No." Finbar glanced across the hut at Atla for support, but his friend pointedly looked away.

"Yes, Finbar, you ought."

"I can't."

"As man to man, all right, but you'll make it harder for us here. They may even throw us off the island."

"What difference does that make to me? I'm staying here until I get a boat home, you know that. Anyway, what of their Christian charity in that case?"

"Charity is of a more subtle nature than that. The Christian must help the innocent sufferer, but he may cast the devil aside. A refusal to allow us to stay here would come because they think you are an agent of Lucifer."

When Finbar raised his voice to object, Brendan rode over him with, "Witting or no, Finbar. Witting or no. If they make us leave, they are hardly likely to allow you to stay on for a year or two. It's you they have the quarrel with, not us."

In the silence that followed, Atla asked, "What difference might it make to Barinthus if we had to put out to sea right now?"

Finbar turned to him angrily. "Unfair, Atla. Please!"

"Listen, Finbar. Listen to the gale. Do you want to shove off into that?"

"Atla, I don't want to shove off into anything. I hate the sea."

Brendan, rising from his bed and holding arms out in a gesture for peace, took the conversation back. "We have not been asked to leave. In all likelihood, we never will be. Father Asolf is a kind man, and a wiser one, Finbar, than you may think. I merely appeal to you as a friend, that's all.

"I haven't said a thing about your beliefs in the months that we have known one another, but now I appeal to you. The Christian faith will sustain you, if only you can allow it to do so. I offer you a new dispensation, Finbar. Your logic is unassailable, but only in your own human world. What Father Asolf said is true. This is a world of God. Here, a new and a wonderful idea holds sway. Suppose, Finbar, just suppose that what we believe is true. Think! The world is saved. No more eternal round. God is active in history, directing events toward His glorious conclusion. Right now is the time, Finbar. I am offering you magic, mystery, faith, hope, joy, all those things if only the Christian belief were true. You have a hard and a sober pragmatism to sustain you; you have logic and power, but what if the miraculous is true? Isn't that better? To put it in your terms, I am saying that your iron might become gold. Not that it will—I don't ask you to believe that it will, because it would be as much as to set a time when it must happen, to be disappointed, and to fall from belief. The Bible states that we must never test God, for to test Him is to try to trap Him with logic. I say to you, Finbar, believe that it *might* be so, that's all. No tests, no logical traps. Don't believe that the iron will become gold; believe that it *might* become gold. That is strength indeed."

Impressed by the speech, but trying to make light of it, Finbar replied, "I've lost my tools. I've no more power one way or the other."

Brendan shrugged aside the humor and answered seriously. "You have the tool that you need, Finbar. In the place of hammer and anvil use your wit."

"If I do?"

Brendan clapped his hands together and barked a great burst of laughter. "Magic! Like this: we winter over and get our rest. Barinthus heals. The curragh is repaired.

Then, in the summer when the seas are lighter, we sail to Paradise!"

"Paradise! Brendan, how can you believe that?"

"It's there, Finbar. I'll make it be there."

"Don't let Father Asolf hear you say that. He'll like your *hubris* as little as he likes my so-called paganism. Not that he understands either."

"He understands by his lights, that's all. That's no different from you or me, or Atla there."

Finbar burst out passionately, "These Nazarenes! These saints! What do they know? They see the world vertical when really it's horizontal."

"What?" Atla asked in a startled voice.

"I've been to places you Nazarenes haven't even heard of, Atla. There's knowledge out there, spread all around, all over the surface of the earth: in Egypt, in Greece, in Persia, in India. What do these Thulean saints know of that? Not one thing. They cling to this rock like monkeys, thinking all the universe focuses through them. They're not like you, Atla, or you, Brendan. You think, but they bear down into their souls as though there was no such thing as a width of knowledge. I know that there is! I can tell them as much about their souls by looking into my forge as they can by pinioning themselves on God's spear. They think everything is straight up and down: just worship their way and everything is in harmony. It's not true! Everything isn't in harmony. What about the traders I used to know in India, with their own knowledge of how things are? What do these monkeys say to that? Nothing. They just cringe on a rock in the ocean looking upward all the time, never to the side, and they wind themselves into contests of self-denial. All they are is competitors in some sort of cosmic austerity contest."

There was silence in the hut for a moment. Finbar slumped away and dropped onto his bed. Atla kicked desultorily at a jerkin someone had left on the ground. Joseph's voice grew louder in prayer. A gust of wind coming through a chink in the wall nearly extinguished the lamp. The air stung the eyes. Finbar felt tears on his lids, but whether they came from the irritation of the smoke or from frustration he did not know.

"Brendan, I'm not a Nazarene," he said in a calm, tired voice. "I can't believe that your Christ was the son of god. I can't believe in his eternal resurrection. I've heard it all, and I've seen your Nazarene faith all over the world, but I don't believe it. You ask me to put my faith in a 'maybe.' That's very seductive, but I am a realist. When I look into my forge, when I see ore become molten, when I pound slag out of it and shape it into bars, when I heat and hammer and bend and shape the bars, then I feel that I have an idea of what the truth is. If your Christ were a forge, then, yes, perhaps I would believe his promise. You asked me to be practical. I am being practical. I am a practical man. I know about iron, and I know how to make steel. That's pragmatism. I'll make you a sword that will slice through armor like the wind through this rotten wall, but I won't wield the sword because I don't know what to hit."

Brendan walked over and sat beside Finbar on the pile of rags and woolens that served for a bed. Together, the two men stared at the tiny, yellow waver of light across the hut. Atla wandered to the table beside the lamp and closed the Testament that the monks had been examining. His shadow, when he drew close to the lamp, was angular on the raw stone of the walls.

"I'm not ordering you to believe," Brendan said.

After a few more moments of silence, Brendan continued, "One must not castigate another man for knowing too little, for one's knowledge is always very little indeed compared with what may be known. Only God knows everything. You can't be certain how He assesses the beliefs of those men in the East you speak of. I certainly don't know the answer. I've seen things that can put your logic to shame during the past two years: the sea is an odd place to spend time. What was logical about Barinthus and the whale? That sort of thing happens all the time. I suggest to you a possibility, that's all."

Finbar laughed. "It's ironic. Aboard the curragh, there was no free space anywhere. We were like too many chicks in a nest. I longed so for the space to take a step or two without tripping over your legs, Atla, or your head, Brendan, that I couldn't wait to get ashore. But, I was free when I was aboard. Now, with hundreds upon hundreds of miles of empty land in every direction, I am in prison."

"Because you are alone," Brendan said, raising his face to meet Finbar's. "You are alone in your refusal of Christ. If you were in Greece, perhaps you wouldn't be such an anomaly, but you are here, now. This is all there is for you. These gales aren't going to go away. We shall stay here all winter, and the sky will be dark, the seas will be rough. What you make of this lonesomeness is up to you. I suggest you think of Christ. I'll shield you in whatever manner I can, but you are alone without Christ. All alone."

The sounds of the storm continued unabated outside, but the fire hissed more quietly as it died down. Finbar rose and limped across the room. He seemed to be at war with himself. Finally, across the flaring lamp, he spoke. His face looked hideous, lit that way, from below. His black cheeks and brows were beetled, his eyes glittered, his scraggy beard was a tangle of black flame. "All right," he said. "I'll keep to myself. I'll be cast out as man is when he doubts the wisdom of the mob. No, Brendan, I mean mob. I'll not disturb our hosts, but I'll find a way to answer you. I shall do that because of what you have done for me. If you save a man's life, he becomes your responsibility forever. I am yours, then, in some way. Also, you are mine, and I may—I say I *may*—seduce even you with logic, in the end. So, Brendan, just as I shall think of what you have suggested, you, too, must look as deep inside yourself as you are able. See if that soul of yours doesn't long for an explanation. Is there some single sinew buried inside all that Christian muscle and bone that doubts? There must be. You've seen strange things at sea. Sometime I'll tell you about strange things ashore. Every one of us lives on the edge of the miraculous, my Nazarene friend, but it's what we do with that strangeness that tells."

And so it was that, as the winter dipped down into its lowest days, Finbar took to walking. The sunlight bled into the sky for only a few hours during each transit, and the monastic community did little work. Instead, each half of the settlement, the monastery and the convent, entered the more carefully into its own religious maze, winding ever more tightly toward a center of doctrine that neither could easily discover. Their few poor huts were backed by immense landscapes of rock and snow, fronted by the cold tumble of the Western Sea. Human life struggled at the seaweed line: for the rest, the blue arctic night held sway. Through the short days and into the long nights, Finbar walked.

The Thule community was situated in a spot that was a good one for walking. Despite the fact that Thule lay in a more northerly latitude than that of Ireland, Finbar discovered the winter weather to be much the same. Along the shore, snow fell now and then, but usually it melted soon after falling; especially snow that lay around the edges of the hot pools and the steaming mud bogs. These latter contributed greatly to the bizarre nature of the landscape. Inland from the cove upon which the community was built was a spot where geysers erupted into the air with regular hissing explosions. The forms of the land were young, it seemed, unrounded. There was little tree cover: the community's buildings were made of rock and sod. Hills rose smoothly, unclothed, into the cloudy sky, the curves of their slopes and the barren excesses of their ridges creating a sort of hollow, soundless echo perceived not by the ear but by the innate senses of the blood.

Walking in the gloaming along the sides of bowls, Finbar began to understand the process by which the tiny community had lost its wit and grown turgid with hyperbolic imaginings of saga-kind. He felt the glimmerings himself as, from one hillside, his eye spanned across empty mile upon mile of grey-green valley streaked with white until—so slowly!—the valley rose again to a distant wall of hills. Over all brooded the slippery, fish-colored sky. Nothing was within the vale save the few gaunt cottages and ricks of the monastery, hardly distinguishable in their insignificant bend of shore. The nunnery, farther along the verge, was little more attractive to the eye. The whole was a scene of space and liquid, heedless air in which, precariously, there dwelt for Christ twenty-two monks and eighteen nuns. The center of the land was impassable, it was said; high, and glacier-buried. Only the birds came there. Wind, and heath, and rain, and naked rock; stunted trees and sudden, fleeing rodents; the lonesome caw of a wintering bird too small before the wind to carry far; a river of melting, steaming mud in which he warmed his feet; coming darkness and slipping return across too many spans of repeated, mushy snow; to Finbar on his walks these things were Thule.

Then there was the Christian solemnity that would greet him at its end hard by the sea. Now it was hymns, and prayers, and meticulous dogmatics he found, which buttressed minds so easily stunned by naked size and air they must, he thought, have had no quickness with which to bridge the gaps of argument on their Irish coastline of home—and so they had run. Run to this solemn place, and clung. And they were looking westward, to the end of the earth, to Paradise—who knew?—but here they dwelt beneath the ever-pressing sky, alone, unswayed, brittle, yet perhaps sublime.

Finbar walked from Christmas to Epiphany. He walked along the shore both north and south. He walked inland as far as he could get while the sun shone. Three times he waited out the long hours of arctic night in order to extend his rambles on the following day. Huddled in his cloak behind some windbreak of stone, his eyes on the faint glimmer of landscape under stars, he was at least as content as he would have been lying lonesome in the darkness of the hut.

By Epiphany, the nervousness that Brother Asolf had been first to voice had grown. Finbar's rambling habit itself was suspect, for who could be certain what mischief lay waiting for a man who skulked among the raw blades of this volcanic land? The man was a smith, as they all knew, one who possessed the dangerous power to transform matter. Occasionally, he was followed during his outings: they knew him, high on the crags, especially in late and driving weather, back to the wind, kneading a lump of bog iron in his fist, and groaning, in some round Mediterranean tongue, a song of aspiration.

"You are wizards, too!" he shouted one night, as the monks clustered around him in a thin rain. His leg ached from the walk just done. He was wet, and the cold slid clever fingers along his ribs. "What of the Host?" He turned from one closed face to another. "What of the transmutation of the Mass?"

"God does that," Brother Asolf answered. "We are His agents only."

"I, too!"

"You are your own master, Finbar; we know what smiths are here."

"If I had a forge, I could show you that there is nothing devilish about the process. Brother Asolf, Brother Cadoc, you, the rest of you . . ."

The monks were turning away from him, forming in procession to make their way to Vespers through the rain.

"My craft is exciting," Finbar called to them, "but it is not evil. How can knowledge be evil? To be able to turn iron ore into a steel hoe is a good thing! You need steel. You use it, I've seen you use it. If it were evil, you wouldn't use it, would you? I know the process is good!"

Brother Asolf stopped, and the trail of monks grew still. The abbot turned back. Wet wind billowed his cloak around him, and he raised his nasal voice to carry against its gusts. "We use steel, yes. Not much, but we do. That is not the point. We are not equal magicians, you and I. My magic, as you would call it, is supported and walled about by God Himself. It was He who gave me the power to transmute the Host. Because I am His servant, my aspirations are no higher. Your magic is different. Yours has no support, no walls, except the whimsy of man. You yourself may not be evil—I doubt you are. Your power, though, is unrestrained, and your aspirations are excessive. When human aspirations exceed human value, and when they have power behind them to realize their desire, *that*, Finbar, is evil. That we abhor." He turned himself away and stepped toward the chapel.

Angry and tired, Finbar limped away.

7

INTER WAS ON THE WANE. The storms were softer now and the land less stiffly frozen. Bogs appeared. The first of the wandering birds, too, returned from the south to their nesting spots along the edge of the sea. The curragh had spent the winter forlornly hauled above the tide and propped with wedges. Snow had covered and uncovered her, and, though her interior had been protected by the oxhide tenting of her deck, she was a sad sight. Brendan announced that it was time to begin refitting her. The encounter with the whale had left her seriously damaged: certain of her ribs and stringers required replacement, an operation only to be accomplished by removing her oxhide skin. She wanted masts and yards, new rigging and new grease.

Brendan stood on her deck, one balmy, fecund afternoon, pointing out to the assembled voyagers the work that needed to be done. "And," he concluded, "I've determined to step the foremast farther aft, so as to provide a better drive to windward."

"You'll get an awful weather helm," Atla began to protest, but Barinthus interrupted him.

The old man straightened from his half-listening, bent posture and smote the side of the curragh with his shellagleigh. "Do you mean to impose your own will on the Will of God?"

"What do you say?" Brendan asked, startled.

"You propose to sail against the wind? That is blasphemy."

"Uncle, she's not a weatherly boat. Think of the struggle we had to make our way to this very spot. Think of what would have happened if we had not made it here."

"God intended the struggle. We are on pilgrimage. Do you expect it to be simple?"

"I'm only talking of improvements to my rig."

"You're talking of changes in the nature of the pilgrimage. To take out of God's hands the conning of the boat and put it into your hands. You may chide me, scoff at my experience"—here he shook his stick at his nephew—"but you must choose: are you a sailor, or are you a pilgrim?"

"I am both."

Finbar interjected nastily, "There is the sinew I spoke of, Brendan. You are both. Flex that sinew, and you will be a free man."

Brendan rounded on the smith. "Get away from me! I'll not be tempted that way."

"It's not I. You tempt yourself."

Brendan took a stance against the mainmast. "I am captain," he said. "I decide. Barinthus, you may think what you like, but I alone am responsible for the condition of my ship. I have studied on this—even theologically, Barinthus—for four months. I say we step the mast farther aft. I also say," and he stared at Barinthus challengingly, "that we will fix bilge keels in place, as a farther assist in windward work."

"You can't," Atla said.

"Why not?" Brendan jerked around to this new quarter.

"You can't. Bilge keels big enough to do the job cannot be attached without major strengthening inside. You'll need proper floors at least, maybe bulkheads."

"What of it?"

"You'll lose all the give in the hull."

"But gain two points to weather, if not more."

"It's been said before: we don't go to weather."

"We will go any direction I say we will!"

"Brendan . . ." Atla's tone was aggrieved.

"Enough." The captain jumped down to the beach. "I know what I am doing. I know what we have before us. We need weatherly qualities in this craft, and I will give us those qualities. Those who object," and here he stood before his uncle, "may stay behind, with this . . . smith."

"I am not a member of this crew!" Finbar shouted.

"No more you are," Brendan answered. "I have said nothing different. You have no interest in our journey. You have said it, thank you very much. We all know that. God be saved, we all know that."

So, on a certain clear and melting day, Brendan, Atla, Joseph and Barinthus, occasionally assisted by brothers of the Thule community, set about the massive task of unstepping the masts, stripping the leather covering from the hull, repairing the damaged members, and then constructing the new curragh according to Brendan's design. Finbar stood aside, or walked, or sought the company of Ide and her nuns. However, he was drawn back continually to the curragh, now bare and vulnerable. The men stripped to their waists as they plaited new thongs around new stringers. There was pleasant talk, mainly, though Barinthus grumbled. Once, Finbar lent a hand at a tough job. The next day, unasked, he put in a morning's work.

A new problem arose. There were no trees along the immediate coastline tall enough and straight enough to serve as masts for the curragh. Thule was not a heavily forested land in any case, but it was thought that the best trees were to be found in the interior. Brendan proposed to set out in one of the monastery's boats for the southern shores of the island, hoping to find a way back into one of the valleys there, toward the central forests. However, that coastline was plagued by sudden squalls and fogs at this time of year, and everywhere it was shoal, harborless and rocky. Eventually, it was decided that an overland expedition from the monastery might have just as great a success and would avoid the logistical difficulties of the coasting voyage.

Brendan and Finbar stood aside from the work at hand.

"You will lead. Joseph will be your lieutenant. Brother Asolf will send four of his monks with you."

"Joseph and I do not combine well," Finbar complained.

"You needn't go at all," Brendan replied, and he turned away.

"No! I'll do it. I want to do it. But why can't I have Atla?"

"Atla is needed here. Besides myself, he is the only

person who truly understands the niceties of the craft."

"I can see that," Finbar replied, "but then why have Joseph at all? I can manage with the monks."

Brendan looked out at the sea. After a minute, he said quietly, "We have a long way to go, Finbar. Paradise is still a long reach before us. If we make it at all, it will be weeks, months—time not measured by time—" He turned to the smith. "And I have been thinking about what you said. I think you should go with Joseph. I think he must see what you are. Perhaps you need to see him, as well. I have hopes . . ."

"Yes?"

"You were a competent crewman, Finbar. Remember that. Remember what you learned from the sea."

Two days later, the six men set out. It was a warm, still morning with the sun hanging low in the eastern sky and throwing its light at them through a golden haze. This was a condition that augured rain, and they looked back over their shoulders now and then to watch dark squall clouds mass above the shore.

To Joseph's quite vocal disgust, Finbar directed their course to the convent. He left the others at the spruce-tree gate and made his own way to the chapel, outside which he found Ide.

"Come with us!" he urged, having explained the mission.

"I can't just leave."

"Of course you can. You weren't even here four months ago."

"That is irrelevant," she laughed.

"Oh, Ide, it would be such a relief from all this."

Ide looked around at the convent, wiping her fingers on her apron. "There's so much to do here."

"You can do it when you get back. It will be the same then as it is now, you know that. Only the seasons change. Human interactions never change. Whatever you want to do now you can do in a fortnight."

"I don't know . . ."

"And the others can plant and take care of the sheep and do the other seasonal things in the meantime."

Ide turned to him. "It's not just politics that I think

about, my friend. You know that. Suppose I get a renewed
taste for the adventuring life?"

Finbar took the trowel from her fingers. He placed it
on top of the stone wall next to them. Looking her straight
in the eye, he said, "If you don't come, you'll never know
whether you really are abbess of this place or simply allowing circumstances to provide you a suitable retreat."

Staring back at him, her head slightly tilted, she replied, "That's not really fair, you know."

"But it's worth a good deal to me to discover the
answer, nevertheless."

Their eyes held each other's gaze for a disorientingly
long time. Ide broke it. She took a deep breath and ran
a hand over the warm stones of the chapel doorway. "I'll
come," she murmured finally.

"Splendid!"

She looked quickly at Finbar and then away. "I've
never done anything like this."

He took her hand and compelled her to look back at
him. "Let us discover whether you will do it some more."

"Don't raise the stakes too high."

"Too high for you?"

"Yes, but, Finbar, also for you. We are of different
kinds, you and I. I am a Christian nun. My commitment
is eternal. Don't use me."

Now he broke the eye contact. He laughed. "We're
making too much of all this. This is a holiday!"

"God pronounces holidays," she said quietly, but she
smiled at him. "Let me make a few arrangements, and I'll
be with you."

Returning to the waiting monks, Finbar reported,
"Ide will accompany us on this journey. She desires to
explore the interior of this country, and Joseph and I both
know her to be a resourceful traveling companion, isn't
that so, Joseph?"

The man sneered and turned away.

Half an hour later, the party was on its way again.
Spring had come to Thule: the great stretches of frozen
valley through which Finbar in winter had made his way
were now invitingly carpeted by flowers; the air was softly
stroked by butterfly wings; the world was suddenly alive

with birds. Phalaropes, dunlins, redwings, snow buntings and ringed plovers whirled and darted in the sky, back to nest and to breed. A patch of greying, late snow, hidden in a north-facing gully, gave the party a sudden, hilarious battle with snowballs. Around them the sun shone, and the world was alive-o, and the storm plotted.

The rain came across them as they hiked along the base of the first ring of hills. Scudding, grey clouds came out of the west, throwing their shadows along the earth before them like fistfuls of sand. The squall was sharp and cold, and the walkers took what shelter they could on the bare ground behind boulders and under their cloaks. For a time, the world was all drip and misery. The explorers mumbled to one another, and their noses ran. Soon, though, the clouds parted, and the sun came out again to shine through retreating rain. Two rainbows arched the land, the lower one clear, the upper one wide and diffusing into the bombilating air. A skua followed the rain, hawklike, and it stooped to drive a raven from a rock. A snipe walked tamely through grass beside Finbar's feet.

The travelers were out of sight of the ocean by this time, cut off from that hurrying and immediate presence. They made their way through a land outside the scale of human time. Now and then came the bark of a fox, happy to see the birds again. There was no other earthbound voice; the sounds were of the sky. Little conversation occurred among the walkers. Only such words as were necessary to determine their path assailed the envelope of air: they listened to other things, glad tidings from the birds, the industry of insects, hollow buffets of the wind. In all, through that first day, they made good ten or twelve miles toward the inner slopes.

After a meal of smoked puffin, they rested. The unfamiliar exertions of the first day made them tired, but they were restless at the same time. Still in thrall to the silence of the land, they huddled by themselves in what hollows they found upon the ground, looking for sleep as the rim of an early moon chased the sun down the western sky. Finbar's leg ached, so that he had a harder time succumbing to the seduction of wide sky even than the others did. Eventually, just after moonset, he rose and walked stiffly through the flowers to a height of land where he squatted and watched the heavens. He had no idea what to do.

Perhaps an hour passed before anything occurred. There was no wind. The land was dark, barely visible in its corrugations under the stars. The sky revolved ever so slowly. He watched the Gemini set, and in time Hercules was over his head. About then his eye caught a dark shape moving up the hillside toward his perch, and when it drew closer to him, he recognized it as Ide.

"Hello," she whispered. "May I sit with you?"

"I should be delighted."

The woman arranged herself upon the ground, cloak pulled around her knees, and silence fell across them for a moment. Then she said, "I saw you climb up and, when you didn't come down . . ."

"You couldn't sleep either?"

"It's so new, this land." Ide gestured in the dark, her hand passing as quickly as a bat across the stars. "It's different from the sea. The sea is more humane somehow. This is so stark, so hard to encompass in the mind."

"Not like Ireland," Finbar chuckled.

"No." He could hear her smile. "Not like Ireland."

The land was very quiet.

"Are you glad you came, Ide?"

"With you?"

"No, I mean, to Thule at all."

"You keep bringing it back to that."

"It's so . . . strange a place."

"This is the edge of the world. There's nothing beyond us. We are sitting in the last place on earth."

"You Nazarenes place a good deal of weight on geography, it seems to me."

"Why do you think I came? To spend two years in an open boat with Brendan and his friends? No, thank you!"

Finbar laughed. "One can spend too much time in that boat, I grant you."

Silence drifted down between them, and it muffled them. Then, in an errant quirk of air, it seeped away, and they spoke of the other half of the question. Ide began it: "Will you be allowed to wait here for a boat?"

"If I go on from here, there's nowhere to go, except with Brendan," Finbar snorted, "to Paradise."

"There are worse places."

"Everyone has a purpose except me. That's the difficulty. You came here because this is the edge of the world. Brendan is partly following Barinthus's lead and partly off on his own exploration, purely for the sake of seeing what's on the other side of the horizon. Joseph follows Brendan. Atla . . . I don't know about him. I guess his purpose is action. But me? I haven't any purpose. I'm a castaway as much as I was before. I can't fish, I can't sail, I can't forge, I can't worship as you do. All I can do is walk!" Finbar slapped his bad leg. "I can't even do that very well, or for very long."

Ide turned her knees in the other direction. "Do you want to know something?"

"What?"

"I used to follow you on those walks, sometimes."

"Did you? Whatever for?" He laughed. "So did the monks."

"I suppose I wanted to see whether you would find a reason for staying in Thule."

The smith and the nun sat on the hilltop for another hour, speaking only occasionally, and then in quiet voices. Little by little, the aurora borealis spread its chilly light across the northern sky. After a bit, it waned, and then they descended and slept.

Morning was still, clear and beautiful. Snow buntings strutted like palace ministers, self-important in their ignorance of the mere human beings beside them. The party pulled itself from its blankets, and Ide and the monks celebrated matins while Finbar kindled fire. In Joseph, Finbar sensed tension which, though it did not surprise him, made him angry.

"I saw the two of you come down from the hill last night," Joseph whispered at Finbar, after eating, as they quenched the fire.

"What of it?"

"I saw you, that's all. You can't hide."

"Joseph, you're wrong. I wish you'd—"

But the man turned away and walked stiffly to his gear.

That day and the next were wearisome. The novelty of walking was gone. The great distances and the silences spoke more of tired legs and parched throats than they did of scenic exultation. Now and then, when they reached the ridge of a hill, they saw that they were leaving the coastal lowlands behind and penetrating into the interior of the country, but these moments of self-congratulation were few. The essential feature of this part of the land seemed to be a series of wide, flat valleys divided by raw hills. As the valleys ran perpendicular to their direction, they were forced to climb one barren row of hills after another, never seeming to make their way out of the same infuriating landscape. The bigness of the sweep caused them problems: a crack in the valley floor, seen as a mere undulation from the top of a hill, might well cost them an hour, as well as a laceration or a bruise, when they tried to cross it.

For lack of any other cohesion in their group, their attention during the days was bent upon the details of the land itself, for they could hardly have conceived a countryside more strange. Finbar perhaps was the most accustomed to it, but even he was shocked by the violence of the place. The heat of creation seemed still to be just under their feet, or so Ide pointed out—literally so, for there were stretches where the rock or the black, volcanic sand was hot to the touch. Steam escaped from vents beside otherwise verdant pools. Lava bulked in the corners of every view. The earth was colored by unnatural tones of greens and blues, streaked now and then by yellow. To Finbar, this was not such a desert as spoke of death, and of the deeds of men long ground to sand: he had felt that way about the Egyptian deserts. These deserts suggested an earth so young that life had yet to begin. History had never stamped it. He made this point to Ide.

"How can you suppose, as a Christian, that creation is done with? Look around yourself," he said.

At the moment, the company was sitting on the edge of a river of hot mud in which they had baked a noontime repast of plovers' eggs. It was the third day, and the tedium of the walk was telling. Tension between Finbar and Joseph was great. Finbar and Ide were separated a little way from Joseph and the Thulean monks, but that vigilant man overheard the question, and his conversation with his fellows stopped abruptly.

Finbar continued, "If God created everything as it is, and if it is good, and if the act is over, then why is this place in such a formative state? Nothing else is."

Ide tossed an eggshell onto the back of the uncanny, boiling river. It lay there, broken edge upward toward the sky, and slid very slowly past the group until it turned a corner around some rocks. She smiled mischievously at Finbar. "Because this is the end of the world. It's Thule. It's supposed to be this way."

Joseph stood up, his voice tight. "Of course, it's supposed to be this way. You can't joke about God's work, as though it were a subject for debate. Who do you think you are, *smith?*"

Finbar looked around. He was sorry to have been overheard.

"I mean no disrespect for your god's abilities—"

"You speak of Him as though He were just another man! We brothers of Christ don't need to compare one landscape with another. To us the landscape that matters is the landscape of God's grace in the world. That is the only landscape that endures, that is the only measure of God's work on earth. This around us is nothing, whether you think it's the beginning or the end. It doesn't matter what you think, how you compare this place with some other place you happen to have seen. That's mere worldliness. We deal in other-worldliness. That's our strength."

Joseph's passion somewhat cooled, and he looked around himself challengingly. "God's ways are not for us to judge," he said.

"I agree with you, Joseph," Ide remarked. "But we *are* allowed sensation. Finbar is right to sense what he does in this." She pointed at the mud river and the wild land through which it twisted its way.

"Not if it places man's judgments ahead of God's."

"It's a narrow line to walk."

"It's the only line to walk. Its narrowness only serves to increase its worth."

Finbar looked at the man. "Do you *not* feel the youthfulness of this place?"

"I'm not concerned with it, youth or no."

"How about you?" Finbar addressed the other monks.

"We aren't taught to feel," Brother Cadoc answered him. "We are taught to remember."

"Then all knowledge comes from the past? What about new impressions?"

"The service of God is the service of the past," Joseph replied, heatedly. "We remember a time when God was here on earth, when He was personally present among us. That's what we remember. That's the explanation for all this question. What happened in the past is true. What happens in the present is possible, that's all, just possible. And possibility is nothing compared with certainty. The Church preserves certainty in a time of flux."

"And the future?"

"The Church knows the future, as well."

"Right here on the edge of the world."

"What better place?" Brother Cadoc's eyes gleamed. "What more suitable spot to begin the work of God than in the very spot at which earth and Heaven become one?"

"Whatever is created is stamped by the Church as your god's own work and, thus, it is good. Is that it?"

"No, no, no!" Joseph was on his feet again, and the other monks were restive. Even Ide looked at Finbar sharply.

"Creation is not a process," Joseph shouted. "You don't see that, do you? You're too tied to your own processes. You think it all resembles a forge. You think God is just another blacksmith! It's not that way. Creation is a fact. It is done. It is ended. It is finished. God's work is in history now. It is not in the creation of new worlds into which the cosmic struggle moves afresh. The struggle is present, everywhere. The Work is present, everywhere. It is finished."

"Isn't your coming here, to Thule, a bringing of the struggle into a world that never had it before?"

"No!" Brother Cadoc answered this thrust. "True, the Church's ministers were not here before. But God was here, creation was here, the struggle was here, history was here. We don't carry those things around with us. We are only men. We come to worship, not to invent. We come here so as not to be distracted by the noise of the world. We look for a spot where we can be still, where we can be devout, and where we can conserve the true forms of our faith. That's all. We didn't bring God to Thule, for He was already here. He has always been here, and He will always be here, long after we are all dead."

Perhaps a minute passed in silence. Then Finbar stood up. "We had better understand one another," he said. "I admit there is a sort of radiance about what you have just said, Brother Cadoc. But, if you will pardon my saying so, it is a radiance of innocence. I respect your Nazarene craftsmanship, your decorative arts, even the legends with which you gird yourself. I have even longed at times for the . . . lenient hours of the cloister, for the incessant chants and prayers. But one would need a simple soul, I think." Here he looked at Ide. "It would be a simplicity which I respect, for its ability, trustingly, to let itself go in the sea of dogma. For myself, I have no such simplicity. I must have the voices of the gods themselves, direct. And I must state that your god has never made any effort to claim me away."

Joseph was on his feet as well. "How could He? You are the most shuttered and closed man in existence on God's earth! How dare you speak of our Heavenly Father in such supercilious terms?"

"I mean no disrespect."

"You *are* disrespect!"

"Joseph—" Ide reached out a hand toward the angry monk.

"Don't take his side, woman. I know you for what you are as well."

Ide rose to her feet. "Your anger has made you irrational," she said, and she turned away.

Joseph turned for support to his fellows. "The idea that such a man as this should guide God's brethren through the wilderness is an abomination. I, for one, will no longer proceed."

"There were those who railed against Moses," Finbar said, with a smile.

Infuriated, Joseph whirled on the smith. "I care nothing for that. Mine is the new dispensation. Jesus Christ is my guide, not some Israelite patriarch!"

Finbar's voice rose. "I'm sorry for you, Joseph. I have tried to explain. I have tried to say that I am a man, like you, and like you attracted to mystical raptures which the gods—and I would say for their own reasons—have made available to man. But finally, Joseph, I must think that you are stupid." He could no longer control himself, and he measured his words with a vicious finger. "I, too, believe that religion will convert the sordidness of ordinary life into beauty, but I insist on basing my religion on something solid, something I can see, something I can hear. Such common sense has deserted you, Joseph, and you persist in this foolish willingness to be astonished at nothing!"

Joseph was apoplectic.

"Stop it," Ide commanded Finbar. "Stop it, you two. Stop it this instant!"

As suddenly as it had overcome him, Finbar's anger drained away. He looked at the monk—the monks—and he saw how easily they could be injured. Knowing his own vulnerability, he was newly compassionate. He took a step toward Joseph.

"Come, forgive me," he asked. "We are tired. We have walked a long way through hard country. We ought not to speak of these things when we are wretched and so very much alone."

Joseph did not respond for some time. Slowly, the Thulean monks parted from him and, one by one, began to gather together their scattered gear.

"Joseph," Ide said, stepping forward.

"Oh, all right!"

Several minutes later, having nothing else to fall back upon, the party was walking again. It was very much strung out. Brother Cadoc and his colleagues led the haphazard way. Alone, pointedly chanting, Joseph made the middle of the train. Though uncertain of one another, Finbar and Ide brought up the rear.

Perhaps a quarter mile passed in silence before Finbar said to Ide, "I'm sorry."

"You were very hard on him."

"I didn't mean to be. His manner makes me so furious. . . ."

"You can hurt," she replied, looking at him with some wonder on her face.

Finbar's reply was bitter. "I know that. I've hurt before."

They walked in silence. Again, Finbar broke it, this time with a chuckle.

"There's one thing I didn't say. . . ."

"Yes?"

"Credo quia absurdum."

She stared at him for a moment, and then she broke into a laugh. "I guess it's better you didn't."

"Yes," Finbar smiled back but still with the hint of bitterness.

Hours wove on, with the greying sky wooly against encircling hills. A sense of desperation at the endlessness of the landscape, and at the powerlessness of his spirit to carry through to its goal, began to harden in Finbar until, like a lump in the stomach, it shortened his wind and watered his bowels.

A day passed, and another. He and Joseph elaborately exchanged no word. In the nights, when Finbar's spirit might perhaps have wandered free, it lay cocooned with him in a rough blanket. He felt abandoned by the earth: he understood no thing of the place he was in, no hill nor drop, no water, no shrub. Nor did he understand his Nazarene companions; even Ide was withdrawn. Then, in the days, when he might have rejoiced in the rapid progress of the party, he stumped lamely along, seeing nothing. That he could hear no whisper of earth's conversation daunted him: at last, at the end of the world, he was castaway from his earth. What he did hear was the echo of his argument, of his anger and his desire to hurt.

The lump in his gut grew heavier, even as his intellect struggled to cast it out. But his intellect had no power over the stone, for his spirit was absent. He had seen the analogous struggle in his forge. Smelting iron with charcoal to create carbon steel, he would strain between too brittle and too soft. And then some . . . what? He had never known what did it, but some . . . something would cause a sudden harmony of earth, fire, air, water; and he would have whelped steel: brilliant steel, and with so dangerous an edge.

On the seventh day, the party topped a ridge and saw before it a wide, white river cutting down the valley ahead, flowing southward to the sea. Turning their eyes northward along the valley, they perceived hills and, in the distance, the high, interior wilds, still snow-capped in the layering air; to Finbar, Olympian. Thirty minutes later, with his feet cooling in the swift melt of the river, and his tongue tingling from its effervescent shock, Finbar looked up, and the sentiment of the heights swept over him. A slight lightening of the weight he carried allowed him his first full breath in days. It was intoxicating.

He looked around. Exhaustion met his eyes. Beside the white river were four monks, shrunken in their hot, brown robes. Joseph was struggling with the stopper of a sheep-belly water skin, but his effort was vague. Cadoc seemed asleep. Ide, a little apart, lay back against an uncomfortable-looking rock with her sandals stripped off, and her calloused feet dangling toward the water. She had not possessed the will to submerge them entirely, and her toes, large and brown, stuck out of the surface, while her heels kicked up a flurry in the current.

"Hey!" Finbar called, and his voice was thick. He cleared his throat and called again. "You! All of you."

One by one, they raised their heads.

"What's wrong with you?" he shouted. He felt a crazy grin on his face.

"What's wrong with *you*?" Joseph muttered at him. "Why so glum?"

"Are you awake?" Ide asked, smiling faintly.

"Awake as ever was. Clean and shining as a new sword."

Ide raised herself onto one elbow. "What an image."

"Not very clean, it seems to me," Joseph grunted.

Finbar looked the man in the eye. "Not clean?"

"No, Finbar, not clean."

"How's this?" Without bending his body, he fell over flat backwards into the river.

The shock of the cold was slow in penetrating the

thickness of his clothes, but the delightful cries of consternation from his companions buoyed him. He sat up, water coursing by his shoulders, and shook his shaggy head and beard.

"Oh, it's good," he said. "Come, try it. It quenches all the fires."

Ide was the first to stand. She gathered her brown habit up above her calves and stepped gingerly down into the stream. At the sight, Joseph turned abruptly away and stared toward the hills.

"Don't be afraid," Finbar taunted Joseph.

"Leave him alone," Cadoc growled, as he, too, stepped into the river.

Joseph was the last to succumb. When all were wriggling their toes in the cool sand, Finbar tried to begin a water fight. This was too abrupt, however, and the mood did not take. The air among them was clearer, though. In addition to the refreshment of the cold water, the evident conclusion of their wandering did much to cheer them. The hills ahead were certainly forested, and the river in which they waded would provide them a means of transporting logs to the sea.

Two days after falling in with the river, the first loose woods were reached. The party had climbed up out of the valley. The river now ran more swiftly down slopes and through grooves in a slanting country. The mountains were close overhead, topped with snow and ice, a wall that gave the impression of beginning a lofty plateau. Birds called, and wind blew with a new, higher vigor; sudden clouds and spates of rain tossed trees in gullies. The ridges, as yet grass-topped, wavered like cloth as the wind sped across them. A few more miles took the climbers into the real forest. The trees crept up on either side, closed across the ridges, and then all the world became columnar and green, with slanting bars of sun gleaming like gold dust. The trees were light hardwood—willow, ash, aspen, birch—with some admixture of softwoods. The heavy hardwoods were not much in evidence. At first, the trees they saw were bent or stunted, but as the travelers made their way deeper into the quiet of the forest, slanting across slopes and fanning through hollows, they found that the trunks grew straighter and taller where they found protection from the wind.

Finbar called a halt, and his troop made its way through the trees into a flat he had found. A stream pooled there before rushing off down the slope to join other tributaries of their river, and it had made a slight shore where the sun would lodge all afternoon. Grassy and warm, the bank invited repose. Finbar directed the pitching of a camp. A fire was kindled and hot food passed round. The remainder of the day was given to rest. Work would commence the following morning.

Not hungry, Finbar climbed upward. He felt compelled by the heights to ascend. He touched the trees. Their skins were smooth, and they shone with a soft radiance that delighted an eye weary of desert scapes. He fingered their leaves and saw the branching of veins within them. He smelled loam and mold. Nothing human was in this forest, and the sounds of his own party had long vanished behind. Occasionally, he saw a bright bird, heard his song. There was also a continual, scarcely heard susurrus of wind high overhead in the slender, upwelling fingers of the beautiful trees. As he went higher, he began to catch an inkling of a new scent, under and behind the organic richness of Thule's high earth. This was a clean and sharp prickle made of ice and raw stone: it meandered down toward him enticingly; even, it occurred to him—in an odd, sensuous inversion—in the manner of some mysterious, feminine enticement. He recalled his Grecian youth, recalled soft laughter and glittering hair disappearing, always disappearing, through pine woods and sun. He smiled as, in his memory, he caught that laughter up, and tucked it into a giggling embrace. He remembered the way she would roll away, and the pursuit, and the capture; the capture that led to a closer pursuit, and that to a closer still, until the entire comedy of surprise and escape was played out in the merest motion of entwined, brown limbs, longing to find, even as they assayed a stratagem to hide away.

Finbar laughed out loud that he should have such a memory in far-off Thule, but he followed the will-o-the-wisp higher and higher until he debouched from the top of the forest onto a bare, stone shield. Before him, fifty yards away, the stone rose from its gentle inclined angle into a cliff. A glimpse upward suggested that it rose at least three hundred feet before its details were lost. There was ice up there, hanging down. Runnels of melt water darkened the face of the volcanic stone, ran down, and slipped steadily and silently underneath Finbar's feet, into the carpet of leaves and thin earth that overlay this edge of the shield, down to feed the roots of the trees, down to fill the streams, down to course through the desert to fill, and never to fill, the sea.

Finbar made a slanting, careful way across the shield, up until he was close under the overhang of the cliff. From there, balancing carefully, he could see out across much of the forest through which he had climbed. The air was quiet, now that the day was old. Bits of ice sometimes rattled down the stone cliff and pattered against the shield by his feet.

The sun was descending through an almost cloudless sky. A sense of timelessness hung there with it, over the western view. His memory still green with Greek recall, the wet rock behind him, and the sun in his face, Finbar savored the air on his tongue. It had the absolute tastelessness of the river water he had bathed in: the same freedom. His lungs strained to take in as much as he could. His spirit came free, and it rose from him, while, somewhere inside, a barrier broke.

He knew the breakage when it happened, the way one knows the end of pain to which one has become accustomed. It was gone; he was free. He knew what he must do. The course, which had been veiled, now was obvious to him. Thankfulness filled him. In relief, he turned and inched along the base of the cliff, seeking a way into the sky.

"Finbar!"

He realized she had been calling his name for perhaps a minute. He turned. "Yes?"

Ide stood on the edge of the forest below him. He could see her face only as a brighter spot against the dark of the trees. Her figure was lost, brown against darker green in the shadow cast by the lowering sun.

"What are you doing?"

"Ide, come with me."

"Where? What do you want?" She started up across the stone of the shield, occasionally slipping on the wetted surface. "Why are you up here?"

She was out of the shadow now, and her face looked up at him, her breath coming quickly from exertion.

He grinned at her. He turned away. "Come on."

"Where are we going?"

"I want to go on."

"There's nothing up there. You can see it."

Without answering her, he pressed forward along the cliff bottom.

Ide watched him go for a few minutes, and then, wearily, she called, "Wait! I'll come, too."

Finbar slowed his scramble a bit until the woman was close behind him, and then he led on. He took them toward a chimney in the rock face gouged out by the fall of a massive boulder through hardening lava. It took some struggle to get around the boulder, partially sunk into the rock at the base of the chimney, but when they were inside, the climbing, for the moment, was easier. They were going straight up now. No top to the chimney could be seen, just the sky open behind their backs and the ragged trench in the side of the mountain.

"Where are we going?" Ide called from below, wiping sweat from her forehead with hands smeared by volcanic dust.

Finbar looked down past his feet to where her pale face showed against the blackness of the rock. "The top," he replied. "You don't have to come."

"How far is it?"

"I don't know."

"It's getting late."

"I want to see the top."

"Can we make it down in the dark?"

"I'm going up." Finbar turned back to his climbing. Again, Ide followed him.

In all, the chimney took them nearly three hundred feet, all the way. Toward the top, the climbing became precarious. They were working up vertically, if not slightly overhung at times, and the walls of the chimney were so narrow that they found purchase only by bracing their backs against one wall and walking upward against the other with their feet and hands. It was terribly difficult, especially for Finbar with his weak leg, and the view below them, straight down through their legs, was dizzying. To add to their discomforts, the surface of the rock was sharp, and they were bloodied when finally the chimney opened up at the top. They found themselves on a long ledge with the slope above them falling back at a more gentle angle, the ice not far above.

Breathless, sore, they flopped away from the chimney and lay gasping on the ledge. It wasn't until some time had passed that they regained possession of themselves and looked out across the miles and miles of Thule spread below them. The day was crouched far down toward evening, but the sun seemed not so low from this height. The horizon was hazed with blue and pale light. Hardly a sound came to them, except the far-away calling of birds from the forest, the tops of which, mottled and green, lay a great distance below. Looking out across the descending tops of the forests, Finbar was able to pick out the upper reaches of the river and to follow it in its course down through the valley they had followed, ambling lower, westward and then southwestward across the countryside. Far to the southwest, he was able to distinguish, he thought, a slight rim of ocean. Westward from the river, the direction of the monastic community, the land was corrugated by the hills they had climbed. He could not see the ocean in that direction.

After they had looked for some minutes, and while their breathing was still returning to normal, Finbar laughed and swept his hand across the view. "I give you Thule. I, Finbar the smith, give you Thule."

"Don't let Joseph hear that."

He grinned, his face streaked with sweat. "I'd better not. He wouldn't take Thule from me."

Ide smiled. Her hair had escaped its confines during the climb, and, sooty, it lay across her cheek. She brushed it aside. "But I will," she said softly. "Thank you, smith."

"It's all I have," he chuckled. Finbar felt himself on the edge of giggling hilarity.

Way below, a hawk soared over the roof of the forest. His scream came to them like the sound that rocks might make, and fire, and steam—thin and eerie at the beginning of the world.

Finbar rose, restless, his leg cramping, and paced along the ledge. Ide was content with the view. He passed her back and forth. Finally, squatting beside her shoulder, he said, "I'm going with them."

"To Paradise?"

He smiled. "Yes!"

There was silence, and then she said, "I think it's the right thing to do."

"Oh, yes."

"If you stay here waiting for a boat, it'll be years. I may have gone as far as I can go, but you haven't."

"All I can do is feel, Ide." He stood again. "I have been walking around underneath this broad, grey sky for months, and the pressure, the dumb yearning has built higher all the time. I stand up here on the edge of Thule, and the sun sets, and I realize that I am changing. Thule is changing me. I don't know how to describe it. It's as though the air is so pure that I gasp. I can't fill myself all the way. I feel my lungs stretching wider and wider, but they can't encompass all the air. I stretch and stretch until I'm about to burst."

Finbar knelt next to the woman. Ide touched him. It was dark. "I'll be a Paradise-man," he chuckled. "There haven't been many of us recently, not since Julian's time."

"What about Brendan?"

"He will be one, too, but another kind. He's tied to the Empire, in the end. Your religion needs the Empire, for it's only by its base in the Empire that you have the freedom to roam. I, on the other hand, have been a roamer all my life. But if I can be in Paradise—whatever it is—I will stop."

Finbar touched her shoulder.

"I must go. You see it, don't you? You followed me through the winter nights. The monks did. They all did.

They know that I am not like them, but they cannot best me, for my magic may bring theirs down: out there, in Paradise."

A star shimmered into view in the dark blue loom of the western sky. A chilly wind puffed at them from the ice above. Finbar touched Ide's hair. It was damp, and he realized she was weeping. He put his arm around her shoulders and drew her head to his neck. "I love you," he whispered. It surprised him to know it.

Her mumble was smothered by his cloak. He pulled back from her, looked down at her starlit face. "I love you," she said.

"Poor, gimp-legged smith that I am."

Ide wiped her eyes with the back of her hand. "You are easy to love."

"Easy as Brendan?"

"Ha!" she barked sourly. "Are you jealous?"

"No. He's a strong man. He is our captain."

A shudder passed through Ide's body. "Hold me," she whispered.

"Yes. It's cold."

"We can't get down, Finbar."

"Perhaps there is somewhere we can be out of the wind."

Searching the back of the ledge, they discovered a crack in the rock, which, after they had tried several positions, gave them a minimum of protection. Ide lay curled into Finbar's lap with her head against his chest, and his arms around her bony shoulders.

"We must switch when you get tired," she insisted. A few minutes later, she whispered, "I can hear your heart."

He said nothing, listening as he was to the language of the land. It was a fey time: he heard syllables of conversation, now and then a sentence, as the roots of the mountain sang to the desert, and the raw rock muttered threats to the stream.

"You're so far away," he heard, and it was a woman's voice, also far away. "Come back, Finbar. Come back. This is all we will have."

He thought it must be the Greek woman. It was: he saw her once again in poses that drew song from the earth. The poor lamp of olive oil sputtered and fumed as, naked, she danced. The air was filled with sweat and the musk of her armpits and buttocks. Her hair was loose. It hurt him, cut his flushed cheek as she swayed close. He knelt on the pallet. He could feel the pulse in his wrists, his groin. He was livid, like Zeus, and she was a Pasiphae cow, all udders and sweet breath. She knelt before him, elbows and knees, and squirmed herself back against him, opening and moist, wider, wider . . . her hair swayed across her back, her voice lowed . . . and they joined in a copulation that stirred the roots of the earth and brought forth the fall of Minos—a bull-man mighty under the palace floor.

"Finbar?"

The voice was nearer than the Greek's might be.

"What is it, Finbar? Am I too heavy?"

His head whirled in the tightening vortex of his memory—the scent, the taste in the air, the gripping, gluesome lust in the woman—until it snapped and spun him out abashed upon the cold, night slopes of the Thulean mountainside with a nun in his arms.

He coughed. He realized that he had become intensely aroused. And, even as he realized it, she felt it as well.

"Finbar, please. There's nothing I can do."

He shifted away from her uncomfortably. "Nothing to do," he grunted. "What do you mean?"

She pushed herself to her feet, and the cold air rushed at him, partly orienting him. "Don't do this to me," she whispered, "please!"

"Do what?"

"You use me, Finbar. Please!" She stepped back another pace. She was outside the crack now, and he knew her only by her silhouette against the stars.

He cleared his throat. "Ide?" he called. "Come back. It's cold."

"Don't, Finbar, damn you!"

"Ide!"

She turned and disappeared. "Damn you, damn you!"

The curse shocked him. He pulled himself to his feet

and went after her. The narrowness of the ledge in the dark, and the enormous well of air to his side, was dizzying.

He found her standing against the rock at the very extremity of the ledge: found her by her set breathing and then felt the grim tightness of arms across her chest.

"What's the matter?"

She rounded on him furiously. "Don't play the innocent. You know how I feel!"

"I'm sorry. I was dreaming."

"I don't mean that. I'm old enough to have felt *that* before. You use us for your own ends, Finbar. I hate that about you."

"How have I used you?"

"Ours is a holy cruise. You have used it for mundane ends."

"But I've changed. I'm going on."

"I know, but again your purpose is your own."

"What else could it be? What is Brendan's?"

"Brendan sails for the Glory of God."

"And himself."

"Not vainglory."

"Agreed. But for curiosity, and that is purely human in your theology."

"Don't debase him!" Her words slapped his face.

Finbar was ashamed. "Forgive me."

"I am not a priest, and you are not baptised."

"I mean, forgive me humanly."

"I love you, Finbar. There's forgiveness."

His hand found hers. "I'm sorry." He drew her closer. "That's the second time I've apologized to you. I must love."

In silence, the two crouched against the wind for a few moments, and then Ide said, "Look at it from our point of view, Finbar. A man leaves us—Sebastian—and another joins. You were not put on that island simply to give us another pair of arms for the sailing of our ship: in the end it is God who sails the ship anyway, so we needed no more arms. There is some other reason that you have been given to us. We have come to depend on that reason, whatever it is, for it is only since you have come among us that we have reached Thule and the end of the world. Now you say that you are going on with the journey. This is as God would want it, surely. But you speak as though it were only for your own sake that you go. You see how you use us? We have come to depend upon you, and you do not see that. God's purpose has come to reside in you."

"Oh, dear Ide, don't put that on me. I can bear the human weight; not the divine."

"You have no choice. None of us has a choice. We are part of God's action in the world, and we cannot draw back from the task. It is as though you were given a basket of food, and you did not serve it out. No matter how fresh the food was when you received it, if you do not use it, it will rot. The same is true of our souls: unless we turn the urgings of God inside us into action, the urgings will stay there and fester, and then they will turn bad."

Finbar nodded. "I have felt the festering."

Ide squeezed his arm. "Now is the time to feed the multitudes with that gift of food, for God."

"And to carry man to Paradise."

"Yes! It stirs me so." She hugged him tighter. "Think of it. Think what God allows us in the Glory of His Work."

Shivering, Finbar asked, "Ide, what is Paradise?"

"The place where God rules completely, and where the struggle with evil is won."

"It's not so clear to me. I only know that in Paradise what is hidden will no longer be so."

"A philosopher's paradise," she commented drily.

Finbar smiled. "I was schooled in Egypt and Greece. What else?"

"You make me laugh."

They returned to the crack, and they were warm, there together. Finbar's imagination began to caress this woman. He saw his hand touch her virginal belly. "Ide," he asked impulsively, "why don't you come, too?"

"I can't."

"Because of the convent?"

"Not just that. There are different orders of inspiration, Finbar. Mine carried me this far."

"And no farther?"

"I have always said so."

"But it could be different, Ide."

"You haven't been listening to me at all. God has a use for me. I am God's creature. Just as he has a use for you."

There was a long silence. Finbar felt the woman's body tense, and he whispered, "What's the matter? Tell me."

"Don't you think that I want to be otherwise, too?" she murmured. "Do you think it's easy being an abbess in these times? These are times of death. My two older sisters died in childbed, another one searching for her husband near Sceilg Mhichil. I'm the last one, the youngest. I am an *oblate*. I had no choice. Do you think I want to live here in Thule—as though wanting had anything to do with it? Don't you think I want to go to Paradise, with you? I, too, would like to adventure with God, or to have a child at my breast. But husbands die, in war, or they drown. Children die. Women die with their children still half inside their bodies. At Ailech, I have reached inside the vagina of a woman and pulled her baby from her body even as she died. You ought to feel that, Finbar, the contractions slowing, the womb tightening on this little life, until you rip it free, and the mother dies. That is the time when you are glad to be an *oblate*, glad that you serve God in the only thing—the *only* thing, Finbar—that lasts. I have no husband. I have never known a man inside me, and I never shall. I long for that sometimes, for the ignorance that was my sisters', because—for all their knowledge of the flesh—they *were* ignorant. I watched them when they were still alive, envied their unknowing, but I do not envy their deaths. To have a man is to die."

She broke off. "Why am I talking about men?" Impulsively, she stood up, and he followed her out to the ledge. "Look here, Finbar. To have God is to live. I serve God in Thule because He would have me here, and for no other reason. That is reason enough, for service to that which is eternal is eternal life, and because there is no other thing that a woman may do who has been cursed—yes, cursed—with a brain. I am as adept as any abbot. At Ailech, it takes the work of thirty-two laymen to support

the contemplation of one of our sisters, and if you take the
monastery into account, the number rises to sixty-eight.
I'm good at that, Finbar. I can run that place so that it
works perfectly, so that the cellarer, and the gardener,
and the gooseherd, and the choirmaster, and the cham-
berlain, and everyone else acts smoothly and efficiently
for the support of the *opus dei* and the *lectio divina*. I
intend to do that here. This convent will be a model of the
working of God in the world that will attest to the fact that
here, at least here on the very edge of the world, as far
away as we can get from the death of our not-so-holy
Mother Rome, there is a community of unity, simplicity
and piety that is a pleasure for God to observe."

Ide's voice had grown fervent as she spoke. She concluded with her arms spread wide, embracing the dim
hills of slumbering Thule. *"This* is my Church; *these* are
the gates through which all men may pass to worship, and
which all men leave rejoicing."

The first bare hint of a false dawn limned her figure
in its archaic posture. Her robe stirred in the chilly wind.
Her hair blew across the fading stars. Her clear, alto tones
seemed to echo outward and outward until they bathed
the forest far below, whose top could not be seen but
whose night exhalation they felt around them in the wild
air.

Slowly, Ide's arms dropped to her sides. She turned
to face the smith, her posture challenging.

He reached for her arms. Close to her face, he
breathed, "You are magnificent!"

A chill passed through her, and her frame relaxed.

"You are a woman! This is a woman. This is a lion!"

Ide began to laugh.

They both laughed and swung their hands like children. Finbar growled at her and gathered her body to his.
There was a hesitation before they kissed, a change from
intoxication to deliberateness. The kiss was long and hard.
Her fingers were in his hair; his flowed down her sinewy
back to pull her waist against him.

They broke apart.

"My dear one," she murmured.

"In another life."

"We have but one life on earth, and then the Life Eternal."

"Perhaps then, then: in Paradise."

She smiled, somewhat sadly. She touched his mouth, almost with curiosity. "You *will* find what you want in Paradise; there will be another sort of lion there."

"Don't speak in metaphors. You are the lion."

"No, Finbar. No, I am a nun."

Their embrace opened, and they stood, arms around one another's waists, looking out over the leagues of Thule. Sufficient light was in the sky by this time for the forest below to be seen, and for the stars almost to be gone. Only the brightest of them could still challenge the coming day.

He smiled at her. "How came we here, Ide? I, from Africa; you, from Ireland. How is it that our lives have led us here?"

"Lucky, and God."

"This is lucky?"

"It is certainly God."

He smiled at her. "I love you."

Her fingers once again traced the lines of his face, as though to memorize it. "You are beautiful," she said.

"No, I'm not."

"You are. That is the luck. You are beautiful to me."

"And you."

From below them they began to hear the sounds of the forest birds waking and singing to the new day. The sound rose and lapped at their feet like a tide, changing the shape of the world.

"We had better go down," Finbar suggested, after a time.

Ide looked at him. "We are warned away from mountaintops."

"What do you mean?"

"In the Bible. Mountaintops are dangerous places. They are the abodes of powers, demons, angels. It is where you go to meet God. Sometimes He comes to you in a desert tent, but more often you meet him up here. Strange things happen on the heights."

Finbar's face lit with a slow smile. "Then I wish we had climbed higher last night."

Ide's laugh, like the rest of her manner, was uninhibited and free. Finbar kissed her again.

The descent down the lava chimney was worse than the ascent, but eventually they reached the flatter land. In a moment or two, they were inside the forest. Suddenly, it was as though they were cut off from the freedom of the heights, and they walked side by side stiffly, not speaking of what had transpired.

"Here we are!" they shouted when they heard their names being called from below, and it seemed to Finbar that Ide flung herself relievedly into conversation with the monks who clambered up through the trees to meet them.

Finbar emerged last at the campsite beside the little pond. Joseph was there to meet him. Ide and the other monks had skirted the water already, and the woman was quenching her thirst from a leather bowl.

"Pagan!" Joseph hissed. "Pagan devil!"

The attack pricked Finbar deeper than otherwise it would have because of the delicious openness of his senses only minutes before. "Joseph, not now," he said curtly. "We've talked it all out before."

"Leave her alone; she's a nun!" Joseph's voice rose in a squeak. The rest of the party turned.

Finbar sighed. "You do her an injustice, Joseph, as well as me."

"I've seen your looks at her."

"We were benighted on a mountain. We slept in a crack in the rock. It was cold. I don't know why I am telling you this. I am thirsty, man. Leave it alone. There's nothing there for you to worry at."

"She's a Christian sister, my sister in Christ. I am responsible for her. I know what men are."

"You may know what you are—"

"Oh! Pagan injustice! Devil-worshipper that you are, you—"

Finbar shoved the man to one side. "Forget this, Joseph. For the sake of your God. I'm tired, I'm thirsty, and there is nothing for you to fear in me." He spun around and stared at the monk. "I am not your enemy! I don't *care* enough to be your enemy." He turned his back on Joseph and stepped toward the group on the other side of the pond.

With a scream, Joseph landed on Finbar's back, knocking him to the ground. The smith roared and heaved. Joseph flipped off and landed on his own back, winded. Finbar pulled himself upright. His face was contorted with anger and he shouted, "Leave me alone! What have I done to you? Leave me alone!"

Joseph pulled himself to his knees. He rose to his feet. A scarlet fever seemed to burn in his unhealthy cheeks. He did not seem to fear Finbar's clenched and meaty fists, rather the reverse. He stared at the black man and panted, "Pagan."

"Leave it."

"Pagan devil."

Finbar raised a fist.

"Hit me. Show yourself, pagan. Hit me."

Finbar unclenched his hands. He tried to stand straighter. "I don't want to hit you, man. I'm not a fighter, but you drive me to it."

"I have nothing to fear from you."

Finbar tried to smile. "And I am not guilty of anything."

"You are no Christian. You deny God."

Finbar was in control again. "Don't you see? I don't deny your god, neither do I acknowledge him. I am indifferent. *You* see only one god. *I* see many gods, so many, in fact, that it's little different from seeing one."

Joseph's limbs trembled. "Then what were you doing all night with Sister Ide?" he flared.

"I told you. There was nothing. We slept on the mountain."

Ide appeared at Joseph's elbow. "How can I reassure you, my brother?"

Joseph took a breath to calm himself. "This man is a pagan. He's glib, witty—but he is a pagan. It is not right for a Sister of Christ to spend the night on the side of a mountain with a pagan." He turned to Finbar. "You accuse me of doing Ide an injustice. Not so. You do me an injustice to think that I have such a narrow, such a specific fear. I have no fears for Ide's virtue. It's for her soul that I fear."

"I'm hardly going to steal her soul."

"It's happened before."

Ide and Finbar exchanged a look.

"I thought Christianity was supposed to make you strong, Joseph. As far as I can tell, all it has done is make you more fearful than you would have been otherwise. I think your religion has hurt you. You would do better to act the part of a pagan for a while. Think free for a minute! The battle you see going on between good and evil may indeed be raging, but your soldiers are not the only combatants. I, too, am a soldier. Don't refuse my assistance, for the enemy is strong, and help other than mine may never come."

"We need no help."

"I think you do, Joseph. Your religion is a young religion. It hardly knows what to do with the world. Your theologians fulminate against one another, anathematize each other. They issue excommunications and rescind them with such bewildering rapidity that anyone outside the Church can see in an instant that they haven't the beginning of an idea what is needed. My gods are two thousand years old, at least. Yours is only a few hundred years old. Which god do you think knows the enemy better? Which has had the time, the experience, the history of battle? Would you cast my gods aside when they are willing to stand up beside yours and fight? I am offering you my help. Don't be foolish. Take it."

Joseph sneered. "A pretty speech. Oh, a pretty speech. That is the sort of pretty, twisting speech that wins the hearts of the sophisticates of the Mediterranean, your friends. Against a real Christian, it says nothing. 'There is no entrance into Heaven but by me.' That is what Christ said. Was He wrong? How could He be wrong? Your gods may be old, but they are dying. They are vanishing into the earth out of which they came. Since there's no hope for you, you try to dilute the purity of my religion by calling for a stand together against a common enemy. That is false logic. You are the enemy that Christ came to slay."

The two men stood angrily on the edge of the pool, their faces bright again with the renewed flame of their argument. Then, unable to sustain the force of it, Finbar made himself relax.

"Joseph," he said, "there's no answer to this. There's nothing to be done. We can't determine the truth. What is truth anyway?"

"Truth is Christ."

"Truth is what you think it is."

"No, Finbar, truth is truth. Don't . . . wiggle."

"I'm not wiggling."

"You are. Your argument is a wiggle. You're always trying to out-argue me, as though this were some game we play for points. I haven't any interest in games. I speak the truth. Everything you say, all the wiggles, all the intellectual tricks, that's just a refusal of the truth. It's not an alternative truth. It's like what we said the other day about Paradise. There can't be two Paradises, two types. There can't be two truths. Truth is truth."

Again, Finbar retreated. He said, smiling, "Well another truth is that, unless we get to work, we'll never have the trees cut."

Joseph was somewhat taken aback, but he rallied. "I'll cut. I'll cut with pleasure because every stroke of the axe brings me closer to the time when we leave this island with you on it."

"Hardly friendly."

"Finbar, I do not feel called upon to be polite. I tell the truth, and all the courtesy in the world will not smother the truth. You may entertain the very devil to dinner, chuckle him up with niceties, but I'll not go. I tell the truth."

With that, the man turned and stalked to where the equipment lay. He seized an axe. "As Christ laid His axe to the root of the tree, so I lay my axe to the root of your sophistication. May you be saved, Finbar, from your cynicism, and may it happen in time for you."

Finbar's frustration suddenly broke. "Damn you, Jo-

seph!" he bellowed, and, grabbing the haft of the axe, he
struggled to wrench it from Joseph's hands. His weight
and strength ought to have given him an easy victory, but
Joseph was animated with a sudden, hysterical rage that
baffled the smith.

"I'll kill you!" Joseph screamed, but the emotion
weakened him, and he shook.

Finbar wrenched the axe away. "You'll do nothing of
the sort, Joseph. You'll calm down, or I'll lay you out with
this fist."

In an agony of frustration, Joseph shivered and trembled, and finally burst into tears. "Oh, why have you
come?" he wailed, making no effort to stem the flow of
water, and then he bellowed, "Brendan loves me!"

There was a long silence as the echoes of this cry
shrank through the forest. Perhaps Finbar had never
been so startled by a sudden revelation. He saw everything, in a flash. He set the axe down carefully. "Joseph,"
he said coaxingly, "please. What have I done?"

"You've taken Brendan from me."

"How? I haven't."

"Shameless."

"What about Brendan?"

Joseph sobbed, "He loved me."

"He does now, I'm sure."

"No! Not since you came. He used to teach me. Now,
he teaches you. I've heard him. He used to talk with me.
He never talks to me now. He doesn't want me. I know
he doesn't want me."

"Of course, he wants you. You're going with him in
the curragh, aren't you?"

"Yes!" The boy looked up, his tears suddenly dry. "I'll
get him back. When you're not there, I'll get him back!"

"Joseph, look, I'm not taking him from you. He and
I talk, that's all. You can talk with us, too."

"Never. When we leave, I'll get him back. You can
have this woman to talk to."

In a quiet voice, Finbar said, "I'm coming with you."

There was complete stillness in the monk's posture
for a second, and then he broke down entirely, dropping
to his knees on the shore before Finbar. In a strangled

voice, he moaned, "Don't. Oh, please, as you love me, God, don't. I can't stand it."

A jay broke the silence that followed this. Finbar looked around at the others. Everyone stood in an awkward posture. No one said anything. In command, Finbar waved them away. Gradually, one by one, they left. Ide was the last. She looked at Finbar, made a motion toward Joseph, received Finbar's shake of the head, and retreated.

Finbar knelt slowly before the monk. Joseph's face was in his hands, his body bent and shaking as though in torment.

"Joseph," Finbar soothed. "Joseph, it's all right."

The monk muttered on, prayers and tears, shaking the while.

"Joseph." Finbar laid his hand gently on the man's shoulder.

"Don't touch me, devil!" Joseph rocked back out of Finbar's reach, staring at the smith, his face a mess of mucus and dirt. The two remained there, face to face, for a long moment. There was no sound.

Finally, carefully, Finbar eased his own posture. "Joseph, I'm sorry."

The monk eyed him, as desperate as a wounded animal before the hunter.

"Joseph, you must believe me. I have no intention of interfering with your friendship with Brendan. I like Brendan, but I am very unlike him. You must see that. Our goals are different, our understanding of the world is different. Believe me. Perhaps he and I could be friends, but he could never love me the way he can love you as one who shares so much with him. Understand me, friend. I have no desire to hurt you. None at all."

Through this speech, the tension in Joseph seemed to relax somewhat. He wiped his nose with the back of his hand. "I . . ." he began and then choked it back.

"Yes?"

His eyes appealed to Finbar. "I have followed Brendan since I was seventeen."

"Yes."

"I have no one else."

"I'm sorry. I understand."

"He is my family. Christ is my Brother. God is my Father."

"Joseph, I never knew my parents either."

"Oh. No?"

"No."

"What did you do?"

"Much as you have done, although I followed a smith. Ansonius was his name, in Hippo Regius."

"In the desert?"

"There, and Egypt, too. You should see Egypt someday, Joseph."

The man shifted his weight so that he sat on the earth, his legs crossed. He wiped his face with his sleeve and combed his hair back from his brow with his fingers. "I'm sorry," he murmured.

"I'm sorry, too. I had no idea you felt that way. You have to believe that I—"

"I know. I don't really believe it. I'm so confused." For a moment, he looked as though he would cry again, but he took a breath and blurted, "I wish I knew how to talk!"

"What?"

"Oh, you know. Like you. You can talk so well, so interestingly. They all listen to you. They never listen to me."

"Oh, Joseph."

"Well, I do wish it!" Joseph looked at the smith for a moment, expressions chasing one another across his face. Then he blurted, "Will you teach me?"

8

EVERY PERSON IN THULE was there. The shore was lined with monks and nuns, all wearing their freshest robes, all carrying sprays of flowers. Hymns were sung, and a long and splendid Mass was celebrated. There was incense on the warm June air. Bluebirds and swallows cavorted above. The grass running back from the shore was lush, and the first roses were just in bloom. Bees droned. Vivid cloths had been laid across the greensward, making patches of pink and yellow for the celebrants to walk upon. Finbar stood aside. It seemed to him in his new perspective an aesthetic draping of the body of the goddess, albeit in Nazarene clothing. That she was present, he had no doubt. Her more ancient hierophancies were attested—innocently he was certain—by sprays of flowers bunched upon the earth and by the feather-woven cloaks of the pale, gay nuns. Finbar had come, at least, to first acceptance of his companions' hope. And that their hope was built of Nazarene liturgics in no way denied that the earth herself was their foundation. In the beauty of the spring, Finbar caressed the earth with his eyes, undressed her of her Nazarene robe, and knew her to be his true mistress at the juncture of whose open thighs lay power.

After Mass there was a banquet. This anchoritic community put aside for the day its severity, and there were tables laden with the harvest of the sea and the seacoast: eggs in profusion, smoked eel, puffin in aspic, salads of the tenderest of garden shoots spiced with goose-tongue, the roe of shad and of sea urchins, shark buried in sand ten days and then smoked over green hay, fried loache with roses and pine nuts, mock entrails made with lentils and served with sorrel sauce, salmon and currant dumplings, and the first of the strawberries wrapped in funnel cakes and presented with duck-egg custard and meringues. To drink, there was Ypocras, a spiced, chilled wine of remarkable potency. There were much chaff and banter through the warm morning, and, as the Ypocras began to tell, there were singing and wild piping and foot races by the shore.

Finbar and Ide walked aside during the afternoon, their stomachs full and their minds a-buzz. They climbed a small rise above the point and looked down at the festival along the beach. Anchored one hundred feet from shore was the curragh, trim, neat, taut and brown. There were strings of ribbons in her rigging, and a stole of daisies hung over her prow. There was a race, four swimmers out to the boat and back, and their slim, white bodies churned splashily through the sea.

"Did they send you off this way when you left Ireland?" Finbar asked.

Ide laughed. "Not at all. It was raining—"

"It's always raining."

"—and they paid hardly any attention to us at all."

The two friends sat down on a rock. Finbar plucked a stalk of timothy and chewed it. Meditatively, he said, "If there were a ship here bound for Greece, I wouldn't go."

Ide smiled.

Finbar threw away his grass stem. "I regret that you won't be aboard, that's all."

"I was bound for Thule, and for Thule alone. This is close enough to the edge for me."

Finbar laughed. "However did I become a mariner, I wonder?"

"You like the food."

He laughed again.

From the end of the point came herring gulls on the wind, bringing their wheeling cry, and under the cry was the groundswell moaning restless against the shore.

"Soon now," Finbar said. The curragh's anchor had been hove short, and Atla was directing several monks in extending the oars.

Suddenly, there were tears in Ide's eyes. "I'll miss you," she said.

"You've got all of Thule."

"Don't be gruff, Finbar, not now. I shall miss you."
Her hand gripped his on the warm rock. She looked away.

"I shall miss you, too."

"Be with the Goddess," she said, turning back to him.
"Ide!"

Her lips twitched toward a smile. "It's who you are,
dear Finbar. Why shouldn't I?"

He grinned at her. "No reason at all. Thank you."

"Being here for the rest of my time may teach me
tolerance," she whispered. "If it does, it will have been
well-spent time."

"Come with us!" he blurted. "You don't want to be
here."

"What has wanting to do with the question? Wanting
is for Brendan, not for me. Besides . . ."

"Yes?"

"If you do come there, finally, come to Paradise, what
will you do then? I don't want to be part of that. I don't
want to choose and plan in Paradise."

Finbar retreated into his own privacy and murmured, "Perhaps Paradise is death."

"Perhaps it is, but I don't think so. Brendan will get
there in this life, if anyone can."

"And then what will we do?"

"That's my question."

"I hadn't thought about it. Paradise ought to answer
the question for us."

"And if it doesn't?" She smiled. "You see why I stay
here."

"You are a wise woman."

"Not necessarily. Perhaps just cowardly. You think
you fit no place now, Finbar. Wait until you have actually
stood in Paradise, actually discoursed with angels and with
God Himself. No, Finbar. I need my sisters too much. I
won't throw them away—and their society—even for the
face of God, and that is not an easy thing for me to say."

Finbar scratched his beard. The curragh nosed
ashore, and the monks shipped their oars and piled out
into the shallow, lolloping sea. Atla searched around and,
when he located Finbar and Ide on the hillside, waved his
long, red arms. Finbar heard the man's high cry of impatience.

"Time to go," he said, not moving.

Ide stood up. "Take care of Joseph," she said. "He needs you."

Finbar looked at her and stood as well. "He needs someone to hate."

"No. He needs someone to be stronger than he is. His faith is weak; not insufficient, just not strong."

"Well, it's not my faith, in any case."

"That does not matter," she said, taking his arm for the descent. "Use the tolerance your pagan religion gave you: try not to be offended by the imperiousness of ours."

They debouched onto the beach.

Ide caught his arm. "I never heard you laugh enough, Finbar. In Paradise, you must laugh."

"Hurry," Atla called, "the wind's fair."

There was a general bustle and scramble around the curragh as final stores and possessions were slung aboard, as the monks and nuns passed forward to touch one final time the ship that would sail to Paradise, and as the crew made farewells and pulled themselves over the gunwales. In the midst of it all, Finbar caught Joseph's eye on him as he embraced the abbess with a rough and awkward caress. Her statement had disturbed him. "I will," he whispered. "I'll try."

"Go," she whispered. "Tell them about me in Paradise."

She turned away and brushed her way out of the crowd.

"Heave along there, Finbar!" Atla shouted.

"Hurry up, smith!" yelled Joseph gleefully.

Aboard, shoving off from the pebbly littoral with his oar blade, Finbar searched for the woman until he found her standing by a tabernacle at the top of the beach. She saw him looking and tossed her head at him, her arms crossed firmly over her breasts. His last memory of her was the firm line of her mouth.

Brendan set their course south and southwest, according to the winds, and for seven weeks the cruising was gay. Sails taut, wake creaming, they skimmed the blue, sparkling sea. Fulmars darted in the draft of their sails. Dolphins wove tight torpedoes at their bow. Whales pondered and basked on the slow, sunny heave of the bosom of the deep. Sunset after sunset drew them ever westward and southward, down the perfect glimmer of the perfect, round, red sun. On occasion, the wind veered west and blew harder with rain. Then, they reduced sail, and stayed below, and piped or spun yarn until the west wind chased itself away. Soon the grey left the sea, the sun returned, and the joy of paradisal voyaging tickled them once again.

After seven weeks, a change came in the wind. For two days it blew fickle, and then, with one final, damp exhalation from the south, it stopped altogether. The curragh was left bobbling in a confused sea underneath a high, pale sky. She rolled and pitched uncomfortably. She jawed and jigged until Brendan in exasperation ordered the oars run out and some way put on her. Moving, she made a somewhat steadier platform. It was high summer at the hub of the Western Sea, and the heat was a surprise to everyone and a serious problem for Barinthus. The old man stayed in the hammock Brendan rigged for him underneath the foredeck through all the hottest hours of the day, while the rest of the crew dragged at oars that grew heavier with each watch. They spent a few days hunting wind, found a slant now and then, but always ran out of the patch of air back onto the shiny surface under the sun. Soon enough, even the confusion of the sea died away, so that by the fourth day of calm they were in the remarkable position of sitting absolutely still in the absolute center of a sphere made up underneath them of flat, bottomless ocean and above them of curved, infinite sky. Save the sun alone, no object of any sort relieved the monotony of the blue expanse. They were as still and as matter-of-fact as a rock in a mud flat. There were no birds any longer, no fish, no dolphins. It was as though existence itself had come to an end, only not for them.

That evening, the last of the pickled onions were served in an effort to cheer themselves up.

Brendan spoke, looking toward the west and picking his teeth with a fishbone. "We have come to the edge of the world. We have passed all the tests."

"Why have we stopped here, then?" asked Atla.

"We are waiting for a sign."

Barinthus looked up from gumming his barley bread. "We shall see it soon, the road. The road to Paradise shall appear before us, and we shall be followers of its path, even as the Israelites were followers from the darkness of their slavery into the light of God's holy land."

The sun went down into the sea. No ripple stirred the waters. The crew sat into the farthest watches that night, each with his own thoughts. When dawn began to spread into the sky, Brendan cleared his throat and spoke again.

"Today we see the sign."

"I hope you're right," Atla said. "I could die here becalmed."

Finbar looked at the captain curiously. "How can you be sure?"

"I know it."

"How?"

Brendan paid Finbar no more attention.

Joseph turned to Finbar, and he said, "He's right. It will happen today. I've seen this sort of thing before." He sighed ecstatically. "Tomorrow we shall be in Paradise."

Finbar was uncomfortable. "How can you be so certain?"

"It will happen," Joseph replied, his eyes shining.

"How do you know?"

"He says it," Joseph answered, motioning toward Brendan.

"But how can he know?"

Brendan turned to Finbar. "You are a smith. When your fire is right, you know it. When the steel is right, you know it. When the blow with the hammer is right, you know it. I am a man of God. When I say that the sign will come to us today, I know it."

With the sun two fingers above the horizon, the rowing began. Brendan and Joseph were at the oars. Everyone was naked. Hours passed. Finbar was steering; it was the hottest part of the day. A canopy had been rigged for the steersman against the sun, and the smith's only activity came when he adjusted its direction over his head.

About mid-afternoon, Finbar happened to glance

into the sea over the side, and his heart lurched. He wrenched at the steering oar and opened his mouth to shout: unknowingly he had steered the curragh onto a reef. Looking once more, though, he discovered that what he had taken to be the glimmer of sunlight on an unexpected reef was in fact the pebbled effect of the sun reflecting off the backs of a myriad of white jellyfish. He called to Brendan and Joseph to look. It was a phenomenon. There were millions of the things, as big across as a man's splayed hand, each with the pattern of a white shamrock on its back. Looking, Brendan and Joseph burst into excited chatter, and began gesticulating at the horizon and into the sea with a sudden vigor that astonished Finbar's sun-dazed mind. "What? What is it?" he called to them.

"The trefoil," Brendan crowed. "We've done it!"

"Done what? What do you mean?"

"The trefoil, the clover. Don't you see? On their backs. It's the clover, the sign of the Trinity. It's a message from Paradise. These fish have come to us from Paradise. White shamrocks! It's the road!"

"It was with the shamrock that our holy brother, Saint Patrick, explained the Trinity to the children of Ireland," Joseph elucidated.

"You mean the shape on their backs?" Finbar's mind was still slow.

"Yes! It's the sign Barinthus has been waiting for."

"They're jellyfish."

"It's a sign," Brendan said definitely.

"I'll get Barinthus," Joseph offered.

Before Joseph got to the bow, Atla stuck his head out into the sunlight. "What's going on? Can't a man sleep?"

"White shamrocks, Atla," Brendan called. "Look over the side."

Atla did so and turned back. "Are you crazy? It's jellyfish."

"With shamrocks on their backs. Look!"

Atla looked again. "Well, perhaps."

"Perhaps nothing. It's what we've been waiting for."

Atla grinned suddenly. "Well, Brendan, I just hope it brings a wind."

"It'll bring more than that."

"That would be paradisal enough for me right now."

"Don't blaspheme."

"I'm going back to sleep. Call me when we sight the Blessed Shores."

As Atla turned around, Joseph was helping the doddering Barinthus out of the cramped hole and to his feet on deck. The old man was not entirely certain what the sudden disturbance was about. He kept looking around in a frightened way and saying, "What? What? A shadow to see? What shadow? I can't see. What shadow do you mean?"

"No," Joseph corrected him eagerly. "A shamrock in the sea! I told you. Look in the sea."

"They have jellyfish for you, old man," Atla rasped. "They want you to look at jellyfish."

"Oh, jellyfish. Very nice."

"Not jellyfish, Uncle," Brendan called. "The sign."

Barinthus seemed to stiffen for a second. He brushed Joseph's assisting hand from his arm and stepped forward, suddenly alert. "The sign, you say, Brendan? Where is this sign?"

"Look there."

Barinthus bent over the rail. He stared for a long time. When he raised his head, his face was eager. "Follow them," he said.

"Follow a jellyfish," Atla groaned. "They're even slower than we are."

"No, no." Barinthus was impatient. "Follow them like a road. They're a road for us to sail."

"A road to row," the other answered, and he caught Finbar's eye with a grimace.

"Row. Sail. What does it matter? Let's go!"

"It matters to me. I have a boil on my butt."

"Atla," Brendan said, "you're going to row."

"I was afraid of that."

"You, too, Finbar."

Finbar stepped away from the steering oar toward the thwarts. Barinthus took up his position in the stern, ready to con the vessel along the shamrock road. Atla still hesitated.

"Do I have to do it myself?" Barinthus asked him.

"No," Atla replied, tiredly. "No." He stepped toward his place. "I don't see why we can't wait for a wind."

Barinthus gave a loud, sudden laugh. "This is the wind!"

Atla sat and ran out his oar. The curragh gathered way.

"What do you mean, this is the wind?" Atla asked, grunting between strokes.

"God's message. His word. His word is the wind. The shamrocks are His word and His wind."

"Much damned good they do us," Atla muttered.

"Oh, shut up," Finbar grunted. "Don't complain so."

"You'd complain if you were sitting on a boil."

Finbar swore. "You joined this cruise. It was your choice! Now what did you expect?"

"I didn't expect to row after jellyfish."

"It's the sign."

"Do you believe that? Well, I'll row. The little floppers will be gone in a few minutes anyway."

In this prediction, though, Atla was wrong. Acres of the sea were filled with the jellyfish. No one aboard had ever seen anything like it before.

The sailors were still following the jellyfish when the sun sank down into the sea. They had found the edge of the school, and they were following along that edge, more or less southwestward. A red sun lit them at the last, and they slowed, to eat and rest, despite Barinthus's protestations.

"We'll follow them in the morning," Brendan gasped as he stood away from his oar.

"They may not be here in the morning," Barinthus objected.

"If they're a sign, they will be."

"Signs only appear to those ready to receive them. If we stop, what does that say about our readiness to receive this sign?"

"I'm sorry, Uncle. What can I do? I can't pull another stroke."

"I'll row."

"You'll not. You'll kill yourself."

"I will."

"You're not fit."

"This is not a struggle to be measured in sinew."

"Perhaps not, but I am captain, and I say we stop. You can't go alone the rest of the way. You need us."

Barinthus turned away and looked longingly toward the setting sun. "That need, my nephew, is man's curse."

The old man moved toward the bow, and, after arranging himself comfortably on the foredeck, he waited through the night, having nothing more to do with what went on aboard.

In the morning, the jellyfish were still there. The curragh had drifted a short distance away from the edge of the school, but a few strokes put the voyagers back on their course.

"How long is this road?" Atla wanted to know.

Brendan answered: "The God of Israel will Himself give valor and strength to His people. Blessed be God."

The tall hunter struggled out of his jerkin. The sun already reverberated off the still sea with enough force to hurt the eyes. Atla shook his head and muttered, "God is wonderful in His saints."

Brendan stared at him. "By which you mean . . ."

"By which I mean, I don't understand you."

"I am not a saint."

Atla dipped a strip of cloth into the sea and then wrapped it around his head as a turban, the end falling down to protect the back of his neck. "You may well be, Brendan."

"I am a sailor, that's all, and a monk."

Atla looked at Finbar, who had run out his oar and was leaning on it, waiting for Atla to ready himself. "We have been at sea more than two years. We have been so far south that the sun stood over our heads. We have seen ocean that is frozen forever, having been so far north as well." Atla turned to look at Brendan again. "For more than two years you have kept us moving, kept us full of the vision of Paradise, kept us fed, protected, clothed, warmed, and free from evil ideas. In that time, you have never once been mistaken in any judgment. Mainly, though, you believe. That's what is so remarkable. You have never ceased to believe."

"The Lord God has given us light. One does not believe. One knows."

"There's the difference. I believe. You know."

Brendan's rough voice was soft when he replied. "You shall know, friend Atla. God has ordained that we shall visit the shores of Paradise. He has shown us so in every one of His works. In the shamrocks we follow, in the winds that blow us, in the very vastness and indifference of the sea: for why should this sea be all around us if it were not the wilderness we need to cross in order to reach Paradise? You speak as though our voyage has been one of trials, which it has been. But our Savior does not reward without trying. Grace is prevenient; salvation is sure. We shall be delivered from this calm—as we have been from all our other trials—in the same manner as David was delivered from the hand of Goliath, as Jonah was delivered from the belly of the whale."

Atla sighed and slid out his oar. "You are a saint."

"Not so. I am a simpler man than you think, than any of you think." Brendan looked around at the crew. Finbar and Joseph were listening with close attention to this uncharacteristic revelation of their captain's thoughts. Atla was attempting to find a comfortable position in which to sit, despite his inflamed buttocks. Barinthus, as he had for twelve hours, sat in the bow and stared into the west. The sun hung low in the breathless, damp air; the sea meandered like hot gelatin.

"In four days, we shall be in Paradise. It has been revealed to me. Since the time I was eleven years old and my Uncle Barinthus returned from his previous voyage, I have worked through my life to reach this spot. In four days, it will be over. The cruise will be done. We shall all stand on the Blessed Shores under the light of Christ's heavenly eye. And I tell you, my friends, that I am less content at this moment than I have been during the entire voyage, less content even than I was when we were sinking. You all know the evil that Barinthus brought to Paradise. Listen, now. This is my evil: I regret our arrival."

Late in the afternoon, the wind came. At first, it was the merest hint of coolness at the backs of their ears, scarcely to be noticed except by sailors exhausted with calm. They raised their heads and stared at one another, then out at the horizon. There was no visible sign anywhere of wind.

"It's out there," Atla assured them.

"But where?" Joseph begged.

They craned their necks. They felt with their ears. Perhaps they had imagined it.

"There it is!" Finbar whispered.

"Where?" Atla asked.

"There. Coming that way."

"No," Joseph argued. "From there."

There was scarcely a ripple on the sea. But, there was a ripple.

"See?" Atla gloated. "It'll be here any moment."

Still, there was nothing more. A minute passed, and another. Then there it was, all around them, filling them, flushing the heat, lifting them. Brendan let go the brails, and in an instant the curragh was twinkling across a sea as vivid and cheerful now as a moment before it had been dead.

Brendan smiled his odd smile. "The God wind," he rasped, and then he fell to musing, with the steering oar in his hand.

Joseph clapped Finbar on the back, and the latter restrained himself from smiling only for fear of splitting his sun-burned lips.

The wind was from the southeast and humid. By the time the sun had set and the stars were making their appearance, the humidity had increased. In another few minutes, Finbar was not surprised to realize that they had sailed into a bank of fog. They enjoyed a good night's sail despite the fog. The wind was steady and the seas were regular. The helmsman was able to keep a good course through the darkness by basing his steering on the angle of the wind and the sea.

They were in the fog three days.

On the third day, the sun set through a weakening haze, and they held their course right down its throat.

After it had disappeared into the sea, the wind increased, having veered in the meantime more into the east. By midnight, the fog was almost completely gone, and the sea was on the rise. Finbar had the watch, and he throve on the sensation of the swoop and glide. Once more, the curragh was a thrilling thing, married to the sea, and the stars overhead reeled with the joy of that wedding dance. When Finbar surrendered the helm at four, there was very little of him left except his skin and his eyes. His mind had gone to bed with the sea.

Though Finbar did not see it, dawn came fast, bright and handsome. Shortly thereafter, the morning canticle was sung. There was a faint tinge of green deep in the blue of the sea, and the crests of the seas broke into the air with white horses leaping. One, and then two, and then three enormous gulls appeared, eyeing the curragh with their amber stare. The birds hung in station off the quarters, sailing easily in their own element above the sea. Finbar came on deck and dashed a bucketful of water into his face.

And then they were there.

The way a landfall appears to a man on the deck of a tiny ship is always a surprise. It does not appear suddenly, fully made; nor does it merge into view like smoke hardening into fact. On a clear morning after months at sea, with the sun behind him and a phalanx of gulls at his side, it appears first as a vision, a mere portent, that starts coyly above the horizon and then is gone. It comes out of a vastness of space, out of an infinity of blue: with its presence it pinpoints that space and gives it shape that it never had before. It disappears almost as soon as it comes, seeming only to have been a low and sidelong cloud. The sailor looks again; there it is! Still there, hanging just above the horizon, almost with humility before the eternity it is challenging and will kill. He is not certain even then. He waits. He rises on a crest again: once more, it is there. Now it is less humble a line. Now, he sees that it possesses the everyday realities of shape and, yes, color. Soon, while he continues to stare, the land becomes so present as to be

seen from trough as well as crest, and his eyes no longer
wheel the seaboard sweep. The very nature of the earth
has changed.

It must have been the smell that brought everyone
on deck. To the senses of the salt-sea men, the perfume
was intoxicating. Since the first moment when land was
sighted, no one had said a thing, save the few grunts
necessary for the almost automatic running of the ship. As
the crew struggled up out of the cabin, one by one, the
hush fell across them. Now they all stood in the cockpit,
leaning automatically into the repeated thrust of the seas,
while the scent broke across their tongues like mint in
summer. There was mud in it, and rock, and seaweed, and
pine. It held warmth, that air, with the sort of cushiony
billow of cotton-like down that the sea's straight-edged
sunlight could never attain. There were flower and berry
and the heavy drone of bees. There was the darkness of
undergrowth and the high clangor of crumbling mountain points. Somewhere in it were river water and pond,
mountain and snow, meadow and daisy. There were deer
grazing in the meadow, and rabbits in the wood; a bear
tore at rotten logs, and a puma sunned herself in majes-
terial arrogance. All this came to the salt-weary sailors on
the wind, some of which they understood, some of which
they did not. And they stood there, sailing unconsciously,
as their eyes watched the hours roll them crest by crest
into the wide arms of an island-heavy bay.

They found themselves nearing an island. It slid past.
Another came near on their other side. Again, it slid past.
Now they saw that there were islands all around, small
ones, large ones, tall ones, islands hardly standing out of
the sea. Some of them were mere humps of rock above
the surface, dotted perhaps with two or three gnarled
spruce, or perhaps with a stunning line of wild rose bushes
deeply green and pink in the horizontal slant of the hot
sea air. Others were hidden, mysterious, draped from
shore to shore in impenetrable cloaks of grey-green pine.
The tide was high, the shore lines clean. White, smooth
slabs of granite rose to low-hanging trees. Or else there
were meadows, here and there: filled with the waver of
silver reeds. The shores were steep-to with granite walls,

against which the sea rumbled and moaned, now spouting high with ecstacies of spray, now arguing with hollow, stone-rolling gasps. What beaches there were had been thrown up of pebbles, and they were scattered with drift-wood and dried lines of winter-tossed seaweed. As the sailors slid deeper into the embrace of the land, the islands were thicker, the sea lanes more tricky. Now, there were ledges just under the surface around which they needed to make their way. In the lee of the islands there were fleets of eider ducks and guillemots. Porpoises rolled along the surface, their black backs appearing with metronomic regularity. There were the curiosities of seals.

It was mid-afternoon, no one had spoken, no one had moved. A chain of islands slid toward them, greeted them, passed by. Inside of them now the sailors no longer saw open ocean over their stern. They sailed in the middle of an archipelago, surrounded by land. The deep swells of the sea were gone. The curragh chopped across wavelets kicked up by a bright mid-afternoon breeze. Still she held her course. Still no one moved. They passed a rock on the top of which was piled a twelve-foot-high seahawk's nest. As they passed, the bird perched on its rim spread her wings and, with a high shriek, leapt into the air. She beat heavily for a moment or two, and then she caught the wind and soared to windward of them, eyeing them. From away in the sky, they heard repeated her thin, wild scream.

They were closing in toward the coastline. It was dramatic in its mountainousness. Five peaks strode north-ward along the coast. The sailors' course lay toward the cliffs of the southernmost peak, and they believed they spied an opening, perhaps a harbor, at its foot.

Speaking with admirable calm, Brendan said, "We shall land."

Slowly, the others came out of their spells. It had seemed to Finbar that they should simply continue to sail on, up the shore and between the mountains, across the forests and the lakes, and ever onward in that same breathless and eternal motion until they should come to the ends of time and of man. Instead, he flaked down the rode.

They crossed the final miles of water. The opening
looked increasingly like a harbor, protected by a small
island at the southern edge and a series of weedy ledges
running out from the northern. It was half-tide, or lower.
A way led between the arms. The curragh made for it.
The breeze scurried them along. They slid between the
island and the ledge. Brendan spilled the foresail, and
they slowed. There was a cove to their right, a point sticking out in the middle, and round the point to the left what
seemed to be the inner reaches of the harbor, narrower
and tucked under the protection of the cliffs. A gust sent
them thither.

The water was smooth, and they heard that new
sound along the hull, the sound of protected water, that
they had last heard at Thule.

They rounded the point and saw the length of the
inner harbor. At its head, a waterfall came down noisily
over ledges. The southern, or left, shore of the harbor was
forested. The northern shore, under the cliff, was clearer,
with an open park of oaks and maples and a sward beneath. Eagles slid along updrafts. Cormorants dove for
herring in the muddle below the falls. Eiders and their
chicks grouped and regrouped among the round boulders
of the shoreline.

Suddenly, there was a hiss of indrawn breath. Barinthus's arm went rigid, his finger at the point. Opening up
among the trees of the park were round, bark-covered
huts, and a line of silent, part-naked men and women
stood along the shore. Children ran quietly to their dams.
Hounds barked and then grew still.

"Angels," Barinthus sighed.

"Men," said Atla. "Don't you see they're men?"

"I see a holy glow."

"Your eyes are old, Brother, or your desire too great."

"I see what I see."

"You see as through a glass, darkly."

"What I see is light."

"Round up," Brendan interrupted. "Back the sails."

The curragh ghosted to a stop, midway between
shores, thirty yards from the waterfall, thirty yards from
the silent onlookers.

"Drop the hook."

Finbar let the rode out almost guiltily, tensely consciously of the eyes of those along the shore. The anchor held. Working slowly, the crew brailed the sails, coiled the lines, snugged her down. Through it, the group on the shore increased in size, but no words were heard. Finbar noticed eight or ten bark boats drawn up on the shore. There were fires still smoldering and there was a smell of smoking fish. There was little movement among the onlookers. Two boats suddenly appeared around the point from the outer harbor, but their paddlers stopped at sight of the strange craft, and the boats drifted to a standstill.

Their tasks done, the crew gathered in the cockpit. Brendan raised his arms outward and bellowed from the drum of his chest, "We come with God!"

A ripple of movement ran down the line of onlookers, as a ripple will flow through a line of birds perched on a rooftop when a new member comes in to land.

"God!" he shouted. "We come from Ireland—that way—and we come with God. We are Christian brethren. We have come a long way to see you in Paradise."

Another ripple shivered the still bodies.

Brendan turned to his crew. "Perhaps we should wait a bit and see what happens."

"What can happen in Paradise?" Barinthus asked.

"They don't know Latin."

"Disinclination to speak is not necessarily ignorance. I shall stand on the shores of Paradise."

"We will wait."

"You have said already, Nephew, that you regret arrival. Do not stand in the way of those of us who go to our promised home with an eagerness you do not feel. Joseph would stand with me in Paradise, wouldn't you, Brother?"

The young man's eyes were wide with awe, staring at the shore. He glanced at Brendan, swallowed, and nodded. "Please, Father," he whispered. "It is as Christ has said: we have come to the Promised Land."

"Atla?" Brendan questioned.

The tall hunter shrugged. Finbar noted that he had slipped a spear from its clip under the coaming. "We'll

have to land sometime," he replied, practically. "We
haven't much water left."

"We could go elsewhere."

"Insult!" Barinthus bristled. "You insult the angels of
God. I am shocked and ashamed. It is horror enough that
you regret Paradise, but to fear the angels is to have listened too long to the whispers of Lucifer. Finbar, raise the
anchor."

"Finbar!" Brendan held up his hand. He turned to his
uncle. "You do not give orders aboard my ship," he hissed.

The other looked back blandly. He, too, raised his
hand, but it was to make the Cross. "You are afraid, my
son, and I forgive you for it. But do not dare blaspheme
God's gift with your anger and fear. Land the ship."

The last sentence was said with such authority that
Brendan, after a moment, turned hotly to Finbar and
barked, "Do as the man says. Atla, you and Joseph—he's
so eager—take the sweeps."

Without crowing his victory, the old man climbed
slowly to the deck and made his way forward. He stood
in the prow as the curragh gained way and then, slowly,
turned her nose toward the middle of the line of onlookers.

As the ship crossed the narrow belt of water, the line
of men and women on the shore fell back in the middle.
When the hull ran up with a smart scrape upon the gravel
beach, the watchers were in two groups. A dog barked
and was silent again, cringing.

Barinthus addressed the assemblage.

"With the help of our Savior Jesus Christ, and with
the permission of God the Father, and under the constant
protection of the Holy Ghost, we have come, we five, to
Paradise. We salute you, people of God, and we ask you
to take us into your favored embrace with the eagerness
of the Father for us prodigals. Many years we have wandered, and our kind has wandered, guided always as the
Israelites in the desert by the luminance of Christ's bright
Light and Word, but wandered nevertheless in constant,
vain search of the miracle of rescue. Grace has been given
us, for which we humbly thank you, but our feet are tired
with the miles, and our throats are raw for lack of the

manna of Paradise. Now, we are here. Our voyage has come to its close. We five are come at last to Paradise, and we are yours, most humbly, as you are God's."

With that, the old man jumped down off the prow onto the shore. His stiff knees buckled, and he fell. A murmur had arisen among the multitude at the conclusion of the speech, no louder than crickets, but it fell still again when Barinthus collapsed. There was complete silence as the monk slowly pushed himself to his feet. He walked two or three steps to the middle of the beach. He stopped. His hands went to his throat and in a second he was naked, standing in the puddle of his fallen garments, his emaciated body pale and trembling.

"Naked I left you," he said, "and naked I return."

He made the sign of the Cross, and then he bent down once more and kissed the stones of Paradise.

9

THAT NIGHT, FOR THE FIRST time in two months,
Finbar slept ashore, and the earth under his buck-
skin-and-sweet-grass pallet tossed him as though he
were beating into a half-gale with a confused sea coming
in from leeward. The fault was not alone the unfamiliarity
of solid ground: his head reeled. He was smoke-drunk.

Finbar was suffering because he and the monks had
been treated to a ceremonial repast that evening, and it
was customary among these people—or so it appeared—
to pass from mouth to mouth a smoldering bowl of
crushed leaves, and to draw the smoke of these leaves into
the lungs through a tube set into the side of the bowl.
They practiced this asphixiating behavior before, during
and after the meal. As though this were not enough of an
affront to the tender nostrils of the visitors, the meal had
been taken inside the largest of the dwellings, where a
smudgy fire sent up a constant fog of smoke. It was a wierd
introduction to the life of the Paradisemen among whom
the sailors had fallen.

The lodge was a long, bark-thatched building. The
fire was in the middle; there was no smoke hole. Hung
from the uprights were weapons, shields and furs, these
latter of very fine quality. Running down each side of the
lodge were raised, earthern couches on which more furs
were strewn. The party reclined on these couches, as
much to escape the thickest of the smoke as for their
refreshment. There were some twenty Paradisemen
among the attendees, and two women. These women appeared to have some ceremonial significance, for all the
others of their sex in the village were relegated to the role

of servers, who passed food in at the doorway and strained to catch a glimpse of the European visitors.

Brendan and company were clustered in the middle, across from the man who was clearly recognizable as the leader of the village. This man, whose name seemed to be Glusgebeh, was as beautiful a figure as Finbar had seen in Greece or the German forests. He was upright of stature and arrogant of eye. Nearing the end of his prime years of strength, he seemed to possess also the aspect of wisdom. In all, he was calm, ceremonious and alert. He had long, black hair, which he wore coiled into a kind of cone atop his head. It was heavily greased, and even in the fuzzy atmosphere, it shone. The primaries of some large hawk dropped from above one ear across his naked shoulder. Encircling his neck was a series of strings, on which were suspended the claws of an enormous carnivore, bigger even than those of the lions Finbar had known in Egypt. Intertwined with the claws were what appeared to be decorations of seashells and some sort of quill. The man wore finely cut leggings and moccasins, also decorated colorfully, and a wide belt made of a rope of ringed tails. His skin color was a deep brown, similar to the color that years of seafaring had given Brendan and Atla. As striking as anything else about the leader was the severe scarring of chest and belly that, obviously, he honored, for it was highlighted in vermilion dye.

It had been this Glusgebeh who started the smoke-breathing. Lighting the long device with a taper from the fire, he passed it across the flames to Brendan.

"Very fine," Brendan said, examining it carefully and passing it along to Barinthus.

The leader's face became impassive.

"I think you should suck it," Atla whispered to his captain.

"Suck the smoke?"

"He did."

Brendan took the smoking stick back from his uncle. Carefully, watching the leader's expression, he sucked. Obviously, it was the right thing. Smiles appeared in the brown faces across the fire. Brendan, however, could hardly stifle the proxysm of coughing it occasioned. Wheezing, he passed the stick to Barinthus. "Careful, Uncle," he choked.

In a few minutes, to their surprise, the Europeans had grown more accustomed to the practice—or so they thought. Finbar realized that he was light-headed when he heard himself singing: he was not a singing sort of man.

With the smoke, the food added to the excitement and the intoxication of the sailors. Clams and mussels they knew, as they knew the earthbound taste of stag. There was a long, red crustacean, the tail meat of which was especially tasty and from the legs of which one sucked meat as one does marrow from a cracked thighbone. Most exotic to their sea-bored palates, however, was a vegetable like a huge ear of rye, from which one tore the kernels with one's teeth. Dipped in oil and strewn with coarse salt, this was a favorite of the evening.

Another favorite, Finbar realized, was a feast for the eye instead of the tongue. As the hours wore on, and the smoking and the singing and the speechifying grew more jovial, he found himself watching the women who were part of this field day. One of them was a crone, whom Finbar took to be Glusgebeh's mother, but the other was a nubile and slender attraction. She might have been the man's daughter, possibly a wife—Finbar knew nothing of the customs in Paradise. Whatever she was that allowed her a place at the festive table, she was also friendly and excited. She sat across from Joseph, but it was impossible for her to make that severe man smile. Her round, pretty face and black eyes instead sought a response in others. Finbar grinned at her, and they waved lobster claws. A little later, when the party began to mix a bit, he was startled to find her at his elbow. Rubbing the corner of her short skirt on his arm, she attempted to get the black off, or that at least was what he finally gathered she was doing. The fact that it did not come off astonished her, and Finbar thought—he could not be certain—that she made a lewd remark to the crone across the fire. In any case, they both laughed while Finbar pretended not to guess what they were saying.

"They are not angels," Finbar heard Joseph muttering to Brendan sometime later. The captain was trying to adjust his singing voice to the gutteral chanting that the Paradisemen used, and he was not especially concerned at the moment with Joseph's theory.

"I showed one my crucifix," Joseph continued, "and he thought I meant the four cardinal points. They are heathens and they are vicious."

Even in the reeling atmosphere of the later stage of the dinner, Finbar was aware of the undercurrent of anomosity that came from Joseph. Something of the same seemed to deepen the face of the crone as the evening wore on. It was a disturbance that Finbar could never quite ignore.

Eventually, the evening came to an end. It was made clear that the sailors were expected to sleep ashore, in this lodge. His head now aching fiercely, Finbar longed for the clean air of the anchorage and the slap of small waves against the hull at his ear. Nevertheless, swathed in unnecessary furs, he and the monks gradually settled themselves for the night, while around him, the Paradisemen snored and scratched.

Unable to close his eyes because of the rolling in his head, Finbar lay a long time wishing he were anywhere else. Now that the fire had somewhat died down, the stench of the village itself was apparent to him: the drying fish, the smoking clams, the salted cod, the half-scraped hides, the offal, the bear grease with which the villagers smeared their bodies, and finally the pine tar they applied as a repellent against biting insects. Each of these belabored his nostrils. The earth was heavy, the air was still and the crickets were deafening. Here and there, and occasionally, a dog barked or a baby cried. Once, far off, a kind of scream in the night, a feline thing, made the hair stand on end until one pulled the fur closer around one's perspiring body.

After a long time, when the drunkenness was less, Finbar flung back his bearskin. His beard itched. The air felt cool, though, as it dried his skin. There was very little light anymore from the fire, and he closed his eyes. Immediately, the image of the young woman came into his mind. It had amused him to watch Joseph's discomfiture,

and it had made him feel superior, but he realized as he
lay there that he was himself just as awkward as the monk,
albeit in a different way. He had not been in a place with
so casual a display of female nakedness since leaving
Greece. It was hard for him to bear. He had watched
while the young woman's breasts grew shiny from dripping oil as she ate. He remembered the weight of her
haunch next to his while she tried to rub away his color.

Eventually, lulled by the soft roar of the waterfall,
Finbar fell into a shallow sleep. He dreamed of a bird: it
was a woman, and her hair was her wings. She took him
in her talons and flew with him high over the hills of
Paradise. He saw the harbor and the waterfall, the hills
and the cliffs behind, all dwindle until they were lost in
the wide sweep of glassy sea and green, mottled forest.
Higher still, and they were among clouds; he could see
nothing except her fierce eyes and her rapacious beak.
Her grip hurt him. He writhed. She turned her face
downward. She opened her mouth, and then she let him
go. It was a long fall to earth. He emerged from the clouds,
and he could see the world once more. He was surprised
that he was not frightened. The winds blew past him, first
from one aside, then from the other. He greeted them as
companions. He realized that he was plummeting nearer
and nearer to what would surely be his death; yet, still, he
was not frightened. He felt his energy pour forth unbrok-
enly. He was bathed in a radiance like heat that came
from inside him. He neared the tops of the trees. It was
this very village toward which he fell. He rolled over in
the air and landed, springily, on his feet. He was surrounded by the Paradisemen, and their faces reflected the
radiance he issued. Then he realized that all their faces
were the faces of the bird-woman, and that their cry was
the cry of early earth before the Goddess had gone away:
they spoke with her voice, and he understood that voice,
and he was sexually stirred. "I am risen!" he called to
them, in Latin, in the hope the monks would hear, and
then he woke. He saw that Joseph knelt in prayer in the
middle of the hut. Finbar's dream had hardly left him. He
stood. The young monk's eyes—empty and sad and ir-
ridescent—swung up from the earth and fixed on Fin-

bar's. For Joseph, there was an awful strangeness in this Paradise to which they had come, Finbar realized. Ashamed, he lay back, covered his tumescence, and hid his head.

In the morning, the sailors made their way to the curragh, and there they found tasks they did not really need to do. Barinthus was the only one who stayed ashore. He unlimbered his shellagliegh and blundered up and down and everywhere, poking into huts, questioning passers-by, and entertaining naked children with feats of sleight-of-hand.

Aboard the curragh, Joseph was fully of entreaty. "They aren't Christians!" he agonized. "We must leave, Brendan, why don't we leave? We must leave before it's too late."

"Too late for what?" Atla wanted to know.

"Did Jesus ever laugh?" Finbar asked suddenly.

"What?" Joseph turned angrily to the smith.

Finbar gestured at Barinthus. The old man was down on all fours in the center of the village barking into the face of a delighted dog. A crowd of children shrieked with glee.

"I said, 'Did Jesus ever laugh?' "

"Jesus Christ is the Son of God," Joseph answered.

"I know, but did he laugh?"

"I don't understand."

Finbar looked at Brendan. "We had better stay."

To Joseph he said, "Look there! If they are angels"—pointing at the laughing children—"*they* laugh, and yet where is the humor in your religion? And if they aren't angels, why are they living in Paradise? *And* if this is not Paradise, what are the meanings of the signs we saw? And, finally, if they were not signs, what did your god put them there for? And us there to see them for? And the wind there to push us here? And the sea there to float us on? Riddle me that."

"Pagan sophistication," the young man said, turning to his abbot. "I'm afraid."

"God is with you, my son."

"No," Joseph hissed. "It is the goddess here. It is the *wrong* Paradise."

When Joseph had gone below, Brendan swung his short legs astride the steering-oar frame. He glanced at Finbar and away. "It does not matter whether Jesus Christ laughed or not. It is the Passion that changed the history of the world. That matters. It is the Church that is important, with her mission of bearing that Passion through history until the Glorious Return. It is the Apostolic Succession that is important, which guarantees the success of that mission in history. All those things are important, but they are important to earth and to her time. In Paradise . . . who knows? Maybe Jesus does laugh in Paradise. But it is *Jesus* who laughs, not Christ."

Atla, astonished, snapped his head round and whispered, "Blasphemy!"

"Maybe," Brendan mused. "Maybe."

"Be careful, my Father, please." Atla's usually easygoing expression had been replaced by a tension that surprised Finbar. "Else, just as Joseph says, something will happen that *is* awful."

Brendan stared at the man. He spoke slowly. "I am already full of awe."

Days passed. The Europeans learned much of these Paradisemen—who called themselves Abnaki—but they did not learn whether they were angels. In the main, the Abnaki proved to be a cheerful people, though serious about their purpose along the shore. It emerged that they inhabited this hunting and fishing camp during the summer months, returning to their homes deep in the forest when the fall came and the animals were driven by diminishing fodder off the heights and into the lake country. It was winter that they feared, and they smoked fish and shellfish as fast and as efficiently as they were able all through the summer in order to survive the snows. That the Abnaki were so caught up in the struggle for existence indicated to all the Europeans except Barinthus that they might not, in fact, be angels. There was little to suggest in the Scripture that the angels got cold when it snowed, and yet, as Atla admitted, not much was actually said about the life in Paradise either. Certainly, Abnaki manners and customs were unexpected, but that might all the more suggest an holy origin.

Regarding their use of metals, a subject of especial interest to Finbar, they were more primitive even than some of the German tribes he had known. Their tools were fashioned from stone and bone, albeit cleverly, and their amazement at the iron fastenings of the curragh's rig was complete. When it transpired that Finbar, whose blackness had already made him noteworthy, was a creator of such objects, their awe of him grew. Especially was this the case with the woman, Talutah, and her companion, the girl Nonanis.

There came an evening when Finbar was treated to a meal in the lodge shared by these two women. From the first, Finbar and the others had been curious about the two women. They were of a different stature in the village from the other women. While others tended the gardens, cleaned and fileted the fish, scraped and tanned the hides and cooked and served the food, neither Talutah nor Nonanis did any of these things. Their roles appeared ritualistic and even medical. It was Finbar's steel that excited them: they had often fingered bronze fastenings and iron hasps aboard the curragh almost with reverence. Because of his itinerant past, Finbar was no stranger to the awe that steel produces in the breasts of those who are not initiated into its secrets. He played up his transformative role in the smelting process a bit, and he even set up a crude bellows and sand crucible in which to smelt some of the copper ore which Paradise boasted along its shores. The result of his demonstration was the invitation to dine.

Some Abnaki speech had been learned by the Europeans, and vice versa. Each adopted vocabulary with which his own language did not provide him: the Abnaki had no words for sailing and its technology, or for iron and steel. The Europeans, on the other hand, found they must use Abnaki vocabulary to refer to the times of the day and the year, to the names of places and natural phenomena, and, most especially, to the spiritual realm. There was a word, *manito*, which was repeated often, and which—though there was some disagreement among the Europeans about this—Finbar felt referred to that web of causes and effects that knitted the Paradiseman to his earth. It was about this concept that Finbar particularly wanted to learn more during his dinner with the two women. To his disappointment, he did not find them forthcoming. On the whole, as he was to discover, the Abnaki were not glib intellects.

By this time, Finbar had grown accustomed to the smells and sounds of the village, and, in fact, he found the interior of Talutah's and Nonanis's lodge light, clean, attractively decorated with furs, quills, and seashells, and pleasantly odoriferous of balsam. He sat comfortably on a couch draped with a caribou skin, smoked, and examined various objects of magical power that Talutah brought out for him. Soon Nonanis produced a piggin of spruce tea, not a bad drink after the first few dutiful swallows. Lazy summer twilight filled the interior of the lodge. Chunks of savory moose nose sizzled over the fire. Nonanis's quick and pretty movements filled Finbar with pleasure, as did Talutah's intense concentration as he attempted again to explain some of the process by which he took the light and heat of the Father Sun and pressed it into the Grandmother Earth, thereby producing the sun-stone that was his special skill. Suddenly he realized, the pipe coming round to him again, that it might have been as many as fifteen years since he had been so entirely at his ease.

He enjoyed long moments of silence with the two women. During them, Finbar felt the twilight darken and the fire in the center of the lodge become his center as well. Or he munched on maize cakes and spoke, in his thoughtful, unelaborate manner, of the Empire, and of Thule, and of the long distances that he had come. He doubted whether the women understood very much of his recitations, but their attention never wavered in any case, and he was grateful for the audience they provided while, in effect, he allowed his legend of himself to catch up with his body.

Before the evening was over, Finbar learned only one thing more about the concept manito, and that which he learned was oblique. It was after the three had eaten. Night had fallen outside, and the only sounds were the final patroling calls of gulls returning to their nests for the night, the ever-present waterfall, and now and again the bark of a dog disturbed by some alarm in his own world.

Talutah, with gestures indicating the portentousness of the moment, took from a place of honor a roll of hide richly decorated with paint and quills. Carefully, she set the package down before the fire and, after purifying her hands with smoke, began to unwrap it. There were several layers of wrapping, each more beautiful than the one before. Finally, she arrived at the last covering. She paused and sang a manito-song, passing the object through and through the smoke of the pipe which Nonanis held out to her. Only then did she open the final seal.

Inside, Finbar saw an animal skull, and, when Talutah took it up in her hands, he recognized it as that of a lion. It was carefully preserved, with painted and life-like eyes in its sockets: its fangs glittered in the steady firelight.

"It is my . . ." Then Talutah used a word that Finbar knew to mean more than friend, in the nature of comrade or ally.

"The lion is your comrade?" he repeated.

Nonanis nodded. "It is manito," she said, and then, while Talutah proceeded to rewrap the skull, she told Finbar a story.

Fleshed out by Finbar's imagination from the halting tale he heard, the story was this: Years before, while Talutah was a young woman with children, her husband had taken ill. It was a strange sickness, for no one could understand its nature. Some evil thing had gotten inside him, and it gripped his heart with painful claws. Before that, he had been a good hunter and provider for Talutah and his other wives, but after the illness set in, they often went hungry or had to exist on the little that other, generous people were able to give them. In every way their luck turned bad: their canoes were holed, their winter lodge collapsed under the weight of snow and ice, their garden never grew. Some enemy must have cursed them, and this illness was part of the wreck he was making of their lives. Talutah's poor husband was a proud man. He did not care to see his children hungry or his wives the recipients of charity. Again and again, he tried to hunt, but always he was unsuccessful, or he was so doubled over with the gnawing inside him that, even when he saw an old doe in a thicket beside him, he was unable to make a kill.

Time passed in this way, and the family's fortunes were falling. Talutah's husband determined one final time to make a hunt and to die before returning empty-handed to the village. This time, though, Talutah persuaded him to allow her to accompany him. They set out and tracked a caribou, for they found fresh sign not far away. A sick man cannot move quickly, however, and it was a long stalk. Finally, high up along the rocky slopes of a mountain, they came upon the caribou they were hunting, but, though he tried, Talutah's husband was not able to draw his bow. Instead, Talutah killed the beast and butchered it on the spot. She fed her husband some of the liver, and this seemed to relieve him somewhat.

That night, camped on the trail homeward, surrounded by as much of the caribou meat as they could carry, Talutah lay beside her groaning husband, and she had a dream. In her dream, a lion came to her, and the lion spoke to her, saying: "Your man's heart will be stopped by the pressure inside him unless you take me as your comrade. I, maker of sharp claws, I, the lion, I shall claw away the obstruction in your man's chest." With that, he taught her a prayer and a song, and then he faded from her, and she awoke.

Some days passed. Talutah was afraid of what she had heard in her dream. Back in the village, the family quickly devoured the caribou meat, and then they were hungry again. In the end, Talutah set out by herself to kill a lion.

At this point in the recounting of the tale, Nonanis stopped and looked at the old woman. Talutah had completed the rewrapping of her skull, and she now sat beside the fire, looking into its flames. "Tell him how you killed the lion, Grandmother." Nonanis's eyes were twinkling with excitement.

Talutah looked at Finbar. Quietly, she said, "He attacked me. I bit his neck with my teeth, and he died."

"You killed a lion with your teeth!"

Talutah grinned. "It was my dream. He came from my dream."

"I can't believe it."

Nonanis giggled. "I show you skull once more?"

After a long moment, Finbar asked, "Then what happened?"

Talutah took up the story. "I skinned the lion and brought home the skull. I lay my man on the bed, and placed the skull at his head. Two days I prayed and sang. Then blood came from his mouth and his nose. He smiled. The hurt was gone. He was never ill again."

A stick popped in the fire, and Finbar shivered. Suddenly, he was a very long way from the Empire, and Paradise was filled with inexplicable things.

"Where is your husband now?"

"He is dead. A bear killed him. I continue to dream."

Later, back aboard the curragh, Finbar sat with Brendan in the cockpit as the moon rose slowly out of the misty sea.

"Do you know what it's like when suddenly the world changes shape and the Goddess is evoked: suddenly, she is there in your midst where she had not been before?" he asked.

"No," the captain replied, "but I have felt the same in the liturgy, and it was God who was there."

Finbar grinned. He looked around at the shoreline and the moon-gleam on the cliffs. A loon laughed near the mouth of the harbor. "For Paradise, it's not bad," he murmured.

Four days later, his twentieth in Paradise, Finbar was alone, exploring the hillside above the harbor. Ostensibly, he was searching for copper, which he had already found in small quantities along the riverbed. In fact, he was idling a private hour or two away from the camp and its demands. These were among the first hours he had been alone since their arrival. The day was still, hot and crowned with high, thin cirrus that portended a renewed southwest wind on the morrow. Out toward the eastern horizon across which he and his companions had sailed, there was a haze that barred his eye. The thousand islands of the bay dotted the surface, but he was unable to see beyond them to open water. Northward, the bay narrowed until it became the mouth of a river, some twenty miles, it seemed, from the spot where he stood. He could see a course for the river penetrating northward into the forest, and he knew that the Abnaki passed that way on their yearly return to their winter hunting grounds. Away far to the north—there was less haze over the land than the sea—he saw that the landscape became crinkled and that it rose to great heights.

He had stripped to his leggings and sandals, and the sun on his naked torso made him itch. Winded by the climb, he sat and stared out across the harbor below and the sea-lanes farther out. He ate a few blueberries that grew near, relishing this new taste to which Paradise had introduced him. In the way the light lay upon it, the country held a memory of Greece, though the flora was wrong. To the Abnaki, he knew, it was Madakamigossek, the Big Ridge Place. Finbar was interested that Abnaki names were not proper designations—as was the European habit—they were descriptions, and in this fact he understood something more of Abnaki connectedness and of the power of manito.

His reverie was shattered by a scream. It came from a spot along the ledge to his left. He leapt up, the hair on his neck bristling. The scream rose in an uncanny way to near inaudibility. Bounding along the rocks, he burst upon a scene the like of which, for unreality, he scarcely remembered. Talutah was balanced on tiptoe on the very edge of the cliff, her head and arms stretched back in a rictus of agony, every muscle in her old torso and legs etched spastically against her brown skin. The scream continued from her rigid throat, penetrated even the boulders, it seemed, and echoed back. She doubled over, almost slipping off the precipice, and then she sprang straight again with a renewed scream. At any instant, she would totter over the edge. What gave the scene its most bizarre quality, though, was the sight of Nonanis sitting calmly on a rock ten feet from the anguished woman, holding her moccasin in one hand and abstractedly scratching between her toes with the other.

Finbar raced forward. Even as he neared, Talutah's scream became so intense that she quivered right off her toes and shimmered at the very edge of balance. Nonanis looked up and saw the approaching smith, his mouth open in shouts of warning. She sprang up, and, to his astonishment, she barred him from getting nearer. The two grappled. Finbar made to cast her smaller body aside, his eyes all the while on Talutah, fearful that he might not reach her in time. Suddenly, with a noise like a hawk stooping, the young woman picked him up off the ground and pitched him eight feet back through the air so that he crashed against a rock and, hitting his head, slithered down in a heap.

For a second, he lay dazed, as much from the blow on the head as from the marvel. He was totally astonished. He stared at her. Nonanis was as he recalled her: a girl of slender physique, for whom only the other night he had needed to carry firewood. But she stood now before him with the intensity of a raptor over a stunned rabbit, and then, figuratively, she ruffled her feathers into place and turned away. Finbar raised himself onto an elbow and shook his head. It is very rare in the life of a mature and powerful male that he is actually picked up off the ground by another person. When it is done by a woman, and a small one at that, it is even more electrifying. Finbar stared at Nonanis in awe. The girl's back was slender and graceful, her hips, under their short, deerskin skirt, canted attractively this way and that as her legs carried her back toward the cliff edge. She gave no sign whatsoever of possessing such strength. She turned slightly when she reached the edge, and she looked over her shoulder at him. Her hair swung forward across her face and twinkled round her high, youthful breasts. A final time, she rustled her feathers, and the ripple of muscle along her spine completed Finbar's capture. The sudden, overwhelming power that she had exerted upon him caused in him a rush of lust so violent in its own right as to make him dizzy. His lungs felt hollow, and his groin ached. He coughed and swallowed in order to clear his dry mouth. He struggled to his hands and knees. He looked at the girl again. She was standing with her weight on one leg looking down at the fallen form of Talutah. Finbar had forgotten Talutah. The woman must have passed out from the intensity of whatever possessed her. Nonanis stood with the sea as her background, brushed her hair aside, and then bent down across the woman. Again, as her face dropped to the woman's, Finbar had the sudden image of the predatory lunge of the eagle when it holds its prey in its claws.

He rolled onto his heels and squatted, shaking his head to clear it. He watched the scene before him. Nonanis had extracted two osprey primaries and a painted bone from a pouch that she carried at her side, and she laid the feathers crossways on Talutah's heart. With the bone, she bent forward, and, using it as one would a whistle, she blew upon the crossed feathers and the heart beneath. Finally, she took from a birchbark vial a fingerful of ochre paint, and she smeared it on Talutah's right hand. This hand she laid upon the crossed feathers, and then she herself squatted back.

Nothing happened for a minute. Finbar's lust raged; he was unable to draw a full breath. Slowly, he stood. The girl looked over at him—warningly, it seemed—and he felt another flicker against his groin.

Talutah's hand began to move. The woman traced a line erratically along her breast and down onto her stomach. Her hand wavered a moment and smeared one more line upward again toward her armpit, then it fell to her side. It was at that moment that Nonanis suddenly grew solicitous and cradled the woman's head in her lap. Talutah drew a few shuddering breaths, and then her eyes came open. She stared around uncomprehendingly and then, gathering herself, she rose to her feet. Nonanis rose as well and steadied Talutah until she had her balance, drawing her slowly from the edge of the cliff. Finally, with the woman alert once more, the two bent over the mark that had been drawn on Talutah's body and conversed in serious tones.

Some minutes passed. Finbar began to detumesce. He felt sick to his stomach. He coughed wrackingly, and the women looked at him as though he were interrupting a religious ceremony—which, in fact, was the case. He recognized now what Talutah did for a living. He looked at her with some awe, for he had rarely seen so powerful a possession, but his primary wonder was still toward Nonanis, who, once again, had taken on the respectful and self-effacing role of the acolyte. He felt the back of his head to find the place where he had bruised it, touching it as a means of reassuring himself that he actually had been picked up and thrown backwards by a girl whose weight seemed hardly to be a third of his own. The passing of the first intensity of his lust had left him prickly and uncomfortable. He felt flatfooted. He coughed again and took a step toward the women.

They had concluded their interpretation of the omen on Talutah's body, and they approached him. He felt embarrassed toward Nonanis, unable to meet her eye. However, it was Talutah who addressed him in the shared language of signs and borrowed words.

"We go to Ktaadn."

"What is that?"

"In the north." She pointed. "A mountain. There we meet Cautantowit."

"Who is he, a king?"

"I don't know this word . . . king."

"Captain, sachem. Who is Cautantowit?"

"The great manito." Talutah struggled with the importance of her information. "Cautantowit is the greatest manito. It is he I speak with here. I am powaw: I dream. I am the greatest screamer of the Abnaki. I speak with Cautantowit, and he tells me to come to him."

"When do you go?"

"No. You go. All of you. Nonanis and I shall take you. We leave tomorrow."

"But—"

"Cautantowit has spoken. We go to him tomorrow. He will tell me what you are and why you have come."

She turned away. Finbar's eyes finally rested on Nonanis' face. The girl stared back impassively; then she grinned. She winked at him.

"Are you hurt?" she asked.

It seemed a challenge, and his stomach churned. "How did you do that?" he muttered.

Her face became blank. "We go to Ktaadn," she said stolidly.

He stared at her for a long time, but her expression

gave him no information at all. Finally, he smiled and told her, "My companions believe they have already reached the end of their journey, that they are in Paradise."

"I hear the old man speak this word, and the thin one who does not eat."

"Yes. They have come to seek Paradise."

"I do not know what this thing is." The question in her mind made her eyes lighter and, Finbar thought, made her pretty again.

"They believe that they have found the spot where . . . where they will go after death."

"No. That is not here. That is to the southwest, many months' journey. Where it is hot all the time, and where Cautantowit has his garden."

"Still, that is what they are looking for. They have sailed, as we have told you, from Ireland, for two years, to find this spot."

"This is Madakamigossek, that's all. This is not . . . Paradise. Your friends have not gone far enough."

Finbar smiled. "That will be a disappointment to them."

"Come," interrupted Talutah, impatiently turning away. "You must sweat."

"Sweat?"

"You do not go to Cautantowit uncleansed. Then we have the ceremony of farewell."

She strode away. Nonanis waited politely until Finbar took a step to follow the woman, and then she, too, fell in behind. Descending the rock face, the party disturbed a fawn, which flushed from cover and darted away across the vertical rocks on improbable, skinny legs. Nonanis burst into laughter, and Finbar turned his face up to share it with her. Instead, seeing her poised above him on a rock, vivid against the luminous sky, he was silenced.

Once in the forest, the three walked side by side. The undergrowth from the base of the cliff to the village had been cleared, and it was a pleasure to walk through the pines on a thick and springy mat of needles.

"How long does it take to get to . . . what is the name of the place?" Finbar asked.

"Ktaadn," Nonanis answered.

"To Ktaadn?"

Talutah gestured three hands of days. "We shall be there when the moon is three-quarters."

"What will we do there?"

"We will meet Cautantowit. I have said so."

"Suppose he does not know what to do with us?"

Talutah had to think about that for a few paces. "He is manito. He will know."

"Is he a person? I mean, will we meet a man?"

"I have seen him so, but he is not a man."

"I do not understand."

Talutah stopped and looked at the smith. Her face showed impatience. She lifted his hand and spat on it. Before he could recoil, she rubbed the spit on his skin with her fingers. "It is not paint," she said. "You . . . this color is manito." She turned away and gestured at the trees around them. "At night, you hear them: it is manito. You see the casts of an animal you don't know: it is manito. You kill an otter, and inside his stomach is a live fish: it is manito. Cautantowit is a name for the greatest manito. Not a man. Not a woman. Not an animal or a bird. Cautantowit is Cautantowit."

"Why, then, must we go to Ktaadn?"

"That is where it happens."

"Where what happens?"

"Cautantowit."

Talutah turned away abruptly and continued toward the village. Finbar looked at Nonanis. His expression was quizzical, and she smiled at him, but her smile did not betoken a sharing of his confusion. It was anticipatory, as though she relished the thought of the meeting between him and this thing, Cautantowit. He grew afraid, suddenly, of what the thing might be. He recalled the Goddess prickling into the air around him in this woman's lodge. He recalled the inexplicable strength of the slender Nonanis. He pictured again the cliffside frenzy of the woman who would lead them. He had not anticipated fear in Paradise.

"Come," said Nonanis, and she laid her hand on his arm. "I have never been to Ktaadn." Her grin was dangerous. "We must clean you."

He and she emerged from the forest into the clearing of the village. It happened that Joseph was there, making a rare turn around the grounds with Barinthus, guiding the old man between rows of squash and beans. Nonanis' hand still lay on Finbar's arm, and she was smiling at him. Joseph flushed angrily and tried to turn the old monk away from the sight. Instead, Talutah, just ahead, caught at his garment and ordered him to sweat, and Barinthus as well.

"Certainly not!" Joseph cried, when he understood her meaning, and he tried to pull away.

Finbar and Nonanis had come up to them by this time. "We had better do it," the smith advised. "It's some sort of purification before the journey they want us to undertake tomorrow."

"What journey?"

"Up the river to a mountain called Ktaadn. We are to meet a being there, some sort of spirit, I think, called Cautantowit."

Joseph sneered. "I have no interest in this, what you call spirit. Nor does Barinthus."

The old man turned his yellow-ringed, dim eyes toward the Abnaki powwaw and said, "Tell her, I shall go."

"You must not," Joseph contradicted, "and certainly I shall not bathe."

Finbar said quietly, "I believe we have no choice."

"I have no responsibility to these . . . beings," Joseph replied loudly. "They do not determine my actions."

Barinthus responded, "You may not speak for me, Brother Joseph. I will do what the angels desire, as you ought to do yourself."

"They are not angels, Brother! See? They flaunt themselves. They make sport of themselves."

Talutah was interested. "What sport?" she asked.

Joseph's voice rose again. "Fornication, harlot! You know the sport."

Talutah turned to Finbar. "What is fornication?"

Finbar coughed. "When a man and woman are together, and, uh—"

Nonanis giggled. "Lying together."

"Yes."

Nonanis said, "But we don't." She indicated Joseph. "You won't. You say you have been at sea for many months, and yet you will not touch us, or our sisters. It is manito."

"I am celibate, woman. I am a Brother of Christ!"

"Are you built as a man?"

"Of course."

"Everywhere?"

Joseph blushed and turned back to Barinthus. "You see! You see how they talk, Brother Barinthus? They would distract a man from what he is bound to do."

"Joseph, don't be an ass," Finbar muttered.

"Why do you not?" Nonanis asked once again, hot on her theme. "It is an insult to us."

"I never have, and I never will. I do it for God."

Talutah looked surprised. "The manito-god you speak about?"

"Of course."

"Is this manito-god, then, not capable himself?"

"He has no sex!"

"It has been cut off?"

"It was never there in the first place, woman!" Joseph slapped his chest in frustration. "Don't you understand anything at all? You are speaking of God! God, do you hear? He has nothing to do with sex, and neither do I."

Talutah asked, "Then why are you staring that way at Nonanis?"

Joseph flushed and jerked Barinthus's cloak as though to go. "I shall hear no more of this. I do not speak with harlots."

Barinthus stopped him. "Christ did," he said softly. "Do not cast stones."

"You say so?" the man sputtered, his thin face growing red with anger.

Barinthus lifted Joseph's arm from his own shoulder. He took a step toward Nonanis and looked her up and down with his vague eyes. "I see a beautiful woman, Joseph. There are things about our calling that you must still learn, even here in Paradise. I am older than you, but I can still appreciate a beautiful woman." His long, veined hand came out from his cloak and stroked once down the

side of Nonanis's hair. The girl was flustered by the gesture, and a shiver ran through her. The old man stood
back, and he smiled at Talutah. "Our sex has not been cut
off," he smiled, "but we have directed that energy to the
hunt for freedom from slavery. We are hunters, and we
must be pure. Can you understand?"

The woman nodded. "Everyone understands a
hunter," she said slowly, and then she directed her attention to Joseph, "but only when he is truly a hunter and not
merely a teller of tales."

Joseph fumed wordlessly while Barinthus led him
away. After they had gone five paces, the old man turned
again and called, "We will be purified according to your
customs. Simply tell us what to do."

Two hours later, the Europeans were ushered to the
sweat-house by Talutah and Nonanis. It was a conical mud
hut on the shoreline away from the village, about which
Finbar had earlier been curious. A small door low down
in the side and a small smoke-hole in the top were the only
openings. A fire had been kindled inside, and Talutah now
stooped to draw the smoldering coals out through the
doorway. Having cleaned the inside, she stood again and
indicated that the men should strip. A wave of heat from
the mud walls played on Finbar as, with some embarrass-
ment, he slipped off his tunic and leggings and, finally, his
breechclout. Brendan was doing the same thing, and Atla.
Barinthus was assisted by Nonanis. No small amount of
snickering and joking was exchanged between the two
women as the white and black bodies appeared. It was
Joseph who offered resistance, but, at Brendan's direct
order, and after Talutah suggested she call five or six Abnaki men to her aid, the ascetic turned his narrow back
and bared his white loins.

Naked, the men were herded into the close, hot
confines of the hut. A wooden door was dropped in place
outside, and barred there. A squat was the only position
possible. The interior was built for two or three persons
instead of five, and the ceiling was low. The novelty of
their position at first kept the men from noticing the heat.
Soon, however, as their legs began to ache, they realized
that they were sweating profusely. Finbar felt oily, itchy

and claustrophobic. His thighs were pressed on one side against Brendan's and on the other against Barinthus's. Across from him, nearly panting in his face, were Atla and Joseph. The heat was making the lice angry, and the men scratched their heads and beards and pubic areas frenziedly while sweat ran in actual streams off their elbows, buttocks and noses.

"You *wanted* to be purified," Atla muttered at Brendan.

"I want to see more of Paradise."

"Look around you," Finbar replied cynically.

"Oh, God, I hate this," Joseph moaned, and he began to pray.

Barinthus was quiet, sunk in on himself, apparently asleep.

It seemed an hour, and breathing was growing more difficult as their bodies cooked, before the doorway was suddenly wrenched open. The men collapsed slowly toward the coolness and hauled themselves out. As Finbar emerged, he felt someone grasp him under the arm and lift him to his feet. It was Talutah. Even as he stood, he was suddenly drenched by a bucketful of cold water poured over his head by Nonanis. His roar of surprise reverberated across the harbor. The drenching was repeated. He turned to wrest the container from Nonanis's hands, but he discovered in that moment that his anger at the shock had evaporated. He felt wonderfully alive. Nonanis was grinning with the excitement of the dunkings, and Finbar, laughing, even went so far as to help her drench his companions as they crawled into the sunlight one by one.

In the course of the next two hours, the European voyagers changed their appearance entirely. Taken to Talutah's lodge, they sat in a row and were shaved of all hair on their faces and chests. Nonanis did this, working swiftly with a sharp edge of clamshell and a flat rock. Barinthus asked her to renew the tonsures that had been allowed to grow out. After their remaining hair had been oiled and combed in Abnaki fashion, the men exhibited a curious appearance, half monk, half paradisal native. Finbar's skin felt tight, and was clean from the sweat-house.

His spirits were high. When Nonanis bent across him to barber him, again he was conscious of her lithesomeness, and again the recollection of her power stimulated.

"Is it good to go to Ktaadn?" Finbar asked, while Nonanis lit sweet grass and showed the men how to wash their hands in the smoke.

"Cautantowit is very great manito. Abnaki never go to him at his mountain unless there is . . . I do not know." She shrugged helplessly. Finally, she said, "There have never been white men here, or a black one, like you. Also, men who sail against the wind. And men who make sun-stone"—here she gestured at a bronze bracelet that Finbar wore—"out of earth. It is manito to us. We must go to Cautantowit. He is calling us there. Talutah knows it. She is a very great powwaw."

"Gibberish," Joseph growled.

"God is often found on mountaintops, Joseph," Brendan soothed. "Remember Sinai and be still."

"What is it like?" Atla asked the woman.

"I have never been there," she replied. "It is not as you think it will be."

"We are in Paradise," Barinthus intoned. "It is exactly as we think it should be."

"Not I."

"Joseph," the old man said, "you are blind. Be silent."

Nonanis blew on the smoldering sweet grass and the fragrant odor filled the dwelling. "We will offer the white caribou to the sun. It will make good medicine for the journey."

"The white caribou?"

"Glusgebeh killed a white caribou near Magabigwaduce before you came. By this, we knew you were to arrive. It was a great hunt. We will offer it to Cautantowit, and that will make our journey a good one."

"Cautantowit is the sun?"

"Cautantowit is manito, that is all."

"Save us, Lord Jesus, from the ignorance of these . . . people, and from our own gullibility."

"Don't be afraid, Joseph," Finbar said.

"I am not afraid! I am a man of God."

"Come," Nonanis urged them, "it is time."

For this occasion, the ceremony was outside. The clearing in the center of the village had been swept smooth and laid with moosehides. A bonfire was built in its midst for later in the afternoon, when the sun would be lower in the sky. Along the shore, fire pits were arched with sizzling venison haunches, moose nose, beaver tail. The dogs lapped at the dripping juices and fought. Handsome young men in their best finery stood around squinting into the distance as though they had no thought for the clusters of equally finely clad girls whispering together between the dwellings. It was mid-afternoon and a hard northwest wind made the greens and blues and stone-whites opaque. Gulls hung high overhead. Big, black crows sharpened their beaks on maple branches and challenged the gulls.

The party of travelers, the two women included, gathered before Glusgebeh and the village dignitaries. Slowly, with enormous ceremony, Glusgebeh unwrapped the coverings of the sacred caribou hide. Singing a different song for each separate wrap, he finally bared the beautiful white hide. It was adorned with eagle feathers, porcupine quills and bursts of brilliant seashells. Everyone in the village sang along with him as, in stately manner, he marched to the four corners of the village, offering the skin to the sky and the earth at each stop. In the center again, he laid the skin open across a wickerwork platform which had been constructed at the end of a long pole. Then this pole, with deliberate care, was raised until the caribou hide was high above all, lying open to the sun. The pole was fixed in a hole already prepared for it, and, at the moment when the offering had thus been made, the fire was lit, and the revelry began.

The dizzying effect of smoking had scarcely lessened for Finbar during the past three weeks, and pipes now began to come at him from all sides. At the same time, accompanied by drums and rattles and Atla's bone whistle, a dance commenced. All the unmarried men and women lined up across from one another and, with mincing and provocative steps, the lines moved closer to one another and back again, teasingly. This subtle flirtation went on for some time, with hilarity erupting now and then from some signal that Finbar and his companions were unable to interpret. Eventually, the pace grew more frenzied, and now and then a girl swept her skirts out at a young man; if she could catch him with her hem, he owed her a kiss. It was darker now, and the bonfire blazed, and the dancers sweated, and the ground shook under the pounding of their excited feet.

Later, the dancing done and the crowd thinned out —there were sudden calls and alarms and discoveries in the warm night under the trees—Finbar lay back and watched the stars grow out of the air, while women passed back and forth between him and the fire, bringing him heaps of lobster and maize, squash and onions stewed in maple syrup, beans and duck eggs baked in bear fat. Through it all the pipes kept making the rounds, and the musicians burst into occasional song, only to stop again as they were handed another boss rib of moose, or as the pipe came their way.

The sun set behind the mountains, and the sky faded to black. The air grew still. The speeches began. Glusgebeh orated at length about the coming of the white men and the black man from across the sea. He spoke of their miraculous abilities. He mentioned also the history of the Abnaki, their relations with Cautantowit, and Cautantowit's pleasure in them, as evidenced by his gift of the seeds from his own garden. He spoke of the manito, therefore, that was in the corn and the bean and the squash that the party had that evening consumed. He encouraged Talutah in her venture at Ktaadn. He commended her and Nonanis as guides to the Europeans, expressing his confidence in their power once Cautantowit should be met. He hoped that the journey might be a swift and gentle one, and that upon their arrival at the great mountain, they should find Cautantowit in a communicative mood. He mentioned that the natives of the opposite shoreline of the bay, the Micmacs, even as they spoke, were encroaching on traditionally Abnaki hunting grounds and fishing ledges, and that the coming of the strangers to the Abnaki at this particular moment of history was apposite. He said he hoped the news Cautantowit had for the Abnaki, and the understanding he had of

the arrival of the mariners, was such that Abnaki owner-
ship of the west bank of the bay, and of their familiar
hunting territories, would be secure.

Naturally, all these messages were not entirely clear
to the Europeans. The language barrier, as well as the
surfeit of tobacco, rich food and new experiences, pre-
vented the subtleties of the oration from being intelligi-
ble. Enough of the thrust of it came across, however, for
Atla to grin and lean across to Finbar at its conclusion and
whisper, "As political a speech as we should have heard
on Tara Hill."

Brendan followed Glusgebeh's speech with one of his
own. It was amusing to Atla—and to Finbar when he
caught it—to watch Brendan struggle against his own
befuddlement in making the speech. A man whose voice
normally cut through a half-gale was an object of sympa-
thy as he slurred his opening remarks. However, once
launched, he beat his way against the winds of the celebration until, figuratively, he rounded a point and could
square away. From then until the conclusion of his remarks, he was as beautiful and as riveting as any proper
ship. He wove the tale of their adventures for his listeners.
His love of the crossing was transparent even through the
language barrier, and Finbar felt that the Abnaki must
have felt a breeze of the Western Sea as they listened. He
himself was treated to the experience of the journey as a
legend in its own time, so much more resonant of myths
and longings than it had seemed in the living.

When Brendan sat down, there remained only a
benediction by Barinthus. The Abnaki, as always, were
impressed by the old man, and, though they apparently
understood nothing of the religious concept presented
to them, they were attentive to the delivery. Indeed,
they had reason to be, for Barinthus's voice was at its
most orotund and majestic there before the bonfire on
the edge of Madakamiggosek harbor. All physical weakness, all blindness, seemed gone. He appeared to tower
into the smoke, and his arms encircled the crowd. His
tones were repeated out of the still air when they came
back again from the cliff.

Finbar lay back on an elbow and watched the old

man as he had watched Brendan through the smoke. The
fire leapt with sparks and glitter against a sky made blank
by its light. Light danced on the faces of the Abnaki, on
their eyes and hands. All wore ceremonial garb: the feathers and amulets and pendants and decorative shells themselves glittered. Beyond the circle of light, unseen, was
the flat harbor, the forest and the cliffs. He could hear the
sound of the waterfall interweaving its roar into the
speeches. Spun on the smoke, his mind whirled round the
scene, seeing it from all angles, all planes. He heard the
holy words, and they merged into the litany of the whole
evening, of Glusgebeh's voice, of Brendan's thrilling tale,
of the gentle whispers of Nonanis as she pressed upon him
hunks of lobster meat and maple sugar dainties. He
looked down at himself and found his chest naked, his feet
encased in moccasins decorated with porcupine quills. He
felt the air move cooly on his shaven chin and lips. Again,
he looked around, and the world spun. He saw the blank,
ponderous wheel of the sky. Fifteen days to Ktaadn: the
moon would be waxing gibbous. Nonanis bent down and
passed him the pipe again.

Later, Finbar found himself vying with young Abnaki
men in contests of balance. He defeated several and then
was himself thrown to the ground. Atla and Brendan suffered the same fate. There were other contests in the light
of the fire, and the village looked on and cheered its
champions. At one point, he and Brendan were paired.
They stood with right feet braced against each other, left
feet back, and tried to pull one another down. In the
frenzy of the moment, it came to both of them, suddenly,
that there was real measurement there. Their bodies
were slippery with bear fat, the footing was uneven, they
were exhausted, but they came to quick sobriety, and the
match was heated.

"Come, Finbar," Brendan grunted. "Try me."

"You're going down."

"No chance of that."

The circle around them grew larger, and the shout-
ing was eager. Brendan's strategems were no lower than
Finbar's. The match was even for a long time, and then
Finbar's desire began to subside.

"Give?" Brendan panted.

Finbar smiled, "I hope not."

Finbar's leg was tiring. He tried a trick that an Abnaki had tried on him, and he was almost successful. Brendan redoubled his efforts. Finbar felt his leg slipping. "Damn," he muttered, and he went down.

A cheer went up. Brendan gave Finbar a hand. As they stood face to face with the crowd milling around them, Brendan panted, "Let's get back on the water."

For a moment, Finbar looked deeply into that round, red face. "Tomorrow," he said, and he clasped a tired arm around the captain's shoulder.

"It's the only place we belong," Brendan muttered, clasping him back.

After that contest, the energy of the celebration seemed to wane. The people began to drift away, eager for rest.

Nonanis materialized beside Finbar and took his arm. "You must sleep," she said.

Finbar looked around for Brendan, but he was unable to find him in the crowd. The fire had died down to a pit of coals, and the night began to seep into Finbar's consciousness. He shivered with weariness. It had been the custom of the Europeans to sleep aboard the curragh each night, after the first one, but Finbar allowed himself instead to be propelled toward Talutah's lodge. He brushed through the rawhide doorway and inhaled the fragrance of balsam and sweet grass. A small pile of embers in the hearth made a faint light, showing him the interior, and gleaming on the claws of the lion skin hanging at the head of the couch. Talutah was not there. Nonanis laid him down on a pallet, and she pulled off his moccasins. She brought him a cup of sweet mint tea. His mind whirled. He gave himself up to sleep.

He was hanging just on the edge of slumber when he felt the bearskins move, and dimly he realized that Nonanis had slipped underneath them. With dawning awareness, he discovered that she was naked. Soon, he, too, was naked. Artfully, she held his attention just on this side of unconsciousness for what seemed an interminable time. Then, just when he thought he must die, he groaned heavily against her breasts and tumbled down.

10

EARLY NEXT MORNING, IN thick fog, two canoes set out from Madakamigossek, turned north along the coastline outside the harbor ledges, and disappeared.

Finbar paddled bow in the second canoe. Ahead of him there was little to see except the pointed stern of the lead canoe constantly wavering and disappearing like the tail of a fish. The surface of the bay was still. No sign of the passage of the canoe before him survived on its silvery meander. The tide was making, carrying the two small boats up into the dark embrace of the land. Finbar saw occasional weedy ledges sucking and bubbling as he passed by. Once there appeared beside him a tall overhang of spruce six feet away out of the fog; then it was gone. Now and then, through the fog from ahead, there would come the careless *thunk* of a paddle haft knocked against a wooden gunwale. Otherwise, there was no sound except the liquid hiss of his own bow ripple and the dripping of his paddle blade as he swung it forward out of the water. Missing a stroke, he turned to glance at his companions. Atla huddled in the middle of the canoe between bales of stores and equipment, his knees drawn to his chin, and his red hair lank against wet cheeks. He looked cold. Nonanis paddled at the stern. She had already cast her mantle aside, and she paddled naked from the waist up. The chill made her nipples hard. She took a stroke and, for a second, muscles tensed diagonally across her belly, and her upper arm flattened one breast. With the fog wetting his skin, Finbar recalled the smell of her. There came a hollow in his belly. The woman, however, seemed indifferent to him, with her senses pricked instead for clues of passage. He admired her skill, saw that her paddle never left the water as she plied it: its blade cut forward parallel to their motion and pressed backward perpendicular.

"Paddle," she whispered. "Micmacs near."

Finbar turned forward again and set to.

He imagined Talutah's leading canoe as he had seen it at their departure: Brendan in the bow, impatient to be afloat again; Barinthus and Joseph huddled together in the middle, antiphonally repeating the psalm of the day; the old powwaw belying her flaccid state by leaping aboard and setting a powerful stroke which soon put Finbar's boat behind. When the fog scaled up for a second or two, he saw the others forty or one hundred yards ahead, now off to the starboard, now to the port, and he saw as well the narrowing arms of the bay, the overhang of silent, patient trees.

His palms, though sailor-toughened, were sore already. All nature dripped. A fleet of porpoises passed them—black, big fish as long as canoes—gasping south. Atla sneezed and was shushed by Nonanis. Finbar changed sides. To port, suddenly, an eerie cry like a bedlam laugh, chopped off: a loon perhaps, or a spirit. Paradise was grey, and wet, and she had no need for man.

The first day was hard, though the fog cleared; the second day harder; the third, the worst of all. At noon on the fourth day, the party reached the foot of the falls known as Penobscot.

This fall was the first milestone. They could not feel the effect of the tidal pulses behind them any longer. They were thirty miles inside the forest, clasped tight in its wooden arms, working their way up a narrow silver surface of heavy flowing river that pressed against them and tried to keep them back. Whereas for the first three days they had paddled during the flooding tides and rested during the ebbs, now they pressed on all through the day. On either side was a monotonous prospect of pine, hemlock, fir, birch, spruce, elm, maple, balsam, black ash and white ash. It was impenetrable. Ten feet inside its body, one might be ten miles from the river. No sound, no movement, no light, no smell of the water came there. The only smells were earth, rock and pine waiting through a dry summer for the return of the cold.

There were forces in that forest that slunk. One knew them there, but saw them little. There were others that shrieked, equally jarring to the spirit: squirrels, jays, harmless things enough, but sudden. And there were inexplicable forces, manitos: there were crashings, night and day, that neither slunk nor shrieked but shook the trees and the equilibrium and brought the women to their feet from sleep or noontime rest, arrows glittering in brave defense.

On the river, though it abraded the spirit in its own ways, too, at least there was movement and a sort of vision. Man left the forest the instant his hasty meal or shallow sleep was done, and he spun out onto the surface, pushing hard against the current, glad of the sight of a strip of sky, and of distance along which his eye could adventure. Where the river was narrow, the forest filled half the sky on one side and half the sky on the other. Only in the center above was there a narrow strip of sky across which clouds sailed, and through which now and then could be spied far-off eagles who might span Madakami-gossek to Ktaadn with a single glance of their wild yellow eyes. When the river was more broad, the sky was wider, and the winds over the forest were felt by those in the canoes; but the river in the main was narrow. The surface was mercurial, beautiful in its way—though always against them. Far away, it had only the colors of the sky and the forest; nearer, it was clear, and they could see the green bottom of the river in eight feet of depth. The biggest salmon and trout were down there, and there were eels everywhere.

Having stopped at the top of the Penobscot falls, the party rested on the eastern shore upon low rocks that stuck out into the water. While Atla tickled trout, Nonanis kindled a fire. It amused Finbar to watch Atla's game: as calm and still as a heron he stood, up to his knees in the eddy below a stone, his hands trailing quietly at the surface. Once he had established his presence, the trout forgot him, and with a splash they were, one by one, flung up onto the rocks. Deftly, Talutah caught and gutted them almost before they had stopped wiggling. The hunter's ability tempted Finbar to try, but instead of a trout, he caught a tumble into the stream.

Standing beside Nonanis, still dripping, he pointed at the smoke from the fire and asked, "No more Micmacs?"

"No. They never come this far into the Abnaki forest. Their winter lands are off there." She pointed across the eastern treetops. "Dry your clothes."

Finbar peeled off his leggings and, with a shrug, his breechclout. He spread them on hot rocks while Joseph sneered.

Sitting down again next to Nonanis, he took a stick from her and turned a spitted trout over the flames. On the other side of the fire, Brendan was peeling hot strips of fish filet for Barinthus, who blew on them awhile and then munched them between his gums.

Leaning close to Nonanis, Finbar murmured, "You never speak much to me, during the day."

The woman shrugged. "We are going to Ktaadn. There is nothing to say."

"Yes, but, at night, you—"

Again, the shrug. Her round face became impassive. "We ought not to speak of the nights."

"I've never known a woman like you before."

"You do not know me now. Perhaps when we return . . ."

Finbar studied his fish and decided it needed more heat. He sat back from Nonanis again and tried to make general conversation. "What will the river be like after this?"

She looked at him over her shoulder. She had the disconcerting ability to turn her head on her neck almost all the way around. "For three, four days there are carries. It is hard work. After that, the land opens out into a wider and flatter country where there are lots of islands and bogs. It will be easier there. Eventually we will come to the lake."

"Is that where Ktaadn is?"

Nonanis began eating her fish. "Across the lake, yes," she replied with her mouth full.

Finbar began his own meal. In silence, he watched Nonanis' profile. He could not fathom the woman. Four days' travel already had meant three nights; three nights, during each of which Nonanis had come for him in the

dark—silently out of the forest, as though she were some
night-hunting owl—touched him on the cheek, and led
him away to a spot she had found, where there would be
sweet fern to lie in, or warm sand, or even, once, the airy
bough of a maple. He had begun to know her. He knew
where and how to touch her, a little, but she was always
silent and cleaved herself to him with intensity that somehow kept him distanced. She did not give, she took, and
he was content to be taken. The whole was so mysterious
to him that he floated along with its demands in a sensual
fog. Sometimes, he was not even certain that he desired
the nightly visitation. He would lie awake, his body tired,
and listen for her coming. He never heard her. Then
would come the touch—no words—and they would be off
into the forest. Her knowledge of their surroundings was
unerring. Soon, he would feel her over him, and her hair
would slide across him, and her breathing would grow
more rapid until it stopped completely, and they would
hang somewhere above the sand, above the trees, among
the clouds, until she sighed, and life came back again.
Sometimes, then, she would talk, but it was very little, and
her voice would have a quality like that of a dove, a
throaty mew. Within an hour, they would wing back
through the maze of trunks and boughs, and he would
discover himself, half-sleeping, lying in his furs with his
head under his overturned canoe, and the intent sound of
the river slipping eternally past, a yard or two away.

Oddly, Finbar was commonly more excited after the
event than during it. He desired her then, as he lay under
the canoe, for he felt the ejaculatory emptiness in his gut,
but he recalled none of the anticipatory fullness he ought
to have enjoyed before arriving at that state. Often
enough, he wondered whether it had occurred at all, and
he thought of her as a dream spirit, until, next morning,
he would discover a welt where she had bitten him, or
smell her musk on his hands.

"Nonanis?" he said.

The woman rose to her feet instead of answering and,
tossing her stick into the fire, led Talutah away for a conference.

For a moment, he joked with Atla about the dunking

he had had, but he felt Joseph's unhappy eyes always upon him, and eventually he struggled into his clothes and wandered off along the riverbank by himself. It occurred to him that Nonanis annoyed him by her manner more than she pleased him with her body, for all its stimulation. He wanted to shake the woman, to make her react to him, in the daylight, where he could see her. In fact, at the moment, he wanted the whole metaphysical charade he was engaged upon to be over. He longed for the simple, straight-forward rapine of a pillaging party of legionnaires, if he was to be marching through the wilderness in any case. He wanted low jokes, and wine, and girls in easy dresses. And he wanted a captain who pointed at a village, and you took it, and burned it, and sent what you could grab of the amber to the woman back home. He had spent many weeks in Gaul attached to such raiding and punitive parties, while making his own way gradually northward and westward, and, for all that in his heart he despised them for their uncouth pleasures, he envied them their clearly understood mission.

Nonanis had been correct about the nature of the river above the Penobscot falls. There were frequent rapids and falls. The carries were many. It was discouraging work to load the canoes after a carry, push off into the river and battle upstream for an hour, only to round a slight bend and see another length of broken water ahead, and to know that within minutes it would be time to land, unload, and shoulder the canoes once again. The process was hard, especially on Barinthus, for, encumbered by his growing blindness, he maneuvered himself poorly along the steep, slippery trails by which the carries were made. On this stretch, the party was often too exhausted to fish or hunt, so its diet was unvaried. Bear pemmican, smoked cod, maple sugar and cornmeal grew boring, and Barinthus stopped eating altogether. Joseph, as usual, was fasting as hard as he could in any case, and his weakness was irksome, for it put that much more pressure on Brendan and Talutah, the only truly able-bodied persons aboard the lead canoe. Atla now and then switched places with Brendan in order to give the captain a rest. However, Brendan resented the intimacy between Finbar and Nonanis, and he was an uncomfortable presence in their canoe. Too, the weather was galling. Hot, still days were the rule, with heavy humidity in mid-afternoon, so that each stroke of the paddle or thrust of the pole was burdensome. For clouds, there were high streaks of cirrus during the evenings and the night, but these never brought a change. The dawns were clear, by contrast chilly, and dew-bedecked. They represented the most pleasant moment of the day's work.

By the time the party had made its way through the country of rapids, Finbar had learned much about such things as staying close to the bank in order to avoid the mightier current in the middle. He came to recognize the spots where a backwash eddy would assist the canoe upstream for a foot or two. He had learned about trimming the canoe in the broader stretches of the river, higher either by bow or by stern, depending upon the direction of the wind. He had come to appreciate an island stop as being one somewhat less subject to mosquitoes than a shoreside rest. He had even adopted an Abnaki trick for drinking that allowed him to keep up his stroke: by tipping up his paddle between pulls, runnels of water would pour down its length and into his mouth. But his knees hurt from kneeling, and his shoulders were burnt, and the current beat against him until he groaned. Nor had he come to any conclusion about Nonanis, despite four more nights of her flesh.

So, four days above Penobscot, the country changed from steep to flat. Talutah was content with the progress made. The party was halfway to Ktaadn, and the omens so far were good. Likewise, the Europeans were pleased. Even Joseph could find no fault with the progress. Brendan observed that it was certainly the sabbath. Accordingly, the canoes that night came to rest on the shore of 'Mskukwal, a longish, bare island in the middle of the stream, characterized by a grassy meadow. A fire was kindled on the leeward shoreline, and the party set about establishing a slightly more permanent camp than was its habit. A hearth was built, for example, and Talutah and Atla baked johnnycakes of cornmeal and bear grease. There was little air movement, and the humidity of late afternoon hung stickily upon the landscape. Instead of the usual blank sky, enormous cumulus puffs built vaguely along the western prospect, and the sun shone red behind them. Brendan took one of the canoes across to the eastern shore and made a hunt in the underbrush. Joseph positioned Barinthus so that the old man was comfortable and able to watch, or at least to feel, the changing light of dusk. Nonanis and Finbar, on friendly terms because of the holiday air, gathered armloads of sweet grass to soften the party's beds. Joseph's sneering references to their offer of bedding angered Finbar, as did the man's always contemptuous treatment of Nonanis. Accordingly, Finbar strolled with Nonanis along the opposite shore of the island.

"That is Mandawessoe there," Nonanis commented, pointing upstream to the tip of a wooded island that showed round a bend.

"What is that?"

"The place where Glusgebeh saw the porcupine."

"I don't understand."

"I show you. Come." Smiling, the woman took Finbar by the hand. She led him back to the camp and set off with him in the small canoc. As the two passed where Joseph knelt among the drooping grasses, the monk lifted his face toward them and called out.

"Those who fornicate shall not inherit the Kingdom. So sayeth Saint Paul."

Finbar stopped paddling and called back, "It is you who are mean of heart. That is the evil in Paradise."

"Pagan, God's sword is long."

"I am an ironsmith, remember. I make swords." Finbar bent angrily back to his paddling.

When they had pulled away from Joseph, Nonanis called softly from the stern, "This is for Cautantowit, this battle."

Finbar turned back to the woman, and he said, "No. Among us, it is for me. It was for Brendan before because he is captain, but we have arrived now. Now, it is for me."

Soon, the couple drew close to the shore of Mandawessoe. There was a spit at its southern end where a canoe might be landed. Finbar swung himself over the side as they came up and dropped knee-deep into the river. He pulled the boat close so that Nonanis could step ashore dry shod, and then the two of them lifted it off the pebbly bottom and beached it above the water. Away from Joseph, Finbar felt in better spirits, and he tickled the girl, which made her impatient.

"Come," Nonanis said, "I show you this place," and she pushed her way through the screen of trees into the wood that covered the island. The island must at one time have been burnt over, for the wood was a thinner one than was common even along this clearer stretch of the river. Here and there, a burnt stump showed by its relative girth the youthfulness of the trees that had grown up around it. Underfoot, the ground was damp, for the island was a low one; but there were patches of dry footing. Thick forests of raspberry canes choked the damper spots. The raspberries were just ripening, and the smith and the woman made a pleasant feast of them as they wended a slow way through the trees. Nonanis seemed to be seeking a particular place. More than once, she retraced her steps or stood irresolute as she attempted to judge her bearing among the new growth that had appeared since the last time she was ashore on Mandawessoe.

"Here it is," she exclaimed finally, and she brought them to an opening beside a large boulder where the ground was cut away and a rudimentary cave had been created. "This is the spot."

"This is what spot?"

The light in the small hollow in the middle of the island was greenish and dimming as the sun dropped into the western overcast. The air was so sluggish that the birds did not even greet the ending of the day with much enthusiasm. Somewhere eastward a fox barked.

Nonanis told Finbar to sit down, and then, curled against his knees, she related a story.

Some years before, Glusgebeh, a consummate hunter, had been camped in this very spot during the course of an autumn's hunt. His luck had been miserable. He had been out ten days, and he had seen nothing more than a weasel. It was manito, for the man's prowess was known even beyond Abnaki lands, and this was the season when the larger game commonly came down from the heights and visited the shores of the river to mate and to escape the cold that killed the fodder in the mountains.

It was evening, and Glusgebeh kindled a fire. The very hearth upon which he did so could still be seen by pulling aside the fallen leaves—Nonanis demonstrated—and beside that fire he lay down to sleep. He was disturbed in the night by a wheezing and scuffling noise, and he awoke to see two eyes peering yellowly at him just outside the range of his small embers. He made a noise, and the eyes turned away. Later, he was awakened a second time. Again, the eyes were staring at him, almost as though fired by a human hatred. It seemed, in fact, that the face—for he could see it somewhat better this time—was one which he knew. However, when he again made a noise to frighten the beast away, he saw when it turned that it was only a porcupine. It was in the early hours before dawn that Glusgebeh was awakened for the third time. It was the same animal, only this time it was clear to Glusgebeh that the porcupine wore the face of a powwaw—the man who was powwaw before Talutah—who was an enemy of Glusgebeh's. Now before he had gone to sleep after the second visitation, Glusgebeh had armed himself with a heavy stick, and he rose up suddenly and threw the stick hard at the face of his enemy leering out at him from the body of the porcupine. His aim was true. He hit the face right across the nose, and the porcupine squealed with pain and tumbled away. At this point, Glusgebeh said to himself that he would have no more ill-luck on his hunt, and, in fact, such was the case, for it was during this hunt that he tracked and killed near Kineo the gigantic cow moose, for which exploit he was most famous.

Finbar was appreciative of the story, and he stroked the woman's hair as she told it.

"That is not the end of the tale," Nonanis said. She turned so that she was staring at the smith, and, with a lowered voice, she reported, "When Glusgebeh returned to the village, he sought out the powwaw, but he was told that the powwaw was ill. Pressing into the man's lodge, he saw that the illness was from a wound, and that the wound was to the face. The man had been struck a hard blow with a stick."

There was still some small light in the dell. Finbar felt a shiver of divinity. The deepening dusk somehow brought the action closer, and he sensed around him the magical forces that the Abnaki sought to manipulate. Nonanis's eyes had grown round, and he was compelled by their darkness. Around the man and the woman the air hung thickly in the leaves, and the sound of the river forever rolling to the sea was loud.

"He had changed himself into a porcupine?" Finbar asked, hushed.

"It is a powwaw's power."

"Is it your power?"

"I am learning only."

"Is it Talutah's?"

"Come," she said, and she reached for his shoulder.

He resisted. "Is it Talutah's?"

"Before it is night, Finbar, come here."

The experience of their bodies was different this time from the way it had ever been. Whereas Nonanis had before been distant, now she was caught with him in the lushness of the senses. They explored one another as they had never done. Nonanis was full of honey, and of glue, and of all things slow and warm. He could scarcely catch his breath. She caressed him with her lips. She bent before him as he remembered the Greek woman bending, with her hair thrown forward in a black fan, and the dim light softening her buttocks. Another time, she knelt above him with her face thrown back, and her eyes closed. She cupped her breasts, and then she looked down at him, and he could see even in the darkness that her nostrils were wide, and her teeth clenched. He had a sudden image of her pregnant, of her breasts and belly swollen, and he strained to reach the inner heart of her, to touch that quick of life.

In the dark, they lay cooling among the rumpled leaves. She had her head tucked into his neck and an arm and a thigh across him. He smelled the bear grease in her hair, and he liked the smell.

"What is Finbar?" she murmured.

"How do you mean?"

"What is the name?"

He chuckled. "It is a hero's name where I come from. It was given to me after a battle. I made the weapons for the winning side. It is not my real name. I was named Adeodatus by my mother."

"What is that?"

"Gift of God."

"Of Cautantowit?"

"It might be, I suppose."

"It is. You are manito. You are powwaw maybe. You have the power to change." She giggled. "You change me."

He laughed, too. "You change yourself, Nonanis."

Suddenly she was uncomfortable. He felt her laughter die.

"What did I say?" he asked.

She pulled her arm and leg away. "You must not speak of it."

"I didn't mean . . . It was a passing comment."

"We are drawing close to Ktaadn. You must not speak of it. Do not speak of the changes."

"I'm sorry. I meant nothing."

"Sometimes I haven't the power to resist."

"Nonanis, I won't mention it again."

There was a pause, and, with renewed good spirits, she said, "You know what Nonanis is?"

"No. What?"

"Small breasts."

He laughed and reached out in the dark and touched one. "Hardly appropriate."

"I was younger then," she laughed.

After a few more minutes, they rose, brushed the leaves from their bodies, and strapped on once more their loin cloths and belts.

"Do you know the way?" he whispered.

"Of course," she replied, but in the dark her voice had assumed again that coolness and distance he recalled during their earlier couplings.

He regretted its return. He would not allow its return. He stopped her as she was about to move away. The continued heaviness of the air, along with the mysteriousness of the island, caused him again to whisper, but what he said was fervent nonetheless. He slipped from his wrist a bronze bracelet that he had fashioned of an old deadeye strop during the slow days of the sail, and he pressed it into her hand. "Take this," he pleaded. "It is mine. I give it to you. I want you to wear it."

The action seemed to shock her. She gasped. "You cannot do that. Oh, Finbar, you cannot do that."

"Why not?" He was taken aback by her reaction. "I care for you."

"Because, with my people, it is . . . I cannot take it."

"I don't care what it is."

"I do."

The two stood with both their hands on the bracelet in such deep darkness as not even to see the loom of the other.

After a few moments, Nonanis released her grip. "I cannot take it."

Finbar took a breath. "Whatever it means, I mean that thing."

"You do not know what you are saying."

"I think perhaps I do."

"But you are manito."

"So are you, to me."

Again, they were silent.

Finally, Nonanis whispered, "After we have come to Ktaadn, and after we have gone away, then we shall speak of it. Not until then, Finbar, please."

"As you desire."

Before they turned out of the dell, Nonanis's hand touched Finbar's chest tentatively. He had not rid her of the diffidence, but underlying that diffidence was an air of curiosity, as though he had penetrated somewhere into the night mystery of this woman and had caught her spirit just before it flew. The spirit touched him now, on his neck, his cheek. It touched his mouth. A last time, it touched him over the heart, and then it vanished.

"Follow me," he thought he heard, and he stepped into the dark where he thought she had gone.

Finbar pushed through a screen of birch leaves and found himself beside the river. The air was somewhat cooler outside the wood than it had been inside, although it was equally heavy. The river was black, reflecting the black sky. He could barely make out the western bank as a blacker silhouette against the heavens. A rustling to his left caught his attention, and he saw Nonanis as she slipped between the water and the land. He followed her. In a few paces, they reached the spit of gravel where they had beached the canoe, but there was no canoe there.

"Are you certain this is the spot?" he whispered.

"They have taken it," she replied.

"Who?"

"The sour one."

"Joseph?"

"He and the one with red hair."

"How can you be certain?"

"I know it, that's all "

Finbar was furious. "Why? For what reason?" he choked. He raised his voice and bellowed down the river. "Atla! Where's my canoe?"

Nonanis hushed him, and, had she not, he would still have quieted, for the yell fell awkwardly upon the black night; it was answered only by an *harrumph* of toads, an increased surge of the endless river, and the sudden squawk of a heron nesting along the shore.

"Why?" he whispered to the powwaw.

"I do not know. You have an enemy there, that I know."

Finbar cursed.

"What shall we do?"

"I want to speak to the bastard. We'll swim."

"The river is manito at night," she warned.

"I don't care. I have my own power, and I need to have a talk with that . . . Joseph."

Nonanis laid her hand on Finbar's arm. "Don't go."

"I will go. You may stay if you like, but I'm going."

He stepped forward until he came to the edge of the river, and he splashed out into its flow. The water was colder than he had expected it to be. He advanced a few more steps. Farther away from the land, the power of the current was more apparent to him. His feet began to bury themselves in shifting gravel and sand. He looked back at the spit. He could not see Nonanis.

"Where are you?" he called in a whisper.

"Here," she answered from beside him.

Finbar turned to stare downstream. "Shouldn't we see the fire?"

"It's a little past the bend." She touched him. "Are you going?"

"I've never liked swimming," he muttered.

"We could stay."

"I want that Joseph." He took two more steps into the river and found himself skidding down a slippery slope. The water rose to his chest before he knew it. The cold took his breath. The power of the flow pressed against him; his balance was gone. "Nonanis," he called, swimming stubbornly.

"Here I am," the woman said, again beside him.

Finbar looked ahead of himself downstream. He could see almost nothing. His eyes were at the level of the water. The swimming was not difficult, once he had oriented himself. He had merely to stay afloat, and the current would speed him in the right direction. The difficulty lay with knowing where he was. The sky and the river banks were dark. The water was cold, silent—now that he was out in it—and swift. He floated in a sitting position with his feet ahead of himself as a bumper against anything he should come against. It was good that he did so, for he rasped across a bar before he could catch hold, and spun, and again he was in deep water. He called out to Nonanis to warn her of the bar, but he heard no reply. He called again. Off to his left somewhere, he thought he heard a gurgling answer, but he couldn't be certain. He slid down a riffle between stuck logs, and he became too busy to call Nonanis again. Once more, he was spun around. He realized he did not know whether he was facing upstream or down. The river surged along at the same rate, whichever way he faced. He began to grow fearful, and his paddling increased. He thought he could tell from the paddling which way was up and which down, but at that moment, he bumped into a submerged rock and realized he had been entirely wrong. He swung around, called the woman, and choked on a sudden mouthful of water. The river was colder by the minute, or so it seemed. It was incredible that so placid-seeming a river should have so much force, once he was in it.

Again, he hit a rock, but this time he was able to grab on as he swept past, and he held himself. His head went under water before he was able to get his feet pulled up against the downstream side of the rock. He felt downward with his toes for a holding place. The rock was slippery with algae, and the current had drilled a deep hole behind it. He prodded without success, and, meanwhile, his grip was weakening. He managed to get one leg wrapped around the shoulder of the rock and had the chance to relax his grip for an instant. The press of the water flowing down from Ktaadn nearly ripped him away. He gripped once more, and this time he had enough purchase to pull himself against the current to the upstream face of the rock and to anchor himself astride it. He was facing toward the current. The water beat against his chest and burst upward across his throat. Carefully, he turned his head in order to catch a glimpse downstream. Over his right shoulder he thought he saw a glow hidden by the loom of a bank, and he took that glow to be the campfire on 'Mskukwal. He had covered most of the distance. He needed to strike out to his right, across the current, in order not to be swept right past the island and onward toward the sea. He wondered where Nonanis was, but he took her to be a better swimmer than he, and he did not especially fear for her safety. About himself, however, he was not so sanguine. To move across the current would be a difficult feat. He realized he was scared. The river was much more powerful than he had imagined; the sky was darker; the night was filled with powers that were manito. His bad leg hurt. The water beating against him was chill, and it seemed to enter him

at the mouth and nose—literally so—and to fill him with
the chaotic energy of this night river. His own will was
being submerged to its. In a panic, he gathered himself for
a push to the right. He tensed. He sprang out against the
current, but even as he did so, he felt it catch him and
throw him back past his rock. He was adrift once more,
and he had made no distance sidewards. Choking, he
raised his head above the water. He stared wildly around.
The glow he had seen was almost opposite him now. He
kicked out. He thrashed his arms. Now, it was moving
past. He tried to fight upwards against the current. He
saw the glow begin to recede. He despaired, and he
yelled. His mouth was full of water: there was no sound
except a wet bleat that was carried away, even as he was
being carried away by the heavy-shouldered roll of the
river current.

He struck a log. He ripped his shins trying to grip it.
He caught it. The current dragged him under, but he held
on. He rose from the water, gasping. He could no longer
see the glow. He held his head above the river until he
had some breath back, and then he experimented by
moving along the log, ever so slowly, toward the eastern
bank. The log held. It gave him purchase. He moved five
feet, then eight, then ten. He began to hope the log might
lead him all the way to the shore. He had pulled himself
fifteen feet when his toes felt the first hint of gravel bottom. Within minutes, he was in water only as deep as his
knees. Unsteadily, he left his grip on the log and stumbled
toward the shore. The water now seemed lazy and warm,
and he cursed it as he dropped exhausted beside the butt
of the log and panted on dry land.

Half an hour later, he had made his way up the river
bank through the tangle of alders and raspberries and
sumac to a spot opposite the fire on 'Mskukwal. He could
see by its light that the company was still enjoying its
evening repast. The sight infuriated him. There was no
sign of Nonanis, and, for the first time, he grew alarmed
for her safety. Joseph, though, was much in evidence,
having apparently broken his fast, for he was gesturing
idiotically with the haunch of a rabbit, and laughing at
some story of Atla's. Brendan lounged on the ground be-

side the fire. Two spitted salmon broiled lazily. Barinthus seemed asleep under his canoe. And the other canoe was drawn up alongside.

The sight of the evidence of perfidy drove Finbar, in a frenzy, across the water that separated him from the island. Fortunately, the river was not especially deep at that point, but it would not have mattered how deep it was, so angry was he. He came charging up out of the river and into the middle of the circle of fire before anyone had the chance to react. He grabbed the thin monk by the throat and shook him.

"You bastard! You miserable son of a bitch! If Nonanis is drowned, I'll kill you, you scum!"

Everyone bounded to his feet with shouts of consternation.

Finbar flung the monk from him against the bank of the island. "I hate to touch such filth!"

"What's going on?" Brendan bellowed, and he gripped Finbar around the shoulders from behind as the smith stepped in to attack Joseph again. Brendan's grip was powerful, but Finbar broke it and turned on the captain.

Brendan held up his hand. "You shall not strike me!"

Finbar lowered his fist. "I'll kill that self-righteous prig."

"It was a joke," Atla was saying. "Dear Jesus, man, it was a joke. Don't you see it was a joke?"

"Where's Nonanis, then? If it was such a joke, where's my—"

"Your what?" Joseph croaked, struggling to his knees. "Your whore?"

"Don't," Brendan cried as Finbar leapt at the monk, but it was too late. The men grappled. Brendan and Atla tried to intervene. The struggle was a short one, with gasped breath, and spitted curses. Finbar got the better of it. He raised Joseph off the ground and turned to the river. Brendan tried to tackle him. Atla hung on his arm. Yet, with a bellow, Finbar flung the writhing monk out over the beach and into the river.

"You fool," Atla shouted, and he jumped into the river after Joseph. "He can't swim."

"Neither can I, hardly." Finbar turned back, and bellowed into the night, "Nonanis!"

"It was a joke," Brendan soothed. "They would have come for you."

"Maybe a joke to Atla," Finbar spat. He gestured at the monk, whom Atla was dragging from the river. "Maybe to Atla, but not to him."

Finbar by now had the small canoe launched, and it toppled against the current as he pawed for a paddle and yelled out the woman's name once more.

Joseph came up, sputtering. Atla steadied him on his feet. The thin man wiped the water from his face and growled at Finbar, "Fornicator. Trafficker with harlots. Pagan nemesis of this expedition. I've known you from the first, even as Brother Barinthus has known you."

"Barinthus has three times your intelligence. He knows me for what I am, not for what his infernal religion wants me to be." Finbar shoved off into the current.

Joseph swelled at this insult to the Church. "Infidel, speak small!" He lunged into the river and, grabbing the stern of the canoe, tipped it until it capsized.

Finbar heaved up out of the water and swung the paddle, which missed. Brendan grappled with him, and the man's enormous arms pinned the sputtering Finbar. Atla clenched Joseph's robe and hair. The two antagonists glared at one another, their faces limned by the fire, their bodies glistening with river water and sweat.

"Finbar?" It was Nonanis's voice.

The smith spun around. Into the light of the fire walked Nonanis. She was dripping, but she smiled. Talutah followed her, offering her a mantle to put on.

Finbar bounded to her side. "Are you all right? I thought you were drowned."

"And you. I thought you were gone as well."

The two smiled at each other, and Finbar helped her with her mantle.

"See?" said Joseph behind him in a clear voice. "See how he flies to his whore?"

"Silence, Joseph!" Brendan commanded. "We'll have no more violence."

"I am not afraid."

Finbar called backwards, never taking his eyes off Nonanis's face, "You ought to be, monk."

Talutah, who had been standing back, suddenly strode forward, and she confronted the bedraggled anchorite. "This land is sacred to Cautantowit. You shall not speak this way while in his land. You shall be silent, you." She spun around and took them all in. "You shall not fight among yourselves. You must carry nothing into his land except your own spirits. You may not carry hatreds, for they hurt you, and they hurt him. What hurts you, he will make you feel. I will not allow this journey to be destroyed by envy and anger."

Joseph said, "You are a woman, and you are a pagan. I need to say no more."

"Have a care," the Abnaki replied warningly. "This is not the manner of speech that is right."

"Your right is nothing to me. I am a *peregrinus* of Christ. He is my master. I am ready at any moment to die."

"You are too ready to die," Finbar said. "You have no life."

"I live in the eternal Grace of the Father."

"Kill yourself, then. Your religion is charnel worship. I have said it before. You all desire to die, for you have no idea how to live. So die. Why stand around breathing up the air?"

"I don't desire to die," Atla replied quickly. "Not all Christians do. It's an unfair accusation."

"Then you have a strong will to resist the temptation. I hate the narrowness of the man who rejects life for fear of its fullness, and then scorns it!"

"By which you mean me?" Joseph asked.

"You, Joseph, may your god help you."

"I'll not be patronized."

"You can't avoid being patronized."

Again, Talutah intervened. She was angry. She pressed her thin old body toward Joseph. Her hands were on her hips. "You are a young man," she said. "Do not be a rabbit in the snow, sitting and counting flakes, saying, 'Coming down, coming down, coming down.'"

"What?" Joseph's response was high-pitched.

"The rabbit does nothing in the snow, and every time he counts another flake, he drops another pellet."

Joseph understood. "I do not simply exist, woman!" he shouted. "I am on a pilgrimage."

"We Abnaki know about pilgrimages. If you are searching out the spirits, you must work. Paddle. Pole. Carry. Hunt. Cook. Tend the fire. I see you do none of these things. The old man I can understand. A young man like you, I cannot. It is not in the manner of our country. This is no pilgrimage."

"I care nothing for your country's manner, woman. I live in God's own land."

"This is Cautantowit's land."

"Your god is folly!"

Talutah walked closer to the monk and looked up at him. Her face had grown grim. "You will regret those words."

"Regret what? The Lord is the only true God."

The woman's voice was intensely calm as she turned away. She stooped to pick up a pebble, and she rolled the stone in her hand. "You seek death, poor man, but you will not find it as you expect it. You will regret that scorn of the manitos of this land. I am powwaw. I have spoken."

Talutah stepped up the bank, and, taking Nonanis's arm, she walked into the darkness. Her words had been so forcefully spoken, however, that the Europeans said nothing for a long moment after her departure. The tableau was broken by Barinthus struggling to his feet and inquiring what all the shouting had been about.

Joseph gave a wild laugh. "Trouble with the whores," he said.

Finbar sprang.

This new melee was interrupted by Barinthus's voice, and here was the Barinthus of the whale and the nocturnal singing. When the men's faces turned his way, he seemed to have swelled. The fight ground to a halt. The combatants broke apart and shifted their weight on the scattered sand. The old man deflated. "Stop," he sighed. "This is shameful."

Joseph was contrite. "Forgive me."

"You are forgiven."

Finbar made a rude noise and turned away.

"Listen to me," Barinthus ordered, and Finbar turned back. "You risk the anger of your companions because of your conduct with that woman."

Finbar replied haughtily, "At Drumhallagh, there were married monks. Even the Abbot sired a family. You have no case against me."

"Married, yes. The Church demands different levels of asceticism from each person, for it recognizes that each possesses a different gift. It does not tolerate fornicators, however. That woman is not your wife."

"She is free within her own people to do what she does."

"Her people are animals," Joseph scoffed.

"Be still!" Barinthus roared. "You, Joseph, have not understood the truth. None of you has understood the truth, except Brendan, I believe. In the middle of the wilderness, in the middle of the river, we are Abnaki, and Christian, and pagan. We are *all* animals. Paradise shaped the wilds, and the wilderness reigns. Look around you. Listen! Don't you hear the sweet, soft voice of God in the rushing of the river, in the trill of the birds, in the snap of the fire? You pray to God at mealtimes and at the hours. You speak to Him when rising and when drifting off to sleep. You have such constant converse with Him, and yet you do not understand. We are in Paradise! We have need of nothing—nothing at all—but to listen to the music to which we listen, to look upon the light which we see, and to be filled with the fragrance that is in the land. *Paradiso semper meior!* Beyond Paradise, in the world, there is meaning in the distinction among Abnaki, Christian and pagan. Here, there is no meaning in such distinction. You, Joseph, are as much an animal as this pagan, even—yes— as that woman you so despise for her lustfulness and for her beauty. You recognize the beauty in a blackbird—I have heard you say it—and in the soft fur of a rabbit. Yet you do not recognize the beauty in that creature, that woman, and she is of your own kind. God made her beauty, Joseph. She is as nearly a rabbit or a bird, *when she is in Paradise,* as are you or I. In Paradise, the man, the woman and the rabbit are as one, for they all dwell equally in Christ's heart and His love shines upon them. Put Christ in your heart, as you are always in His."

The old man's tone changed to peevishness. "I think the weather is changing, and I am tired. Why do I have to explain all this to them, Brendan? Why don't they understand?"

He collected his mantle around his thin ribs and bent his way back toward his bed.

No one said anything for a time. Slowly, the camp was put to rights. Finbar and Joseph came face to face.

"Atla thought it would be funny," Joseph offered.

"Don't scoff at Talutah's power," Finbar offered in return.

The air was as sticky as ever. Finbar lay down on the bed of grass he had gathered with Nonanis. He wondered where she was. There was little sound except Brendan's snore and the river's just-audible rush. Joseph muttered to himself. After a time, the monk quieted, and then there was the sound of far-off thunder rumbling quietly in the west. Brendan turned over and ceased to snore. Finbar found that he could not sleep. He rose at last and made his way out of the tiny glow of light cast by the embers and squatted beside the river, looking blindly into the wet darkness before him. He realized that he was frightened of the wilderness. The swim down the river in the dark had been a shock. Paradise was more powerful than they were, as Barinthus had said. He himself did not have the power to control it. He suspected the Nazarenes also lacked the power, and that Joseph's increased anger was symptomatic of the fact. He hoped that the powwaw could control this, her people's wilderness, for he had heard Nonanis admit her own fear. If Talutah herself could not control Paradise, then nothing stood between the party and whatever did control it, and that, despite the Nazarene claim to the contrary, was terrifying. As he squatted, a spatter of rain fell around him, and then it passed away. It had not even wetted him. The air was filled almost to flowing. It was hard to breathe.

Eventually, Finbar's emotions began to quiet, and he

understood that he could sleep. He began to rise. Even as he did so, there was a soft footfall to his left toward the fire, and he heard a quiet cough such as he had not heard since he was a young man in the Egyptian hills. He froze. Half-erect, he peered toward the firelight. A sinuous shape moved for a second between himself and the fire, and the cough came again, even softer than before. The light was dim, and he couldn't be certain of what he saw. It was gone before he could focus more clearly. Fear made the hair crawl on his neck and back, and he felt a sudden ache in his groin. Whatever had been there was no longer to be seen. He straightened his knees, realizing that his heart was tripping fast, and that he was panting. His nostrils quested for the scent of what he thought he had seen. For a long time, nothing happened. No breeze stirred to carry a scent. No sound came that was not the pacific sound of the night river. Gradually, his heart slowed and his breathing stilled. He shook his stiffened legs and took a step toward the camp. He walked several paces. He was on the edge of the firelight. Just then, the cough was repeated, and, across the glow of the fire, he thought he saw a sudden flicker of feline eyes. Fear rushed back. He froze. The lion blinked. Its eyes seemed to peer deeply into his own. Then it was gone.

Finbar roused the camp. Dry grass flared in the fire, and the night moved back. Cautiously, within the circle of their torches, Finbar, Brendan and Atla patroled the perimeter. There was no spoor. Great footprints in the dry earth might as well have been something else. Atla bent to sniff them but could catch no lingering scent. Finbar wondered whether he had been asleep and had dreamt the beast: so much was fearsome in this wild. The men gathered in the middle of the camp.

"Joseph is right," Finbar whispered. "We should turn back."

Brendan caressed his crucifix. "In Paradise?"

"I don't care any more for that. There's a power here. I have felt things like it, in Greece, in Egypt . . ."

The monks looked round at the hovering night. Finally, gesturing at Brendan, Atla whispered, "He has power, too."

Finbar did not know whether his friend meant Brendan or the Nazarene god.

"Suppose no one can control it," he asked. "What then?"

"I put my faith in Brendan."

"Isn't this tempting your god?" Finbar whispered. "You've come to Paradise. To go farther is challenging god. Even in Paradise there has to be somewhere more paradisal."

"We must go on," Brendan said, deliberately settling down once more into his blankets. "God made this place; we are here in it. He would not have put us here if he did not intend us to continue."

Finbar looked at Atla. "Come with me. I want to check about Nonanis and Talutah."

"There is no lion, Finbar. I'm going to sleep."

Finbar crept across the flat of the island, alone, spear and torch trembling in his hands. He thought he knew the place where the women slept, but when there, he found no sign of them.

"Nonanis!" he whispered into the heavy air.

Something was watching him, but he saw no eyes.

"Nonanis! Where are you?"

The something was closer, he felt. He spun. Nothing. The river signed heavily down from Ktaadn to the sea. Dry grasses brushed his calves. His bad leg suddenly ached. "Where are you?" he whispered again, softer.

There was a sound behind him. He whirled around, spear brandished, and his torch snuffed out. Terrified, he dropped to the ground. No more sound came. No motion was transmitted by the sand under his cheek. No scent alarmed his searching nose. But it was there, whatever it was, closer still: he knew it. His lungs could draw no air. He felt he must die a little.

Then it was gone; like that. Sensation rushed back to him. He rose to his knees and was dizzy. He tasted vomit at the back of his throat.

Warm fingers closed suddenly over his throat from behind. He made a strangled cry.

"Finbar?" The fingers relaxed a little. "Is that you?"

"Nonanis?"

He spun and caught her in his arms.

"I thought it was the thin one."

"Why? What would he be doing?"

"He will come one night, Finbar. To kill me, or to lie with me. I know it. He has no way else to live."

"Nonanis, there is something here."

"What do you mean?"

"Something I couldn't see. Something . . . at first, it was a . . . I think it was a lion, but—"

Nonanis had gone rigid. A moment later, she whispered into his chest, "Not now, not yet."

"What did you say?"

"Nothing."

"But what did you say?"

"We are still eight, ten nights from Ktaadn, and he is here."

"Cautantowit?"

He felt her nod.

"Who *is* Cautantowit?"

"The greatest manito."

Finbar looked around into the scarcely penetrable darkness. The hair on his neck stirred once more. "You are invoking him."

"I do not know that 'invoking.' This is his forest, his river, his night. We are here, and this is his."

"Where is Talutah?"

"She is not here."

"Where is she? What do you mean?"

"It is better not to ask."

"I have to ask! Brendan will not listen. I have to know."

She shook her head. "There are powers—"

"I have power, too!"

"Not this kind, Finbar. Nor does Brendan, nor anyone. Talutah is of the lion-kind. It is her dream."

"This is crazy," he said, but he clung to her. "What dream?"

"Her dream. The lion is hers. I told you."

For a long time, the man and the woman stood clutched together beside the invisible river. Finally, Finbar relaxed his arms. "Poor Brendan," he sighed.

She nodded. "All of us are small, and he is big."

As before, knowing exactly where she was in the darkness, Finbar's night-owl woman led him back to his side of the island until he could see the glow of the fire. She parted from him there.

Brendan and Atla stirred as Finbar came out of the darkness into the light of the fire. The latter was dozing with a spear across his thighs, back propped against a canoe.

"Are the women well?" the hunter asked.

"I was right," Finbar replied tiredly, slipping out of his leggings and arranging his bed, "but there is nothing we can do about it."

Atla looked at him uncomprehendingly, and Finbar said no more.

At dawn, because this was Brendan's sabbath, Mass was celebrated. Joseph choked on the bit of johnnycake that was being used for the Body, and the sacrament came to a halt as one and then the other of the Europeans tried to help him get his breath back. It was a brooding, colorless, strangely cold day. No birds sang.

Talutah and Nonanis watched the awkward ceremony. Finbar stood by Nonanis, but when he made to speak to the powwaw, the girl pulled him away. "Not now," she whispered. "Do not mention it. Please, Finbar. Not now."

"Why not?"

"Do as I say. I know this land."

"Only because you ask it," he agreed grudgingly. But he watched Talutah watch the Nazarenes, and there was a hint of . . . something—he could not identify it—beneath her impassive expression.

By common and unspoken consent, the camp was broken soon after the morning meal, despite the fact that the plan had been to rest all day, and the party was glad to leave the unhappy shores of 'Mskukwal. Passing up the western side of Mandewessoe, Finbar searched for the spot where he and Nonanis had spent their dusk hour, but he was unable to identify it. Nonanis gave him no clue, her attitude being distant, exactly as it had been at the start of the journey. Finbar fell to brooding about the lion, and about the ill timing of its appearance.

That day passed, and the next. The weather continued to be depressing. Low, furry clouds sent down spatters of tiresome rain, but there was no break. The humid atmosphere stripped the world of color: grey water flowed between banks of grey trees, and the grey sky drooped overall. The camp that night was a sorry one, perched between forest and river, and life in it was dull. Atla tried once to lighten their spirits with the music of his pipe, but even he saw that it was inappropriate to the place and gave it up. No one troubled much to fish. Though having twice bathed in the river, Finbar felt dirty. Most disconcerting, however, was the sense of a beastly presence that hung over the camp from dusk to dawn. The sense was ubiquitous, but the evidence was only in one hollow cough that bumped its way through the trees when the fire was low. It was manito. And in the night Nonanis did not come, though Finbar desired her intensely.

Two nights later, the party camped on a muddy spit where a small creek meandered from the west into the main stream. The mosquitoes were especially bad in this spot, for the land behind the spit was mucky and swampy. The men lay in their beds, hoping not to hear what by now they knew they must hear from the night forest. Of them all, Joseph was the most restless, though he denied the presence completely. Nevertheless, his prayers were loud and garbled, and Brendan had several times needed to quiet him down. The hours of dark passed one after the other, and there was no sound of the ghostly lion. Eventually, Finbar fell into a shallow sleep. In it, he could hear Brendan's snore and Barinthus's octogenarian wheeze. From across the river, he heard repeated the low, unsettling *whoo* of the screech owl. The river itself gurgled past a rocky obstruction with the sound of water running perpetually down a deep drain.

A shriek rent the air. Finbar leapt up. He was disoriented by milling bodies. Joseph whirled in the center of the camp with a flaming brand in his fist. Sparks sang through the air. The lion was monstrous in the flaring light, hissing and spitting at the fire that the monk thrust at its face. Finbar's eyes caught the sight of corded muscles quivering under tawny fur. He felt a momentary

relief that, at last, they had seen it—and then the beast
was gone.

Each man spun, searching, straining. Atla panted for
a chance to use his spear. Barinthus felt the darkness
around him with his crooked hands, blind eyes grey in the
holes of his face. A spark from the brand sizzled against
a pile of reeds hacked away from the sleeping area,
smoked, and began to grow.

The lion burst into the camp from the forest behind
the canoes. It swept one of the boats aside. It roared.
Joseph screamed as the animal bore down on him. Atla
flung his spear and missed. Brendan bellowed at Joseph to
run. Barinthus was knocked off balance and fell into the'
lion's path. The lion stopped, its enormous, feline head
lowered threateningly inches from the prostrate man's
face and neck. All movement ceased. Everything was frozen for one moment in time, except the lion's tail, which
lashed from side to side. The moment drew out into another moment. The fire among the reeds grew, and with
it grew the illumination of the scene. The lion's fangs
were bared. Saliva dripped on Barinthus's neck. The muscles of the lion's haunches were trembling.

Then a curious thing happened. Barinthus raised one
hand until it was just below the lion's breast. Gently, he
laid his palm on the lion's fur. He pushed. There was a
moment's hesitation in the beast, but Barinthus's firmness
persisted. Then the lion's head rose. Its attention turned
from the old man and swept the camp, its fierce eyes
lighting on each man by turns. It lifted a forepaw and
stepped casually away from Barinthus. The monk rolled
onto his side and drew his legs up, clasping his knees.

The lion stood still in the middle of the ring of men.
The fire grew. Again, the lion swept its eyes from face to
face. It stopped when it reached Joseph, and the monk
began to wither under its stare. It took a step toward the
man. Finbar saw that Joseph's face was dead-white, and
that he would at any moment collapse. Atla saw the same
and stooped toward a rock. The lion twitched its head in
the hunter's direction, and Atla's movement ceased, but
he had gripped the rock. The lion turned again toward
Joseph, one step closer. Joseph backed away, his teeth

chattering. Atla gathered himself. Then the lion suddenly shook its head and turned and stalked out of the camp.

Joseph groaned and fainted. That brought the camp alive. Atla armed himself. Brendan bent over the unconscious Joseph and lifted him into the circle of the fire. Finbar armed himself as well, and then he and Atla controlled the fire among the reeds. When they turned back, Barinthus was sitting with his knees drawn back into his shoulders, rocking on his buttocks, whining tiredly and drooling. Joseph had wet himself. There was the acrid smell of urine in the air. Brendan was attempting both to soothe his uncle and to prop Joseph up so that he might regain consciousness more quickly. The captain nodded at Atla, and the hunter drifted out of the circle of light, on guard. Finbar came forward and bent to attend to the old man. He held Barinthus's shoulders and kneaded his tight, stringy muscles. Gradually, in the course of a quarter of an hour, the monk's moaning ceased, and he began to be aware of his surroundings. Joseph remained unconscious.

Barinthus shook himself free of Finbar's hands. The smith sat back on his heels. Only then did he realize how frightened he was, for he felt the trembling in his own limbs. Barinthus opened his eyes and stared toward his nephew.

"Are you there?"

"I am, Uncle."

"I can't do it again," the old man said. "I haven't got the power."

"You won't have to."

"God has been good to me, but my strength is gone now. I used it all."

"It won't happen again."

"It will, Brendan, for we are not there yet. I think we are not truly in Paradise."

"It won't happen, Uncle," the captain repeated.

Barinthus shook his head. "Something is keeping us away," he whispered.

Joseph woke up and screamed.

Taking up a brand from the fire, Finbar made a cautious way along the spit until he came to the women's camp. It was a now-familiar scene. Though the bedding was laid out, neither woman was in evidence. He knelt to feel the furs, but he could discover nothing by any heat they retained; it was too muggy at any rate even to use furs when sleeping. He stood and peered into the darkness. He could see nothing outside the flicker of his torch.

"Nonanis?" he called in a whisper. "Nonanis, are you there?"

He waited. There was no reply. Reluctantly, he decided that there was little he could do.

"Come back, Nonanis," he called again. "Please."

When again there was no reply, he returned to camp, to discover Joseph on his knees before the fire. The monk beseeched his god that the beast might not come again, and Finbar recognized language that arose from the Book of the Revelation of John. Atla leaned on his spear and poked the embers with his moccasined toe. He was quiet, out of apparent respect for Joseph's entreaties, but he grinned a wolfish grin at Finbar when the smith emerged from the darkness. Brendan was examining the canoe that had been battered in the attack. Already, Barinthus had dropped back into boneless sleep.

Brendan came to stand beside Finbar and Atla. "The canoe is not badly hurt. We can repair it tomorrow."

"You still want to go on?" Finbar asked.

"As much as before."

"This time, you saw it."

"It was a lion, that's all."

"I don't think so."

"If Barinthus could do what Daniel did, how could it be other than a lion?"

Finbar shook his head. "You are stubborn."

"I've gotten this far."

"And you may get back. But at what cost?"

"It was only a lion, Finbar."

"And you're only a man. Remember that."

As the three stood at the edge of the firelight beside the heavy flow of the river, it began to rain.

At dawn, Finbar woke to feel Nonanis crawl under the canoe where he and Atla were sleeping out of the rain. "Where have you been?" he asked sharply.

Her face showed the obstinate blankness that he hated. "It is wet. I would like to get dry."

"Do you know what happened last night?"

Before Nonanis could answer, the gunwale of the canoe was lifted again, and Talutah wriggled underneath. Four bodies were as many as the canoe could shelter, and they were pressed closely together.

"Talutah," Finbar began, and he felt Nonanis's fingers close on his foot in warning. Taking no heed, almost with his voice shaking, he went on, "Where were you last night? I must have an answer. Where do you women go? We were attacked! By a lioness."

Talutah nodded. "We have heard sounds, all of us."

"Don't be so bland, woman! This is your country."

"It is Cautantowit's country."

Atla, who had been listening, spat in disgust. "Brendan is going on," he said. "We must have information. What kind of country is this?"

"Your captain has no choice but to go on. Cautantowit calls him. He calls all of you. He calls Nonanis and me. We are in his land."

"What about this lion that has been stalking us?" Finbar asked. "Nonanis doesn't want me to speak, but I must."

"I have nothing to say," Talutah replied.

"Please, Finbar," Nonanis whispered. "Please, don't."

"Barinthus could have been killed! We all could have been killed."

"Cautantowit will decide," Talutah answered Finbar. "It is for him, not for us. You are a man who makes the sunstone. Have you never been tested before?"

"Our God tests us," Atla replied, "but no one will be tested beyond his ability to endure. And only God understands what that ability is."

Talutah shrugged. "Perhaps Cautantowit is like that, too. Perhaps not. You white men seem to speak for your god always. We do not do this for Cautantowit. Cautantowit is manito."

Though both Finbar and Atla attempted to press more information out of the women, nothing at all was forthcoming. Eventually, out of frustration and exhaustion, they fell asleep.

It rained for two days, hard. The wind blew cold from the east. The river was grey, the sky white-grey. The forest dripped, and there was no place to lie down. The party huddled together under its overturned canoes, men and women in musty proximity. When it was day, they pressed forward up along the river, despite the rain. When it was dark, they were more miserable still. Barinthus retreated into his coma-like state. Joseph sniffled annoyingly. He did what he could to avoid the women and Finbar. The reed of Atla's pipe got wet, and he fumed for an entire day until Brendan exploded at him, saying that the music of Paradise ought to be music enough. He himself, he said, had once spent twenty-four hours listening to the song of a blackbird perched in the window of his clerestory at Clonfert, and he had never after that desired any but the music of God. Atla told Brendan how many times he had heard that particular story, and how tired he was of it, and how he wished everyone would just leave him alone.

There was no sign of the lion. "Too damned wet, even for a magic lion," Atla grunted when Joseph tentatively made the observation. "Better the lion than this," and he tried to stretch his long legs, but there was no more room under the canoe. He settled for wet feet but straight knees.

On the third day, the storm broke. The wind shifted into the southwest and then the west. Finally, it came in briskly from the northwest, and the clouds were chased away. The party pushed off again upon the river. Colors came back. The air was delicious. The sun lit everything in silver. For an hour, they paddled in ecstacy and then, as though all this had been orchestrated by some powerful hand, the canoes broke from the river and coasted out onto the ruffled surface of a wide lake. In an instant, the oppression both of the sky and of the curtailing forest fell away. The vista was endless. The lake's width exceeded the limits of Finbar's river-stunted imagination. Its length could only be guessed at, for it appeared to go on forever into the eye of the wind. It was dotted here and there with islands, small ones, and its shores were lined with hills. It was intensely blue. The sky was blue. The shores were white, or reddish, or the luxuriant, soft greens of fern and sasparilla. Ducks flocked along the shores, their voices loud and neighborly. Talutah and Nonanis whistled and clapped their paddles against the gunwales in excitement.

"Look!" called Talutah, her voice a clear reed across the water. "Ktaadn."

There it was. At the end of the lake there rose from the tableland an irregular mass of mountain that seemed to bulk higher and higher into the sky, stretching wide. It was impressive not for any steepness of slope, for it was not especially steep, or for any regularity of shape, for, again, it possessed none. Its power came from its monumentality in a landscape created on so much more restrained a scale. Where the shoreside hills were useful but approachable, Ktaadn was purposeless and beyond the pale. Where the lake was flat and reflected the friendly blue of the sky, Ktaadn was crenelated and had only an austere darkness about it. Where the sky all around was clear, Ktaadn so much existed in its own world that it was plumed with a long streamer of cloud across its summit. The mountain dominated all observation of the scene. Once noticed—and one could not be ignorant of its presence for more than a few moments—nothing else appeared to the eye, for nothing else was worth the visual trouble of looking.

"Manito," Nonanis breathed, and she was right.

That night, they camped on an island in the middle of the lake. Ktaadn seemed no closer to them than it had when they first saw the heights, but it dominated the scene even more certainly than before. The west-falling sun showed its corrugations as red stone, and the plume of mist was pink. The celebrative atmosphere among the paddlers had quieted somewhat, but there was a lightness among them still that buoyed them upon the expansiveness of the landscape. They stood around a merry fire and broiled trout, the fish so fresh they required to be spitted lengthwise to keep them from curling round into tight circles in the heat. With their sticks, the travelers were all as spokes to a wheel, and the warmth played upon their faces, and they bantered in happy conversation. Joseph sat apart and fasted.

The following day was like to the last. The mountain did not draw closer; it merely assumed more greatness. Islands passed them on all sides, and the lake was sportive with birds and fish. The wind was still in the northwest, and it kicked up a merry chop into which they bent their paddles with relish at the flurry and splash. Barinthus was awake again, and his sere face turned this way and that as he drank what he could of this vivid paradisal wine. Another island stop closed the day: the lake was becoming narrower, and they saw that the following day's run should take them to its end. Again, there were trout and several big bass. There were late-season blueberries, so thick in one spot on the island as to bow down the bushes. Mountain cranberries boiled with maple sugar made a delightful sauce for the bass. Far from shore as they were, the night for once was free of biting insects, and they stayed awake around the fire longer than was common with them. Talutah was excited by the near completion of their journey, and she held them in thrall with the tale of Abnaki beginnings and of Cautantowit's generosity to the people he had chosen above all the rest. The tale fit the surroundings, so high and wild were they.

The Europeans heard about the cloud world above the sky, and about the mighty tree that had grown in its center. They learned how the grandmother of all peoples had been pushed through the hole in the floor of that world when the tree was uprooted, and how she had fallen to earth. She landed far in the southwest, and there she gave birth to a daughter. As she had fallen, the thunder, and the lightning, and the winds of the various quarters had given her gifts, that she might not be without the necessities to sustain life when she landed. These gifts her daughter planted around the spot where the birth took place, and thus the garden grew with all the things that men eat. As her daughter grew, the mother noticed that the girl was happy and understood that she was pregnant and would have two children, their father being the western wind.

When the time came, the birth was hard. First came

a boy, strong and hale, and then came another, but this one was angry and poorly made—he killed his mother as he passed from her body. The first, the good one, whose name was Cautantowit, drove the evil brother away for a time, and he and his grandmother lived together in the garden.

Cautantowit grew tall, and, when he was a man, he left his grandmother to search for his father, the wind. It was a harrowing pilgrimage, but in the end he found his father, and his father gave him three leather bags to take back to the garden. The bags contained the animals, the fish and the birds, and, when Cautantowit released them, he named them for their chief characteristics, the elk for his antlers, the moose for his nose, the weasel for his cunning, the muskrat for his swimming.

By that time, however, the evil brother had returned, and, being anxious to make trouble, he caused briars to grow where before there had been only ferns, and he took some of the beings from the bags before Cautantowit could name them, and he created the rattlesnake, and the mosquito, and the loathly worm.

Then the grandmother saw what transpired, and she warned Cautantowit of his brother's intention. A battle grew between the brothers. Cautantowit triumphed, but, being compassionate toward his brother, he did not kill him. Instead, he sent him out upon the face of the land and ordered him to try his hand at good. Cautantowit knew that it might take a very long time before his evil brother learned good, so Cautantowit made for himself a place where he might pass the hot season, a place his brother knew nothing about. That place was Ktaadn. In the warm season, Cautantowit came to Ktaadn, and there he ruled over the other manitos of the land, and the evil brother did not follow him. As the year grew colder, however, Cautantowit longed for the warmth of his garden away in the southwest, and he departed. Then, in his wanderings, the evil one made his way into the Abnaki lands, and all was destroyed. The lakes froze, and the forest was covered with snow. The cold wind howled through the trees. The game was scarce. All life came to a stop, and only by the thoughtfulness of Cautantowit in giving his people fire—that memory of the heat of his garden—did they survive the evil one's destructive power.

By the time this tale was done, night ruled Ktaadn's world. The moon was gibbous and setting, sending a silver streak across the water, which had grown still with the evening death of the wind. A sound could be heard for miles and miles across the water. The stars were tiny chinks in the dome of the sky through which the light shone down from the cloud world above. Complete stillness reigned. Ktaadn itself could be seen only as a black spot among the stars. The fire had dwindled to a few small coals into which now and then Talutah dropped a twig. Then light would flare yellow for a moment, and the quiet, etched faces of the travelers would be illuminated. Barinthus's was cadaverous, and his lank hair hung against his cheeks. Brendan sat with pursed lips; his beard bristled with fire lights. Repeatedly, he passed a hard, square hand across its scratchiness. Atla seemed fascinated. His red hair snarled around his face. His eyes twitched this way and that with the excitement of such an odd tale. To Finbar, Nonanis was beautiful; he thought she might well be hearing the slow, croaking voice of Ktaadn as, from under the earth, it echoed the tale that she must know as deeply as she knew her own name. And the speaker: Talutah was animated, and there had come into her old body a feline arrogance that it commonly did not possess. The moment lasted for a long time, with all of them there. Then Joseph made a noise as of a snort. Suddenly, across the water, there came a scream. The scream was repeated, and then it degenerated into a coughing grunt.

"Lion," Atla breathed.

The women looked at one another, questioning.

"The lion is still there!" Joseph's voice was frightened.

"No," said Talutah. "Not the lion."

Joseph jumped up. "What do you mean?" He could not stand still. "Of course it's the lion."

"It's not. I just know. Don't be alarmed."

"I'm not alarmed!"

Talutah rose to her feet. "Be truthful. You must be truthful here. This is Ktaadn."

Joseph turned away disgusted. Talutah stared after his dark form as he made his way through the sparse trees to the opposite shore of their small island. Her curiously feline manner was pronounced. If she had had a tail, it would have twitched in anger.

Dawn found the party already in the canoes with paddles wet from early effort. Their island lay half a mile behind them. There was no wind. The surface of the lake rippled only with the burbles of feeding trout. Mist rose thinly from the water into the still air. Ktaadn wavered above the mist, as though it were no part of this lower lakeland world. Two kingfishers chased one another across the surface, and higher, an early eagle hung south, beating his wings. His shriek came down to them like the crack of organic destruction: granite split by slow ice, an elm torn by lightning. He was angry at the lack of a supporting wind.

The shore of the lake came toward them. They distinguished its features. A stream emptied into it, coming from Ktaadn, and toward that mouth they bent their line. Soon, they were out of the lake altogether, and the forest closed in around them again. The sudden force of the stream against them reminded them of the river up which they had come, and it made them long for the easy water of the lake. They dipped harder and pulled more strongly. They relearned in a moment the lessons of reading a current. As the stream grew more narrow, poles were unlimbered, and that more efficient but more difficult technique was employed to press them on. No sight of the mountain came to them. The air in the forest was colder than it had been over the lake, and the early light was deep green. The columnar spaces echoed with the delicious *a-tee-hee-hee* of the white-throated sparrow. They progressed another mile or so, and the way became steeper and more boulder-chocked. Finally, Talutah bent her prow against the forest verge, and she stepped out. Her face radiated the eagerness she felt; her body was clothed in green shadows. She pulled the canoe up onto the shore and overturned it between yellow birches. Brendan, Barinthus and Joseph stood awkwardly in the shallows as the second canoe nudged the land and was emptied. Nonanis, too, had the trembling excitement that her mentor embodied.

"We go now," Talutah announced when all had shouldered burdens.

"Where is Cautantowit?" Brendan asked.

"We go to Ktaadn. He will make himself known when he desires."

"You are certain?"

The question need not have been asked, so radiant was the powwaw's face. Without answering, she turned and plunged into the forest, following the line of the stream.

At first, the walking was not difficult, though the forest floor was still wet from the recent heavy rains. Feet sank now and then into dark holes of rich earth and pine needles. At other times, the footing was across boulders sticking roundly from the earth. Lichens made for good gripping on the rock surfaces. The trees were spruce, in the main, and fir, with an admixture of birch and an occasional cedar. Sign of moose and of bear was frequent, of rabbits ubiquitous, but no wildlife was actually seen. Many of the younger trees had been stripped of bark as high as nine or ten feet by the hungry moose. Now and then, a bear-tree was passed, showing the claw marks of a violent embrace. Small tributaries to the stream seeped down from the higher country and crossed their path. Gradually, the party became strung out, until, in time, each member seemed to be walking alone in the world of his own beginnings. Talutah led. Atla and Brendan vied for second place. Joseph, assisting Barinthus, walked in the middle. Finbar, though eager to reach an eminence and to see again the compelling massiveness of Ktaadn, was attracted nevertheless to Nonanis and paced her at the end of the column.

After two or three miles had passed in their meandering journey, both the sides and the bottom of the vale through which they walked grew steeper. The travelers were pressed closer to the banks of the stream. Finally, even as the party tightened in upon itself, it found that it must cross the stream at a log-and-boulder jam. In fact, crossing and recrossing the stream as the way led higher, the group discovered that the stream itself was the most desirable highway, for all its being a wet one; and the march continued slowly, ankle- or thigh-deep in the cold water, or else poised upon tumbled logs or great, split granite humps. A glimpse of the sky and even of the sun stimulated the climbers as they made their way across the boulders, but the aspect of their route was somber and baleful enough for all that. The way seemed to go upward ever more steeply and more precariously, as though up a giant's staircase down which a river happened to run. Especially for Barinthus, but also for the thin, nervous Joseph, the climbing was difficult. Yet, whereas Joseph tended to hang back and to relieve his anxiety with loud prayers, Barinthus pressed forward despite his dim sight, and seemed not to mind the surprise inundations with which an uninstructed step rewarded him.

At midday, Talutah called a halt. The party gathered on a shelf of rock in the sun. Below their feet, the stream leapt out from a ledge and dropped fifteen feet into a pool. Mist from the fall hung below their perch like a cloud. They were soaked, having just made their way up that waterfall with the water battering against their chests and heads, and they were chilled. Barinthus stripped himself naked and lay clutching the warm rock, his thin shanks shivering and pale in the sunlight. The others dried themselves with cedar feathers and concocted a meal. Save for the roar of the waterfall, the forest was silent. Far away and below them, through a small break in the trees, a corner of the lake could be seen, like a bit of mirror broken off and cast down on a green rug to shine in the sun.

Finbar finished his johnnycake and maple sugar and set out by himself to find a tall pine from the top of which he might get a view of their surroundings. He found a monarch and climbed its ladder-like limbs until he pierced the canopy of the lesser spruces and firs. The air suddenly came alive. The top of the tree swayed under the pressure of a northwest wind. He wormed his way still higher, until the land all about fell away, and he was alone in the sky.

Ktaadn was off to his left, looking as far away as it had

from the lake, as though it were receding from them as they approached. Its summit was still plumed in mist. He saw that between them and it lay a ridge, and that their stream was below the ridge. They would have to leave the stream and climb the ridge before they could reach the true slope of the mountain. In the other direction, he saw the lake stretching out with its myriad islands. He saw what he thought was the outlet of the great river up which he had come. Far to the south, he saw a blue highland that might have been the hills near the seacoast. Beyond that seacoast lay Thule; and it seemed to him that he could hear his own words on the wind. "I, Finbar the smith, give you Thule." And another voice, the strong, sweet voice of Ide: "You *will* find what you want in Paradise. . . ." He lingered in the treetop for many minutes, one with the sun and the wind, before he descended into the green depths of the forest once more.

Talutah and Nonanis were on their feet when he returned, while the monks still rested.

"We must go," the powwaw said. "Get up now. We must go on."

"There's a ridge between us and the summit," Finbar commented, shouldering his burden.

"We leave the stream soon," Talutah nodded.

"You've been here before?" Atla asked.

"I know the way," the old woman said. "Cautantowit shows me the way."

Indeed, after another mile or so, there appeared on the left a massive rock slide, which had torn a scar through the forest from the ridgeline Finbar had seen.

"This way," Talutah motioned, and, belying her aged appearance, she sprang away from the stream.

The men were not so quick to follow, however. Flinging his pack down angrily, Atla collapsed against a boulder and panted, "Let's have a rest."

"It is late; there is far to go."

"The mountain will stay where it is," Atla called back.

Seeing that the other men were stopping, Talutah returned the distance she had covered. She was angry. "Do not lose height unnecessarily," she said. "It is how we climb."

Barinthus was badly winded, however, and the pow-waw took time to press her hands upon his neck. Quietly, she hummed a manito-song beside his ear while the others brushed sweat from their faces and passed a water skin back and forth.

The first hint of the afternoon's waning was in the air as the party readied itself again and then flung itself at the slide. It was clear that this slide was indeed the road to the upper slopes, but the climb was difficult and even precarious. Looking up, the climbers saw that only the plume of cloud showed iself above the shoulder of the ridge before them. Ktaadn's actual slopes were still hidden.

Brendan and Atla led. Talutah and Nonanis came quickly after. Finbar lingered behind to assist Barinthus, doubting Joseph's competence on such a shifting and irksome slope as the slide appeared to be. It was well that he assisted Joseph in this, for the old man was an awkward burden, although an eager one. The rocks over which they made their way were hot from the all-day sun, and they were sharp. Soon, sweat again streaked their faces, and blood welled along the scratches and barked shins that such climbing costs.

The others of the party were rested and impatient to be off when Finbar and his companions scrambled up the final slope and dropped exhausted to the ground at the crest of the ridge. It was late afternoon.

"You might have helped," Finbar complained generally. "It's not easy for Barinthus."

Immediately, Brendan's face showed his concern. "Of course, it isn't. I'm to blame. I was too eager. From now on my uncle will climb with me." The captain made his way to the ancient figure draped against a rock and cradled Barinthus's shoulders in one huge arm. "Are you ready, Uncle? We are nearly there. Feel the wind."

In a moment, Brendan had departed off the ridge, supporting Barinthus. Similarly, the others pressed on. Left behind, Finbar and Joseph stared at one another. Then they looked out at the heavy, cloud-hung summit of Ktaadn dominating the sky above them. The slopes were no more than half a mile away across the gulf of air. Between the men and the summit, hawks soared on up-

drafts, tilting this way and that, their fierce eyes filled with
nature's yearning for food. It was an elemental scene.

"I love Christ," Joseph said after his panting had
ceased, "but I have sinned. I am not worthy of this."

Said casually and without rancor, the statement was
as uncharacteristic of Joseph's manner toward Finbar as
the scene was stupendous, and it was almost certainly
derivative of that sensation. "How have you sinned?" Finbar asked equably.

"I have doubted God's mercy."

"Surely not."

Joseph looked at Finbar and then turned his eyes to
the scarf of mist before them. "It says to me, 'Why have
you come? I have not called for you. Why have you come?'
The others do not hear that. Those women, they hear only
the voice of their Cautantowit and the memory of their
race. Brendan is mad: he hears nothing but the grandeur
of it, and he thinks the grandeur God. Atla is the same.
Barinthus, perhaps, truly hears the voice of God speaking
softly to him, for Barinthus of all of us understands the
mercy of God. One must understand the mercy of God
before God will be merciful."

There was silence. Into the silence came a scream
like the scream that had followed them for days. Joseph
stiffened. "I hate it," he moaned. "I hate it."

"That was an eagle," Finbar soothed.

"It matters not."

"It wasn't the lion."

Joseph's face turned toward Finbar, and the smith
saw that the monk was tormented by devils. He took
Joseph's hand and raised it to his lips. Feeling awkward
but tender, he kissed it. "Be calm," he said, but he knew
that the abjuration was in vain.

"I love God!" Joseph sobbed, standing.

Finbar rose beside him. "Come," he said. "We should
find the others and eat. Food will make you feel more
human, less of the heights."

"I don't eat," Joseph murmured, as, docilely, he was
led down off the crest of the ridge. "I never eat. God loves
me, for I do not eat."

Finbar made a way down into the forest toward the

area where he guessed the night's camp to be. At the bottom of the saddle he and Joseph crossed a stream smaller than the one that tumbled down the other rise of the ridge. They turned upward along this stream, and soon they emerged from the trees into a high meadow. They were on the very shoulder of Ktaadn now, and the curtain of mist hung only a few hundred feet above them. The stream they were following fell literally out of the clouds and made its way between banks of grass and blueberries to the spot where Finbar and Joseph stood. To their left, the meadow spread out along the shoulder. Enormous grey boulders punctuated the green. To their right, a tongue of aspen and birch curved up from the forest and challenged the bare rock of the mountain's steeper slope. Before it reached the mist, however, it was defeated by altitude, and it dwindled to a miniature forest. From everything that Finbar could see, the upper slopes of Ktaadn supported nothing more than mountain cranberries and open rock. No vegetation clung to a landscape that looked as though it had been heaped up out of colossal stones in some playful gesture of Cautantowit's. High as they were, the wind was penetrating and cold.

One hundred feet away from where they emerged, in the lee of a massive boulder, the rest of the party had set up its camp. Finbar and Joseph walked across. There was a small fire sputtering and struggling with resinous wood, and there were furs laid out, and there was food on the spit. Atla had killed three fat partridge, which, when they came to be eaten, tasted of spruce buds. The travelers drank condensed cloud by the cupful. They made a dessert of blueberries.

High in the air, the sun was long in setting across their perch. The lowlands were dark before the sky cooled from blue to grey-blue and the western horizon glowed yellow. The rocks above them were washed with red, and the plume likewise. The wind dropped. The moon could be seen setting after the sun. Finbar wandered upward across the bouldery meadow until he was close under the roof of fog. He felt awesomely alone. The fire, which he could see as a small spark two hundred feet below him and off down the slope, burst this way and that with the dying wind. Now and then he saw the form of one of his companions pass before it. The sky's light faded still more, until there was no color division between the rocks and the grass, and until, later, the sky took on the grey coloration of the mountain slopes. Last to go was the band of pale light along the horizon. Then he was in darkness. Then only the star of the fire recalled him to his world. He hurried downslope, faster than he thought. He stumbled and hurt his weak leg when it snubbed against a low, gnarled spruce only two feet high.

That night, there was no talk of Abnaki origins, or of the god of the mountain. Even the mountain's name was withheld from what little conversation there was. To Finbar's surprise, Brendan, who had seemed entirely engrossed in his own exploration of the height of Paradise, spoke inquiringly and privily to him about his climb with Joseph, and about Joseph's state of mind. There was little that Finbar could say to enlighten his captain. As Joseph had understood, Brendan did not seem to sense the anger of the mountain at their presence. Atla reminisced about the journey for a few moments, but, as no one would follow his lead, he rolled himself into his bearskin and lay back watching the stars as they dipped in and out of the covering mist.

The camp grew still. The fire sputtered. Talutah tended it. Finbar positioned himself close to Nonanis, but the woman paid no attention to him. He lay down. They all slept with their feet toward the fire in an effort to stay warm. The air was quite cold by this time. Now and then a whisp of the foggy mantle would blow down low enough to engulf the campsite for a moment, and all would be damp and echoing, and then it would blow away. Finbar fell asleep.

In his sleep, he seemed to hear the groaning of stone and the springing of grasses. He heard the entire awesome ponderousness that was Ktaadn. The mountain seemed to purr, to roar, to moan. He opened his eyes. It was deep night. No one was by the fire, which had burnt low. In a half-conscious state, still hearing the grinding moans of Cautantowit's world, he rolled onto his side and sat up in order to throw a log across the fire. What he saw shocked him so totally that he had no idea whether he dreamt.

Near the fire was the lion, a tawny coil of writhing limbs. It was she who moaned and purred. She was in monstrous heat, it appeared, slavering herself along the ground. Her claws tore at the sods, her back arched, her loins rippled, her tail was like lightning. Astoundingly, bending over her was a form Finbar thought he recognized, one that he knew he knew. The man's mantle spun wide with the intensity of his own dance. The man's hands gripped the lion's fur at the neck, tore her skin, rasped her with nails while she mewed and panted. Her tail twined around him. Saliva flew from her fangs as she swung her head from side to side. The smell of sweat and blood mingled in the clear air, and the fire sputtered, and the sleepers stirred and raised shocked faces. The mating dance grew more frantic. The man's thin form writhed, its muscles lit by the fire. The lion slid herself along the ground. Her fur met the fire, and the singed smell of hair creased the night. Her screams mated with the hoarse grunts of the man, and together they echoed in the night. The man neared his peak. His moans merged into a bellow that shook the very rocks of Ktaadn.

The man collapsed across the lion's body. Finbar blinked. The mountain shivered in silence after that prodigious sound. The bodies slid apart. Finbar swallowed. He shook his head. He moved his hand. Joseph lay curled into a ball with his knees drawn up into the fire. Talutah was naked and bloody under his feet.

Brendan coughed. Finbar sat up straighter. The smell of burnt skin filled the air, and suddenly Joseph leapt back from the fire and landed on toes and hands, his face inches from the steaming form of the unconscious woman. His face hung uncomprehendingly for a second and then he shrieked. As though pulled backwards by a rope, he flew to his feet away from the powwaw's body. He was naked from the waist down. His groin was covered with blood, dark in the firelight. In horror, he stared at the woman. He crooned and held himself. Surprised, he gazed at the blood on his hand.

"No!" he cried. He turned and ran.

Finbar found himself streaking across the black
meadow into the clouds. Brendan panted beside him. "Joseph!" they shouted as they ran. "Joseph, come back!"

There was no reply from before them, just the sob-
bing of a wounded animal retreating into the fog. The
sound was without substance. Now, it came from this direction, now from that. In absolute darkness, Finbar fumbled forward across boulders wet with the weight of the
mist. He realized that he was no longer beside Brendan,
and he called out to the captain. He thought he heard a
voice answer the call from along the slope to the right, but
he thought he also heard the crackle of brush ahead of
him that might be Joseph battering his way through
stunted trees. He pressed ahead. His feet and shins were
bruised. His bad leg began to ache. He felt heavily the
thinness of the air. "Joseph!" he called. "Where are you?
Come back!"

He ran on. He bumped into a boulder and hit his
forehead on its surface. There was more wind in the fog,
and he stood beside the stone rubbing his head and realized that he was cold. Sweat dried instantly, or was blown
away. He groped along the stone with his hands, looking
for a way past. It was massive. He crunched over dwarf
spruces, walking on their tops, off the ground. He followed the stone to the right. Its surface was smooth, wind-
worn. A weakness in the surface ahead warned him too
late, and his leg broke through the spruce tops and
scraped down against slow-growing, iron-like branches. It
hurt, and he was awkward about pulling it out. He realized he was bleeding when the limb came free. With his
fingers, he could feel a rip in the skin. He stripped off his
loin cloth and bound it around his thigh for a bandage. He
pressed onward along the face of the stone, but he realized from his pained walk and from his dizziness that he
was growing disoriented and that he should stop. Even as
he thought this, he fell once more through the surface,
only this time his whole body dropped into the hole. He
found himself wedged between rocks a full five feet under
the canopy of the wind-planed spruces. The canopy effec-
tively shut out the wind. It was warmer there. He had not
been further hurt by this last fall. He determined to wait

there until enough light came in the sky to show him the way. He could not have found his way back to the camp had he wanted to. Nor could he have followed any further the wraith-voice of the stricken monk as the latter stumbled on through the fog.

He arranged himself as comfortably as he could. The bleeding seemed to have stopped, and now the leg throbbed. He huddled inside his mantle. He did what he could to keep himself free of thought.

Eventually, dawn came. The trunks of the trees around him could be perceived, then their foliage against a white sky. He moved. He was stiff. He realized he had slept a little. His leg hurt when he flexed it, but, as he hoped, the bleeding had stopped. His loin cloth, however, was soaked with blood. He dared not remove it, for fear of dislodging the scab. Because of this nakedness, he felt unprotected, ridiculously so, as he wormed his way up out of his hole and onto the springy, precarious footing of the top of this midget forest. He called to Joseph, knowing it was no use, and then to Brendan. He hoped Brendan might answer, but nothing came back except the whirling of the wind around cracks in the rock. He saw his way past the boulder that had defeated him the night before, and he limped upward, following the vague belief that Joseph must have gone that way.

He climbed for hours, it seemed. There was nothing to see. The boulders over which he dragged his hurt leg were identical, one with another. The fog sometimes drew back—once he even climbed in a funnel of sunlight, and there were colors all around him—but as soon as it opened, the fog closed in again, and he was lost. He had long ago ceased calling for Joseph. He struggled onward in silence, his miserable effort some sort of expiation for the evil that had befallen the monk.

He was on the summit. He paused, dazed. There was no more *up*. He sat down. His leg was bleeding again. His heart hammered, and his breath wheezed through lungs unaccustomed to such heights. Blackness swept over him. He must have fainted, for he discovered himself on the ground. He groped to his feet. Only by the direction of the wind could he tell which way he had come. Befuddled, he turned and stepped toward the descent. A sound came through the fog, a voice. He stopped, suddenly alert. He cocked his ears. It came again. It had something of the resonance of Brendan's seaman's bellow. It seemed to come from beyond him, down on the opposite slope. He turned once more and crossed the summit. He stopped to listen. Yes, it came again, and he distinguished the name of Joseph. He stepped down into the fog. "Brendan," he called, and was surprised at what a croak his voice was. "Brendan, I'm coming!"

He fumbled his way down. The rocks were cold, the fog thick and speeding. He saw that the summit was intersected by a ridge, but that this was no such ridge as he had ever seen. There must be another summit out there, he realized, for this knife-edge had to lead somewhere. Or perhaps not. In this madness of fog and wind and holy terrors, it was possible that the ridge led nowhere that a man would go. It was two feet wide and sheer down on both sides. He could see little along it. As this strange landscape came into view, he practically bumped into Brendan, who was hidden by a twist of fog.

Brendan faced out across the void, into which the knife-edge penetrated, and he bellowed to Joseph.

"Is he there?" Finbar panted.

Brendan spun around, his eyes wild. "Yes! I saw him disappear that way. At least, I think so."

"We should go after him."

Brendan looked more closely at Finbar and saw his bandaged leg. "Are you hurt?"

"Not badly, I think. I ripped it against a tree last night."

Brendan nodded. "It was an evil night."

Finbar gestured back toward the boiling mist. "Has he answered you?"

"No. Nothing. I only saw him by chance. I was about to give up."

"So was I."

The two men stood at the end of the knife-edge and peered into fog. The narrow bridge disappeared some ten feet before them. The wind whipped across it from left to right, from west to east, and streamers of mist caught against rocks and flapped their edges, just as though they had been more substantial stuff. It was cold. Finbar shivered. The eerie scene frightened him. He thought that this was the proper backdrop for a myth figure, not for a wounded, half-naked smith and a beached seaman. Even as he thought this, there came out of the fog a wail of such anguish as could issue most reasonably from the throat of a god.

"We'd better go out there," Finbar said.

"Yes."

Together, they inched out onto the stone arrow, and soon there was nothing behind them except a few tattered feet of rock, and nothing more than that before them. The wind tore their bodies and set their hair awhirl. They clung to one another for support. They moved forward, crouched and tense. The eastern side, the leeward side, now and again was revealed to them. Some quirk of mist would open a hole down five, six, seven hundred feet, and all there was to see was the sheer drop of grey rock and the boiling of this cloudworks of the world. Once from overhead came a slant of sunlight, but it was gone immediately, replaced by billows whipped by wind that massed against the western slopes and was forced upward, upward, until it poured across the knife-edge with the force that a river has when it finds itself narrowed to a tiny cut. They were struggling forward through air rapids, and the task was no less formidable than doing the same through white water. The air was a tangible element wishing to creep under them and lift them unawares until they toppled over the edge and fell down, down, through rioting clouds to smash their lives away upon granite.

They had progressed perhaps three hundred interminable yards in this manner when the mercurial nature of the fog opened a slant before them. In an instant, their eyes sped forward along the bridge. Fifty yards away, there was a bulk upon the bridge, and, when it moved, they saw that it was Joseph.

They shouted together. Joseph made no sign of hearing. They bellowed again, and the fog swirled in. Like that, he was gone.

Eschewing caution, they pressed forward faster. Finbar's leg delayed him, and he dropped slightly behind the captain.

"Wait!" he called, but the wind snatched the word away and blew it out east, over the great, empty bowl.

Finbar stumbled and fell. He caught himself on the brink. A violent nausea and dizziness swept across him, for the way below had opened at that instant, and he had seen all the distance down. His head reeled as he pulled himself back into the center of the narrow causeway. Blood was again seeping from his bandage. He looked ahead and discovered that he was alone, completely solitary, in the world of titanic forces. He scrambled to his hands and knees and crawled as quickly as he could after Brendan.

Looking at the rocks before his face, his consciousness narrowed to miniscule scope, he came upon the captain and did not know it until his head bumped the man's back. Slowly, almost paralyzed by the enormity of his fear, he gripped the captain's mantle and, pulling himself to his knees, pressed himself against Brendan's solid torso.

Brendan, meanwhile, had paid little heed to this, and Finbar saw the reason when he looked forward across the captain's shoulder. Joseph stood naked, looking east, his flesh pale in the fog, his eyes closed.

"Does he know we're here?" Finbar whispered.

"I think not. I'm afraid to speak. He might fall."

"We have to do something, or else he *will* fall."

The monk was only a dozen feet before them, but they were separated by a gulf more yawning even than the depths to each side. While they clung to the rock for fear of their lives, Joseph existed in a state of divine madness in which he teetered upon the edge of destruction without the slightest qualm.

Brendan crept a foot or two closer, and Finbar hugged the man's movement to himself.

A crisis seemed to be approaching, for Joseph's breathing was growing faster, and his eyes had opened. What those eyes saw, neither could tell, but they stared into the eastern fog with otherworldly brilliance.

"Joseph," Brendan called softly. "Joseph, come away."

There was no response.

"Joseph!"

Still nothing.

"Brother Joseph! It is Brendan, your abbot, calling you."

This was heard. The monk swung his head. His eyes were blind to ordinary things. Slowly, vision returned to them. He saw the two men crouching close to him on the knife-edge. He hissed and coiled into himself like a serpent. His voice was cracked and savage. "Come no closer, Brendan. I am evil."

"You are forgiven, my son. Come away."

" 'You shall not lie with any beast and defile yourself with it; it is perversion.' Thus sayeth the Lord."

"It was a trick. It was the woman," Finbar called.

"I know what I have done."

"You have done nothing you could keep from doing. It is no sin to be tested too hardly," Brendan said. "Come away with us, and we shall leave this awful place."

"This is Paradise!" Joseph laughed hideously. "I have been unclean in Paradise. I have lain with a beast. It shall not happen again," he cried.

"Joseph, what are you doing?" Brendan shouted, starting up.

In Joseph's hand was a ragged shard of rock. The monk grasped himself and raised the shard.

"Joseph, don't!" Brendan was on his feet moving forward.

The piece of shale swept down in the monk's clenched fist and bit into his offending flesh. Blood started like wine from a burst skin. Joseph made no sound. He hacked again. Frozen with horror, Finbar and Brendan hung just outside the range of the terrible act. Joseph slumped forward. The blade slipped from his hands and fell over the precipice to disappear in the clouds below.

Brendan and Finbar stepped forward again. Joseph reared back. Blood spattered his lower body and gushed from the hideous wound.

"Oh, merciful God," Brendan began, but he had no time to finish the prayer. Even as Brendan stepped within range of the monk, Joseph stood up, and, looking right into his abbot's eyes, he walked off the edge of the world.

There came a long, long scream floating up from

below, a scream that was terminated many seconds after Joseph disappeared.

Finbar whirled and was sick.

Minutes later, he pawed his way off the ground and knelt before Brendan. The monk was weeping, and Finbar realized that he, too, was wracked with sobs. The two men clung to one another, arms powerfully embraced, faces looking either way along the fatal stone, and each felt the life in the other.

"Oh, God, give him peace," Finbar heard himself saying, over and over, and Brendan answered, "Amen."

11

Hours later, Finbar and Brendan descended from the clouds and found themselves again on the high meadow where the camp had been. Atla, Barinthus and the Abnaki women were gone. The hearth was cold. The two men took a little time to drink from the stream. They had said very little during the descent, and they said little now. They stared at each other occasionally, but then their eyes slid away. They were cold, exhausted and terrified. It was midafternoon or later, and the sky was overcast. Finbar's leg still oozed blood, and he was weak. The two did not speculate upon the whereabouts of the others. There was nowhere to go but down.

Climbing the ridge and descending the slide were difficult activities, especially for Finbar. He leaned heavily on Brendan's strength. They reached the river, which would eventually lead them back to the lake. They stopped on the ledge over the waterfall where they had lunched the first day of the climb. The sun had set by that time, and, in the forest, the darkness was thick. Their anxiety to be off that mountain vied against their tiredness, and lost. Huddled together against the faint sun heat that the rock still retained, the two men passed a restless night. There was nothing to cover them except an exiguous blanket of spruce boughs. Beneath them, the falls roared a constant roar. Mist filled the air. A slow rain came down before dawn. Their stomachs complained of hunger and kept them awake. In their minds, imprinted forever, was the image of Joseph's final, fogbound step.

As soon as there was any light in the air, the two rose and continued their descent. Finbar's leg was stiff, but the bleeding seemed to have stopped. In and out of the

stream, balanced and slipping off logs and boulders, the
men dove deeper into the forest, and the angle of the land
flattened. The rain stopped. Hours later, limping over
almost flat ground, they were aware of streaks of sunlight
penetrating the foliage above them. The smells were
those of an ordinary forest. Around them was the matter-
of-fact hammering of woodpeckers. Finally, they dropped
down one final slope and broke out of the trees along the
river where they had left the canoes. Without much gladness, they collapsed among the startled members of their
expedition. There was little talk, except for the exchange
of a bare report concerning Joseph's fate and the cause of
the larger party's flight from the heights: Barinthus had
collapsed after Joseph's horrible enchantment, and the
old man's breathing was labored in that rarified air.

Some time later, Talutah was ministering to Finbar's
leg. Finbar looked down his body at the woman bending
over him. The wound had been exposed, and it was a
serious gash. Nonanis was preparing a poultice of effica-
cious herbs for the dressing, and Talutah was bathing the
wound in preparation for its application. The powwaw
looked wrinkled and brown, and her face was passive. She
blew smoke on the wound.

"It was you? The lion?" Finbar asked, more in wonder than in question.

She looked up at him. "Cautantowit has spoken."

Finbar dropped his head to the ground. He felt the
gentle fingers massage the wound with warm water and
oil. In his mind's eye, he saw the naked, unconscious
figure of this same woman, bloodied and firelit. He was too
exhausted to bring the two pictures together into one
person.

Two days later, the party was camped on an island in
the lake close by the mouth of the great river that would
lead it once again back to the sea and to Madakamigossek.
The weather again was fine, and Finbar's physical recu-
peration was proceeding swiftly. The body and the spirit
are not always housed in the same mansion, however.
Finbar's spirit was continuing to struggle desperately
against the blows it had sustained high inside the cloud,
which sometimes he stared at as it streamed away so pret-

tily to leeward of Ktaadn's peak. He said little to anyone, and he kept much to himself.

Brendan's attention was focused on his uncle. Barinthus was dying. There was no doubt of it. It was not a painful death, and it was a lucid one. The ancient man had pressed himself finally beyond his power, and the life force was gone. He lay all day in the sun on a soft mattress of balsam and sweet grass that Atla had prepared for him, and he was so thin as almost not to be there at all. Talutah blew smoke over him, and Nonanis made secret signs with osprey feathers. The old man spoke softly to Brendan sometimes, but mainly he was content with the sun and with his nephew's hand.

Two days passed, drawn out in a long trajectory of death. The camp was centered on Barinthus. Only once did Finbar and Nonanis speak privately.

Nonanis came to the smith as he sat on the opposite side of the island, under Ktaadn's weight. Tentatively, she sat down beside him. She touched his bandaged leg. "Are you in pain?"

"No." He did not look at her.

"What then?"

He shook his head.

She sat still and looked out across the flat, summer lake. Pintails and teals cavorted, and the surface was dotted with the circles of trout feeding. Mist rose toward the everlasting flag of Ktaadn's wind.

"You have been awake all night."

"When Joseph fell, I thought it was over, but it is not."

She nodded, "Not for you." She touched him, but she received no response. She smoothed her skirt and stared at her hands.

"Nonanis," he said, "I have always allowed my life to direct me to this place and that: I have been a pilgrim. Oh, a smith's life is a traveling one, I know; but that is mere rationalizing. I have never directed my own life. Joseph directed his own life, poor man, and he followed his life to its end."

"And he is dead. Cautantowit killed him."

"Every one of us will die."

"Not every one of us may go then to the Sandhills where Cautantowit has his garden."

Again, Finbar shook his head.

"That thin one was a half-man, and he could not be cured. Cautantowit saved you because you may be cured."

"Cautantowit?"

Nonanis touched his wound. She nodded.

"Cautantowit had nothing to do with it. I fell."

"So did the thin one."

Finbar's eyes swept up to the cloud. He shivered. "I can still feel the wind," he whispered. "It blows on me even down here. It pushes me toward the edge."

"It is manito," Nonanis agreed, "yet you may be cured."

"How?"

"You have been touched by Cautantowit. You have seen what is manito, but it has made you meek. Seeing what is manito, your spirit has again become that of a pilgrim, as you say it has been in the past, not that of a man. A pilgrim is forever going somewhere else. That is a useless indulgence. To be cured, you must stay and fight. The heart of a man is the heart of struggle, and a man's heart flows free because every struggle is his final struggle in life. The outcome matters not at all: the outcome concerns pilgrims, not men. The redhaired one and the one you call the Captain, they are pilgrims. The old one is a man."

"I must become a man? But I am a man."

"In some things it is easy to be a man."

"But what must I do?"

"The choice is yours. Be a pilgrim and always need something that you have not got, or be a man and let your heart flow free. I am powwaw. To be powwaw is an encumbrance, but it is to be free, and a woman."

"I always think I will be free."

"Not while your spirit is meek. Cautantowit has hurt you: fight back."

He turned to her. "You are a fierce woman."

"I do not allow the Grandmother to frighten me, nor

Cautantowit either. They will, if you let them, and then you will be a pilgrim."

"I carry too much weight with me," he replied, glancing toward the Ktaadn-shroud.

"Only because you desire to."

"But I don't desire it."

"Then cast it off."

The man and the woman sat for a long time watching the lake. Finally, Finbar touched Nonanis's hair. "And if I do?"

She looked at him. "I am not a prize." She stood up. "Delight in your own power and do not try to make it something it cannot be." With that, she walked away.

Finbar was present at the moment of Barinthus's death. It came as the sun dipped down out of the sky that evening. The old man lay flat. His face was sunken. Everyone knew that the end was near, and they sat around him. Brendan held one of his hands, Talutah the other. Atla had just moistened his lips with a damp cloth. Suddenly, Barinthus's eyes snapped open, and his entire body went rigid. His blindness was gone; those eyes were clear and bright, but what they saw was in the sky above and was obscure to mortal eyes. It seemed that every sense was straining upward to catch the fullness of the sight, the sound, the smell. This lasted for several seconds, and then he was dead.

Talutah and Nonanis began to wail. Brendan dropped his forehead onto his uncle's chest. Atla stood up and wandered away, kicking at pine cones. When Finbar looked again, the wrinkles were deeper; the body, a stick.

He looked at his companions. He heard Atla off by himself. He heard Nazarene prayers over the body, and through them were manito-songs. He remembered other deaths, his on his island, and his in the sea. How many deaths can a man have? And why does he hang onto the weight that he carries even so? Had he not learned enough? Had he not exhausted all learning? Here he was in Paradise, and still he squeezed and squeezed and squeezed that weight, as though he could force *it* to answer him.

He staggered away from the others. On the shore of the lake, he stopped and looked at the sky, and a vortex began to whirl inside his head. In ever-expanding circles, he saw himself on the island, the island in the lake, the lake in the forest, the forest in Paradise, Paradise beside the Western Sea, the Western Sea beside the Empire. And he knew that in the Empire were the separate whirls of the Nazarene, the Gnostic, the Jew, the Druid, the Zoroastrian, the Eleusinian, the Mithran. The great babbling vortex spun faster still, and all the world blurred with man's—his!—yearning for an answer, man's ceaseless need to stop it, to stop it, to stop it—to stop the whirl of brute existence, the dance of light, and fire, and earth, and sea, even of the Goddess herself, so that he could once, just once, *know why!*

And then the top whirled too fast, and an eccentric wheel began within the blur, and another one off that, and another, and another, until the whole chaotic, sparkling, furious universe shattered and blasted and fell twinkling to the ground.

And there at the end, there in the middle, there in the red twilight of an island in the lake of the world, there was Finbar, the smith, and he looked at himself, and he thought, 'What in the name of all that has just gone smash am I doing here?,' and he began to laugh.

He laughed, and he laughed, and he laughed, and then he fell down like a tree and slept.

The following morning, the fourth day after the party's arrival at the island, Finbar awoke, and the sparkle of the world rushed into him with a gladness he had never known before. He rolled over and stretched. His companions were up already, preparing for the ceremony of Barinthus's passage into the next world. It was thought appropriate, and that Barinthus would find it so, for Abnaki manners to be observed, with only a recitation of a psalm to tickle the Grandmother with the knowledge that there might be another way. During the night, the women had prepared the body: cleaned it, purified it with smoke, wrapped it in caribou skin, decorated it with feathers, and quills, and seashells. Now there was little to do save sing its manito-song and put it in its final resting place, so that Barinthus could begin his journey to the Sandhills, or to whatever destination he had.

Through it all, Finbar's spirit soared.

The downstream journey was much easier than the upstream one had been. The canoes took turns shooting rapids that spun them along breathlessly until the exhilaration was as finely tuned as Finbar recalled it when rushing ahead of great ocean combers. It took them four days to get to Penobscot. There, with salmon backed up by the falls, they rested half a day and gorged themselves. They pressed on and, now in the tidal stream of the river, welcomed the new brackishness of the stream as a harbinger of the broader prospects and grander winds of the bay. Soon, the canoes passed from the mouth of the river into the sea, and the paddlers saw the hills of Madakamigossek ranged before them along the western shore. It was a fine, hot, blustery day. The surface of the sea was blue and white, and the islands were green. The air was salt, and clean, and streaming from Kingdom Come.

"My uncle should be here!" Brendan called from the other canoe, slapping his paddle against the gunwale.

"He is!" Finbar called back, and the two canoes set off on an impromptu race down the bay. There was laughter as they rounded the ledges neck-and-neck and skimmed into Madakamigossek harbor under the shadow of the high stone cliffs.

But Barinthus was not there. The old man's body was tied in the top of a huge oak tree beside the mouth of the Ktaadn river. Neither was Joseph there, and where his smashed spirit lay, no one of the travelers could say for certain. It was unlikely that, even now, it wended its way toward the Sandhills far to the southwest. More likely, it haunted the knife-edge ridge of Ktaadn, vying still with Cautantowit's judgment.

These were the fates upon which Glusgebeh and the old men of the Abnaki smoked and chewed through the evening following the return. Finbar, Brendan and Atla had little to do with these deliberations. After a short ceremonial meal, they retired to the safety of the curragh, and the familiar oxhide walls were pleasing to Brendan and Atla. It soothed their spirits once more to lie upon woolen blankets, once more to feel the scratch of hemp cordage against the palm. All it would take to depart would be to draw up the anchor stone and to let go the brails. The Empire was there-away; not far a sail, and a known one.

But for Finbar it was irksome to be thus enclosed. After the first night, he slept ashore in Nonanis's lodge. For the time being, Talutah stayed with a cousin of hers. In the daytime, he was made much of by Glusgebeh. Pompous and powerful, the man smoked with Finbar, served him choice bits of beaver tail and lobster, and intoned about the manito of the Black-One-Who-Makes-Sun-Stone coming to the Abnaki from the other side of the sea.

It was four days later, and red tinged the leaves of the maples. There was a cider-colored wind. The wood smoke smelled good. Finbar and Nonanis stood on the edge of the harbor watching eiders and old squaws group and regroup under the falls. A conference of the elders of the tribe was being held in the long lodge, and both their minds were on it.

"If Glusgebeh allows it, I shall stay," he concluded.

"And if he does not?"

Finbar sighed. "My friends set off in a few days. Perhaps I will go back to Thule."

Nonanis huddled her mantle around herself more tightly as a gust carried across the harbor and pressed against them. "There will be much snow this year; Talutah knows."

"I shall make a forge. With steel axes, we can cut great amounts of wood."

"I am afraid of your . . . steel."

"My manito, no more than yours, is simply the art of getting results." He smiled at her fondly. "You, a pow-waw, should know that. It's only a trick. There is very little to magic, once you know its trick."

She grinned. "And that of your friends?"

"Brendan's is the same, but his needs a history in time

and place. That's its limitation, and I think Paradise does not have that history."

"This is not Paradise; this is Madakamigossek."

Finbar looked around the harbor shore, and his eyes went farther, out across the surface of the bay. The colors were hard in the brittle wind. He laughed. "I don't know what Brendan thought it would be, but Paradise is blue, and birds fly in it."

The man and the woman stood for a while longer, and then they turned away.

Glusgebeh met them as they strolled into the center of the camp. They stopped beneath the sacred tree on which the white caribou skin had been raised more than a month before. There was little left of the skin, ripped by wind and crow, except tatters. The elders of the tribe were ranged in a semicircle.

"Black-One-Who-Makes-Sun-Stone desires to stay in Abnaki land," Glusgebeh said. "Cautantowit desires that it be so. Our people will have tips for their arrows made of sun-stone. It is right that it be thus. The fire, which is Cautantowit's, and the earth, which is the Grandmother's, shall join to make our people rich in meat this winter. Black-One-Who-Makes-Sun-Stone knows the way to make the fire and the earth one. As children of the Grandmother, the Abnaki welcome the black man's manito."

Finbar squeezed Nonanis's arm.

"Let us smoke together," the sachem concluded.

Later, Finbar and Brendan canoed down the harbor to its mouth. There was a small island off the southern point connected to the mainland by a half-tide bar. The canoe crossed to seaward, scraping over gravel in the chop coming up the bay from the southwest. The tide was making. Finbar held the canoe just feet away from the steep, granite edge of the island while Brendan trolled for cunnar. The smith enjoyed the delicate play with current and wave and paddle. The slightest flick of his wrist allowed the canoe to slip past projecting rocks, or to meander on the wash of a wave between half-submerged boulders. The wind propelled them along the shore at a rate of perhaps ten feet to the minute.

After boating a few fish, Brendan spoke. "I guess I got what I wanted out of Paradise."

Finbar smiled. "I did, too."

"The difference between me and you is that I want to tell everyone about it."

"There's only one person I want to tell."

"Ide?"

"A good guess. You're going to Thule?"

"It's the best way home."

"Brendan, tell her that I've seen the lion . . . but I chose the owl."

"Will she understand?"

"If she's still the woman I knew." He took a stronger stroke to propel them around a particularly large outcropping. "I thought of her once as an owl," he said, half to himself.

Brendan dropped his line overboard. "Did you know that . . . when I was a young man, before—"

"She told me."

There was a pause.

"Why did you become a monk?"

"More than anything, I wanted to experience God directly. I could not have done that on my family's land, not even if I had shared it with Ide." He swept his hand around. "I could not have done *this.*"

Finbar looked out to windward a few minutes, watching the seas break on a ledge a mile or so offshore. "You know, I've puzzled myself over your religion for more than a year—your own religion, I mean, not the Nazarene faith. Until recently, I could not understand the truth of it. Now, I think that you are a simpler man than I think you are."

Brendan laughed. "Jesus Christ was a simple man; it is man makes Him elaborate. What is hard is to serve Him —it was hard for Joseph—but it is hard because we forget the simplicity: consider the lilies of the field."

The two friends stared at one another for a moment or two, and smiled.

"Got enough fish?" Finbar asked, breaking the contact.

"Sure."

"Come along for dinner tonight, then. The tribe is building us a lodge of our own. Nonanis will broil a moose nose."

Brendan picked up his paddle as the canoe rounded the outer point of the island. The current swept them quickly along and shoved them under the lee.

"Will you marry her?" Brendan asked, over his shoulder.

"I think I already have. She wears my bracelet."

"Do you want my blessing?"

"No."

A few more strokes put them back in the smoother water of the harbor. Brendan said, "We both won the challenge we made in Thule, do you realize that?"

"Then you do doubt?"

"Not Jesus Christ, no. But I doubt geography, and for an explorer, that is no small doubt."

"At least you return chastened."

"No, Finbar. *Deus semper meior.* We have come to Paradise, and God is still greater. *That* is what I have found. That is why I say I doubt even geography's greatness in the face of God. I return to Ireland gladder in my heart than I had ever hoped to be."

"Well," said Finbar, bending their course in so that they sidled gently up against the shore by the village. "I still doubt. But on Ktaadn, I did pray to your god, just once."

Brendan grinned at him. "I know. I remember."

"Of course, that was for Joseph."

"I don't think so, friend. At that moment, I think it was for you."

Ashore, Brendan handed his catch to a woman for cleaning, and wandered with Finbar into the center of the village. Atla was there, lending a hand in scraping a bearskin.

"Come to our lodge tonight," Finbar invited.

"As soon as I clean some of this grease off."

"Want to have a sweat?"

"Why not? Brendan?"

"No. I've got things to do aboard."

"Until later, then," Finbar said, and, with Atla rubbing at the offal on his arms, the two walked off toward the shore.

When the mud was hot, and they were inside, Finbar and Atla contented themselves for a while scraping each other's backs and thighs with bundled twigs to stimulate perspiration. The heat slowed the brain and made one pant.

Eventually, Finbar asked, "What will you do in Ireland?"

"Maybe I'll stay in Thule."

"Why?"

Finbar could see the gap in Atla's teeth when he replied, "Maybe you'll see me back here someday."

"Yes?"

"Not to stay, no. I'm not like you. I wouldn't be content as smith—or whatever—to the Abnaki. But I would like to see that garden of Cautantowit's southwest of here."

"Still looking for another Paradise, eh?"

"Let's get out of here. I'm cooked."

After they had dashed water on each other and dried themselves, Finbar repeated his question.

"It's not Paradise so much." Atla skipped a stone out across the still harbor. The sun now was low over the cliff and, in the cloudless sky, there were pinkish and greenish tinges. Sounds of the village behind the two men wove in and out of the ubiquitous murmur of the waterfall. "It's just that being back there in Ireland will be too confining for me, no matter what Father Brendan says. I've come to love margins."

"All you would have to do would be to sail a bit, though. Just move around, to Iona, to Skye; tell them about Paradise."

Atla shook his head and smiled gently. "No. I mean real margins: you can truly get somewhere when you are out of the world."

"I like that." Finbar clapped Atla on the back. "Come on. Let's go find Nonanis. Glusgebeh had a lodge made for us today."

"Lots easier with saplings and hides than with stone."

"Let's find Brendan first, and then see how it's been fitted out."

Nonanis had moved much of her property into the new hut by the time Finbar, Atla and Brendan arrived. She was purifying the interior with smoke and manito-songs. Her possessive and domestic manner pleased Finbar far more than he would have thought possible, and he was proud of her before his friends. It was a merry evening, and Atla played his whistle until long after the fire had died down, without Brendan's raising any quarrel.

In starlight, Finbar walked the two men back to the shore. Brendan said, "Only remember that she is powwaw, Finbar. It will be like being married to a . . . a saint, perhaps."

"This saint will give me sons."

"The sons of the powwaw."

"I have power, too, you know. Just think what sons they will be!"

Brendan and Atla stepped into their canoe to paddle out to the curragh. A strip of black water widened between them and the shore. "I shall tell them about you at home," Brendan called, softly, out of the darkness.

"Don't," Finbar replied. "Don't burden me with that. I am a free man. Only tell Ide. But for the rest, never say you left a man behind in Paradise. I do not desire to be 'examined' by your philosophers, as such a man would surely be."

"As you wish," came the voice.

"It is you," Finbar blurted out. "It is you who should be remembered . . . and will be."

"Goodbye, smith."

Finbar heard the canoe bump quietly up against the curragh's hull. "Fare well," he said softly, "and may the Goddess go with you."

Finbar's last sight of the curragh came on the following morning. Pressed by a vigorous autumnal breeze, the craft had reached out of the harbor, tacked twice, and then settled down on a slant that would pass her to seaward of the first screen of islands. Instead of following in a canoe as others had done, Finbar and Nonanis raced through the forest to the cliff. A quick scramble took them to the top. From there, the curragh was a brown fish on the blue sea, alone, for the canoes were heading back. Finbar strained to see Brendan and Atla. The Irish boat merged with a swell, disappeared, reappeared again. For a moment, Finbar thought he could still make out the specks that had been his companions, but he was not certain. Then, after a time, he was certain they were gone.

He turned to Nonanis. "So," he said.

She waited for him to go on. When he did not, she said, "Now you are mine."

"Yes," he replied. "But also you—you, Nonanis, pow-waw, wife of my lodge and of my bed, mother of my brave black sons to come—you are mine." Then he felt a grin spread across his face until he could do nothing but tip up his head and laugh. He grabbed Nonanis around the waist and, there at the top of the mountain, he roared forth such a bellow that the eagles flew down and gathered around him, and the trees tossed up their branches, and the Grandfather Sun himself stopped in his tracks and poured down his fire upon the earth, so that the very waters ran gold and the rocks tumbled into the sea.

Designed by Barbara Holdridge
Composed in Gael, with Bernhard Modern
  initials and display, by ComCom, Allentown,
    Pennsylvania
Printed on 60-pound Glatfelter Antique
  Offset by Haddon Craftsmen, Bloomsburg,
    Pennsylvania
Endpapers printed on 80-pound Light Natural
  Blue Hill Offset Vellum by Haddon Crafts-
    men, Bloomsburg, Pennsylvania
Jacket color separations and printing
  by Capper, Inc., Knoxville, Tennessee
Bound in Holliston Sailcloth and
  Holliston Novelex by Haddon Craftsmen,
    Scranton, Pennsylvania

fInBAR's world

PARADISUS